THE RAPIDS

Part II—*Le Québécois Series*

DORIS PROVENCHER FAUCHER

Doris P. Faucher

ARTENAY PRESS

All rights reserved under International and Pan-American Copyright Conventions. Published in the United States by
ARTENAY PRESS
P.O. Box 664, Biddeford ME 04005
http://home.maine.rr.com/artenayp/
artenayp@maine.rr.com

First Edition

Library of Congress Control Number: 2002094340

ISBN: 0-9679112-4-9

Manufactured in the United States of America.

For my immediate and extended family members—
for their patience and support,

for our many friends, old and new—
for their generosity in sharing their expertise and valuable references,

and for our early Canadian ancestors—
whose faith, courage, determination, and decisions,
led us to be where and who we are today.

Author's Note

Bastien and Marguerite had successfully settled on land he had cleared and tilled from the Canadian virgin forest. As part of the first Canadian-born generation, their sons and daughters would share challenges and experiences which were quite different from those of their French-born parents.

During the twenty years of peace that followed the French-Iroquois peace treaty of 1667, Jesuit missionaries and beaver fur traders moved ever westward, leading French exploration throughout and past the Great Lakes area, and southward by way of the Mississippi River to the Gulf of Mexico.

That period of rapid territorial expansion was achieved through the early Canadian's use of the Algonquin birch bark canoe, a sleek, lightweight craft that could be easily patched en route, and could safely transport heavy loads of trade goods and fur packets, as well as men. Historians tell us that this river craft could weigh less than three hundred pounds, yet could carry five tons.

During the French regime, early canoes required a two-man crew. Later trading versions would accommodate a crew of ten to twelve men, provisions, and up to nine hundred pounds of cargo.

Whether the canoeist was an explorer, an unlicensed coureur, a voyageur employed by a licensed trader, or a militiaman, ideally, he was lean, strong, resilient, adaptable, and no more than five feet, five inches tall. His summer traveling day often started at 3:00 a.m and ended at 9:00 p.m., averaged 57,000 strokes, and covered 45 miles. Ten-minute smoking and resting breaks (*pipes*) were called by the bowman's command *"Allumez!"* every three miles or so.

At night, the voyageur slept under his overturned canoe for no more than four to five hours while partially exposed to all kinds of weather, and to the ever present mosquitoes and black flies.

Except for whatever small game he might pick up along the way, his diet typically consisted of dried peas or corn, and pork fat simmered in water overnight, over an open fire. In early morning, he usually added a biscuit to thicken the mixture while he reloaded the canoes. Cold leftovers and pemmican were eaten during travel.

Most fur trade voyages started from Montréal and headed up the Ottawa River to the upper Great Lakes, or traveled by way of the upper Saint Lawrence River to lower lakes Ontario and Erie.

The French-Canadian voyageur often faced sudden violent storms and cold winds even in summer as he paddled across the Great Lakes, but the river rapids represented his most arduous challenge.

These travelers often had to unload the canoe, then carry it and the cargo past the many rapids and waterfalls they encountered while moving upriver. The traditional route from Montréal to Michillimackinac required fifty separate portages.

Portaging meant that the voyageur must repeatedly lift and carry two ninety-pound packs on his back while ascending difficult wilderness terrain. A single portage could be as long as 45 miles, but was divided into delivery stages called *posés* which were located about a third of a mile apart. Thus, a 10-mile portage could require as many as thirty *posés*.

The canoeist never climbed into nor out of the frail birch bark canoe while it was on dry land; he boarded, loaded, and emptied it while it was afloat.

All habitants, ages sixteen to sixty, were required to serve in the militia, and they could be mustered by the French governors of New France to build western forts, or to join in the several overland campaigns against the Iroquois villages south of Lake Ontario. On such occasions, the Canadians traveled by canoe but were also directed to assist in the movement of soldiers and military equipment by means of the heavier wooden bateaux.

It is important to note that governor-generals Frontenac, La Barre, and Denonville left no descendants in New France. Although they each had at least one son, none of these came to Canada but spent their entire lives in France. Denonville returned to the homeland with his wife and their three unmarried daughters at the end of his governorship. Callières remained a bachelor; he died and was buried in Québec as was Frontenac. Two of Rigaud de Vaudreuil's six sons would pursue their military careers in North America. Pierre would become governor of Louisiana in 1742 and of Canada in 1755. François-Pierre would become governor of Trois Rivières in 1748 and of Montreal in 1757.

D. P. F.

To the Reader

Over time, many French words have been absorbed into the English language. Italicization of this text has been reserved for French and native American words that are not found in *Merriam-Webster's Collegiate Dictionary, 10th Edition.*

A glossary of French words or idioms, and a chart of characters outlining family relationships have been provided at book's end.

I am most grateful to Ken Rapple who so graciously provided the cover photo for this sequel to *Le Quebecois: The VIRGIN FOREST.* He tells us that:

> "Moose Rapids is a class 3-4 drop about 40 meters long. You will find it on the upper Ottawa River, about a day's paddle downstream of Lac Granet, just inside the northern boundary of Parc Verendrye, Quebec. The late August morning that I took the picture was a classic northern Canadian day with cool wind and warm sun. The river up there is clean flowing, quiet, enshrouded, and thoroughly satisfying. The deep woods of northern Quebec and Ontario still hold a certain magic, a timelessness that keeps drawing me back again and again."

Homecoming

One

Late August 1672

Bastien's yearlong journey to the northern sea had finally come to an end, and news of his arrival had quickly spread through the community of Cap-de-la-Madeleine. An afternoon and evening celebration with family and friends had also come to an end. The guests had left, and the children had fallen asleep, exhausted by the day's events. The house had grown quiet and peaceful.

Marguerite's great joy, relief, and gratitude for her husband's safe return now gave way to the realization that life would be easier now. She hugged him warmly, and welcomed him home again.

They sat on the door stoop and contemplated the adjustments that his renewed presence would bring to their lives. He took her hand and told her that he had greatly missed her.

She nodded. "Home is not the same without you," she confessed.

"I hope never to leave you and the children again."

He asked about the crops, how she and François Morni had managed during his absence, if there had been any illness, how the sale of the second concession had been fulfilled. But his eyes grew heavy—time enough to discuss these things after a good night's sleep, in his own bed, lying next to Marguerite, he thought.

She rose, still holding his hand. "You must be tired," she said with her gentle smile.

That simple, intimate gesture smoothed away the physical and emotional vestiges of his long overland journey to Hudson Bay. He marveled at this calming effect she continued to have on him, and he sensed that she had grown stronger, less dependent, during his absence.

Marguerite also recognized a subtle change in him, even as she caught that softening look in his eyes.

"That bed seems very inviting…" he murmured, and he guided her toward it.

That night, they reunited in passion, love and deep personal intimacy, and regained that awesome beauty, warmth, and comfort they had always found in each other. And they both slipped into a deep, relaxing sleep.

Bastien awoke the following morning to the familiar sounds and scents of a family breakfast. The children had waited patiently, and now jumped happily into bed with him. He hugged and frolicked with all of them, then suddenly, the nine-year old "temporary" cord web he had fashioned as a mattress support began to give way. His namesake, two-year old Sébastien, giggled at the speed with which his father reacted, thinking that he was running away from them. But eight-year old Madeleine, six-year-old Marie, and four-year old Louis were puzzled and shaken when the mattress collapsed under their combined weight and activity.

Marguerite was shocked but as soon as she realized that no one was hurt, she began to laugh at all of them.

"You shouldn't feel badly about this; I should have strengthened it long ago," he tried to reassure them.

"I want to help!" Louis volunteered.

Bastien studied him briefly. "And so you shall, *mon gars*—as soon as I've made a complete tour of the farm." He turned to Marguerite, whose hearty laughter he had always thoroughly enjoyed, and with mirth in his eyes, he assured her that he would repair the bed as soon as possible.

François Morni joined them for breakfast and reported that all of their crops would yield a better than average harvest because of favorable summer weather. The grain at l'Arbre-à-la-Croix would also be theirs as part of their sale agreement. Marguerite assured Bastien that there had been no problem with the contract.

He turned to François. "Did you experience any problems during the transfer of harvest and animals from there last autumn?"

"We had a lot of help from the neighbors and things went smoothly," their engagé replied.

Marguerite nodded in agreement. "We also had help from Jacques Massé, who was working that lease next-door for Jeanne Dodier."

"Then I must find him and thank him. He wasn't here yesterday."

"He and his wife are busier than most with their own projects. I've gotten to know Catherine during this past year; she also spins and weaves, you know. We've become good friends."

"I'm glad to hear that. Perhaps we should invite them over for Sunday dinner?" he suggested.

"I'd like that," she replied.

Bastien walked his property with François while the family dog, Métis, ran ahead, and Louis ran close at their heels, trying to keep up with his newfound father. The grain fields would soon ripen; the vegetable and fruit gardens thrived; the animals browsed contentedly in their outdoor pens and enclosures. The barn and equipment showed some neglect, but that was understandable. "Everything seems to be in good order, François. I'm impressed with the upcoming harvest. This couldn't have been easy for you."

"I had a lot of help; it seemed as though your friends and neighbors anticipated our every need."

"I appreciate that."

They heard a rustling in the brush. Bastien stiffened. François called out: "Ho there! Jacques!"

Bastien recognized Massé the moment he emerged from the woods into the adjacent clearing. "*Bonjour, mon ami!*" he called back.

The younger man approached them energetically. "*Bonjour, voyageur!*" he hailed back.

Bastien told him: "I have much to thank you for, Jacques. I understand that you and your wife have helped my family while I was away."

The young habitant shrugged his shoulders. "Whenever we

could—I can't imagine having to leave my wife and child for a year, as you have—How was your journey?"

"I'd like to tell you about it over Sunday dinner. Can you come? I look forward to meeting Catherine and thanking her also. Marguerite tells me that they've become good friends."

"We'd be happy to."

Bastien noticed that Joliet's clearing had grown noticeably larger. "I see that you've already cut down a good part of Jeanne's forest."

"As required by my contract—I hope to get out of that soon, because I've signed a permanent lease on a farm that's much closer to my own property."

"You'll have to tell me all about that."

Jacques turned to walk away and called over his shoulder: "We'll see you at Mass next Sunday."

"He's a hard worker," François remarked as they continued their tour of the farm.

"He arrived late in the summer of '65—Captain Rivard's high praise of him convinced me that it was time for us to hire a helper; that's when we first met you, François."

"Happy day for me, Bastien. I was so relieved to find a home in this new land. I was quite young then, and you were very patient with me."

"It worked out well for both of us. Have you ever thought of striking out on your own?"

"I'm still not ready for that. I'd prefer to stay on a bit longer, if you'll have me."

"That's good news!"

Louis stumbled, reminding the two men that they had walked as far as the boy could manage. Bastien bent down and hoisted him up onto his shoulders to carry him the rest of the way, then he took leave of his engagé.

Louis had never entered the forest until now. Adding to the perspective he had from sitting high on his father's shoulders, this was a completely new experience for him. He felt safe, and he was curious; his senses immediately focused on the different sounds and scents of this strange new world. They entered an area thick with pines, a dense mat of aromatic brown needles covered the ground. The rippling sound of running water reached them from beyond the trees as they started down a small banking. When they reached the water's edge, his father stopped to set him down.

Bastien examined the hemp, while Louis looked up and wondered what was so special about this plant which grew taller than his papa. A plopping sound drew the boy's attention to the running water; he turned in time to see a fish swimming upstream, feeding on insects that wandered close to the water's surface.

His father explained: "I need to repair the bed, Louis, and this is what I must use. I hope we still have some in the barn, because if I have to cut this down now, it won't be ready to use for a long while." He collected one stalk, lifted his son onto his shoulders again, started up the banking, and they headed home.

Marguerite tended the vegetable garden in the dooryard, and upon seeing the hemp that he carried in his hand, she told him that their supply of processed fiber lay untouched in the barn. "Can you make your own rope?" she asked.

"I know I can, but it would be easier and faster to start with spun yarn. Twisting it together by hand is a long, slow process, and I'm eager to replace that mattress support. I'm surprised that the original one lasted as long as it did."

"My spinning wheel is in the barn."

"That's where I'll set up my rope-making equipment."

While they spent the rest of the day working on this project, Bastien saw their two daughters routinely share many of their mother's chores, and he noticed that her namesake, Marie seemed to have a special way with young Sébastien. All four of the children were fascinated by this process of making rope out of hemp. Madeleine seemed quite adept at feeding the fiber to her mother, who spun it into yarn, then counter-twisted six long lengths of this yarn together into strands. Bastien improvised some equipment to tightly twist three of these strands together, again reversing direction in order to lend strength to the rope.

They set their mattress on the floor that night when they realized that they would need another day to produce enough rope to weave into the bedframe. "It's just as well," he admitted, "because I think we should weave through twice as many holes as we originally had, so we'll need to make more rope."

The following day, Louis continued to follow at Bastien's heels, and mimicked his every move and gesture. The girls teased him, and their mother chided them for it. She took them aside and quietly reminded them: "You two are old enough to remember your father; Louis was too young when he left. Be patient with your little brother until he gets used to having his papa around the house."

They spent the morning producing additional rope, then after the noon meal, the boys watched as Bastien bore more holes into the bed frame with his spoon auger. When he began to thread the rope through the head of the frame, he started at the middle, measured off equal lengths at either side, and worked out a way for Louis to help him by feeding one rope end into its holes at the foot of the bedframe, and carrying it back to his father. Bastien was surprised by how quickly his young son learned, and how seriously he worked at this task. He recalled how Métis had complicated this work when he had first attempted it. That seemed so long ago—before their wedding day. Today, their mongrel dog lay by the hearth and occasionally dozed off while he watched them work.

Once the warp had been set tightly and securely, Marguerite joined Bastien in weaving the rope from side to side. By then, Louis had grown tired and restless, and had gone out to do his minor chores. The girls and young Sébastien, however, were fascinated by this part of the project. Madeleine could see that it was similar to her mother's work at the loom, but less refined, where the strength of the rope became more important than the closeness of the weave. Marguerite interlaced from one side while Bastien worked from the other. Finally, he strongly pulled the web taut and anchored it securely.

They managed to reassemble the bed in time for the family to sit outdoors and watch the sun set in the west. It was then that Bastien finally opened his knapsack, and removed several packets. He gave the first and largest to his wife.

She looked at him quizzically, as she handled it and saw that this was something soft and light. Yet she caught her breath when she unwrapped it to find that he had given her a white fur muff. "But these are so expensive!" she protested.

Delighted by her response, he replied: "I only wish I could have given it to you last Noël. I made it myself, you know, during those long evenings in our winter shelter—you were very much in my thoughts. We trapped many white hares; they were a major source of our meat, and their winter fur was too beautiful to throw away. I'm glad you like it; you certainly deserve to have one."

She passed it around to Madeleine and Marie who were both enchanted with its softness and warmth; they took turns rubbing it gently against their cheeks.

Bastien took out two slightly smaller packages, one for each of his daughters. They grew very excited, looked at each other, and opened their gifts. They too had muffs, not quite as white as their mother's but certainly like hers in every other way. They both ran to Bastien to hug and kiss him.

Louis grew restless and watched expectantly as his father reached into the bag again and withdrew a fourth present, which he handed to him.

The boy was puzzled by what he saw.

Bastien explained: "These are sea shells, Louis. They can only be found on the shore of the great northern sea. The natives who visit that area consider these to be very special. A small fish lives its entire life covered by one of these shells. The natives eat the fish for food, and some will trade these with other tribes who live far away from the sea. The natives decorate themselves with them. Some shells are large enough to use as knives and scrapers. I picked the prettiest ones that I could find for you."

Louis followed his sisters' lead and hugged his father. He showed the shells to his sisters, and they, in turn, allowed him to try out their muffs.

Bastien called Sébastien over to him, gave him a gentle hug, and helped him to open the smallest of the packages. Inside the wrapping was a carved set of miniature cups which fit inside each other.

While he helped his youngest son to fit these together in a series, Louis asked him: "Papa, where did you sleep in the woods?"

"Mostly on the ground, covered with a blanket, and under an overturned canoe."

"What if it rained?"

"Even then."

"Who cooked your food?"

"I did, over an open fire."

"Can we try that sometime?"

His parents exchanged a look of surprise.

"Why would you want to do that?" asked Marie.

"I think I'd like that—What did you eat?"

"Corn cakes, oatmeal, some dried vegetables and fruits, pemmican, whatever meat we could find on the trail."

The boy's eyes widened. "Did you see any big animals?"

"The biggest I saw was a white bear that lives near the northern sea."

"Bigger than ours?"

"Yes."

"Was he close?"

"No, because it was safer for us to keep our distance. But we watched many of them fishing with their claws."

Louis' eyes opened wider as he pictured this scene.

"How did you spend your winter?" Marguerite asked.

He answered all their questions: how he had built a small log cabin with a stone fireplace, and elevated cots for him and for his two traveling companions; how he and their native guides had processed the skins of moose and caribou to serve as fur coverings during the much colder winter nights, and had stored their meat in stone caches which they placed a safe distance from their camp. He told them that the farther north they had traveled, the earlier winter had begun, the shorter their daylight hours had been, and the colder the weather had become. He explained to Marguerite that their messenger to Québec, who had carried instructions for Cusson to arrange for the sale of their second concession, had also carried back to them extra provisions, and the necessary survival gear to provide for heating, cooking, and lighting in their rude cabin through the long winter nights.

"Did you see any Iroquois?" Louis resumed his questioning.

"No, we didn't. You know that we're at peace with them, don't you, Louis?"

"Yes..."

"And so are all of the other nations that we met along the way."

"*Maman* won't let us go into the woods. She says that it's too dangerous."

Marguerite quickly reminded them: "It's no safe place for a little one!"

The parents exchanged glances.

"She's right, you know; it's very easy for children to get lost in the forest and never find their way back. You must never go in alone."

The children thought about this; they had heard many stories of people, even grownups, who had disappeared into the woods.

Their father continued: "The natives learned long ago to adapt to the forest and live off of it. They can travel great distances with few supplies, and they meet their needs from what the forest provides for them: shelter, clothing, food, tools, and weapons. This is your Canadian heritage, and is not to be feared by men. I'll teach you all you need to know when you're ready to learn."

Louis asked: "How did you learn to live in the forest?"

"An Algonquin friend taught me much of it, and I also learned from marching to the Mohawk villages with the Carignan Regiment."

The children listened intently.

Marguerite added: "You've all met Red Dawn—He brought us meat last winter."

Bastien smiled at their signs of recognition. "He also joined us in that march to the Mohawk villages.

"Life is very different here from what it was in France for *Maman* and me. We've learned new skills every day since we arrived. We'll start teaching those skills to all of you, as soon as you're old enough and strong enough to use them."

He studied the effect of his words on Louis who seemed to have an endless curiosity about his world.

Two

September 1672

The following Sunday, Bastien and his family walked to the
small village church of Sainte-Madeleine where he and
Marguerite had exchanged vows in January 1663. His family
listened proudly while the Recollect priest praised Bastien's
service and sacrifice for the Church and the Colony, then
welcomed him back from his yearlong voyage to Hudson Bay with
Jesuit Father Albanel. Bastien nodded to the Franciscan priest,
but was simply happy to be home among family and friends.

After Mass, militia captain Nicolas Rivard announced from the
church steps that France was now at war with the Netherlands;
that Count Louis de Frontenac had arrived to replace both
Governor-General Courcelles, and Intendant Talon at Québec.
Bastien and his wife regretted this, because they knew and
appreciated how much progress the colony had made under Jean
Talon's administration.

Notary Cusson approached them. "It's good to see you, Bastien!
You've been gone a long time!"

"I'm glad to be back, Jean. Thank you for handling that sale for
us. Marguerite tells me that all went well…"

"I was glad to be of service. We received your message that
you'd be spending the winter near Lac Saint-Jean, but by the
time I was able to share that news with your wife, your messenger
had already left Québec. Marguerite was greatly disappointed

that she couldn't reply to your message. We agreed that it would be best to postpone the sale until spring in order to find the appropriate buyer for you."

Bastien recalled that Saint-Simon had hurried back because the rivers and lakes had already begun to freeze. "It was the right decision—Tell me, Jean, do you still offer lessons in reading and writing?"

"Why yes, of course! What do you have in mind?"

"At what age do you recommend that a young boy begin instruction?"

Jean scanned the children and focused on Louis, who was the most likely candidate. "Our Michel is about his age. Another two years, perhaps, depending on how easily he holds a pen. In the meantime, he can practice the basic strokes to train his hand and eye."

"What would he need for practice?"

"Chalk and slate are best—but a stick and a sandbox will do to start."

Bastien laid his hand on Louis' shoulder. "I think this one will be eager to learn. I'll be in touch with you about this. I thank you again."

Several of his friends congregated about him, including Guillaume Barette, Nicolas Leblanc, Louis Lefebvre, Jacques Vaudry, Michel Rochereau, and the Bigots. They talked for a while as the children played together, then Marguerite spotted Catherine and Jacques Massé.

The woman approached them with a toddler in her arms. She was well-dressed for an habitant's wife; judging from her eyes, she seemed capable and strong of character, yet at least a decade younger than her husband. "Bastien," Jacques said simply, "this is my Catherine."

Bastien smiled at her and said: "Marguerite speaks very highly of you. I understand that you've become the best of friends."

Marguerite chuckled as Catherine's cheeks flushed and she replied: "We've learned a lot from each other—I'm sure she missed you terribly, Bastien."

A bit flustered by Catherine's reaction, he turned toward his wife. "But she's done quite well on her own while I was gone; there doesn't seem to be much work piled up for me to do."

"We'll soon be harvesting our crops," Jacques reminded him.

"I look forward to that."

Jacques' family had traveled to church by oxcart, now the women and younger children rode together while the men walked alongside with Bastien's daughters. The girls entertained the toddlers while their mothers chatted. Bastien could already see that their two families had much in common.

"This past year must have been filled with new and exciting experiences for you," Jacques remarked.

"Yes, and there were some difficult times. I wouldn't want to repeat the journey, but I do appreciate having made it."

"Your world has certainly grown larger because of it."

"Yes, and now I'm quite happy to be back home."

"You have a good man working for you."

"I know, and I can't help but wonder how much longer we can keep him." Bastien picked up Louis, who began to lag behind the others, but resisted joining the mothers and toddlers in the cart. "You mentioned the other day that you've signed a permanent lease on property closer to your home?"

"I signed at mid-summer. It's located this side of Champlain, next-door to where we live. I won't have to travel as far, and the land is already cleared."

"How much longer does your lease run with Jeanne Dodier?"

"About a year, but I'm not sure I can manage it in addition to my own farm and this new lease."

"Why don't I speak to her and see if I can set up a lease of my own, releasing you from that agreement."

Jacques showed some surprise at this prospect.

Bastien continued: "Now that we've sold our second concession, and with François to help me, I see no reason why I couldn't work a farm next door to ours. I could speak to her within the next few days, if Marguerite agrees."

"I'd really appreciate that—I hope it works out, Bastien; it seems like the ideal arrangement for all of us. You should know that although her husband Antoine Baillargée will negotiate the contract, she controls this farm and will expect eighteen *minots* of wheat each year, delivered to their home nearer the village."

"Has that been a problem for you?"

"No, but in addition to that, she requires that pine trees be cleared in payment of *cens et rentes* to the Jesuit *seigneurie*."

Jeanne's conditions were less than what Louis Lefebvre had required; this prompted Bastien to enthusiastically introduce this possibility to Marguerite, who approved of the commitment.

During their dinner conversation about developing the land, Bastien found Jacques to be most intense about his hopes for the future. He personally had never experienced that sort of ambition. Although he and Marguerite had carried a four-year lease with Louis Lefebvre, and had developed a second concession at l'Arbre-à-la-Croix, those were unexpected opportunities that had conveniently become available to them. Bastien admired the younger man's enthusiasm, but he felt satisfied that he and Marguerite held more land now than they could have hoped for in France, enough to pass on to their children and grandchildren.

Perhaps this contrast between the two men was due to their difference in age—or to his weariness from the long journey. Yet he looked forward to the autumn farmwork: the harvest of grain and vegetables, sturgeon and eel-fishing, the hunt of migratory ducks, geese, and passenger pigeons swarming south to warmer climes. All of this gathering of food stores would see them through the upcoming winter—one which no doubt would be more comfortable and less isolated for him than the last.

"Marguerite told me that you make your own cider and wine, Bastien."

"My father always made his own cider," he explained, "and Marguerite tends a thriving fruit garden. *Père* Allouez made us a present of imported grapevine cuttings on our wedding day, but they didn't survive the first planting. We experimented with the native elderberry a few years ago, and we still enjoy its wine."

He rose to search for a bottle he had left cooling before his departure, and soon returned with it. "*Sieur* Boucher gave us this calvados as a wedding present. Did you know that Marguerite sailed with him when he returned from France?"

Catherine turned to her friend. "You never told me!"

"It seems so long ago," she replied, and wondered what Bastien was up to.

He winked at her. "We've always kept this for special occasions, and I think this qualifies, don't you, Marguerite?"

He wiped the bottle clean of dust and showed it to Jacques. "Have you ever tasted this?"

"No, I haven't, but I know how special it is. You mustn't waste it on us."

Marguerite had already produced four small cups. "Two special occasions," she declared, "my husband's homecoming, and an afternoon with special friends."

The following day, Bastien promised his wife that he would be especially careful about Louis' safety as he navigated his canoe close to shore on his way to the cape mission in search of Red Dawn. He also told her that he would teach the children to swim the following summer.

They arrived at the cape mission where they found the Algonquin chief teaching two of his grandsons the art of bow-making. His wife, Blue Bird was away, working in the fields.

The chief's hair had begun to show gray, but his bearing was as strong and straight as ever, his manner serious and thoughtful. Bastien had learned to read his dark eyes, and on this day, he knew that the chief was delighted to see them.

He saluted Red Dawn in his native language.

"You now speak my tongue," the Algonquin observed.

"I am honored to know a few words."

"You have learned much while you were away."

Louis had never been in a native teepee, nor this close to a native chief. He sat quietly as he watched and listened to his father who used strange words and sounds to communicate with the native.

Red Dawn noticed the boy's interest in his shaping of the bow and arrows. He set these aside for now and signaled his grandsons to show Louis around the mission grounds.

"I have seen much," Bastien told him after the boys had left.

"What have you seen?"

"A longer, colder, darker winter."

The chief nodded in agreement.

"A great white bear, larger than any I have ever seen. He fished with his claws at the end of winter."

The chief's eyes widened, and he leaned slightly forward to hear more. "I have heard of this *makwa*. You have seen him?"

Bastien tipped his head. "I regret that I could not bring you his claw. My musket was not strong enough to kill him, and we did not need meat at that time."

"You did well."

"I brought you these." Bastien handed him a leather pouch containing several perfect shells that he had gathered on the shores of the northern sea. Red Dawn's eyes studied them closely, one at a time. "Blue Bird will treasure these," he said.

"The tools you gave me helped me through the northern winter. Our Montagnais guides were curious about them."

A barely audible grunt escaped the chief's lips. "Do you still have them?"

"Yes. Our guides were surprised to see me using such tools. They helped me to prepare sleeping furs for *Père* Albanel, *Sieur* Saint-Simon, and me."

Blue Bird returned with the children, and while she prepared corn cakes and honey for all of them, she offered an herbal tea. Louis approached the bow, to study it and the stone tool that Red Dawn had been using.

"Your son is eager to learn our ways."

"He has much to learn, but he is still young."

"Old enough to learn to make a bow and arrows."

"Too young to shoot an arrow."

"Old enough to practice and to learn."

"I cannot teach him."

"I will teach him."

This offer took Bastien completely by surprise. "You would do this?"

"Your son is like you; he appreciates our ways. He will learn with my son's sons. I will teach him how a bow and arrows are made, and he will have these to practice with my grandsons. When he is old enough and strong enough, I will lead him into the forest and teach him as I have taught you."

Bastien's face shone with pleasure. "May I come too?"

Red Dawn laughed as he rarely did, and tapped him on the back. He took out his pipe and shared it with his French friend.

Before returning home, Bastien traveled across the Saint-Maurice River to Trois-Rivières where he delivered letters and news to Elizabeth Radisson from her brother Pierre-Esprit, and to Marguerite Hayet from her husband Médard Chouart Des Groseilliers. The women were relieved to receive word that the two men were both alive and well, but they were disappointed that Bastien had no information as to how much longer it would be before the two adventurers would return to their families.

Marguerite stood anxiously at the top of the bluff that overlooked the river, and watched the point of land beyond Louis Lefebvre's lot until she finally saw their canoe. She breathed a deep sigh of relief, and turned away from the riverbank. She had fought her fears most of that day, to no avail. Of course, Bastien would be careful with Louis, but children were always unpredictable; one quick movement...

The boy ran into his mother's waiting arms, and couldn't speak fast enough to share his news. Marguerite quickly learned that he had enjoyed this day, traveling alone with his father, visiting the Algonquin mission, meeting new people. She knew that she must get used to having him out of her sight, but this first experience had left her totally exhausted.

Two weeks later, Bastien paddled his canoe to royal notary Jean Cusson's office to make his mark on a nine-year lease contract with Antoine Baillargée. His first payment of eighteen *minots* of wheat would be due late September of the following year, and he would fell pine timber to pay the seigneury its yearly *cens et rentes*. Baillargée promised to provide six working days to assist him in clearing existing brush from the property.

Once the Baillargées had left, the royal notary invited Bastien to bring Louis to his office in the village so that he could introduce the boy to the preliminary handwriting exercises of circles and diagonal strokes.

"Isn't he too young?" Bastien asked.

"He might struggle with it at first, but if he's as interested as I think he is, he'll accept the challenge and work at it until he's mastered it. If he does, this exercise will certainly improve his handwriting."

"Very well then; I'll bring him the next time I come to the village. *Bonjour*, Jean."

A crowd of people had gathered near the village pier, drawing the two men toward the scene. A large party of uniformed guards had just landed.

"What's going on?" Jean asked one of the men nearest the water's edge.

The store clerk replied softly: "The new governor-general has come from Québec to inspect the iron mines."

Frontenac walked past them, behind his military escort, quickly and keenly scanning the crowd with his sharp eyes. He strode to meet Nicolas Rivard, who had been alerted to his arrival. The new governor personified the French aristocrats of Versailles: he stood taller than the militia captain, and wore gray, lightly damasked cloth, and boots of fine gray leather. A scarlet silk-lined, wide-brimmed hat, decorated with a fine arching plume, topped his curly wig. In a strong, imperious voice, he asked to be led directly to the mines.

Never having seen the local iron mines that Intendant Talon had opened the previous autumn, Bastien blended into the crowd with Jean, and moved among the villagers who followed the governor's party.

They reached an area where six massive piles of rusty ore had been deposited. Frontenac reacted exuberantly as he examined the quantity and quality of the metal. "Why there's enough here to furnish two iron smelters full-time for three or four months— Enough for us to produce our own cannons! And this source runs all the way to Champlain!"

Bastien and Cusson exchanged puzzled looks. Once peace had been established with the Iroquois nations, Intendant Talon had planned to turn a major portion of this domestic source of iron into fittings for the six merchants ships he had under construction at Québec. He had hoped to develop a triangular trade route to the Antilles, then to France, and back again to the North American colony. He had expected the rest of the ore would meet domestic needs. This new military governor apparently envisioned a different future for Nouvelle France.

FRONTENAC

Three

The fields of grain had ripened to a golden color. Their vegetables would soon be ready for storage. Bastien prepared his tools and equipment for the gathering and storage of their summer bounty. Then, while Marguerite and the girls picked garden onions and herbs to dry in the loft, he and François repaired the oxcart and sharpened the scythe and sickle in preparation for the grain harvest.

The men reaped their winter wheat, oats, and rye, setting aside the straw for use as thatch and animal bedding. The girls and their mother collected the sun-dried retted flax, and tied it into bundles which they hung to dry in the barn.

Bastien and François added to their supply of firewood, and piled brush and debris for the autumn burning. Some of the wood ash collected from that fire would provide the lye they needed for soap making; they would spread the rest over the new clearing to enrich the soil for growth of their winter wheat.

Two weeks later, native and French canoes crowded the Saint Lawrence River as Atlantic sturgeon made their annual run upriver. Bastien and François went fishing, while the girls set up the temporary outdoor tables on which the adults would clean, fillet, and cut the man-sized fish. They feasted on this seasonal treat all that week, and continued to dry the cut-up fillets on outdoor drying racks set over a bed of red coals.

Shortly after they completed harvesting, processing and storing their sturgeon catch, adult eels began their frantic migration downriver. Bastien's family spent the next couple of weeks drying and salt-processing their bountiful catch, filling their bins and barrels with a supply of fish that would feed them through February.

Early in October, Bastien and François tilled and harrowed the fields at the two adjoining concessions, where they sowed winter wheat and rye. They scattered oat grain over the previous summer's corn field, and reserved the other tilled ground for the following spring's corn planting. Meanwhile, Marguerite and the girls prepared the squash and pumpkin for harvest and storage.

Daylight hours grew shorter as the family joined together in collecting apples, grapes, and currants. Most of the grapes and currants would be preserved by drying, but since their supply of cider had run low during his absence, Bastien delivered a generous batch of apples to the cider mill and prepared his barrels and kegs for refilling.

As the weather turned cooler, the girls gathered wild walnuts, chestnuts, and sweet acorns of white oak. Marguerite rendered a fresh supply of cooking oil from some of these and culled the rest for storage in the house loft.

At the first white frost, the family collected and stored dried beans and corn. While the younger children dug up and brought in the parsnips, turnips, and carrots, Madeleine and Marie threshed, and their mother winnowed the grain.

Great formations of ducks, geese, and passenger pigeons flew overhead during their massive southward migrations. The men hunted these large birds, and Marguerite taught the girls and Louis to strip and collect their feathers while she gutted, cleaned, and prepared most of their meat for storage in the salt barrels. Meanwhile she reserved several of them to bake into the traditional meat pies that she had learned to make in Pithiviers, France.

Late that month, Sunday announcements informed the parishioners that newly-inaugurated Governor-General Frontenac had convened a full session of the Estates-General of Nouvelle France. At the newly completed Jesuit church of Québec, all members of this governing body had pledged their allegiance to the royal authority, and the following day, the Hurons and

Abenakis had voluntarily pledged their loyalty to the king and the new governor.

The people murmured among themselves. What was to become of the King's Sovereign Council? How could this governor install a form of council that had been abandoned in France over fifty years ago?

A rumor swept through the colony that Intendant Talon had granted the concession of a sizable island to his niece's husband, Montréal's royal Lieutenant-Governor François-Marie Perrot. Île-Perrot was located upriver from Canada's major fur trade center, and straddled the route normally traveled by native traders and coureurs who annually delivered their furs to the merchants of Montréal.

Before leaving for France on the last ship to sail that November, Intendant Talon recommended to Governor Frontenac that Louis Joliet would be most qualified Canadian explorer to search for the long-sought land route to the Mississippi River. Talon then carried a letter from Frontenac to Minister Colbert, in which the new governor stated: "I never saw anything more superb than the position of Québec. It could not be better situated as the future capital of a great empire." The new governor announced that he had accepted Courcelles' and Talon's advice to build a fort on Lake Ontario, stating that they were all convinced that such an installation would protect the Sulpician mission at Quinté, and safeguard the colony's fur trade from the Iroquois who delivered to the Dutch of New York those furs which they obtained from the Ottawa tribes.

Frontenac requested the assignment of French troops to Nouvelle France in order to maintain peace with the Iroquois who were becoming insolent toward the French, and to control the lawlessness of the illegal French traders who grew in number every day. He accused these coureurs of abandoning their farms, thereby jeopardizing the strength of the colony. He warned that these outlaws were joining together, threatening to build their own trading forts, and that many of them had already traded their furs at *Manatte* and Fort Orange of New York, thereby jeopardizing the colony's export. He promised to deal severely with them upon their return to Montréal in early spring.

A second letter from Frontenac recommended to Colbert that an iron forge be built at Champlain, on the Pépin River, downriver from the Cape. The governor requested that iron workers trained in the production of cannon be sent to Nouvelle France.

Frontenac had no troops, money, munitions or boats at his disposal. Anxious as he was to build his new fort, he devised the means to assemble what he needed without waiting for the French minister's reply.

Before the end of November, militia captains read a letter from the governor-general to the parish settlers, which ordered a general mobilization of all militia units, and corvées to construct a fort on Lake Ontario. The militiamen were called upon to provide boats, canoes, several hundred armed men with ample food supplies, artisans and their tools to clear the forest and build the fort, all at their own expense. Furthermore, the aristocratic governor-general called on all Carignan veteran officers and soldiers to join in this enterprise, and furnish their own canoes and supplies at their own expense. He explained that his purpose of this project was to impress upon the Iroquois nations an overwhelming sense of French power. He ordered that the expedition be prepared to leave immediately after spring sowing.

Bastien tensed upon hearing *corvée* which always reminded him of the unpaid years of labor he had served in wartime to satisfy his family's feudal obligation to their French landowner.

The cape habitants were shocked by this unexpected summons of the militia to build a garrison fort in the northwestern wilderness. No such campaign had been organized in Nouvelle France since Marquis de Tracy's venture into the Mohawk homeland, and even then, militiamen had served on a voluntary basis in spite of the direct Iroquois threat to the very survival of the French colony.

Marguerite was stunned. "How can this be? We're not at war with anyone—Does this mean that you must leave us again, Bastien?"

"I certainly hope not...." he muttered hotly, and left to join others who angrily questioned Nicolas Rivard on the church steps. Their militia captain had no answers for any of them.

Finally, Bastien asked him: "How will this fort be built in the wilderness?"

Rivard seemed relieved to have an answer to that query. "The structure most likely will be built of timber which will be cut and hewn on site. Metal fittings will be required in certain areas such as the gate and doors of the fort, its fireplaces and gun emplacements. Planks will be required for flooring and walls, wooden shingles for the roof of various buildings."

"Can any of these materials be prepared beforehand and carried to the site?"

"What are you suggesting?"

"Whenever we've been called upon to build a fort, or a redoubt, a basic plan was followed. Most parts of that structure were precut and pre-hewn to specific markings. Can we do any of that work this winter and transport these to the worksite?"

Rivard saw that this tactic might lessen the number of men who would have to travel as part of the workforce. It might also lead to quicker construction, but more difficult portages. "I'll pass that on, Bastien," he replied.

The village blacksmith, Michel Rochereau, came up behind him and tapped his shoulder. "I wish I could believe that your recommendation would permit me to stay home with my family, but I'm sure they'll still need me to fit the metal to the wood."

"Maybe so," Bastien reminded him, "but wouldn't you rather do most of your work at home?"

François Morni joined them. "This campaign may be what I've been waiting for; it's time for me to see what Canada is like beyond this village!"

Bastien thought this over and realized that he might be right. His engagé had never strayed from his employ. He had joined them as a very young man; seven years had already passed, and it was only natural that he should consider starting a farm and family of his own.

In London, Radisson and Des Groseilliers were called to answer Governor Bayly's charges that they were responsible for the rapid increase of French traders into Hudson Bay Company territory. Although they were innocent, Bayly knew that during their encounter with Father Albanel at Hudson Bay, the Jesuit priest had delivered letters to both of them from French Minister Colbert, offering proposals for their return to French service.

By the end of November, the weather turned colder as f winds blew in from the northwest, and snow began to fall for days at a time. The evenings grew longer, and Bastien made a small sandbox for Louis, who worked at scratching his diagonals and circles every evening. Marguerite weaved homespun and the girls did needlework to provide the family with warmer clothing. Young Sébastien played with his wooden cups and frolicked with Métis, while his father smoked his pipe and told François as much as he could about life on the trail. Louis listened attentively.

When their neighbor, Antoine Baillargée, died a month later, his widow Jeanne Dodier set additional conditions for the lease of her farm. She and Bastien met with Jean Cusson to negotiate a codicil to the original contract which required that Bastien's first yearly grain payment be delivered to her on February 2nd, rather than the following September 29th as had been agreed, and that any improvements he might make to the property were not to be undone at the end of the nine-year lease.

Martin Foisy fulfilled his purchase agreement for the concession at l'Arbre-à-la Croix by delivering twenty *minots* of wheat to Bastien on Christmas Day. This year's holiday was a happier occasion for them; not only were they all together, but the girls contributed their own gifts for each of the children, adding to those small treats that the parents placed in Louis' and young Sébastien's wooden shoes while they slept.

When their neighbors joined them for the traditional *réveillon* party after Midnight Mass, the men congregated in one corner of the room, where they speculated as to nature of the governor's future instructions. Michel the blacksmith and Nicolas Leblanc had already accepted the fact that they would be required to take part in this project. François Morni spoke with great enthusiasm. Bastien listened quietly, still hoping that he might be excused from this service because of his recent expedition to Hudson Bay.

This topic continued to cloud conversation at Jacques Massé's home where Bastien and his family shared Christmas dinner.

Marguerite and Catherine exchanged their own concerns with each other while they prepared the meal; Bastien and Jacques sat near the hearth and discussed the situation. The girls helped their mothers, and the younger children played in the far corner.

"Are you expected to take part in this?" Jacques asked.

"I still don't know. Although I'm weary of travel, I doubt that I'll be excused. This new governor-general is even more militant than Courcelles; he has much grander ideas for the growth and development of Nouvelle France. I expect that this is only the beginning of his plans for us."

"I know I'll have to go, but I hate to leave my wife and little ones."

"It's never easy—If François and I both have to leave, I can't help but wonder how Marguerite will manage on her own."

"Or Catherine."

Shortly after New Year's Day, Captain Rivard announced that the Carignan veterans who had settled in the country would join the expedition. He informed the settlers that project engineer Raudin had designed a log fort and palisades which could best be produced on-site from timber that must be cleared before construction, but he added that some of the materials needed to build several of the buildings within the enclosure could indeed be hewn ahead of time. He delegated to Bastien the responsibility of organizing the production of cedar shingles for the roofs; this construction component would be light enough to transport, yet time-consuming to produce.

Bastien split the shingles; Michel cut and formed the nails; François drilled a single hole in each shingle to receive the nails and bundled the roofing material together; Nicolas provided containers for the nails.

Bastien asked Rivard if he could be excused from the militia call-up.

"I'm sorry, *mon vieux*, but we've been told that everyone in our age group is to respond. Grandfathers and new recruits are the only exceptions."

That night, Bastien reluctantly shared the news with Marguerite.

Fear and anger crowded her dark brown eyes; she remained silent as she considered the repercussions of this second assignment which she felt to be terribly unjust. Marguerite had come to believe that he would not have to leave his family again. She felt very vulnerable.

Bastien could sense the tension of her body as they lay beside each other that night. He sought that calmness that she had always shared with him, and there was none offered through words or touch. Her reaction was quiet and unrelenting.

Finally, he told her gently: "You realize that I have no choice; I must go."

"And François? Will he also leave us?"

"It was never really his choice either."

"How will we manage on our own—one woman and four children?"

"Our neighbors will help, as they always have."

"Won't most of them be going with you?"

She was right, of course. Nicolas and Michel would certainly have to join the expedition. He didn't know about Guillaume Barette, or Jacques Vaudry, or Louis Lefebvre—Louis' carpentry skills most likely would be needed.

"This will only be for the summer, much like Marquis de Tracy's campaign into the Mohawk homeland. We'll sow the grain before we leave. The major task will be to harvest the winter grain in July. The girls can help you with that; it will take longer than usual to bring it into the barn, but if the weather holds up, I'm sure the three of you can manage it on your own. You'll just have to do the best you can—For all we know, I might be back by then."

"And what about the concession next door?"

"You're not to worry about that. Jeanne Dodier will just have to make her own arrangements to have it done."

"We can't hunt or fish..."

"I'll hunt for meat so we can process a new supply of pemmican before I leave. Then I'll speak to Red Dawn, and see if he can furnish some fresh meat or fish. He promised to take Louis hunting with his grandsons."

"Is Louis old enough?" she asked quickly.

"I trust Red Dawn's judgement about such things; Louis will be safe with him. He's already training him to hunt with bow and arrows."

Although his coming absence still weighed heavily on her—it seemed as though they were repeatedly being pulled away from each other—the impending burden did seem to lighten once they talked it over.

"I promise you, Marguerite, that I'll do everything within my power to see that you won't run out of anything that really matters, and that I'll come back to you as soon as I possibly can."

"I know you will, Bastien, but I miss you so much when you journey into that forest. I can't help but worry about you."

"I know this will be difficult for all of us, especially for you and the children, but hopefully, this will be our last separation."

The prolonged absence of sunspots continued to affect their weather; snow depth had already reached nine feet, and river ice was five feet thick. The weather limited the settlers to working indoors. Except for Michel who worked by the heat of his forge, the men prepared the shingles together in Bastien's barn, leaving occasionally to warm themselves by the hearth.

When the family's supply of eels ran out in February, Marguerite turned to the salted sturgeon and pigeon meat to provide their protein needs. She baked beans twice a week, and whenever the sun shone, Bastien ventured out to hunt for elk or moose. He and his neighbor Nicolas now had to travel deeper into the woods each time they went hunting on their *raquettes*.

At the end of February, François hitched the oxen to the long sledge and helped deliver the pine logs to the Jesuit seignory as land rent on Jeanne Dodier's concession. The men prepared for the collection of maple sap, and the process of boiling it down to syrup and sugar. This still remained the principal source of sweetener for the settlers, although cane sugar, molasses, and syrup were now available from the Antilles. Most of that supply came through New England, and was difficult to obtain through barter; coinage continued to be scarce in Nouvelle France.

By mid-March, the snow had begun to recede, although its depth remained unchanged in the shadows of the evergreen forest. The sugaring season lasted three weeks, during which time they boiled the sap around the clock, taking turns at continuously maintaining the fires under the large iron kettles they had suspended over the open stone hearth of their sugar hut.

By the end of April, the habitants feasted on spring fowl, when the sky filled with the honking of Canadian geese heading north to nest and rear their young. Soon afterward, dense flocks of mated mallards passed overhead.

A few weeks later, tree buds signaled that it was time to till the soil and sow their wheat, oat and barley crops. Militiamen throughout the Saint Lawrence River valley prepared for their long overland journey to Lake Ontario.

When deciduous trees leafed out in late May, the settlers planted corn in their partially cleared fields, around the stumps and girdled trees.

Bastien and Marguerite outfitted François for his overland trek. Bastien gave him his extra backpack, and lent him that set of voyageur hand tools that Talon had given him. But he packed in his own knapsack the special gift Red Dawn had given him as he prepared to leave on his long journey to the northern sea. That complete Algonquin traveling kit consisted of a tinder-horn, and a set of bone and stone hand tools.

There was every indication that Frontenac would complete his mission by the end of summer, so they would not require much extra clothing, and that would lighten their burden. Each man would carry his own musket, knife, hatchet and axe. Bastien fashioned rawhide covers to protect both the canoe and the cutting edges of his axhead. He provided two long poles which he laid in the bottom of the canoe, birch bail-out containers, and a waterproofed canvas to protect their belongings.

Marguerite prepared an emergency supply of pemmican for each of them. Bastien decided that he also wanted to carry a portion of ground cornmeal which he could bake into cakes while traveling through the forest. His older daughter Madeleine gave them extra pairs of stockings that she had sewn during the winter; Marguerite sewed two pairs of deerskin slippers for them to wear in the canoe; the men made their own rawhide moccasins and leather straps for trekking and carrying through the rough portages.

Late that month, as berry bushes and plants budded and leafed out, Jean Cusson prepared, and Bastien signed, a second procuration granting Marguerite power to act as his legal representative during his absence. It was through such an agreement that she had been able to sell their second concession during his yearlong absence.

The following day, Louis came running from the edge of the

bluff overlooking the great river, and called excitedly to his parents and sisters: "Come see! Come see the funny boats!"

Bastien picked up Sébastien and followed the rest of the family toward the edge of the bluff overlooking the river. They arrived just in time to see two barges, armed with small cannons and garishly decorated with red and blue paintings, heading upriver toward Montréal. As the two flatboats moved closer, Bastien recognized Governor Frontenac who was dressed in darker and hardier clothes than when he had inspected the mines; he was surrounded by members of his staff who wore colorful garments, and his own guards, all of whom wore burnished breastplates and swords. A flotilla of canoes followed close behind with regular troops from the garrison of the Chateau Saint-Louis; the soldiers were armed with muskets and wore metal helmets that reflected the sun's rays. Another group of canoes carried native scouts and militiamen.

Bastien and Marguerite glanced over at each other. Their hearts sank as they realized that the time had come for him to leave.

Four

June 10, 1673

Just before dawn, Marguerite awoke and turned toward Bastien's sleeping face. He was her love, her warmth, her security—and he was about to leave her again. She had discovered an inner strength during his long absence; that had come as a surprise to her, yet she felt it even now. I've been through this before and I've managed, she reminded herself.

She slipped quietly out of bed to prepare his hot breakfast.

Bastien and the children stirred from their slumber at the sounds of kitchen activities. The girls came down from the loft to help her, while both boys slipped beside him in bed, knowing that he would soon be gone again.

"Take good care of each other," their father admonished them. "*Maman* will need your help now, more than ever, because François is also leaving."

"Don't worry, Papa, we know what to do," Louis and Sébastien solemnly promised.

François joined the family for breakfast, but left early to help the other men who loaded the bundled shingles, nails and the metal fittings that Michel Rochereau had brought with him. While some held the birch bark canoes steadily afloat in the shallow water along the shore, others carefully and evenly distributed equal shares of their cargo into the three light river vessels.

Bastien stayed behind long enough to reassure Marguerite and the children that they would be well-taken care of during his absence, and reminded them that he would return as soon as possible, hopefully before the mid-summer harvest.

The children followed their mother's example and hid their sorrow while he prepared to go. Bastien kissed and blessed each child, kissed his wife and reluctantly left for another journey.

Jacques Massé, Guillaume Barette, and Michel Rochereau boarded the first canoe. François Morni, Nicolas Leblanc, and Louis Lefebvre got into the second. Bastien, Pierre Guillet, and Jacques Vaudry mounted the third.

They traveled together toward the cape village where they reported to Captain Rivard, who checked their supplies and those of the other eighteen militiamen. Then, with his two Algonquin scouts, he led the seven cape canoes to Trois-Rivières where they merged with Frontenac's main force. The governor's two garishly painted barges stood out in the predawn light.

Their mixed fleet of bateaux and canoes left for Montréal immediately after sunrise, and followed in the wake of the two Québec barges. The most experienced canoeist sat on a narrow seat at the bow where he watched for obstacles ahead of them and guided the steering; the least experienced sat in the middle position until he gained enough understanding to rotate positions with the paddlers; the helmsman responded to the bowsman's signals and moves. The only real break from their repetitive strokes came at midday, when they disembarked to stretch their legs and tend to their needs onshore.

Bastien explained to his aching friends that this first day was always the most difficult because of the length of the paddling sessions, and the awkward position they must maintain to ensure the stability of the heavily loaded canoes.

They disembarked again at dusk, at a sheltered, uncleared area, and while the lead man held the canoe in place, the others emptied it of its supplies and equipment. Then, while one man set up their camp fire, the other two lifted the birch-bark vessel out of the water, carried it ashore, and tipped it over to serve as partial shelter during the night.

Rivard kept his group close together while they traveled upriver for three more days.

At dusk on June 15th, Montréal's Lieutenant-Governor François-Marie Perrot, Charles Le Moyne and his Blue Coat militia greeted the arrival of Governor-General Frontenac with a full military salute. The local judge and head councilman welcomed him with their speeches, then while the Sulpician priests led a solemn procession to the church for the congregation's recitation of the Te Deum in honor of the governor-general, the soldiers and militiamen began to set up camp for the night.

Jacques Massé was impressed. "That was quite a ceremony! But who are these 'Blue Coats'?"

Bastien replied: "Montréal's elite militia, our most highly skilled fighters against the Iroquois warriors. They led the Carignan Regiment to the Mohawk villages. I'm glad to see that they'll be with us; they know the Iroquois better than anyone other than the missionaries, and they've earned their respect. *Sieur* Le Moyne knows their language, and I expect he'll be serving as translator during the meetings."

Massé asked: "Does anyone know how long it will take for us to reach Lake Ontario?"

Bastien understood his restlessness. "The only part of this journey that we can speed up will be the construction of the fort. Once that's done, they won't need us anymore."

"Then we'll be on our way home?"

Guillaume had also become restless. "If the Iroquois cooperate, *mon ami*—But right now, I'd like to see what Montréal is like at night. Will anyone join me?"

Bastien reminded him to talk that over with Captain Rivard. He did, and was warned to be back by the 9:00 p.m. curfew. Then François left with him.

Louis Lefebvre confessed that he was weary from the day's paddling and was just about ready to bed down. "Where does that man get all his energy?" he asked.

Bastien chuckled. "Guillaume was the first man I met when I arrived at Québec. He laughed at me because I had to catch my breath halfway up the hill to the fortress. I had trouble keeping up with him then, and I always will."

Pierre Guillet's eyes grew heavy. "I'm tired too, Louis. I feel as though I've spent a heavy day at construction. It won't be long before I fall asleep tonight."

Bastien sat puffing at his pipe. "Don't worry about it, you two. You'll get used to it soon enough. Give it a couple of days, then you'll more than keep up with the rest of us. Go ahead and rest."

Bastien kept a smoky fire going in an effort to control the dreaded mosquitoes that plagued them at night along the riverbank. The group huddled around it and talked about family, farming, and what lay ahead of them.

Jacques Vaudry spoke softly: "I can't understand why the governor called the militia when we've had no problem with the Iroquois at any of the settlements."

Bastien continued to smoke quietly, staring into the flames.

Massé added another log to the fire. "What I don't understand is why we need to build a fort so far into the forest."

"He told us that it's to protect the missions," Nicolas offered. "Surely, if there's any trouble brewing with the Five Nations, the missions would be the first to suffer."

Bastien looked up and said: "I think this may be an effort to control the coureurs. The priests always protest that these traders corrupt the missions with their cheap liquor. You know how eau-de-vie affects the natives—We saw it at the cape a few years ago."

"Well Bishop Laval and the king have certainly set a lot of strict penalties against that trade."

"But each year, more and more young men are leaving their farms to run through the woods to make more money."

"It must be a very difficult way of life in the woods."

"They claim that there's more freedom for them in the forest."

"Are they right, Bastien?"

"If they wish to live by their own rules."

"And in the meantime, the lands they have cleared and leave untilled are reclaimed by the forest."

Their friends returned from the village minutes before the fortress cannon sounded the curfew.

Bastien eyed them quizzically. They had been drinking, but not overly so. "How was it?" he asked.

François answered: "Not as big as I thought it would be—mostly one narrow street with small houses, palisaded seminary buildings, a hospital, and a windmill, mostly built of stone. The windmill has loopholes for defense, and there's a bastioned fort where Governor-General Frontenac and his party will stay with Lieutenant-Governor Perrot until we leave."

"Very crowded," Guillaume added, "but we heard some interesting talk."

They drew closer together and listened intently as he reported his news.

"A lot of grumbling against the call-up of the militia and the corvée."

They nodded knowingly.

"A lot of questions as to the governor's motives for building the fort."

Bastien glanced over at François, who nodded in agreement.

"Some say it might help to restore the flow of furs to Montréal—That's really slowed down during the past two years."

"Others say that the coureurs and the Iroquois are trading with the Dutch and English of New York."

Bastien's thoughts turned to Hudson Bay, where Radisson had complained of a drop in native fur deliveries. He recalled Radisson's speculation that the French coureurs were intercepting the northbound native traders, and diverting their furs east toward Nouvelle France.

The troops remained two weeks in Montréal, while Frontenac organized another corvée for the construction of a dry road extending from the frontier settlement to Cavalier de La Salle's former seignory at Lachine, a good three-hour distance on foot. He justified this project on the grounds that it would provide a safe overland route for transportation of their supplies, equipment, canoes, and two painted barks past the difficult Lachine rapids. During this time, the governor-general also organized his militia forces, received the Carignan veteran officers, and dealt with their mutual jealousies regarding lines of military authority. He reiterated that the call-up of the militia, and the corvées were necessary in order to convince the Iroquois of the overwhelming strength of French power.

Once the four hundred armed men, one hundred twenty canoes, some mission Indians, and the two armed barks had reached Lachine, Frontenac left Montréal on June 28th, and Lachine the following day.

This next portion of the journey proved to be extremely difficult to accomplish because of the series of rapids and falls that interrupted navigation on this section of the Saint Lawrence River. Poling proved to be impossible in many instances. Not only did the militiamen portage their own canoes and cargo, but they also hauled and pushed the heavy, awkward flatboats along the shore, sometimes in water knee-deep or up to their armpits, as they ascended the white water current. The men from Cap-de-la-Madeleine were already exhausted.

They reached Long Sault on the night of July 5th, when heavy rains brought them to a halt, and Frontenac grew concerned that his supply of biscuit might spoil; such a loss would have ruined his carefully thought out plans to impress the Iroquois. The biscuits survived, but because of the further delay, he sent a messenger to Onondaga to announce a postponement of the parley with the leaders of the Five Nations, moving it forward to July 15–20th.

A few days later, having passed that last rapid at Long Sault, the French forces finally reached calmer waters. Word spread through that evening's encampment that Frontenac had sent two Sulpician priests ahead to Quinté to relay the order that the parley would take place at Cataracoui, nearer where the waters of Lake Ontario flowed into the Saint Lawrence River.

The habitants were relieved to learn that they were now closer to their final destination. Bastien realized that the lake outlet would provide an ideal location for the fort, yet he wondered why it had not been the governor's original choice.

They reached the Thousand Islands area, where their canoes glided through a series of channels that flowed between what seemed like an endless number of rocky islets. These showed a variety of environments: some with lush coves, others dry and craggy, still others damp and covered with moss and ferns.

On July 12th, they sighted the open waters of Lake Ontario, and the troops broke out with a cheer.

Governor Frontenac called them to order, and immediately set their canoes in battle formation. The lead position included the four divisions of Montréal Blue Coats, and uniformed Carignan veterans and regulars with polished helmets. The two brightly ornamented flatboats followed close behind them with their loads of supplies and armament for the fort.

A second line of canoes carried Frontenac and his entourage, whose colorful clothing, polished chest armor, lances and swords were meant to dazzle the Iroquois. Regular troops with shining helmets followed in canoes holding musket to shoulder, with the Trois-Rivières contingent covering their left flank, and native allies covering their right. Two more squadrons of canoes, paddled by armed habitants and woodsmen, formed the final line.

Several Iroquois chiefs approached in an elm bark canoe to greet them. Their haughty spokesman announced that the leaders of their five nations awaited Governor-General Frontenac at Cataracoui and offered to lead the French official to the meeting site.

They reached an area where a large number of Iroquois camping sheds stood at the edge of the forest. The French disembarked nearby, and while some of the troops unloaded the canoes, bateaux, and barks, others set up camp under the direction of their officers. Frontenac spent three hours briskly walking the site with his engineer Raudin, scrutinizing its features from a military point of view, while the Iroquois chiefs watched quietly from a distance.

Meanwhile, the governor's guard set up his grand pavilion, and installed the standard of France at its entrance. Raised high on its pole, the silken white flag, emblazoned with several golden fleurs-de-lis, flapped majestically in the wind. Once this was done, Frontenac retired to his quarters for the night.

While the governor and Raudin reviewed the final construction plans for the fort, regulars and habitants began to level an adjoining area of the forest according to the engineer's demarcation lines; they worked furiously with axe and saw throughout the night, driven by concern for their midsummer harvests. Others dug a trench for the erection of the palisades. Still others set up a pile of firewood to be lit the following morning, and prepared an area for the next day's initial meeting by spreading the barges' sails on the ground in front of the governor's pavilion.

The sounds of axe, saw and shovels continued throughout the night.

Cape-de-la-Madeleine, mid-July 1673

Winter wheat fields lightened in color, and the women and children at the cape prepared for the mid-summer harvest. Marguerite had seen how Bastien handled the scythe, but found it too heavy and cumbersome for her own use; she was more experienced with the lighter sickle. Since she only had one of these hand tools, she purchased two more and taught Madeleine and Marie how to use them.

Marguerite regularly inspected the fields and, when the grains had fully ripened, she and her daughters moved forward to reap in parallel swaths, each moving forward slightly behind the other. They worked awkwardly at first, but gradually developed a smooth and effective rhythm of motion. In this fashion, they advanced through the four-foot high wheat, oats and rye, while Louis remained nearby to watch over his younger brother.

When they tired of cutting, they bundled their harvest into sheaves, binding each of these with a thin handful of grass, tying both its ends together with knots. Madeleine and Marie worked through a great deal of frustration before they finally mastered this task. They were all exhausted by the end of the first day.

Five

Cataracoui, mid-July 1673

French drums beat a sharp tattoo at dawn, calling the formally dressed troops to attention. They marched in single file to form a row on either side of the space which separated the Iroquois encampment from Frontenac's pavilion. More than sixty chiefs walked warily through this corridor to the place of council, and sat on the carpeted ground; none, even among the most elderly of the natives, had ever seen a French soldier in full dress uniform.

Amid the silence, Frontenac emerged from his tent. Dressed in full military regalia, with plumed hat and sheathed sword, he strode to a highly gilded and ornamented chair facing his semicircled adversaries. He sat and studied the inscrutable faces before him; they in turn surveyed the elaborate and colorful setting he had prepared for this opening ceremony.

Finally, their chosen spokesman, Onondaga chief Garakontié, opened the council meeting with a long respectful greeting to the French governor. Then each Iroquois leader came forward to present the customary porcelain necklace to the *Onontio*.

Frontenac ordered that the campfire be lit near the chiefs, and Charles Le Moyne de Longueuil came forward in his role as interpreter between the two parties.

"My children," the governor began his address, "I am pleased to see you here where I have lit a fire by which you can smoke your pipes while I speak to you. You have done well, my children, to follow the orders of your father. Have no fear, my children, for my words are gentle and full of peace, words that will fill your cabins and villages with joy."

He signaled that ten armfuls of tobacco be distributed among the chiefs, then resumed his address.

"Be reassured that I have come here to meet with you because it is only just, that a father know his children and that the children know their father." He promised to be kind to his children as long as they obeyed him, and he expressed his regret that they must communicate through an interpreter.

During Le Moyne's translation of this message, Frontenac signaled that a musket be presented to each nation, and generous portions of glass beads, prunes, and raisins to the women, along with wine, brandy, and biscuit.

Immediately following the noon meal, French workmen began to dig the trench that would encircle the fort.

Once this introductory meeting was over, Frontenac fraternized with the chiefs and their families during the next several days. He dined with their leaders and entertained them, befriended the children, and gave gifts to the the wives and children.

Meanwhile, his conscripted laborers worked at a furious pace, fully within view of the natives.

Cap-de-la-Madeleine

Despite their exhaustion from several days of harvesting, Marguerite and her daughters began to move their grain into the barn while the weather remained favorable. Once they had enough sheaves to justify hitching the oxen to their cart, Marguerite struggled to remember how to accomplish this task. She lacked Bastien's strength but, with her daughters' help, she managed to lift the yoke into place. They soon realized that they could not master directing the oxen, so the three of them loaded the old hand sledge, and manually transported as much as they could on their own.

Cataracoui, July 17th

By the time the grand council reconvened at Cataracoui on July 17th, the governor had already demonstrated an instinctive understanding of the Iroquois mind. Age implied wisdom to these bold native warriors, and on this basis, they had already accepted Frontenac's fatherly manner.

He urged them to adopt the Christian teachings offered by the Black Robes. He cautioned them that if *Onontio* had come so easily with this great a force merely to visit them in friendship, what would he do if they angered him? He warned them not to molest his Indian allies, or he would chastise them. He advised them not to trust "bad men" who might seek to lead them astray, but to trust "men of character" such as French explorer Cavalier de La Salle. He asked that they allow their children to learn French from the missionaries so that they might become one people with the French, and he invited their children to study at Québec.

The following day, Frontenac presented fifteen muskets, powder and shot to the leaders of the Five Nations. He counseled them to trust in his kindness, the proof of which was this storehouse at Cataracoui where they could obtain all the trading goods they needed. "I will soon furnish it with a wealth of merchandise so that you need not carry your furs as far as you have in the past. I will offer these goods to you at fair prices and I will enforce fair trade. I will punish any of my men who might attempt to cheat you."

The Iroquois chiefs asked that the French assist them in defeating their enemy, the Andastes, who lived in the Susquehannah valley and the Chesapeake Bay region. "It would be shameful for *Onontio* to allow his children to be oppressed as they soon expect to be," declared one Iroquois leader.

They also wanted to know what value the French would now place on their furs. As for their children learning the French language, the chiefs replied that they must return to their villages before reaching a decision.

Two days later, the French completed construction of the fort.

Three days after the end of the council meeting, the Iroquois left, and the governor sent many of his forces home by detachments, beginning with the habitants and craftsmen whom he no longer needed. The first to leave were those from Québec, then Trois-Rivières, and finally Montréal.

Frontenac repeated his admonitions to another group of Iroquois who arrived later from their villages north of Lake Ontario.

By August 1st, the governor appointed his new ally, Cavalier de La Salle, as commandant at Cataracoui. In addition, he assigned enough men to defend the fort, received delivery of a year's provisions and merchandise for the storehouse, and gave orders for additional tasks to be completed through the winter. Then he embarked with his guard to begin the return journey downriver to Québec.

Montréal, early August

Bastien and his friends arrived at dusk, a full day earlier than they had expected, due to their rapid progress with the downriver flow, riding some of the rapids, and carrying much lighter loads.

Rivard invited Bastien to venture into town with him in search of bread, wine, and cheese, while the others stayed behind to rest and set up camp for the night.

They had walked a third of the distance in silence, when the militia captain asked: "Are you always this quiet, Bastien?"

Bastien seemed startled by the question. "Forgive me, Nicolas; I've been worried about my family, and how Marguerite has managed since we left."

"I can understand that. I'm sure our families will be very tired by the time we get back."

"I didn't expect to be away this long."

"Neither did I, but that road construction, pulling those barks upriver, and the weather really slowed us down."

They were quiet again, then Bastien asked tentatively: "Were you surprised by any of it?"

Rivard hesitated, and eyed him thoughtfully. He knew Bastien well enough by now to be confident of his discretion. "Yes, I was."

"Did you expect this to be a trading post?"

"Never. "

"Does the king's edict still stand—that all fur trade must be conducted only at Montréal, Trois-Rivières, and Québec?"

"I've never heard otherwise."

Montréal was rife with heated debate and rumors. Word of Frontenac's performance had already spread as a result of the

Québec contingent's passage through this settlement on their way home. Rivard did not want to become involved in the debate, nor to be questioned. He and Bastien quickly obtained the food and slipped back to their encampment.

That night, François Morni told his employer that he would soon join his soldier friends in the Richelieu valley.

Bastien had suspected as much, because Morni had spent most of his free time with the two veterans while at Cataracoui.

"I'm happy for you, François. You're more than ready to start a life of your own. When will you leave?"

"They offered to recommend me for a land concession near theirs, and once they take care of their summer harvest, they'll come for me."

"That should take at least a couple of weeks. "

"I think so. "

"I wish you well. I'm sure you'll get a good start with their help. They're good men."

"They also told me that their wives have a few unmarried young women who would like to meet me."

They both laughed at this, and toasted the occasion with some of the wine that Rivard had managed to find.

Bastien had been impressed by Frontenac's diplomatic performance with the Iroquois, yet he remained troubled by it. He saw the governor as a man imbued with aristocratic power who relished any opportunity to wield it. Although he couldn't identify the cause of his discomfort, he felt threatened by this change in method of colonial governance. The entire project at Cataracoui had reminded him of the peasant status he had rejected by leaving his homeland. He now sensed that feudalism might have followed him across the sea.

He and François arrived home to a warm welcome in mid-August, too late to help with the harvest, but able to finish up the midsummer chores and relieve the stress on the family. Jeanne Dodier's grain field remained untouched by the sickle.

Marguerite huddled close in his arms; her eyes filled with tears as she saw him look disappointedly toward the neighbor's field. "I'm truly sorry, Bastien, but it was physically impossible for us to do anything about it."

He realized that she was exhausted, and so were the girls. "Don't you worry about that. I told Jeanne that she must take care of it herself. François and I will salvage what we can; I think we can gather enough for the lease payment. Meanwhile, I insist that you get to bed—all of you. We'll have plenty of time to talk after you've rested."

She yawned. "Aren't you tired as well?"

"Don't you worry about us; take care of yourself and rest." He guided her toward the bed; she collapsed onto it, and immediately fell asleep.

Seven-year old Marie hugged him. "It's been really hard, Papa."

His eyes moistened. "I know, Marie. You did really well. I'm proud of all of you. Go to bed now, and I'll have a hot meal ready for you when you wake up."

Bastien sent François to assess the condition of the crops and fields, while he rummaged through their food storage for the makings of a meal. He found dried sturgeon, fresh vegetables and milk, onions, butter, but no bread.

While he set about mixing a batch of dough, and preparing the ingredients for a fish stew, François returned with his report.

"They did better than I expected, Bastien. I don't think you need me any more." He smiled as he continued: "Your wheat, oats and rye are in the barn. That storage will need to be straightened out. The crops next door are surprisingly in good shape. The weather has apparently been good for us. Three days of work with the scythes and we should salvage at least half of that grain."

These were good news. "Why don't you get us some beer from the cellar while I prepare the food."

"I didn't know that you could cook and bake, Bastien."

His employer looked up from mixing the bread dough, and matched his smile. "This came in handy until I found myself a wife."

By the end of the first week, the girls had completely recuperated from their ordeal, and life fell into its normal routine.

Marguerite and Madeleine harvested the peas and beans. The field of flax had flowered; Marguerite pulled out the three-foot plants and bound them into *chapelles* which she placed upright to dry in the field. Bastien took Louis duckhunting along the reedy south shore.

Everyone regretted that they would soon lose François.

"We'll all miss him, of course, but will you be able to work both farms without him?" Marguerite asked.

"I know I will—after all, we managed quite well during our lease of Louis Lefebvre's land."

"Would it be difficult to replace him?"

"It would be an extra burden right now not only to look for the right person, but also to train him in our way of doing things."

Bastien went alone to the village to ask Jean Cusson to prepare a document recommending François Morni for a concession, vouching for his industry, honesty and reliability. He made his mark on it, and was about to leave when the notary held him back.

"Have you heard that a crew of the king's cannon-makers have arrived, and that they'll make use of our iron ore?"

"No, I didn't know that. They must need those guns for the ships that Intendant Talon was building at Québec."

"I've been told that that project has been discontinued because of our short shipping season. We can't compete with Boston ships that sail year-round and are closer to the southern sea."

"Then maybe we'll be producing them for France."

The royal notary shrugged his shoulders and changed the subject. "Several of your neighbors have asked that their sons be taught to read and write."

"We talked about Louis' lessons during the voyage, but I didn't know how serious they were about it."

"Barette, Vaudry, Rochereau, Leblanc, Lefebvre have already approached me. My son Jean could help me with the lessons, but first, I believe that they should all practice circles and strokes as your Louis has done. Then it would be more productive for them to get together as a group at least twice a week—perhaps at one of your homes? The formal lessons won't begin until late next spring."

"That's fine with me, Jean. Do you want me to tell them?"

"You'll have to agree where the sessions will be held, then either Jean or I will travel to that location."

"Will they be using ink and paper? I understand that they can be quite expensive."

"Oh, no. We'll furnish the ink, but you fathers must provide the birch bark and quill pens with which they'll practice—We'll teach you how to prepare those at our first lesson."

A week later, while Marguerite and the girls laid out the flax in the field to ret naturally with the morning dew, and Bastien topped and nipped the flower buds and axillary growth off his tobacco plants, the boys came running from the edge of the bluff.

"Two men just arrived in a canoe, and they're carrying it up here!" Louis reported breathlessly.

Just then, his parents recognized two of their former soldier-pensioners who called out: "Ho there! *Notre jolie canadienne!*"

The veterans had not changed very much in the six years since they had left the bunkhouse; their banter with François seemed to continue where it had left off. They teased the girls and entertained the boys, yet Madeleine was the only one of the children to remember them.

While Marguerite baked fresh bread and berry pies, and prepared a meal of fresh fish and corn on the cob to share with their friends, the soldiers told Bastien that reports of Frontenac's last speech to the Iroquois had preceded his return to Montréal.

The corporal told him: "The fur merchants were very upset by his surprise announcement at Cataracoui." He grinned and went on: "Since Intendant Talon had granted Lieutenant-Governor François-Marie Perrot that island upstream from Lachine, he had already grown wealthy through dealing with the fur convoys before they reached Montréal. Governor Frontenac's new trading fort at Cataracoui threatens the operation at Île-Perrot."

His companion continued: "Governor Perrot immediately confronted Governor-General Frontenac when he arrived. Perrot reminded him of the king's ordinances regarding the fur trade, and accused him of engaging in illegal trading activities by setting up a trading fort at the head of the Saint Lawrence River."

The corporal added: "Governor Frontenac stationed his military representative at Montréal, with written orders to arrest any coureur de bois who traded furs without his express permission.

"A few days later, a royal sergeant arrived at the home of a friend of Perrot—a man named Carion—to arrest two coureurs who both managed to get away. When Perrot heard of the incident, he chastised the local judge who had issued the arrest warrant without having consulted him as governor of Montréal."

"When Frontenac learned of this, he ordered the arrest of Carion who had given refuge to the two coureurs. Perrot arrived in time to protest this action against a member of his government. When Frontenac's lieutenant of the guard presented his governor's written order, Perrot threw it in his face. He in turn arrested the officer and kept him under guard."

Bastien remembered that during his first few years in Canada there had been a similar quarrel between the church authorities of Québec and Montréal when papal representative Bishop Laval and Sulpician abbé de Queylus had both claimed authority over church affairs in Canada. Laval had ultimately won with Jesuit support. Now, he saw that a similar power struggle had extended into the sphere of government.

The two Carignan veterans had married and had children. They expressed their pleasure at having François join them in the Richelieu River valley where hunting and fishing were good and the soil yielded bountiful crops.

They asked Bastien about his yearlong voyage to Hudson Bay, and were amazed at what he had to say. Their conversation continued through most of the night.

The following morning, François Morni had very little to carry, but he did have several coins that he had saved over the years. Bastien's notarized letter of recommendation brought a grateful hug from his engagé.

"I'll never forget everything you've done for me, Bastien."

Bastien replied. "We feel as though we're losing part of our own family, François. May God be with you always."

After another series of hugs, the three men left by canoe and headed upriver to Montréal.

"Will we ever see him again?" Louis asked.

"I don't know," Bastien replied.

Just then, they saw two travelers walking toward them from the direction of the village.

René le Cordier

Six

Late August 1673

The two men seemed vaguely familiar to Bastien, but he knew that they were not from the cape nor from Trois-Rivières.

"Ho! Bastien! They told us that we'd find you here!"

The voice was familiar…

"We told you that we'd come to visit once you settled down!" said the other man.

Another vaguely familiar voice…

"Do you still play chess?"

"Of course!" Bastien ran toward them. "René le Cordier! François le Charpentier!"

He enthusiastically welcomed them to his home, relieved them of the weight of their packs, and introduced them to his family, telling Marguerite: "These two served as ropemaker and carpenter on the ship that carried me here from France!" He turned to them. "How long has that been? I'd given up hope of ever seeing you two again!

"Marguerite, François made that chessboard and gave it to me when we arrived at Québec; and René gave me that special hemp seed that we shared with Intendant Talon!"

She welcomed both men, knowing now that these must be very good friends of her husband if they had come to visit him after such a long time.

They moved into the house and began to exchange their news over a cup of cool cider and a wedge of berry pie.

Bastien took out his well worn game board, and told them: "You know, I made one of these last winter to pass the time during our long evenings up north."

"We heard about your voyage to the northern sea—that's quite a way to travel by land," René remarked. Then he asked: "Tell me, did you ever make rope?"

The children giggled, and their parents smiled. "Yes, I did, twice for the same project," he replied.

"Did the seed produce good fiber?"

Marguerite rose and retrieved a sample for him to examine. He seemed pleased with the quality. "I've woven it into burlap for seed bags," she replied, "and into cord which Bastien twisted into rope for the bed support."

"May I see that?"

He judged that the final twisting could have been wound tighter with better equipment and planned to look into that, but not right now.

Bastien and Marguerite noticed that he looked very tired, and heard François ask him: "Are you all right, René?"

"Just tired from the walk—I envy you, Bastien; you have a fine family."

Bastien took his wife's hand. "Marguerite and I have been blessed, René."

"How did you two meet out here in this wilderness?"

"We met and committed to each other before I left France, but it wasn't until five years later that I managed to build a home for us."

"And you waited all that time to marry? That took a lot of patience," François remarked.

"She was worth waiting for."

"And so was he," she added. "Of course, we had a lot of encouragement from our friends and Bastien's family."

"Yes," her husband acknowledged, "*Père* Allouez for one—A Jesuit priest who granted this concession, supported, and encouraged me during a difficult time."

"And also *Sieur* Boucher, and Madame Dousset."

René's eyes grew heavy.

"Would you like to lie down on the bed and rest?" Marguerite asked.

"I'd appreciate that," he replied.

François signaled his approval to Bastien. "Perhaps this would be a good time for you to show me your workshop, my friend."

Marguerite sent out the children to do their chores while she quietly tidied up the kitchen. René soon fell asleep under the blue blanket.

"Is he sick?" Bastien asked as they walked to the barn.

"He's been granted a leave from duty because this last trip was very difficult for him. The doctor at Québec told him that he should no longer sail across the sea."

"I'm sorry to hear that."

"The problem is that he has no family left in Normandie, and he's never married, so he's alone in the world. The ship was his home, the crew was his family; now he's grown too old for sailing— You know how powerful those ocean storms can be. I brought him here hoping that you might be able to help him."

"When does your ship sail?"

"In early October."

"Perhaps all he needs is plenty of rest and Marguerite's cooking."

"I think it will take more than that, Bastien."

"Then we'll think of something."

When they reached the barn and workbench area, François immediately focused on the collection of carving tools. He was surprised to learn that Bastien had made most of his furniture and had carved a periwinkle design on many of those pieces. "These are well done, Bastien. I didn't know you could carve like this."

"It's mostly been a family tradition." He added that he had learned to hew timber to specification during his indenture.

"I look forward to seeing some of your work—You once mentioned to us that you hoped one day to make rope for the colony—Have you done that?"

Bastien shook his head. He had never had the time nor the expertise to fulfill that ambition, but he remembered that during the terrible summer drought following the great earthquake, it had been difficult for him to find the heavy rope he needed to haul river water up the bluff to irrigate his crops. "There's a chronic shortage of it in the settlements. What we do have is mostly imported from France."

"Consider this: If I were to build a ropewalk with these tools, and René helped you to produce the rope, could you sell it?"

"I'd have to ask the local merchants, but, yes, I believe so."

"You'd need some samples to show them."

"How long can you stay?"

"We were given a six-week leave—The captain knew that René couldn't travel alone. My apprentice is filling in for me, but I should return earlier, if possible."

"That doesn't give us much time, yet if this should work, I think I could talk him into staying here with us. I doubt that he'd want to, unless he felt he could contribute in some way."

René reacted enthusiastically to their proposal, and he examined the hemp that Bastien had accumulated over the years. "I could work with this, but first, it must be processed to release the fibers."

Bastien told him: "We can all pitch in to accomplish that; Marguerite and I have often prepared our own flax and hemp."

They immediately planned the construction of a ropewalk for twisting the rope and cable, and decided to set up the new equipment in the barn so that it could be used regardless of the weather. While René drew up his plans and specifications, the others used the flax brake, then scraped and combed the fiber.

Meanwhile, Marguerite and her daughters gathered the retted flax into bundles and hung these to dry from the loft rafters.

Québec, late August 1673

Upon his return from Cataracoui, Governor Frontenac received a letter from Minister Colbert which was dated June 13th of that year, yet it had just recently reached Québec. In it, the king's minister reprimanded him for having called the Estates-General, a form of representative council that had been long avoided in France as being overly democratic, and a threat to the king's absolute authority.

The governor immediately wrote to the king and Minister Colbert, offering a detailed report of his expedition to Cataracoui, in which he stressed the strategic importance of that site. He described the fort and promised to develop control of lakes Erie and Ontario by building another fort at Niagara, and a ship for each of the two great lakes.

Frontenac also received a full report from his Lieutenant of the Guard Jacques Bizard, who had been summarily prevented by the governor of Montréal from carrying out Frontenac's arrest order against Philippe de Carion. Upon learning of this incident, Frontenac sent a conciliatory letter to Perrot, inviting him to Québec to explain his actions.

Cap-de-la-Madeleine

Early that September, civil announcements revealed that Jesuit Father Marquette and Louis Joliet had discovered the great Mississippi River.

Militia Captain Rivard also announced to his fellow parishioners that Québec's Sovereign Council had registered a new royal ordinance declaring that under penalty of death, none of the inhabitants of Nouvelle France could leave their homes and enter the forest for more than twenty-four hours without the express permission of the governor-general of Canada.

Upon receiving their instructions from René, François cut and marked oak logs to length, and Bastien hewed them to the ropemaker's specifications. They trimmed the joint ends, and drilled the trunnel holes with the hand auger. Then they all worked together to assemble the various parts of the ropewalk equipment.

During this activity, they heard loud honking and squawking overhead, and saw the earliest signs of the autumn geese and duck migrations.

Bastien told his guests: "You'll soon witness something very special that's never been seen in France."

He began to carry his musket with him whenever they worked outdoors, and Louis practiced with his bow and arrows, hoping that he might go bird hunting with his father.

The men built four separate solid oak sections with transverse pieces of equal height. François securely anchored the two largest and heaviest units at opposite corners of the barn floor.

The first unit was securely anchored to the floor; its heavy cross-piece allowed for the controlled feeding of three strands which would be counter-twisted into three-stranded rope. It could also allow the secondary processing of three ropes for counter-twist into a nine-stranded cable.

The second unit had two transverse pieces and stood on a four-wheeled base. Its first transverse secured a large wooden spool which tapered its feed, and had three lengthwise notches from wider to narrow end; these notches served to guide the three strands or ropes that would be counter-twisted together. Its second transverse, about a foot beyond the first, held two upright trunnels to keep the rope aligned after its of counter-twist.

The next and lightest unit stood free, and was shaped like a sawhorse with upright trunnels to keep the rope or cable properly aligned; its function was to allow René and Bastien enough room to stand on either side of it in order to manually smooth the counter-twist with iron rods.

The fourth and last unit was also secured to the floor and had a large hole in its transverse part which allowed the rope or cable to pass through for its controlled twisting. The rope or cable also could be held firmly in position here while it was being smoothed on either side of the the third section.

Just as they successfully completed this ten-day project, massive autumn bird migrations flew overhead on their way south for the winter. The two sailors stood in awe as they watched dense clouds of Canadian geese flying and honking boisterously in V-shaped formations, casting their shadows upon the land.

The birds passed too high for Louis' bow and arrows, but Bastien easily shot a few which Louis insisted on carrying home to his mother. Later that day, however, some of the birds landed in their field to feed on dropped grain seed. Five-year old Louis stalked them from the edge of the woods, and shot at a few, but his stealth proved to be more effective than the power of his shot; although he hit two of the birds, his arrows merely glanced off his prey.

René and François shared a new experience that night as they feasted on freshly roasted goose.

"Do you eat like this all the time?" asked the carpenter, as he deftly cut into a thigh piece.

"Only during the spring and fall migrations, when we can also enjoy fresh duck, sturgeon, and eel," Bastien replied.

"I wouldn't expect sturgeon in these waters," René reflected.

"Oh yes, they're man-sized, and they fill the Saint Lawrence from shore to shore as they swim toward the sea. Great schools of eels will follow them downriver soon afterward."

"I've never eaten eel," René told them.

"You're in for a treat. We cook them fresh whenever we can and dry the rest to feed us through the winter. They're an excellent source of oil."

"How are the winters here?"

"Very cold, very snowy, but beautiful. Time for us to catch up on our maintenance chores, clear the forest, and hunt for meat."

René remained quiet for a long time while the others continued to talk.

"We haven't had much news from France. What's happening over there?" Bastien asked.

François answered: "More wars with the Dutch, the Spanish, and the Holy Roman Empire; France is forever pushing against its borders. Do you know about Versailles?"

"What about it?"

"A few years after you came to Canada, King Louis XIV and his court began to spend their summers at Versailles, just outside Paris. He eventually created a major construction project there as a permanent residence for his government and the aristocracy. They say that hundreds of men died or were injured during its construction. I've been told that it's become the finest and most expensive royal palace in all of Europe, attracting artists from many other countries. I've also heard that there are more servants there than the entire French population of Canada. Those people spoke of a great room with mirrored walls that repeat, against each other without end, the reflections of candlelight and of the room's occupants."

Bastien's scalp prickled. "Isn't that about the time when the peasants of Blois were starving for lack of bread, and epidemics raged throughout the countryside?"

The anger in his voice silenced the conversation.

Marguerite touched his hand as though to calm him; she had seen the effects of that period of famine and disease while she was still at Pithiviers, just before she had left France. She knew that he had been deeply worried about the welfare of his four brothers and a sister whom he had left behind.

She rose abruptly to clear the table of dishes, and announced: "It's almost time for sunset, shall we go out and enjoy it?"

A few days later, René told them that he was ready to try out the equipment. "We have enough fiber now to run samples. We should twist a length of rope and another of cable that you can show to your merchants."

He demonstrated his techniques, and in doing so, made a few minor adjustments. This practice run also helped to determine how large a crop of hemp Bastien must grow the following year.

Bastien and René introduced samples of their rope to merchants at the local village and at Trois-Rivières; these contacts generated immediate demand for their product. When Jean Cusson prepared equitable agreements that proved to be acceptable to all parties, the combined results of their efforts greatly cheered René and François just as they were about to return to their ship at Québec.

Bastien finally asked his friend: "Will you stay with us, René?"

The ropemaker hesitated only briefly as he considered the import of this invitation. "It would give me great pleasure to remain here with your family, Bastien, but would I be able to pay my way?"

"If you stay, Jean Cusson has recommended that we share the profits. You would sleep in the bunkhouse, but you would be very much a part of our family, sharing meals and daily activities with us, with the freedom to retreat to your own quarters whenever you need to rest from our hectic schedule. I know I couldn't produce enough rope on my own without your experience and guidance; you need a home and workshop right now. Your product has been very well received—Will you stay?"

The ropemaker's eyes revealed his emotional relief and gratitude. "Of course, I will. It's very good of you and your wife to ask me."

Marguerite and the children hugged this man who had already become a part of their family in the few short weeks that he had spent with them.

François expressed his gratitude. He could now return to Québec knowing that the ropemaker had found safe haven.

The carpenter packed his few belongings, but before he left, he presented young Louis with a carved replica of the ship that had carried his father to Canada. All of the children examined this very closely, for it was much different from the sailing shallops that they had seen on the river.

When François headed toward the village to board Toulin's river vessel, Bastien and René walked part of the way with him.

"I'll most likely never see either one of you again and that saddens me, but having experienced a little of the life you'll share here, I know that everything will go well for both of you. There were times when I was almost tempted to stay myself, but it's too early for me to give up the sea. I wish the very best that life can offer to both of you—and to your family, Bastien. I thank God that we met you so many years ago.

"And you, René. We've been shipmates for longer than I care to remember; you were always a good friend and like a brother to me. I'll miss you, and so will our fellow crew members, but I'm confident that you're in good hands—I wish you health and happiness in your new home. God be with you."

They hugged each other and said their final goodbyes. Bastien and René watched François le Charpentier walk away from them, then turned toward home.

After supper that evening, Bastien took out his calvados to share with his Norman friend. While he and Marguerite officially welcomed René into the family, Madeleine, Marie, Louis, and young Sébastien joined the toast with their own cups of apple cider.

"I'm very much surprised to have this here in Nouvelle France. I vaguely remember that this was a very special brandy in Normandie."

"Yes, it's very rare to find it here. My first employer, *Sieur* Boucher gave this to us as a wedding present. Thanks to him, Marguerite also had safe passage across the sea."

"Where are you from?" she asked the ropemaker.

"A small village on the coast of Normandie—I was born to a large family of fishermen, the youngest of many boys."

"Do you still have family there?"

"I don't know—I left home at an early age and never went back. I loved sailing, but had no wish to spend my life fishing in the

North Sea; I was old enough to know that too many men never came back at the end of the day."

The children listened quietly.

"I joined a merchant ship as a young cabin boy. Fortunately, the ropemaker showed interest in me and took me on as his apprentice. A few years later, I qualified for my first job on a small sea-going vessel. Ever since then, I've been sailing across the sea."

"Have you ever regretted that choice?" Bastien asked. "It must have been lonely for you at times, without family."

"There was a certain camaraderie at sea which more than made up for it," René replied thoughtfully. "You made a similar choice by leaving your family and Marguerite behind."

"There seemed to be no future for me in France. Taxes were so high that a peasant labored for everyone's benefit but his own and never had enough of his harvest left over to properly feed and clothe his children—that too was a difficult life to face. I was forced to serve a long time in the army, and when I returned to Orléanais, everything had changed for the worse. I spent a year trying to get back into it, but found that I no longer took pleasure in farming someone else's land. When a visiting priest spoke in church one day, the colonial life he described just seemed right for me, so here I am."

"But it still took a lot of courage."

Bastien shrugged his shoulders. "I knew that Marguerite would join me one day." He and his wife smiled at each other, and the children basked in the warmth of their obvious affection.

Seven

Bastien turned over to René the entire supply of dried hemp that he had collected and stored in a corner of the barn. Although the ropemaker would have preferred a fresh supply of the fiber, they had their first order to fulfill, and this would be the true test of all their equipment. Bastien worked his flax-brake to break open the straw, and a wooden swingle knife to clear the fibers from the inner bark and the remaining gummy substance that had bound them together.

Although Marguerite lent René the graduated series of hatchels that she normally used to comb her flax, this bast fiber was thicker and stiffer, and therefore initially required a coarser, stronger carding tool to separate the longer fibers from the shorter tow. Michel Rochereau provided the iron spikes for the construction of just such a tool for Bastien and René.

Once everything was assembled, the ropemaker began to comb the long hemp fibers by slapping the crushed stalks against the stationary comb and pulling their fibers through the spikes.

Meanwhile, Bastien used his scythe to harvest their grain crops, while Marguerite and Madeleine followed behind him to bind the sheaves and stand them in the field. Then, while he tilled and harrowed the soil for his autumn sowing of winter wheat, oats and rye, Marguerite gathered her onions and herbs and hung them to dry in the house loft. The girls began to collect nuts in the nearby forest, and Louis kept watch over young Sébastien.

One leisurely evening while the men sat watching the children's activities, it occurred to Bastien that his friend had gradually become a natural extension of his family.

"You know, René, we had just bid farewell to our long-time engagé when you came down the road with François. Morni and four Carignan soldiers were the only other occupants of that bunkhouse."

"We had heard that Nouvelle France was in serious danger from the Iroquois; François and I worried about your safety."

"It was a very bad time—No one was allowed to sail back to France, because none could be spared from defending the colony."

"Then the Carignan Regiment was successful?"

"There were two campaigns: one in mid-winter, then another that following autumn which proved to be the more successful. We reached the Mohawk villages with a force of 1200 men."

"Papa joined in that march," Louis said proudly.

"Papa had no choice," Bastien told him soberly.

"How far was it?" René asked.

"Five weeks of travel overland, much of it upstream by canoe and portage. We had to carry our own food supply for that period of time, and it ran out before we got there.

"Our drums made quite an impression on the Mohawks; they ran deeper into the woods every time we approached another of their forts.

"We took from their storage caches whatever food we'd need to feed us on our way back home, and we followed their example by destroying their winter shelters and food supplies. The rivers had flooded, but we managed to get back before they froze over in mid-November."

"How thick does the ice get to be?"

"Thick enough at Québec to crush an ocean-sailing ship."

René caught his breath when he realized that his friend was quite serious.

Bastien prepared for the great fish migrations by checking and adding to his weirs, spears, and traps, then he set up his drying racks and picked up a supply of salt for his barrels.

A few days later, the Saint Lawrence River teemed with canoes, as gravid female eels began moving in great numbers toward the sea. This event never failed to fascinate Marguerite and the children. René was enthralled by the spectacle; he gladly joined Bastien in his canoe and soon learned how to use the trident spear.

"This is the easiest fishing I've done since my first sailing to the Newfoundland banks," he told Bastien.

"I remember how easily you sailors caught the cod with hook and net when we first sighted land"

"You have to wonder where they all come from!"

At the end of that first hectic day of fishing and processing their catch, Marguerite introduced René to pan-fried fresh North American eel, and was rewarded by his comment: *"Superbe!"*

The ropemaker soon learned that autumn was probably the busiest season of all for this farming family, as its members harvested and stored the food and firewood that would see them safely through the winter.

Bastien sowed his winter wheat, oats and rye, rotating his wheat field with those of corn and oats.

Later that month, they picked wild apples and grapes, some of which the girls set out on their drying racks. Bastien made his elderberry wine, and René took charge of making cider Norman-style, while Marguerite and her daughters collected, cleaned and stored their garden vegetables.

Then Bastien selected and marked the pine trees that he would cut down that coming winter on Jeanne Dodier's land. The family gathered firewood, threshed grain and stored rye straw in the barn. Bastien checked their thatched roof and clay chimney, and found a few spots on both that needed to be patched.

At the first white October frost, the men went shopping at Gatineau's store for René's winter clothing and new blanket. They chose a heavy hooded blanket coat, sweater, homespun trousers, oiled winter moccasins that laced more than halfway up to the knee, wolf skin mittens, and a woolen toque, then charged these against the supply of rope that they would deliver to the merchant within the following year. Bastien bought wool fleece to replenish their supply; the girls had already knit heavy woolen socks, mittens, toques and scarves for all members of the family, which now included René.

As the days grew shorter, and the evenings longer, Madeleine gained experience at processing and spinning the wool into yarn, while Marie helped by feeding the fiber to her. Their mother, now grown heavy with child, guided the girls in setting up the linen warp, while she prepared to weave a fresh supply of warm homespun on her loom. Meanwhile, Bastien made new *raquettes* for himself, René, and a smaller set for Louis.

When the first winter blizzard struck in mid-December, René was stunned by the severity of the weather, and the isolation that the cold and snow imposed on the inhabitants of this land which was no farther north than his childhood village in northern France.

Bastien had forgotten how miserable he had been during his first Canadian winter.

Marguerite alerted him: "René's always cold; he stays close to the hearth all day long."

"Does he have enough heavy clothing?" he asked.

"I could probably knit him another woolen sweater, but that takes time—I do have some woolen homespun that I could sew into a warm shirt for him to wear over his sweater."

"I'm sure that would help." He paused as he considered the problem. "I worry the most about him at night."

It became evident to both of them that René should not be expected to spend the winter alone in the bunkhouse. They agreed to make room for him in the main house, even though it already seemed filled to capacity. They screened off their sleeping area that night, and made space nearer the hearth for a pallet that they could fold up against the wall during the day.

Then they invited the ropemaker to move in with the family during the winter season.

"I don't wish to intrude on your privacy," he protested.

"Not at all, René," Marguerite reassured him. "We'll sleep much better having you in the house than by worrying about your comfort and safety, sleeping alone in that bunkhouse. You'll find that next winter won't be as difficult for you."

"And by then," Bastien added, "you and I will have built a lean-to addition to the house which you can use as a more comfortable bedroom, with direct access to the main room."

René was obviously relieved.

The family began to plan for the winter holidays and learned that the ropemaker had not enjoyed a family holiday since his childhood.

"What was Christmas like in Normandie?" Madeleine asked.

"It was a happy time for all of us, starting with the Advent wreath."

"What was that like?"

"Many generations ago, during the cold December darkness of Eastern Europe, the German people made wreaths of evergreen, and lighted many candles as signs of hope for the coming spring and shorter nights. My people borrowed that custom from them."

"Can we make one of those?" Louis and Sébastien asked.

"What did they look like?" asked their mother.

"The Advent wreath was made of four candles in a circle of thick balsam fir branches decorated with pine cones and dried red fruit. Three of the candles were purple, and the fourth, the last to be lit, was pink. Each day, we lit the candles and said a short prayer before the evening meal. The circle held one candle during the first week, then an additional one each succeeding week until Christmas."

"I'm sorry, but we don't have purple and pink candles, Louis," Marguerite reminded him.

"But we have everything else—Can't we use regular candles?" Louis asked.

The ropemaker hesitated. "I don't see why not, but that's up to your parents to decide, *mon petit gars.*"

Bastien and Marguerite both smiled their approval. The children grew excited over this new custom.

"Then you must all help me make the wreath tomorrow," René announced.

Everyone contributed to the project, and Sébastien lit the first candle with the help of his father.

They began to plan their Christmas Eve celebration. Madeleine and Marie looked forward to helping their mother prepare the traditional feast for the *réveillon* that followed Midnight Mass. Since many of these dishes had evolved from Orléanais, and others from Canada, they would be new to René.

While the two men smoked their pipes by the fire one evening, and watched the family's activities, Bastien admitted: "This year's Christmas will be a special one for us too, René. As you know,

Marguerite and I also left our families and friends behind. Both of us had already lost our parents before we came to Canada; our children have never known a grandfather. You seem to have made up for that by extending our family by another generation."

These words had a sobering effect on the ropemaker. He hesitated for a brief moment while his eyes moistened, then said: "And yours is the younger family I never had."

"Will you attend Midnight Mass with us this year?" Bastien asked him directly.

"I've thought about it."

"You haven't been attending Sunday masses, and I wondered why."

"I just fell out of the habit."

"Would you like to join us Christmas Eve?"

"First, let me tell you that before we came here to see you, François and I visited Sainte-Anne-de-Beaupré. Did you know that that church was built and dedicated by Norman fishermen?"

Bastien nodded.

"The doctor had just told me that I shouldn't sail anymore. I was completely at a loss as to what I should do with the rest of my life—All of that changed at Beaupré. I found myself completely at peace when I entered that church. For whatever reason, François and I both thought of finding you. We spoke to the captain, and here I am."

Bastien smiled in recognition. "I've heard of such things happening. The nearest I've ever come to that feeling was when our expedition stalled halfway to the northern sea just as winter began to set in—We had just learned from a group of returning natives that the English were already there and were settling in for the winter.

"I hadn't volunteered for that assignment, and I couldn't wait to get it over with so that I could return home to my family. *Père* Albanel asked me if it was possible for us to winter there, if we could obtain passports from Québec. Faced with the option of turning back, I suddenly realized that I'd be turning away from a chance to explore an unknown region of this vast country—an opportunity that few men are ever offered. I also realized that somehow, I had adapted to living in the virgin forest. Once I learned that I could send a message to Marguerite, I assured him that I could shelter and feed us through the winter. So we stayed and continued our journey the following spring."

"That took a lot of courage."

"You think this winter is hard? You should have been there!"

Marguerite frowned as she looked up from her stitching. "So that's how it really went?"

Bastien's ears turned red. "I'll never know what came over me, Marguerite."

She shook her head in dismay, but she looked into his eyes and resigned herself to the unpredictability of this man whom she had married.

"I'll definitely attend Midnight Mass with you," René finally replied, "but first, I must visit the priest."

Guillaume Barette, Nicolas Leblanc, and their families shared Christmas dinner with them. When the two men offered to grow the hemp on their land, Bastien considered buying all of the processed fiber that his friends could provide, but he and René finally decided to wait another year while they measured the ongoing market for their product.

In London that winter, Radisson and Des Groseilliers negotiated for an increase in wages from their English employers. Although the Hudson Bay Company had realized 100 percent profit on its investment, its owners refused to raise the French voyageurs' joint annual stipend beyond their current one hundred English pounds.

Frontenac's letter to Montréal Governor François-Marie Perrot had appeared nonthreatening. He had also written to Sulpician abbé Fénelon, pressing him to encourage Perrot to accept his invitation to come to Québec. When Perrot asked the abbot to accompany him, Fénelon accepted in the belief that he could reconcile the issues between the two governors. They walked on *raquettes* the two hundred ninety kilometers (one hundred eighty-five miles) from Montréal to Québec and arrived at dusk, on January 28, 1674.

Perrot presented himself before the governor-general the following afternoon, and was immediately arrested in Frontenac's chambers by Lieutenant of the Guard Jacques Bizard, the same officer whom he had challenged at Montréal. Perrot was then summarily delivered into solitary confinement at the Chateau Saint-Louis. Abbé Fénelon's protests rankled Frontenac and proved futile; he had no choice but to return alone to Montréal. On his way upriver, he stopped to say Mass and spend the night at Trois-Rivières. Word of Perrot's fate quickly spread throughout the surrounding communities.

A few nights later, Marguerite roused Bastien from a deep sleep.

He jumped out of bed in total confusion. "What is it? What's wrong?" he asked loudly.

"Don't wake the children," she whispered.

"But what's wrong?" he repeated softly.

"The baby's coming."

"Oh!—What do you want me to do?"

"You should start boiling some water, and tell Madeleine next door. She'll know what to do."

"Do you need her right away?"

"Not yet, but soon."

"Are you all right then?"

"Yes. I only wish it were daytime, so that the children could be out of the house."

He listened to the sounds of snoring coming from beyond the cloth partition they had strung up around their sleeping area. "René wouldn't mind taking the boys out to the bunkhouse."

Marguerite caught her breath for a minute, then said: "The girls are old enough now to learn about such things. But if the boys should wake up, we don't want to frighten them—Please speak to René."

Bastien stoked the fire and set the water to boil, then left on his errands. Meanwhile, René retreated to the bunkhouse to provide privacy for Marguerite and to warm up the cabin.

Madeleine came down quietly from the loft. "Where did Papa and René go in the middle of the night?" she whispered. "Are you all right, *Maman?*"

"Yes, *chérie*, the baby should be born before daylight."

Madeleine's eyes widened, and she smiled. "How can I help you?"

"You can stay if you like; your papa has gone next door to get

Madame Leblanc. Help her if you can—Are the others still sleeping?"

"They're all snoring up there."

They laughed together, and hoped that this would continue throughout the night.

Bastien returned and reported that he had been successful in his errands. "René's really excited about the new baby. He hasn't seen a newborn since leaving Normandie."

He sat beside Marguerite and held her hand. "It's been four years since young Sébastien was born. How are you doing?"

She squeezed his hand. "Everything feels normal, Bastien. I don't think it will be long now—a quarter of a cord of firewood, I think," and she smiled at him.

His cheeks colored a bit as he remembered her first delivery, and the amount of wood he had split in an attempt to relieve his tension. Madeleine, their firstborn, wrinkled her brow, and wondered what this private little joke was all about.

Jean-François was born before daylight, and his first cries finally woke up his sister and brothers who had slept through the night. Nine-year old Madeleine held the baby just minutes after he was born and felt awed by the event and the unfamiliar sensation of bonding. It was a special experience for the entire family, and for René who got to hold the infant boy a few hours after his birth.

Later that day, their new pastor, Recollect Father André Richard baptized François in the presence of his godmother Marie-Marguerite Volant, daughter of Françoise Radisson, and therefore Pierre-Esprit's niece.

René was re-energized; he took over Marguerite's chores, and gently continued to bond with the boy.

A week later, without consulting with the Sulpician *seigneurs* of Montréal, Governor Frontenac arbitrarily installed his friends Thomas de Lanouguère as lieutenant-governor, and Gilles de Boyvinet as judge at Montréal. From his cell, Perrot challenged Frontenac's right to make these political moves, and appealed to the Sovereign Council.

On the last Sunday of March, abbé Fénelon gave a sermon at the church of Montréal. In the presence of 600 parishioners, including Cavalier de La Salle and Governor Frontenac's

Brigadier of the Guard, he preached against political pettiness, officiousness, and the calling of corvées for projects which were of no benefit to the population. He indirectly described as autocratic and despotic the manner in which Frontenac had handled this situation with Perrot, had called the corvées to build the fort at Cataracoui, and the road between Montréal and Lachine. An indignant Cavalier de La Salle stood up and warned the parishioners and the priest against public incitement.

The Sulpicians disavowed the sermon that following week. An outraged Frontenac, convinced that a slur against the king's representative was a slur against the king himself, demanded that the Order of Saint-Sulpice eject the preacher from their society. Abbé Fénelon fled to Lachine, where few dared to offer him shelter.

Eight

Spring 1674

Once the maple sap ceased to flow, and river ice began to break up, Bastien and his friends organized the neighborhood classroom at Louis Lefebvre's empty bunkhouse, where all had agreed that the boys' lessons should take place. Jean Cusson would travel to the site for the initial and other formal lessons, but he informed the group that his son, fourteen-year old Jean, would supervise most of the practice sessions.

Seated at the back table were the oldest boys of the group: François Vaudry and François Rochereau who both took this instruction quite seriously, and Laurent Barette who was naturally restless and mischievous, yet determined to work hard in order to keep up with the others. At the table in front of them sat the younger group: Louis, Nicolas Leblanc the younger, and Jacques Lefebvre who was the youngest at age five.

The fathers waited with their sons, and when the instructors arrived, the notary immediately addressed the adults. "Here are the ink and inkwells that I promised to provide for the first lessons: each student will have his own, but each must also learn to prepare his quills and white birch bark for writing. This first lesson will be as important for the fathers as for the boys; once you learn how to heat and shape these long feathers into writing quills, you can provide your own."

"Where do we get these feathers—must we buy them at the store?" Bastien asked.

"These are goose feathers, but quills from crows are better. Feathers of the eagle, owl, hawk, and turkey can also be used. The geese will be flying overhead very soon; this is the best time of year to collect their feathers, immediately after the bird falls. The five outer wing feathers make the strongest quills, but I prefer those from the left wing because these will curve away from the right-handed writer."

"How long will a quill last?"

"That depends on how it's used. I keep several ready at all times, and I change from one to the other as a nib wears down and needs to be re-cut."

"Do you need a special tool to form the writing point?"

"I shape it like this with my penknife..." Jean Cusson demonstrated as he spoke.

"Did you all collect the outer birch bark?" he asked the boys.

They proudly showed him what they had.

"You'll notice that there are straight lines running across it; that will help you line up the letters—Have you stripped it into single layers?"

They all nodded their heads.

"You'll learn to write with the quills and master several letters every week. Then we'll teach you to join the letters together into words. You'll eventually learn to write the words that you hear, but the first words that you'll master will be those of your full name.

Louis looked up at his father and saw how happy he was that his son would learn to read and write.

Bastien recalled his own grandfather's beautiful handwriting, and again regretted that he had not shared this gift with his sons or grandsons.

Notary Cusson carefully filled the inkwells from a small bottle of ink. He told the group that he mixed his own, and that he would show them how to do this with the same indigo that the women used to dye their cloth. "We can start with this much, and when you need more, I'll show you how the dye and water are mixed to produce a dependable ink," he promised.

In early May, the Sovereign Council of Québec held a hearing into the affair of the Montréal sermon. When the Sulpicians refused to testify, abbé Fénelon was summoned to appear before the Council.

A few weeks later, Radisson and Des Groseilliers reached Québec aboard the first ship to arrive from France. Word soon spread to the Trois-Rivières area that these local heroes had met with Minister Colbert. A strong advocate of mercantilism and naval power, the minister had successfully recruited them into the French Navy by offering them 300 livres for their joint services. The explorers had readily accepted his offer, which was triple that of the English.

At the cape, Bastien and René densely sowed their hemp field. The ropemaker judged that Bastien's sandy loam, and the average amount of summer rainfall that his friend had described to him, would provide ideal growing conditions for quality fiber. Although he had never personally raised a crop of his own, he had often visited and viewed the fields in which hemp had been cultivated, and had learned that dense growth encouraged the production of straight, long fibers.

In late August, abbé Fénelon appeared before the Sovereign Council and wished to be seated. Governor Frontenac, who presided over the proceedings, insisted that he remain standing to hear the charges made against him. The abbot countered with the demand that he be tried by an ecclesiastical court as was allowed under French law. The Council finally referred his case to the king.

François-Marie Perrot, who had already been imprisoned for eight months, continued to challenge Frontenac's and the Sovereign Council's authority over the governance of Montréal. He also sought justice before the king.

At about that time, Frontenac received a letter which Colbert had written on May 17th, in reference to his report on the expedition to Cataracoui: "It is not his Majesty's wish that you undertake great voyages up the Saint Lawrence River, nor that in the future, the habitants extend themselves as far as they have in the past. The King prefers that you let the natives deliver their furs to you, without the French having to travel so far to accommodate them. To the contrary, he wants you to work tirelessly…to concentrate the settlers in towns and villages, so that they can better defend themselves…He would prefer that you concentrate on developing the most fertile areas, closest to the sea and to communication with France, rather than exploring deep into the continent in places that can never be inhabited nor possessed by the French."

Bastien and René found that the hemp grew well without branching, and stood taller than either of them. Some stalks bore small, greenish-yellow flowers, others freely shed pollen; both signs alerted René that the plants would soon reach full maturity when the strongest, longest, and greatest number of fibers would be ready for harvest. A week later, they cut the woody stalks to several inches above-ground and prepared them for water-retting, a process that would rot the outer bark, and release the inner layer of fibers.

After consulting with local carpenter Louis Lefebvre, Bastien outlined the base of the lean-to addition which would serve as René's winter quarters. Then he and the ropemaker walked into the woods to search for the pine logs they would use to build the walls.

"How far does your land reach into the forest?" René asked.

"Would you like to see?"

"Why, yes, of course, if you promise we won't get lost."

Bastien chuckled at his apparent concern. "Don't worry, I have a marked trail to follow, and I have my musket primed in case we should run into a bear or a wolf."

René's eyes widened and his neck stiffened before he recognized the humor in Bastien's eyes.

Bastien spoke more seriously: "There's not much danger around here, *mon vieux*. The Iroquois are converting to our Christian faith, and the more dangerous animals are deeper into the woods than we'll be going."

As they walked on, the trees appeared much taller, the underbrush more dense. The ropemaker became deeply impressed by the beauty and wildness of it all, and by the distance that they traveled before reaching Bastien's corner marker.

"This is forty arpents from the riverbank." Bastien pointed to the southwest and added: "Our concession reaches two arpents in that direction as it does along the river. I've never cleared any of this area, but it's been good for winter hunting."

René examined the width and height of the virgin trees. "I wish François could have seen this."

"Perhaps he'll come back to visit with us."

"I doubt that he's ever been in such a forest."

"Are you tired, René? Would you like to rest before we start back?"

They both realized that he had walked quite a distance today; he had obviously regained his strength. "I couldn't have done this last autumn," he admitted. "Marguerite's cooking is obviously working its wonders on me. Do you realize how lucky you are, Bastien?"

Bastien smiled and nodded. "You don't miss the sea?"

"Not at all, and that surprises me. But then, it had been such a long time since I'd been part of a settled family. This is a good life, my friend."

On their way back toward the river, Bastien selected and marked the several young trees they would need to cut down for their construction project; these all stood close to his clearing and would be easily accessible from the worksite. He planned to work at this project as time permitted, but sowing and harvesting the crops would necessarily be his top priorities. René did as much as he comfortably could; the family expected no more of him.

The following week, they hauled the soggy hemp stems to an open field and laid them out in the heat of the sun, turning them every day or so to ensure even drying.

Soon after they had safely stored the dried hemp in the barn, their parish priest announced that Monsignor Laval had been named by the Pope to be the first Catholic Bishop of North America.

The following month, François-Marie Perrot and abbé Fénelon sailed for France under military escort. Two weeks later, Frontenac sent his loyal ally, Cavalier de La Salle, to France to convince the French authorities of the strategic importance of Cataracoui. La Salle carried a letter of recommendation from the governor to Colbert which praised him as "a man of intelligence and ability, more capable than anyone else I know here to accomplish every kind of enterprise and discovery which may be entrusted to him, as he has the most perfect knowledge of the state of the country."

Versailles, Winter 1674-75

Minister Colbert separately interviewed the three new arrivals from Canada, and gave thorough reports of his findings to King Louis XIV. The monarch sentenced Perrot to three weeks in the Bastille, to chasten him for his defiance of royal authority. He then allowed him to return to Nouvelle France as lieutenant-governor of Montréal on the condition that he apologize directly and sincerely to Governor Frontenac, the king's direct representative in all of North America.

Sulpician Superior Bretonvilliers forbade abbé Fénelon to ever return to Canada, and he addressed a letter to the priests of Montréal cautioning them to remain neutral in all political matters. The king endorsed both decisions.

Minister Colbert wrote to Frontenac that the ten months Perrot had been imprisoned at Québec, and the three weeks he had spent in the Bastille were punishment enough. He ordered the governor-general to accept Perrot's apology and to forgive him. The king additionally warned Frontenac that he must not supersede the authority of Montréal officials unless it was absolutely necessary, and he admonished him to live harmoniously with the Sovereign Council and with the ecclesiastics.

Louis XIV and Colbert recognized that they must rein in Frontenac's authority to govern and administer all of the French colonies of North America. The king therefore reformed the Sovereign Council and finally named a new intendant, Jacques Duchesneau de la Doussinière et d'Ambault.

Cavalier de La Salle made two petitions to the king: one asking for a patent of nobility, in consideration of his services as an explorer; the other for a seigniory at Fort Cataracoui. He offered to: repay the 10,000 francs that the fort had cost the king, assume the expense of upgrading its defenses and labor force, establish a French colony around it, build and support colonial parish and mission churches in that area.

The king accepted his offers. He raised La Salle to the rank of the untitled nobles, and granted him the seignory of Fort Cataracoui, with its adjacent lands and islands extending four leagues along the lakefront and half a league in depth. He also invested the explorer with the government of the fort and settlement, subjecting his jurisdiction to the orders of the governor-general of Nouvelle France.

Cap-de-la-Madeleine, Winter 1674–75

René slept in the lean-to addition during severe winter weather, but preferred the privacy of the bunkhouse whenever it became practical. Bastien had removed the extra bunks, and had installed a sleeping pallet which the ropemaker could fold up against the wall during the day, as in the main house. The little cabin now served as a small daytime workshop.

Both men worked in the barn to release the fibers from the retted, dried hemp. While Bastien used the flax-brake to crush the woody layer, René removed the remaining woody portion with the wooden swingle knife, first by beating and scraping the root ends, then the tops. They continued the cleaning process by dashing, each in tandem with the other, a handful of dressed fiber against their spiked board, thus aligning the fibers parallel to each other, completing the removal of foreign matter and small loose fibers at the end of the strick, and separating the long fibers.

The girls took over the rest of the process by combing first the root ends, then the tops, to refine the fibers. They sorted these by length into slivers or ribbons, giving each a slight twist in preparation for their subsequent twisting into yarn.

Based on this experience, the two men decided that raising and processing their own hemp required too much of their time, which could be spent more efficiently at making rope. Therefore, they accepted Guillaume Barette's and Jacques Massé's offers to grow the following year's crop on their adjoining farms, and committed themselves to buying all of the fiber that the two farmers could process within the following year.

The rope-making project had already realized a small profit.

Upon his return to Cataracoui that summer, La Salle renamed the fort in honor of his mentor and ally Frontenac.

In 1675, King Philip's War broke out between the English and Algonquian tribes of southern New England. Hostilities began in the town of Swansea, then quickly spread from New Hampshire to Connecticut, as the Wampanoags, Nipmucks, and Narragansetts raided the rapidly expanding English settlements.

Major cultural differences in customs and concepts of land use had caused tension for many years. Rapid colonial increases in population led to intense competition for natural resources such as farmland, hunting and fishing. English hunger for land, as well as the heavy-handed treatment of native tribes by government officials, led to one of the most disastrous wars in America's history.

Québec, August 1675

Intendant Jacques Duschesneau's arrival aggravated the situation with Frontenac. They quarreled over the presidency of the Council; the Intendant sided with Laval against the liquor trade, and accused Frontenac, La Salle, du Luth, and other notables of illegally engaging in the fur trade. The Canadian population soon split into two factions supporting one or the other of the two powerful rivals.

AUBIN

Nine

Twelve-year old Madeleine had already developed a reputation within the local community as a mature, responsible individual, well-trained in domestic and child care skills. In mid-February 1676, the parents of Pierre Brunel invited her to serve as godmother at their son's baptism.

Two months later, from his palace at Saint-Germain-en-Laye, King Louis XIV signed an ordinance forbidding all habitants to travel to the outlying native villages to engage in the fur trade; the governors were not to grant them any official permits. This new law stipulated severe penalties for those who left their farms to illegally profit as coureurs-de-bois: the first conviction would result in confiscation of the furs and a fine of 2,000 livres; the second offense would be judged, and its penalty determined, by Governor-General Frontenac. Since most public officials, including the governor and his allies, routinely profited from this trade, these penalties were not enforced.

The Montréal merchants reacted to the diversion of their fur trade to Fort Frontenac by establishing their own trading post at Michillimackinac, which was located farther west, on the strait between lakes Huron and Superior. The new post soon became the delivery point for the Ottawas (upper Algonquins), Hurons, and French coureurs who collected prime skins from other native tribes living north and west of Lake Superior. The licensed merchants then hired their own voyageurs to travel to

Michillimackinac, pick up this cargo, and deliver it to the warehouses at Montréal.

One summer afternoon, Louis returned home from his writing lesson, and showed his father that he had written his own name. Bastien picked him up off his feet and gave him a big, long hug. "This will open up all kinds of opportunities for you, *petit gars*. You'll be able to guide your brothers and sisters in their public dealings, and sign as witness to their public contracts."

Louis listened soberly. Marguerite seemed a bit upset. "That's a lot of responsibility to assign to an eight-year old boy, Bastien."

He looked deeply into her eyes and told her: "As the oldest son, Louis must be willing to accept it."

The boy sat at the table and practiced his additions and subtractions, while Sébastien and François looked on. Their older brother's life was already quite different from their own; he could communicate in the Algonquin language with Red Dawn and his grandsons, and hunted in the woods with them on a weekly basis. He learned quickly and well, and easily tolerated cultural differences.

Only one Jesuit priest remained at the cape mission. Since peace had been established with the Iroquois nations, Catholic missionaries had moved away from the Saint Lawrence River parishes and had established their missions farther afield, among the native villages located to the north and west of the French settlements.

The Sisters of the Congregation from Montréal organized small schools at Lachine, Pointe-aux-Trembles, Batiscan and Champlain, but very few of the rural children could attend classes, because they were needed at home.

At the end of August 1676, Michel Rochereau told Bastien and Marguerite that he had just been granted a new land concession within the Seigneurie de Villier on the south shore.

"The soil is less sandy there," he explained, "so it tends to hold moisture better than at the cape."

As they discussed the conditions of the agreement, Marguerite became concerned about Bastien's growing interest. During his long absences, her experiences at managing both farm and family had caused her to become more conservative toward assuming additional commitments.

"These lots run four arpents wide and from the riverbank to within one arpent from Lac Saint-Paul. They're located almost directly across the river from us. As you can see from here, there are marshes along the shore—Of course, we have hunting and fishing rights."

Bastien considered the value of an undeveloped forest and marsh for winter, spring, and autumn hunting. "When are the *cens et rentes* payments due?"

"November 4th of every year."

He considered these facts. The timing was good for him: Jeanne Dodier's lease payment came due in early February. The rope-making venture had proved successful and manageable now that Jacques and Guillaume provided a reliable supply of fiber. René seemed to thrive since he had joined them. The ropemaker seldom required his help, and they had a steady flow of orders for his product.

His thoughts turned to the amount of labor that a new concession would require: to clear more woods, build another house within the coming year, and till enough land to raise a first crop of grain. He wondered if he could manage these additional responsibilities.

"Well, Michel, do you have a particular lot in mind?"

"There's one available next to mine—We could work together."

Bastien sensed Marguerite's reaction and grew more cautious. "Can you show us that lot?" he asked the blacksmith.

"I can do that right now, if you like."

Marguerite caught her breath and nodded; she knew that this meant crossing over by canoe.

When Bastien carried her ashore on the southern riverbank, the first thing she noticed was that it seemed cooler here in the shade of the great trees that shielded them from the heat of the midday sun. Lush undergrowth filled the edge of the forest. A beautiful wilderness of undeveloped land, she thought, Bastien must have experienced just such a sight when he first came to the cape.

He caught her facial expression, and was grateful that she

shared this thought with him. But now he must decide if he could take on another concession.

From the southwest, the quietness of this scene was interrupted by the unmistakable sounds of a broadaxe chopping into one of the mighty trees.

"That must be Maudoux clearing his woods," Michel told them. "Come, let me introduce you."

Aubin Maudoux appeared to be in his mid-twenties, lean and energetic. Bastien noticed that his axe strokes did not cut as deeply as his own. At first he thought that Aubin must be new at this work, but soon realized that the young man had been chopping alone. He knew it was always easier to work in pairs.

Michel introduced them to each other, and informed Aubin that Bastien and Marguerite might apply for the middle concession.

"It's a good piece of land," said the younger man, "one arpent wider than mine. May I walk it with you?"

They started out by following the boundary line between Aubin's and the available lot. Bastien held on to Marguerite who was hampered by her long skirt and struggled to keep up with them. He noticed that she obviously enjoyed the beauty of the scene. Lac Saint-Paul teemed with fish that gently rippled the surface of the water while feeding on low-flying insects; otherwise, the lake was clear and still. Soothed by the muted sounds of the birds, and a gentle breeze flowing through the trees, Marguerite now understood her husband's enjoyment of the undisturbed forest.

Bastien considered the contractual obligations of the land-rent agreement as they followed Michel's boundary line on their way back to the river. Both of the concessionaires agreed that they were reasonable: a home must be built within a year; a twenty-foot wide road must be allowed along the high tide line of the Saint Lawrence River; one live capon, or its monetary value of twelve deniers per arpent of frontage must be delivered to the seignior in early November of each year; and their grain must be ground at the manorial gristmill.

"The habitant must not disturb the marshland except to hunt or fish," Michel added, "and the seigneur reserves the right to hunt and fish on all concessions."

These were standard conditions. Bastien kicked free a handful of soil, sniffed at it, and tested its texture. He walked alone with

Marguerite toward the marshland that bordered the riverbank, and looked across the river to their home concession to confirm his assessment of the distance by canoe.

He assured her that he could safely move his oxen across the winter ice to haul lumber from forest to building site.

"It's really quite beautiful here, Bastien, but you already have so much to take care of already; are you sure that you can take on another major project like this?"

"I don't know yet," he replied with his usual frankness.

"I finally see how hard you must have worked to get that home built and furnished before my arrival. Could you manage to clear and till the land, then build another house without the oxen? Would you want to move here?"

"This soil is more fertile than our own; I've noticed that our harvests are yielding less than they did at the beginning. I've cleared wild land before, when I was younger and closer to Aubin's age.

"Jacques Vaudry and I worked well together. I'm sure that Michel, Aubin and I could help each other with the heavier work— Michel and I are more experienced now, but Aubin seems to be new at this. I'm not certain yet. I'm thinking in terms of selling this land at a profit later on.

"No, I don't think I'd ever want to move away from the other side. How do you feel about that?"

She seemed relieved. "We're raising our family in the home you built for us—the only real home I've had since I was a child. I would hate to leave our friends and what we have to start all over again, wouldn't you? Shouldn't we take some time to talk this through before you decide?"

He agreed, and told the others that they needed more time.

On their way back across the river, Michel Rochereau told them that Aubin had previously worked as a domestic somewhere near Québec, and that this was his first concession.

"Where is he living now?" Marguerite asked.

"I don't know. He can't have much money saved. I wonder if he's set up camp at the site…"

"That's too wild an area to be camping out alone," Bastien told him.

When they reached home, Marguerite asked: "Could we afford to hire an engagé?"

"Yes, I think so, and I've already been looking for one, but they're hard to find now that so many young men have turned to the fur trade."

"Then why don't you make an offer to Aubin?"

Early the following day, Bastien traveled alone to Villier, to learn more about Aubin Maudoux. He found him working on his land, and saw that he had made little progress.

"Have you decided already?" the young man asked.

"Not yet. How long have you had this one?"

"Two weeks."

So it hadn't been that long after all. "Have you ever worked at clearing the forest before now?"

"Not really. I spent most of my indenture working in the fields."

"Where did you spend your indenture?"

Aubin continued to swing his axe as he answered. "I worked for René Mezeray, at côte Saint-Ignace-de-Sillery." His strokes seemed less effective than they should be for a man his size.

"Here, let me see that axe." Bastien tested its weight and balance, felt the edge of the blade and found it to be dull. "When did you last sharpen it?"

"I haven't. It's as it was when I bought it."

"Let me try it." Bastien stood in position and gave the tree a mighty whack. The axe bit into the wood at half the depth that he would normally get. "Do you have anything to sharpen this with?" he asked.

Aubin shook his head.

"Then I think you should come home with me so that I can renew the edge."

Aubin was grateful for the offer, and accompanied him across the river. He told Bastien that he had signed on as an engagé at age fifteen and had crossed on one of the king's ships that had returned to Canada to pick up the Carignan soldiers.

"Were you with the army then?"

"No, but I looked older than my age, and no one questioned it. I signed an indenture contract with René Mezeray, then I mostly farmed rented land; there wasn't much profit in that. I worked with a butcher for awhile, until I had the opportunity to sign a contract as a voyageur to the Ottawas for Jean Péré and Gabriel Bérard who shared a trading permit. I was at Sillery during all of that time. When more land became available in this area, I took advantage of the concessions being offered at Villier."

"Did you say that you signed a contract?"

"The notary read it to me, but yes, I signed my own name."

Bastien was intrigued by his ability to sign, and by his having arrived alone at such a young age.

"Where are you living now?"

"I've set up camp on the concession," he casually replied.

Aubin grew quiet as they approached Bastien's landing. Louis and his brothers came running down toward the water's edge, calling: "Papa! Papa!" They helped carry the canoe onto the shore, and followed the men to the barn, where Bastien introduced Aubin to René who was working at the ropewalk.

The older man took a break from his work and came over to talk to them. "I've been looking for you, Bastien. I could use your help this afternoon—the rope is ready to be twisted into cable for Gatineau. Will you be available?"

Bastien nodded, and Aubin watched him sharpen the axe head on his grindstone. "You've obviously had more experience at this than I've had," he admitted.

"My indenture required that I learn to do this during my first winter in Nouvelle France," Bastien explained.

"You have quite a collection of tools."

"Many of which I brought with me from France."

"How long have you been on this land?" Aubin asked.

"Since '62."

"That was before my arrival—Weren't you threatened by the Mohawks?"

"Yes, clearing the land was much more dangerous for us then." He gingerly tested the edge of the blade, and seemed satisfied. "This is how that edge should feel—You really should have at least a sandstone to keep it sharp."

Just then, Madeleine appeared with fresh water for the men, and announced that a hot meal would soon be ready. Bastien introduced his daughter, and invited Aubin to join the family for the midday meal.

Ten

Bastien's extended family gathered around the table with their new guest. The children, especially François, were very curious about this stranger among them. When Aubin caught the toddler staring at him, he winked, and the boy broke into a giggle.

Bastien introduced his guest. "*Maman* and I met Aubin Maudoux while we were on the south shore yesterday. Now I want each of you to stand up, one at a time, and introduce yourself to him. Let's start with the oldest."

The older daughter rose from her seat with a slightly flushed face and said: "I'm Madeleine. I'm almost thirteen."

Marie got up and shyly explained: "They call me 'Marie' because I was named after *Maman*, and that can be confusing at times. I'm ten years old."

Louis gave his name and mentioned that he was eight.

His next younger brother took his turn and said: "I share Papa's name, but everyone calls him 'Bastien', and they call me 'Sébastien'. I'm six years old." He turned to introduce his younger brother: "He's Jean-François, but we call him François. He's only two years old—that's why he giggles a lot."

The family chuckled over this while Marguerite and Madeleine set the food on the table. Once they had taken their seats, Bastien led the group in a solemn prayer of thanksgiving for their many blessings of food, shelter, safety, family and friends.

As the men took their portions of food, René asked Aubin: "Do I detect a Norman accent in your speech?"

"I'm from Saumur, Anjou," their guest replied.

"You must try some of this Norman-style cider," the ropemaker offered as he reached over and filled his cup.

Bastien and Marguerite were pleased with the ease of conversation, as they reminisced about the old country. Aubin freely answered the boys' questions, offering the adults the opportunity to learn more about his background. They learned that he too had been born to a large family, the youngest of twelve children.

While the girls and Marguerite cleared the table, Aubin reached into his pocket for a length of twine, and entertained the younger children with a few tricks he had learned in the old country.

Madeleine watched him from the corner of her eye while she washed the dishes with her mother. Marguerite noticed this and sighed, as she considered how much her daughter had matured during the past two years. Focused on his performance, Aubin was unaware of this exchange.

Meanwhile, Bastien and René returned to the barn where they counter-twisted three lengths of manila rope into cable, the most demanding aspect of their craft.

"What do you think of him?" Bastien asked his partner.

"He seems like a good man, and he certainly has a way with the children."

"Marguerite and I are seriously considering that concession on the south shore, but we'd need to hire a domestic—perhaps Aubin."

"I can see how one decision might lead to the other."

"He's camping out in the woods on the south shore while he's clearing his land; that must be difficult for him, but he has no other shelter right now."

"And you're wondering if he and I could share the bunkhouse?"

Bastien appreciated his friend's directness. "Yes," he replied.

"That would be no problem for me—I'd welcome the company. Besides, this is your property, not mine; it's yours to do with as you wish."

"No, René," Bastien protested, "this is your home as well as mine. We wouldn't expect you to share your limited living space and winter workshop with someone unless you felt comfortable with him."

"I appreciate your thoughtfulness, Bastien, but don't trouble yourself over this. If this is an arrangement that works well for you, then I have absolutely no problem with it."

Bastien led Aubin on a tour of his land and buildings, and invited him to spend the night in the bunkhouse with René and share breakfast with them in the morning. The younger man gratefully accepted.

During their crossing that following morning, Bastien discussed his tentative plans. "We've all enjoyed your company, Aubin. As you know, Marguerite and I are very much interested in acquiring that concession next to yours, but we're already committed to several other projects—I'd need to hire extra help.

"If you'd consider working for me for room and board, I could continue to work on my present concession and the lease next door, while I help René with his rope-making. Michel, you, and I could still work together to clear and build on the south shore— that type of work is usually done in late autumn and through the winter."

Aubin knew that he still had much to learn, and Bastien seemed willing to teach him. He welcomed this opportunity, so he quickly agreed to Bastien's terms and prepared to move his meager belongings that same day.

On September 12, 1676, Bastien accepted a third concession, his first on the south side of the Saint Lawrence River.

Once they had completed the autumn grain harvest, Bastien and Aubin joined with Michel, and began to clear the brushy undergrowth of their adjoining forested areas at Villier. They hoped to harvest enough timber that coming winter to start construction the following spring and summer.

Aubin energetically participated in the autumn harvest and storage of the garden vegetables, and assisted the girls in collecting apples, grapes, currants, and nuts. Although he was eleven years her senior, he and Madeleine easily became good friends. The children continued to find him amusing, and he was patient with them. Madeleine, however, grew to be more than amused; adolescent yearnings had begun to surface. Aubin's interest in spending time with her flattered her, but more than that, serious and responsible as she was, his joie de vivre fascinated her.

One night after the children had fallen asleep, Marguerite expressed her concerns: "Shouldn't we be a little more careful about those two spending so much time together?"

"I see nothing wrong with their friendship," he replied casually.

"Oh, Bastien, it's already becoming more than friendship— Madeleine is quickly developing into a young woman."

Her observation startled him by its implications; he began to view the relationship in a new light. Finally, he said: "I trust him to be honest and responsible. He's older than she is, but he wouldn't harm her; I'm sure of that."

"She's already grown very attached to him."

"We must remember that King Louis requires that our daughters marry by age sixteen."

"What do you know of Aubin's past?"

"Only that he was quite young when he arrived in Canada. I know him to be conscientious and eager to learn. He holds a concession on which he'll soon build a home. The children greatly enjoy his company. He can sign his name—that counts for something."

"So can Louis," she reminded him, "but he won't marry for a long while yet."

He chuckled at this; she was right, of course, but she also understood that writing was an accomplishment that he greatly respected. Louis had tried to teach his father to sign his own name, but Bastien had been totally frustrated by the effort. He felt it was too late in life for him to master this task; his hands felt too clumsy to control the pen.

They lay in silence for a while, then he promised her: "If this really worries you, I'll speak to Aubin tomorrow."

His conversation with the younger man went more smoothly than Bastien had expected. The very next morning, he posed several questions while they worked together in the fields.

"You've never spoken much about your past, Aubin, except that you're originally from Anjou, and that you were younger than most when you first arrived at Québec."

"There really isn't much to tell—I worked at Sillery and Cap Rouge until I was granted a concession at Villier."

"I had already committed to marry Marguerite when I was your age, and I sailed to Québec soon after, to serve indenture, settle, build a house, and earn her passage so that she could join me here."

"You accomplished a lot in your early years here."

"You've never married?"

"I signed a marriage contract while I was at Sillery, but my bride-to-be had the opportunity to marry an older man who already had a farm. So we annulled our contract, and she married him a week later."

"I'm sorry to hear that."

"I was eighteen years old and working as a domestic, Bastien— much too young to assume the responsibilities of marriage."

"You were wise to admit that."

"I was greatly disappointed at the time, but it turned out for the best. Now that I have a concession and the opportunity to build a home, I find that there are very few girls of marriageable age—it's not easy to find a bride."

"Are you considering that possibility then?"

Aubin's ears flashed red as he looked away from Bastien. "Yes, I am."

By mid-November, they had safely stored their food harvest in the barn, attic, and cellar, had neatly piled most of their firewood for both buildings, and had sheltered their animals in the barn. Then bitterly cold northwesterly winds and snow flurries blew in from Hudson Bay, signaling the change of seasons.

By now, Marguerite had resigned herself to the fact that regardless of her youth, Madeleine, her firstborn, was seriously drawn toward Aubin Maudoux. Although they had discussed the repercussions of such a decision, Madeleine in all seriousness, argued that she was ready to assume the responsibilities of marriage. Bastien stood by, sympathetic to both sides of the debate, and understood that the king's decree must be obeyed, regardless of parental sentiment. He also felt that his daughter was too young for such a commitment, but, as he reminded Marguerite, the signing of a marriage contract did not necessarily mean immediate union in the eyes of the Church. He and Aubin concurred that such a document represented a promise to later marry before a priest, that the final exchange of vows could be postponed until all parties agreed that Madeleine was truly mature enough to leave her home and family to live with Aubin. Meanwhile, her fiancé would work toward establishing a home for them.

On the morning of November 15, 1676, friends and family of the couple gathered at Bastien's house with royal notary Antoine Adhémar to witness the signing of the marriage contract. The bride's godfather, Guillaume Barette, and family friends Jean Crevier, Michel Rochereau, and Louis Lefebvre heard the terms by which the couple promised to marry within a reasonable time as determined jointly by the parents and the couple. Des Groseilliers' son-in-law, Jean Jalot, signed as an official witness to the agreement.

At age thirteen, Madeleine had officially committed to marry twenty-four-year old Aubin Maudoux and eagerly planned her trousseau with her mother's guidance. Meanwhile, Bastien showed her fiancé the carved wooden chest that he had constructed for Marguerite's linen collection before he had left France. He now offered to help him build one for his future bride, if he wished to do so.

Marguerite, Madeleine, and Marie began to spin and weave their flax fiber into large quantities of linen thread and cloth. They planned to sew and embroider hemmed towels, tablecloths, pillowcases and spliced sheets for Madeleine's trousseau during the coming winter months.

After the first snowfall, Bastien and Aubin collected pine lumber on the neighboring concession as required by his lease contract. Now that René no longer lived alone in the bunkhouse, Bastien and Marguerite were less concerned for his comfort and safety. Only during the worst storms, which would isolate them indoors for a number of days, did he and Aubin move into the smaller lean-to addition to the main house.

René worked in the bunkhouse or the barn whenever the

weather allowed. Bastien, Michel, and Aubin traveled across the river to their new concessions when the ice proved to be solid enough to support the movement of their oxen sledges. These carried the men's equipment and tools, and allowed for easier movement of the harvested logs from forest to building sites. The first crossing required the most caution, since currents at mid-river unpredictably created thinner sections of ice which might prove to be especially hazardous under the weight of the animals. The men probed ahead, marked their way with evergreen trees, and repeated this probing at every crossing.

On one of these earlier excursions, they met Nicolas Perrot who also prepared to build a house at Villier. The voyageur, and master interpreter of native languages, was warmly respected by the native nations of the western Great Lakes region. Perrot was well-known in the Trois-Rivières area, and throughout Canada, a legend of his time whom the western natives called "the man with the iron legs" because of his repeated overland travel at any time of the year.

In late spring and early summer 1677, Bastien and Aubin completed their routine farm chores, and began to travel by canoe with Michel to Villier. Aubin learned from Bastien how to hew his own lumber for construction. And it was during this time that they got into the habit of sharing noonday meals with Nicolas Perrot, whose lot was located close to theirs.

Perrot asked Bastien about his overland voyage to Hudson Bay, and as they exchanged stories of their experiences, it became clear to both of them that they shared an appreciation for the Canadian wilderness, but that the welfare of their families always remained their top priority.

"Isn't there a Jesuit mission located alongside a river near here?" Bastien asked him one day.

"Yes, Saint-François. They've set up a small village for the Abenakis on Rivière Puante. That mission has grown rapidly during this past year. The Jesuits occasionally ask me to help as an interpreter—the Abenaki language is similar to that of the Algonquin, you know."

"Where do they come from?" asked Michel.

"From southern Acadia. The English colonies are growing faster than ours, and their settlements are spreading into the traditional

Abenaki hunting grounds. They once traded muskets, powder and shot for native furs, and the Abenaki became dependent on these for hunting, but the English began to mistrust them and withheld ammunition in trade. They turned to offering rum for furs; as a result, alcoholism began to corrupt Abenaki society and family life. The native chiefs recognized this, and have been leading their people to this Canadian mission where the use of liquor is forbidden."

"Isn't that what the coureurs are accused of doing to the western Jesuit missions?" asked Aubin.

"Yes, and that's why the Jesuits and Bishop Laval continue to appeal to the king to ban the liquor trade with the natives. The Jesuits built this local mission in '69, but during this past year the southern cousins of the Abenakis have been at war with the English colonists. Although the northern Abenakis have tried to remain neutral, *les bostonnais* don't trust them. These poor souls are caught between their native allies and the English in a war that they don't want to be a part of, and they've had to flee to Canada with their families, leaving behind their harvests, and their hunting and fishing grounds. They're trying very hard to create a new home for themselves, but they've also had to shelter and provide for an increasing number of refugees from the war in southern New England. This only increases the suspicion of *les bostonnais*."

Bastien recalled his ship's arrival in North America. "I thought that Acadia consisted of several large bodies of land that we sailed past before entering the Saint Lawrence River. I remember the great fishing fleets from so many countries, and my first taste of fresh cod."

Perrot explained: "Acadia also extends southward from Gaspé, on the mainland to the east of us. It shares a frontier with that part of northern New England called Boston whose fishing vessels harvest much of their catch near northern Acadia."

He rose to gather his belongings. "It's time for me to get back to work—What troubles me is that we're beginning to lose our distance between Nouvelle France and New England, and English attitudes toward the natives are quite different from ours."

Eleven

1677

Marguerite and both her daughters decided that Madeleine's new clothing would first require the production of finer linen, and homespun cloth. While the men spent long days across the river working on their new concessions at Villier, the women spent every spare moment at the spinning wheel and loom. Both girls had already become quite adept at both crafts; Marguerite's skill, however, was still required for spinning and weaving the finer thread and linen they would use to sew into many of the clothing items.

Once they became involved in this part of the project, Madeleine displayed a newfound interest in her parents' courtship, and about what life had been like for both of them in France. "You waited five years to marry?" she exclaimed.

Her reaction immediately caught the attention of her siblings.

"Life was very different for us in France," Marguerite replied with a faraway look in her eyes. "It wasn't any easier for us then than it is for you now, *chérie*. I had no family—my parents had both died when I was six years old. I grew up working in a convent as a fille du roi, then as a domestic at the local manor in the small town of Pithiviers. One day, your papa came home after a long military corvée. His parents had died, but somehow, his brothers had kept the family together. By then, his younger brother and his wife had taken charge of the family farm."

"Did you know him then?"

"We met shortly after he returned home."

"Did you marry in France?"

"No, because he had no place of his own. That was why he decided to come to Nouvelle France, when he heard that there was free land available here."

"Couldn't you marry and come here together?"

"He had to serve thirty-six months of indentured service to a landholder before he could apply for a concession and then build a home. We waited another two years because all of the French settlements were under constant attack by the Mohawks. It was a very dangerous time for Nouvelle France, and for your papa."

They had heard about the Mohawks, and could not imagine living under that kind of stress.

Marie asked: "How did you manage to travel alone across the sea?"

"I had no means to pay for it, but your father borrowed the money and arranged for me to sail with his former employer *Sieur* Boucher, who had been sent by the governor to petition the King Louis for military support. If he had failed in his mission, I couldn't have come."

"After waiting five years, you wouldn't have married?" Madeleine asked.

"That's right—So have patience, *ma fille*, our lives are always in God's hands."

Marie, who had been quiet during this conversation, added. "You and I would not be here today."

Madeleine and Marguerite both turned to her, surprised by her comment. Marguerite smiled. "That's right, Marie. Perhaps none of us would be here. The colony and your papa were in great danger."

"Had Papa managed to finish the house by then?" Madeleine asked.

"He had started late, and had worked very hard, but then he received my letter telling him that I was coming, and he worked even harder. When I finally reached Cap-de-la-Madeleine, I stayed and worked at the Jesuit manor for a few months until the house was finally ready, then we were married."

Except for Madeleine, who vaguely remembered the presence

of the four Carignan soldiers living in the bunkhouse, none of the children had ever known anything but peace in their lives.

All that summer, rumors circulated throughout Nouvelle France concerning the constant political turmoil engendered by Frontenac and La Salle's continuing expansion of the fur trade toward the west and south of the Great Lakes. Since close to half of the male adult population remained unmarried because of the chronic shortage of potential brides, there was little incentive for younger men to develop new farms. Although life on the trail could be brutal, it offered much greater financial rewards than did clearing the forest and cultivating the soil. This exodus of manpower left many fields untilled and many crops unsown, thus weakening the colonial economy.

Despite the increasing harshness of the King's penalties against unlicensed trade, young men continued to flock into the deeper forests of western Canada. Intendant Duchesneau estimated that there were at least five hundred of these independent coureurs roaming through the Canadian wilderness. The Jesuits continued to protest against the increasing debauchery of these renegades who corrupted the lives of their native converts. Bishop Laval supported those charges. The intendant also reported to the king the names of those government officials who, he believed, were profiting from the illicit traffic.

Beleaguered by the growing number of negative reports and complaints from the Canadian clergy, merchants, seigneurs, and government officials, Louis XIV wrote new laws forbidding the habitants to hunt beyond one league of their cleared land, or to deliver liquor to any native village located a distance away from the French settlements. He also restricted hunting expeditions to the winter period of January 15th through April 15th. And he warned Frontenac to avoid causing any suspicion of his taking part in illegal commerce.

The work at Villier progressed more slowly than Bastien, Michel, and Aubin had anticipated. The soil on the south side of the Saint Lawrence River proved to be much more fertile than at the cape, its forest growth more dense. Its larger trees required more labor not only to cut down and root out, but also to cut to length, split, and hew into lumber.

By the end of summer, Marguerite had almost completed her production of fine linen cloth, and the girls had already spun much of the wool needed for weaving the heavier homespun.

With the help of Nicolas Perrot's domestic, Louis Lefebvre and Pierre Guillet completed construction of the explorer's house at Villier late that autumn, allowing Perrot to move his family across the river on December 2, 1677. But Bastien, Aubin, and Michel estimated that they would need several more summer months to complete their own houses.

Early winter proved to be especially severe that year. René grew restless as he became housebound. He spent more time with the children, and although he truly enjoyed their company, he desired most of all to be making rope. Finally, he insisted on returning to work in the barn, an unheated space which took its toll on his health. He began to cough, and found it difficult to sleep through the night. When he eventually lost his appetite, and could barely sip the special broths that Marguerite prepared for him, Bastien and his wife insisted that he move to his original winter accommodation near their hearth.

Despite their herbal potions, the ministrations of the village physician, and spoonfuls of the last of their remaining calvados, René's condition continued to deteriorate until one night when Bastien stood vigil and desperately attempted to fight the fever with whatever traditional remedies he had at his disposal.

The ropemaker opened his eyes briefly and saw his friend dozing off in his chair by the hearth. "You must be very tired," he whispered.

Bastien was startled to hear his voice. "Are you feeling better?" he asked hopefully.

"I'm weaker than I've ever been in my life—It's become very difficult to breathe—I must tell you…"

Bastien gently took his hand. "Save your energy. You must rest quietly, René."

The ropemaker weakly protested, and spoke haltingly. "No— You've been a good friend—I don't know what I would have done— if you hadn't invited me into your home—You're a good man— Wish I had more time—to teach you more—but you're the ropemaker now—You'll do well, Bastien—God bless you and your family…"

His hand went limp; his eyes lost their luster.

Stirred by the sound of their whispers, Marguerite sensed that something was wrong. She heard a single sob from her husband, and immediately went to him to hold him and comfort him. "He's with God now, Sébastien."

Marguerite turned to René, whispered a prayer for him, and closed his eyes. Then she drew his hands together, and wrapped his rosary around them, inserting the base of its crucifix between his thumb and palm. Together, she and Bastien knelt beside their friend's body, and softly recited their rosaries.

Soon after the winter burial, the family shared subdued Christmas and New Year celebrations. They attended Midnight Mass, had a lighter meal than usual, and went to bed early. The house seemed imbued by their common grief. Although René had been with them for a relatively short period of time, they all sorely missed his company.

Now that Aubin lived alone in the bunkhouse, he and Madeleine yearned to exchange their vows. Marguerite remained adamant that her daughter was too young for this; Bastien agreed with her, and cautioned the young couple to be patient.

"We won't give our consent until you've completed construction and furnished a home for her," he told Aubin one day, confident that because of the young man's inexperience as a builder and his inability to pay someone to do it for him, this project would take a while longer than he expected.

Yet Madeleine continued to plead with her parents.

In early spring 1678, Marguerite, now heavy with her sixth pregnancy, finally relented. She insisted, however, that if they were to marry now, the young couple must live with them by sharing the bunkhouse until Madeleine could manage on her own. On this agreed basis, they announced the Church banns, and prepared for a summer wedding.

Marguerite recalled her own innocence on her wedding night and struggled to decide whether or not she should prepare her young daughter for this pending marital relationship. She studied Aubin and Madeleine whenever they were together, and saw that he was quite gentle with her on all occasions, that she was obviously very trusting of him. Perhaps, she thought, this was something that each couple must discover and work out for themselves. She discussed this with Bastien one night.

"Do you think I have a responsibility to talk to her about what to expect?" she asked him.

Bastien sensed the depth of her genuine concern. He remembered their own innocence on their wedding night. "Was it that difficult for you?" he asked gently.

She smiled at him. "Oh no, Bastien! After all, we had waited much longer to be together; they've only known each other for less than two years."

"But they've seen each other every day during that time."

"I was also older."

"Yes, but you had spent most of your life in a convent."

"I trusted you and I yearned for you."

"And I for you." He drew her closer to him in the night. "I believe that they both share such feelings, Marguerite, but if it will make it easier for you, I'll speak to Aubin tomorrow, and remind him that she's at a very tender age—It may be easier for men to talk to each other about such things."

In mid-April, Madeleine served as godmother for one of Nicolas Leblanc and Madeleine Dutost's twins. A few weeks later, she and Marie Bigot-Rochereau assisted Marguerite during the birth of her sixth child. On the following day, Aubin and Marie Bigot served as godparents at Marie-Catherine's baptism, and the children rejoiced at having a new baby sister.

The family continued to prepare for the church wedding. Marguerite opened her carved wooden chest and took out her wedding dress, but the heavy homespun skirt and shawl were too warm for a summer wedding. Therefore, she took out a length of string and took Madeleine's measurements for a new wedding outfit, setting knots in the string whenever it extended to a point of measure such as from neck to waist, elbow to wrist.

Marguerite showed her daughters how to use the string measurements to mark off a pattern for each of the required garments. Then she guided them in stitching together out of the fine white linen: two chemises, an inner skirt, a light, square shawl which the bride would drape over her shoulders on her wedding day, one white apron and another colored one from heavier linen.

While the two sisters worked companionably on these garments, their mother boiled and dyed a square yard of heavier wool cloth to a light blue, shrinking and matting it before setting it out to dry flat in the sun. Once it had dried, she cut and sewed this fabric into a fitted, laced bodice for Madeleine, who had outgrown most of her clothes during the past year.

Since she would also need heavier clothing for the fall and winter, Marguerite dyed, marked and cut pieces of homespun to sew into two outer skirts, and a short hooded cape.

Their sewing extended through the late spring and early summer evenings.

"I'm so happy not to have to do this on my own!" Madeleine confessed. "I could never have managed this by myself, and I promise to help you with yours when your time comes, Marie."

Her younger sister blushed slightly as she replied: "I can't imagine ever working on my own trousseau, but I'll remember that promise." She turned to her mother and asked: "Did anyone help you with yours, *Maman*?"

"I had a very close friend at the manor who was married to Papa's brother," Marguerite replied. "It was she who introduced us to each other, and it was at their wedding that your father and I first spoke to each other. She was like a sister to me."

Both girls had come to realize just how lonely their mother's life must have been before she married.

On a Monday morning, in mid-June 1678, Bastien escorted his fourteen-year old daughter down the short aisle of the church of Sainte-Madeleine, and placed her hand in Aubin's. The bride's light brown hair was neatly, yet loosely pulled and coiled on the back of her head, and covered with a white, finely woven, starched headdress. Soft white linen sleeves extended down the length of her arms and were gathered into slight ruffles at her wrists; delicate white embroidery decorated the edges of her neckband and lower sleeves. The front lacing of her light-blue felted bodice was covered by the pointed bib of a white linen apron, which displayed her own embroidery of a periwinkle flower, stems, and leaves in their natural colors. She wore a pale blue outer skirt of lightweight homespun that reached down to just above her ankles. Her fine linen shawl draped over her back and shoulders, its ends were neatly tucked into the front of her bodice.

Bastien and Marguerite leaned slightly against each other; their thoughts dwelt on that other Monday, fifteen years earlier, when they had exchanged their own wedding vows in front of this same altar. Twelve-year old Marie looked on starry-eyed, eliciting another motherly sigh from Marguerite. The rest of the children watched proudly and quietly; their oldest sister seemed suddenly transformed into a beautiful adult.

Michel Rochereau and his wife had spent the previous day helping the twenty-six-year old groom prepare for the occasion. His face was freshly shaven, and his light brown hair neatly tied back with a new leather thong. Marguerite had washed and freshened his Sunday clothes: a white linen shirt that Madeleine had made for him, and breeches of natural-colored homespun. The tops of his linen stockings reached under the bottom hems of his breeches and were held up above the calves by a tied drawstring enclosed in each top hem.

Aubin watched the candlelight dance in his bride's dark brown eyes as they exchanged their vows before God and his Church. They held each other's hands, and relished each meaningful word. He noticed a single tear escape from the corner of her eye, and lightly squeezed both her hands. They smiled happily at each other.

Following the church ceremony, their guests followed the newlyweds to Bastien's house for the outdoor reception. The village fiddler provided the music; their invited guests brought food, beverages, and gifts for the couple. Bastien had set up an outdoor rotisserie which someone had volunteered to tend for him. The roast pork had already become fork-tender.

Their wedding guests included Guillaume, his wife Louise Charrier and their four children; Nicolas Leblanc, his wife Madeleine Dutost and their five children; Jacques Vaudry, his wife Jeanne Renault and their six children; Louis Lefebvre, his wife Catherine Ferré and their son Jacques; Jacques Massé, his wife Catherine Guillet and their three children; Michel Rochereau, his wife Marie Bigot and their three children. Other fellow parishioners dropped by with gifts and were invited to join the celebration. Jean Jalot dit Des Groseilliers, who had witnessed the marriage contract, came by with his wife to congratulate the young couple and wish them well, as did Nicolas Perrot and his wife from Villier.

Their party lasted through the afternoon and until late evening. Parents danced with their children, and with the bride and groom. The men took turns tapping rhythm with the spoons. The boys congregated in one corner, the girls in the other; they had all grown up together, yet were now unusually shy with each other.

That June evening, as the sun reached low on the western horizon, the bride and groom began to spend a lot of quiet time together, and seemed to lose interest in the festivities. The children grew tired and the youngest became sleepy. The guests gradually wished them well and left. Madeleine and Aubin thanked everyone for their good wishes and gifts, hugged Marguerite and Bastien, kissed the children goodnight, and retreated together to their temporary home.

Twelve

The young couple transformed the bunkhouse into their own space with linen curtains at the two windows, a linen cloth and flowers on the table, sheets, cased pillows, and a clean blanket on the bed that Aubin had constructed for them. The small chest he had made for her stood nearby and was filled with her clothing and linen. Madeleine insisted that she prepare their own meals, and so Aubin purchased the necessary equipment to upgrade the cabin hearth to a small cooking center, fully expecting to transfer these kitchen accessories to their home across the river once it was fit for occupancy.

He continued to work as Bastien's engagé, but he also maintained his efforts toward finishing their own home at Villier. Because of their involvement in so many other projects, the construction of their neighboring houses on the south shore progressed very slowly for both men, even as they watched Louis Lefebvre's progress on Michel's house at the new site. The carpenter understood their difficulty, freely answered their questions, and guided their efforts.

Marguerite admonished the children to respect the young married couple's privacy, yet Marie and the boys remained close to Madeleine. She continued to help her mother during the day while the men worked on both sides of the river.

Bastien found little time to spend at rope-making. By now, all of René's equipment had been transferred to the barn, and the bitter winter cold remained as restrictive for him as it had been for René. He could not produce as much as his old friend had because there was so much else he needed to accomplish. In an effort to meet continuing demand from the local merchants, he began to train Louis and young Sébastien to feed the lighter strands at one end of the ropewalk while he twisted three or four of these together through the opposite end of his equipment. The manufacture of cable remained beyond his resources.

Late in May 1679, Marguerite and Madeleine Dutost-Leblanc assisted Madeleine with the delivery of her namesake. As is true for most first deliveries, but especially so for a fifteen-year old mother, the process of childbirth proved long and difficult, leaving her weak enough to postpone the baptism for a few days. Marie-Madeleine Maudoux was baptized by sixty-nine-year old Jesuit Father Gabriel Druillettes, who had recently retired from missionary work and had stopped to visit at the cape. Louis Lefebvre and Marguerite served as godparents.

The birth of their daughter greatly affected Aubin, who felt frustrated by his rate of progress in building his own home and developing his own farmland. He greatly admired the loving family environment that his wife had enjoyed and yearned to provide as much for his own family.

One Sunday in late September, Jean Lemoine, seigneur de Sainte-Marie, greeted Bastien after Mass. "*Bonjour!*" he called. "I see that your family has started a new generation!"

"Yes, Jean. We're very proud of our first grandchild."

"Tell me, Bastien, have you done any traveling since your voyage to the northern sea?"

"No..."

"Well, I'll tell you, I'm looking for an experienced voyageur to accompany my domestic to Michillimackinac to pick up a load of furs. It pays well. Would you be interested?"

"I thank you, but no. My family needs me at home."

"I'm sorry to hear that—Can you recommend anyone?"

Bastien was about to reply negatively, when Aubin moved forward and said: "Excuse me, *Sieur*, but I may be interested in applying for that job."

His unexpected offer surprised everyone.

Aubin continued: "After my indenture at Cap Rouge, I took part in a voyage to the Ottawas for Jean Péré and Gabriel Bérard."

Lemoine eyed him speculatively. "Who are you, young man?"

Bastien explained: "Aubin Maudoux is my daughter's husband, and he's the father of this grandchild."

"Do you vouch for him then?"

"Yes, I do," Bastien replied, "But he's also my engagé, and we should take time to discuss this among ourselves."

Lemoine quickly sized up the situation, and told Aubin: "Once you've talked it over, and if you're still interested in applying, come and see me at Sainte-Marie. I'll give you two days to decide. I have a great deal of respect not only for your father-in-law, but also for Jean Péré."

The women were unusually quiet on their way home that Sunday. The children ran ahead as they usually did, but Madeleine and her mother remained sullen. Both men knew what their wives were thinking and dreaded their arrival home.

When the young couple reached the privacy of the bunkhouse, Madeleine broke down and cried. Aubin did not know how to cope with this outburst, except to apologize. "You feel that strongly that you don't want me to go?" he asked.

Between sobs, his young wife shot back at him: "You'd abandon the baby and me so soon after she was born!"

"But I wouldn't be abandoning you!" he protested. "I'd be doing this for both of you, so that I can offer you a better future."

She clearly remembered how stressful her father's yearlong absence had been for her mother and the rest of the family. "What kind of a future will we have if something should happen to you while you're traveling through the wilderness?"

"Madeleine, I've never been able to save any money. We're living now on your father's generosity. I don't know how much longer it will take for me to finish our house and barn at Villier. It's already been over two years, and I feel as though I've made so little progress. If I sign on as a voyageur, that one journey would allow me to pay Louis Lefebvre to finish our house, we'd be able to move into our own home, where I could develop my own land, grow my own crops."

Her crying had dropped to a whimper, but she was not convinced.

"You'd be safe here with your family. I wouldn't lightly abandon you for the sake of adventure." He approached her and held her in his arms, but stress continued to grip her body.

Meanwhile, Bastien had sent the children out to do their chores, and he and Marguerite were also debating the issue.

"It's downright irresponsible for him to consider leaving them right now!" she protested.

Bastien lit his pipe; he had learned to listen quietly on such occasions.

"What can he possibly be thinking of," she continued, "leaving his fifteen-year old wife and newborn child to go traipsing off into the woods?" She ran out of breath.

"Is that what you think he's doing?" he calmly asked.

She looked earnestly into his eyes, and was puzzled by what she saw. "You don't?"

"I haven't talked to him yet, but I'm sure he has good reason."

"You're so trusting."

"I've worked with Aubin for over two years now, and I respect him enough to want to hear his side of the story."

His simple logic quieted her.

The children monopolized the conversation during the noonday meal. Immediately afterward, Bastien and Aubin took a walk down to the stream, to privately discuss this problem with each other.

When they reached the bottom of the hill, they sat by the running water, and Bastien lit his pipe. "Do you want to talk about it?" he asked.

Aubin quickly responded: "Yes—it would be such a relief to explain this to you. Madeleine is so upset that she refuses to talk to me."

"She's young, and feels abandoned."

"I've tried to explain to her."

"First, tell me about your voyaging for Jean Péré."

"Do you know him?"

Bastien shook his head slightly and replied: "I know of him, that he's a fur trader and merchant at Québec, and that his family maintains a warehouse at La Rochelle. His brother Arnaud met me at the quay when I arrived from France. It was he who held my indenture contract and passed it on to Pierre Boucher here at the cape."

"Jean was a fair man to deal with, but I was nineteen at the time, and others who were involved in the deal took unfair advantage of me."

"How so?"

"I promised to pay 100 livres to the man I was replacing, because he was giving up his position to me."

Bastien scowled at this.

"I had worked with that man as a butcher at Sillery. He was my senior; I felt I knew him, and I trusted him. He told me that since I would be leaving the trade, he'd have to go out of business, and he told me it was only fair that I should pay him over 100 livres for the merchandise and equipment left over from our partnership."

"Did you?"

"I signed an agreement against my future earnings in order to do so, but on the advice of the notary who sympathized with me, I annulled that contract the very next day. Needless to say, my former partner was very upset with me."

"Served him right."

"I had also rented a local farmer's land, two weeks before signing up for the voyage. That farmer's family name was the same as my former partner's, but I don't believe they were related. I had to promise to pay him more than 60 livres for the balance of the lease I owed him, once I returned from the Ottawas."

Bastien drew a deep breath. "That's much more than I've ever paid for any farm lease."

"I learned a lot from those experiences."

"As well you should have. Now tell me why you feel that you must go on a second voyage at this time."

He listened quietly, while Aubin repeated most of what he had told his wife.

"I tried to explain to her that I knew she'd be safe here during my absence. She's afraid that I won't come back, and fears what life will be like for her and the baby if that should happen.

"Bastien, I haven't the slightest doubt that I'll return, and with enough money to hire Louis Lefebvre to finish our house at Villier so that I can work my own land. For the past ten years, it seems as though I've done nothing but work for others. I've seen what you've accomplished here—I hope to do the same for my family."

Bastien continued to smoke in silence. He realized that his son-in-law's absence would make things a bit more difficult for him, but he also realized that Aubin had legitimate reasons for signing on as voyageur to the Ottawas.

Finally, he told him: "Go then, with my blessing. Don't worry about Madeleine and the baby; Marguerite and I will take care of them."

Aubin breathed a sigh of relief. "I'm sorry that you'll have to work alone during my absence."

"Don't worry about that either; I'll do as much as I can, probably not accept any rope orders for the coming year, and I'll stop construction at Villier. I hope nevertheless to sow and harvest crops there next year, in addition to those here on the north side. I'll have to speak with Jeanne Dodier and see if she might accept a lesser clearing of her land this coming winter. I expect that we can work around your absence, but I hope you and I can continue to work together for a while after you return. I expect that Jeanne will want me to make up the difference in felled trees the following winter."

Aubin nodded his agreement.

Bastien taught his son-in-law many of the basic skills he would need as he voyaged through the wilderness, but Jean Lemoine would completely outfit and equip him.

By signing a procuration document notarized by Jean Cusson on October 29, 1679, Aubin granted Madeleine power of attorney during his absence. And he willed all his earthly belongings to her should he not return from his voyage to Michillimackinac. Late that season, he left with Jean Lemoine's hired crew.

Originally created by Jesuit Father Marquette in 1671, Michillimackinac had long served as a northern refuge for the Hurons and Ottawas whose villages had been devastated by the western Iroquois. Because of its location between lakes Huron and Michigan, it had gradually developed in the intervening years as a vital fur trading center serving the Montréal merchants. Since the creation of Fort Frontenac at Cataracoui, native trappers now prefered to barter their furs directly at the western forts, rather than travel to the Montréal fairs.

ANTOINE

Thirteen

1680

Early in January, Madeleine and Michel Rochereau served as godparents to Marie-Catherine Massé, daughter of Jacques and Catherine Guillet.

Louis routinely accompanied Bastien into the woods to hunt for meat. The boy had already fired a musket, but lacked the strength to control its accuracy, so he continued to rely on his bow and arrow, and his well developed tracking skills. By now, he could easily identify the prints of the various animals, and knew the habits and characteristics of the smaller prey that he had stalked with his Algonquin friends.

Madeleine and her baby wintered in the main house with the rest of the family, and helped her mother and sister begin to fill the wooden chest that Bastien had made for fourteen-year old Marie.

In mid-April of that year, an impatient King Louis XIV wrote a stern message to Frontenac which listed the multiple complaints he had continued to receive from all quarters of the Canadian population. He scolded the Québec governor: "I've heard from the bishop, the ecclesiastics, the Jesuit fathers, the Supreme Council. They all complain of you. Merchants and tax collectors complain of lost commerce and claim to suffer from the flight of the coureurs into the woods; they also claim that they receive no protection, that you delay ships from leaving when they are ready, that navigation of the rivers are entirely restricted by your permits and passports. But I am willing to believe that you will change your conduct and act with necessary moderation to encourage growth of the colony, which will be completely jeopardized unless you change your ways."

By now, the French king had once more favored Cavelier de La Salle, by granting him five years to find the outlet of the Mississippi River. Sunday civil announcements revealed that he and Recollect Father Louis Hennepin had already begun this search.

Inter-tribal warfare had depressed the level of the fur trade in the Great Lakes area. In order to satisfy the ever-increasing European demand for beaver hats, French explorers and coureurs now pushed farther west and south of Lake Superior. During the summer of 1680, Daniel Greysolon *Sieur* Du Luth visited that area in an attempt to settle matters between two of the major resident nations, and succeeded in negotiating a lasting peace between the Sioux and the Assiniboin. He had already discovered and befriended the native tribes called the Dakotas and the Sioux, thus opening up these regions to French missionaries and traders.

Accompanied by four Frenchmen and one native guide, Du Luth explored the land of the Brûlée River (Wisconsin border) and descended the entire length of the Sainte-Croix River (northeastern Wisconsin to the Mississippi River), becoming the first white man to have made that trip. After he established a trading post at the mouth of the Pigeon River (northeastern border between Minnesota and Ontario, off western Lake Superior), he explored the Wisconsin and Fox Rivers, and Lake Michigan. In recognition of these accomplishments, Governor Frontenac appointed him commander of the forts at Lachine, Cataracoui, and Michillimackinac.

Young Sébastien and his older brother worked alongside their father in the fields and barn; Louis assisted with the plowing and seeding, while Sébastien especially enjoyed working with the animals. Although Louis seemed drawn to the forest, Sébastien preferred to work the farm. Marguerite and her daughters joined them during the mid-summer grain harvest.

Peace with the Iroquois had allowed the extension of French exploration deeper into the hinterland, multiplying the number of Christian missions and French alliances among the newly discovered native nations. This growing presence of Jesuit missionaries in the Great Lakes area drew these priests away from the Saint Lawrence River settlements. The Algonquin mission at Cap-de-la-Madeleine closed its doors in late summer of 1680.

Red Dawn and his entire family prepared to move to Sillery, closer to Québec. Bastien and Louis were greatly saddened to see them leave.

"You have taught me many things," Louis told the aging chief.

"Like your father, you have learned well," Red Dawn replied.

"Your grandsons have also taught me many things."

"You have taught them as much. They now speak your language."

"We will miss you," Bastien told him.

"You have been like a brother," answered the chief. "Your son can now hunt with you in the forest."

Bastien smiled at this old friend whom he expected never to see again. "He prefers the bow and arrow to the musket."

"They make less noise." Red Dawn smiled back.

"May God be with you always..." Bastien wished him with misty eyes.

"And you..." The chief uncharacteristically approached both of them and hugged them, then turned toward his tent.

Louis ran after him and handed him a gift of tobacco that his father had brought for this occasion. He saw into the Algonquin's sad eyes and said: "I will never forget."

Red Dawn put his hand on the boy's shoulder and said: "Neither will I."

By early autumn, the Illinois and other allied tribes had settled near the upper Illinois River, in the area of La Salle's new Fort Crèvecoeur (Peoria). Their renewed presence in that area resulted in a rapid depletion of young beaver in the Ohio Valley, thus setting off a violent reaction among the Miamis and the powerful Senecas whose villages formed the western door of the Iroquois confederacy. Forewarned of their intentions to attack, and vastly outnumbered, La Salle's colleague Henri Tonti at first attempted to mediate a truce, but was unsuccessful and was wounded in his attempt. He and the other French traders fled to Green Bay, while thousands among the Illinois families who remained in the valley were massacred. The Iroquois peace of 1667 thus came to a violent end with the beginning of the second phase of the Beaver Wars.

The Senecas, the most powerful warrior force among the Five Nations, were well-armed through trading furs with the Dutch and English merchants of New York; now they resumed their attacks against their western neighbors in their attempt to gain control of that fur-rich area. Their growing dependence on trade with the New York merchants drove them to neutralize those western tribes who delivered their furs to the French forts at Illinois and Michillimackinac. As they conquered, they absorbed warriors into their own forces, gaining strength with each conquest. Their eventual goal was to become middlemen between the western tribes and the Albany traders.

That September, Aubin returned home to his family and had much to tell about his year's experience. He was amazed by the change in little Madeleine, who toddled toward him from across the room. His wife thoroughly enjoyed watching the two of them rediscover each together.

Bastien found that his son-in-law had grown stronger, more energetic and self-confident.

"Was your voyage a success?"

"More so than the previous one," Aubin replied as he picked up his daughter. She tested his beard, not in the least intimidated by this amiable face which she had no way of remembering.

"Then everything went well?"

"Yes," Aubin reassured them.

"What was it like, in the deep forest?" Madeleine asked, wide-eyed as she sat close beside him.

Aubin described his experiences while traveling through the rivers, rapids, lakes, wilderness, and inland seas of upper Canada. "It seems to go on forever—and it's such a quiet place."

Bastien nodded in agreement.

Aubin continued: "It was hard work at first—the loads were so heavy to carry—but it became easier with time."

Aubin helped his father-in-law with the autumn grain harvests, and he hired Louis Lefebvre to help him complete his house at Villier. While working on the south shore concession, he met Antoine Cottenoire who had served several years as a domestic for Jean Lemoine.

"Didn't you recently return from Michillimackinac?" Antoine asked.

"Yes, I did, and your name was often mentioned as having been on such voyages yourself."

"I couldn't go last autumn because I was negotiating to buy this land concession, and the contract wasn't settled until last January."

"It looks as though we'll see quite a bit of each other from now on—Are you married?"

"No, I'm not. Are you?"

Aubin nodded proudly and replied: "We have a daughter."

They talked about life on the trail, moving west toward Michillimackinac, and they discussed the quality of the soil at Villier.

Aubin asked Antoine: "Would you like to join us for our evening meal?"

"It's kind of you to invite me—I look forward to meeting your family, but I must clean up first."

Aubin pointed out the location of Bastien's farm across the water, and told him that they usually ate shortly after he reached home and washed up.

When Antoine landed his canoe on the cape shore, three young boys ran down to the narrow beach to greet him, but they drew to an abrupt halt halfway down the bluff when they came face to face with a stranger.

"I'm looking for Aubin Maudoux," Antoine explained. "Is this the right landing place?"

The three boys answered in unison: "Oh yes!" Then the oldest boy continued: "He married our sister. Come, we'll show you where he lives."

His guides ran up the sandy slope with twice as many strides as Antoine needed in order to keep up with them; all except for the smallest boy who struggled against falling behind. Antoine slowed his pace and introduced himself.

The six-year old replied. "My name is François, and I'm happy to meet you. Do you know papa?"

"I've heard of him, but I've never met him. Did he really voyage all the way to the northern sea?"

The boy nodded his head vigorously. "He was gone a long time! He said that winter was much colder there."

"I can well imagine. You see, the deeper into the woods and the farther north you go, the colder it becomes in the winter, and the nights are longer, too."

"That's what he told us. Have you ever spent the winter in the forest?"

"Yes, but not as far north as your papa did."

François grew quiet then spotted Bastien. "There he is!"

Bastien waved at them as he approached to introduce himself, and to ask if he could be of service.

Antoine had barely returned the introduction and stated his reason for being on Bastien's land, when a lovely young girl approached from the farmhouse.

"Papa," she called, "the meal is about ready, with just enough time for you and the boys to wash up."

"Thank you, Marie." Bastien turned toward the new arrival, and told her: "This young man is Antoine Cottenoire, a friend of Aubin."

"Ah—yes!" the visitor added. "I met him on the south shore today, and he invited me for the evening meal. These three boys were leading me to his home—I'm pleased to meet you, Marie."

She rewarded him with a glowing smile.

Bastien directed him toward the bunkhouse and told him that they would most likely see each other again, when he started working at Villier during the coming week. Before leaving, Antoine noticed how the boys crowded around Marie as they walked back to the house together. They obviously enjoyed being with her.

Upon his return to Fort Crèvecoeur, Cavelier de La Salle discovered the slaughtered remains of his native allies, and feared for the safety of his friend Tonti, whom he had left in charge of the trading post.

The evening of December 29, 1680 was crisp and clear, when La Salle's party saw a great comet blazing over the ruins of the

Illinois villages. Later reports coming from Europe as well as New England described it as the largest ever seen. The explorer postponed his search for the outlet of the Mississippi River and returned northward in search of his friend.

At Cap-de-la-Madeleine, Bastien, his family and neighbors also watched the unusual spectacle in the night sky. They knew this comet to be more spectacular than those seen in 1664 and 1665.

Bastien recalled several other unusual celestial phenomena that had preceded the unified threat of the Five Nations against the very survival of the Saint Lawrence River settlements. A sense of foreboding enveloped him as it did all others who had witnessed those previous events. He viewed this comet as a warning from God, as did the Puritans of New England, the natives, and most French settlers of that time.

Yet Bastien did his best to conceal his reaction from his family, and quietly took measures to prepare for any eventuality. He trained Louis to improve his musketry skills. Louis, in turn, fitted a set of bow and arrows for young Sébastien and taught him how to use them. Aubin and the boys helped to strengthen the farm's palisades. Bastien and Marguerite prepared to increase their food storage.

Aubin and his father-in-law built palisades around their unfinished buildings on the mostly unsettled south shore, and decided that the younger family should remain in the bunkhouse for a while longer. Aubin continued to work as Bastien's engagé, but concentrated his efforts on developing their fields at Villier, and commuted by canoe across the river on a daily basis.

Although they spoke little about it, in order not to alarm the children, Marguerite understood the reason for such activities, and quietly encouraged the children to participate in any way that they could. Meanwhile, she prayed that her husband and sons would not be caught up in a war over a stretch of unoccupied land far removed from the cape.

These changes did not go unnoticed by their friends and neighbors who approached Bastien individually on separate occasions to get his assessment of the situation. As a result, Nicolas Leblanc, Michel Rochereau, Guillaume Barette, Jacques Massé, Jacques Vaudry, and Louis Lefebvre consulted with militia captain Nicolas Rivard about restoring the old redoubts that dated back to 1660. These had been neglected and had deteriorated to the point where they were totally inadequate. They would need to be torn down, and others would have to be built because French settlement had spread eastward along the river into Batiscan and Champlain. The settlers voluntarily and cooperatively contributed to this project.

In early February 1681, Bastien served as godparent for the first time, along with Catherine Guillet as godmother, at the baptism of a neighbor's son who was named Sébastien.

That spring and early summer, rumors of an impending war with the Iroquois repeatedly spread throughout Nouvelle France, fueled by reports from Jesuit Father Jean de Lamberville, long-time missionary to the Onondaga, who warned Québec authorities of Iroquois belligerence and preparations for war.

The Senecas were finally at peace with their southern enemy, the powerful Andastes. By 1681, their attacks against the Miamis and Outagamis had killed six hundred warriors, had captured and absorbed another seven hundred, thus swelling their fighting strength to half the total force of the five-nation Iroquois confederacy. They now turned their fury against the Illinois nation, and actively recruited warriors from the other Iroquois tribes to wrest control of the fur trade in the Great Lakes area, along the Mississippi River and all of its tributaries. The combined power of the Iroquois Confederacy already counted twenty-eight hundred English-armed warriors, the strongest military force in North America.

The Great Comet of 1680 disappeared late that February, having been visible in the night sky over a period of eighty-eight days.

Young Canadian-born men continued to range through the western forests without official license, lured by the freedom of the frontier, and the enticing financial rewards of the fur trade. In May 1681, the king granted amnesty to the young coureurs-de-bois, and simultaneously authorized more serious penalties for the incorrigible law-breakers: public whipping, branding with a fleur-de-lys, then finally, a life-sentence spent rowing in the Mediterranean galleys. These harsh measures also failed to control the illegal trade.

Intendant Duschesneau's census of 1681 reported a colonial population of 10,000. The population of Cap-de-la-Madeleine had outgrown that of Trois-Rivières: the cape showed a count of 38 houses and 204 inhabitants, as opposed to 26 houses and 150 people at Trois-Rivières.

The census also reported that 370 (11.6 percent) men between ages twenty-one and seventy were engaged in commerce, various trades, and professions; 800 (24.9 percent) as trappers, voyageurs, coureurs. The remaining 63 percent worked in agriculture.

Antoine Cottenoire was still listed as a domestic employee of Jean Lemoine, although he now lived at his home at Villier. Over time, he had become a regular guest at Aubin's Sunday dinners to which Marie was also invited. Eventually, these events included the rest of the family and were held in the main house. As time went on, a bond developed between Antoine and Marie which became apparent to her parents and sister, and they all approved of the match. Antoine was a farmer, but also a fur trader, an occupation he had learned in Lemoine's service. He was also a literate man with an established farm on the south shore, and already seemed a part of the family.

In another attempt to control the coureurs, Colbert now convinced the King that fur trade must be limited to no more than twenty-five licenses a year, allowing three men per canoe to barter with the natives only at specified fort locations. This new royal edict had little effect, as long as Frontenac continued to benefit from the trade.

La Salle had spent the winter of 1680–81 at Fort Miami, with the continued hope that Tonti had escaped the Iroquois massacre at Fort Crèvecoeur. During that long winter, he had developed a strategy to unite the western tribes into a strong defensive league against their common threat, the Senecas. He planned to establish this confederacy as a colony around a new, stronger fort that he would build in the valley of the Illinois, and he would supply these native allies with arms and goods in exchange for furs.

From that base, he also expected to continue his search for the Mississippi River outlet, intending to provide a safer, more convenient year-round port for the French delivery of furs to Europe. This plan of his further alienated the Montréal traders who now sent their voyageurs to pick up their furs at Michillimackinac.

La Salle set out to begin his negotiations with the Miamis in early March 1681, when he began his ascent of the Saint-Joseph River to reach another of their villages which was located on the shores of Lake Michigan. He found no sign of Tonti there, but he did, however, find Abenakis and Mohicans who had migrated from near the English coastal colonies, and had wintered with the Miamis. These eastern exiles from King Philip's War against the English colonists of Rhode Island, New York, and Virginia had arrived as strangers in this western world; they were easily convinced to join other forces in alliance against the Iroquois menace. In addition, a Shawanoe chief and his one hundred fifty warriors from the Ohio valley promised to join La Salle at the new fort that following autumn. The explorer reconciled the Miamis and the Illinois, then late in May, he left for Montréal to deal with his creditors.

La Salle finally reunited with Tonti at Michillimackinac, where he and Father Zenobe Membré had recently arrived from their safe haven at Green Bay. These three men then safely traveled the remaining 1000 miles east to Fort Frontenac.

At Montréal in August 1681, La Salle wrote his will in favor of a cousin to whom he was deeply in debt. Then he gathered the supplies and equipment he would need to carry out his grand plan for the Illinois country.

That September, Bastien and his family celebrated the end of his nine-year lease of Jeanne Dodier's farm. Louis and Sébastien were now strong enough to help him both in the fields and forest.

In early autumn, Aubert de la Chesnaye, Cavalier de La Salle, Louis Joliet, and Charles Le Moyne held a secret meeting at Montréal, at which they jointly formed *La Compagnie du Nord* in competition with the Hudson Bay Company. Radisson and Des Groseilliers agreed to lead its first expedition to the northern sea, on condition that they be awarded 25 percent of the profits. La Chesnaye promised to finance the expedition, and to provide two fully-manned ships. Radisson and his brother-in-law agreed to wait out the winter season, then move to Île-Percée in the spring to await delivery of the two vessels.

Meanwhile, La Salle and Tonti set out again with heavily laden canoes for the Illinois country, from where the explorer planned to resume his exploration of the southward flow of the Mississippi River.

La Salle and Tonti journeyed to Toronto, arrived at Lake Simcoe two weeks later, at Lake Huron in October, and finally at Fort Miami the following month. The explorer carefully selected a small, but loyal party of twenty-three Frenchmen and eighteen immigrant Abenakis, then led this group to the country of the Illinois, where he left Tonti in charge of building Fort Saint-Louis. On December 21, 1681, he and the rest of his party left by canoe to continue his southward exploration.

Fourteen

1682

On April 9, 1682, René-Robert Cavelier de La Salle claimed French possession "of the country of Louisiana; seas, harbors, ports, bays, adjacent straits, and all the nations, peoples, provinces, cities, towns, villages, mines, minerals, fisheries, streams, and rivers, within the extent of the said Louisiana, from the mouth of the great river Saint-Louis (now called the Ohio), as also along the river Colbert (now called the Mississippi), and the rivers which discharge themselves into that river, from its source beyond the country of the Nadouessioux (Sioux), as far as its mouth at the sea, or Gulf of Mexico, and also to the mouth of the River of Palms, upon the assurance we have had from the natives of these countries, that we are the first Europeans who have descended or ascended the said river Colbert; hereby protesting against all who may hereafter undertake to invade any or all of these aforesaid countries, people, or lands, to the prejudice of the rights of his Majesty, acquired by the consent of the nations dwelling therein."

Thus, France gained on parchment an enormous section of the North American continent which included the present state of Texas, the Mississippi River basin from its northern beginnings to the southern outlet into the Gulf, from the Allegheny mountain range in the east to the Rocky Mountains in the west—vast fertile regions of North America from Hudson Bay to the Gulf of Mexico, and up to 1000 miles west of the Great Lakes.

On the morning of April 27, 1682, royal notary Jean Cusson met at Bastien's house with sixteen-year old Marie, and Antoine Cottenoire to witness their signing of a marriage contract, through which the groom-to-be pledged the bride a widow's legacy of 300 livres. Among the other witnesses were cape merchant Pierre Le Boulanger *sieur* de Saint-Pierre, his wife Marie-Anne Godefroy, Ignace Lefebvre *sieur* de Belisle, Louis Lefebvre, Jacques Massé and Catherine Guillet.

The religious wedding took place the following day at the small church of Sainte-Madeleine, where Bastien and Marguerite, Madeleine and Aubin had also exchanged vows and received the priest's blessing. Marie wore homespun clothing and fine white embroidered linen as had her sister and mother during their special ceremonies. Her face glowed with joy during the exchange of vows.

Antoine stood fully a head taller than either Bastien or Aubin. He wore a matching suit of gray serge breeches, vest, and frock coat; a white ruffled shirt, a neck cloth and clocked stockings of fine white linen, and a pair of French leather buckled shoes.

The proud parents of the bride stood close together and shared strong emotions; his eyes moistened, and she dabbed at the occasional tears that seeped down her cheeks. They knew that they would miss both of their daughters in their daily lives, but they were confident that, young as Madeleine and Marie were, they had found devoted husbands who truly cared for them. They looked forward to enjoying their second Canadian-born generation.

The local fiddler's music led a large party of wedding guests to the bride's family home in celebration of this event. Family, friends, and neighbors contributed to the food table, which already offered meat pies, roast pork, root vegetables, cheeses and jams, fresh-baked breads, home-churned butter, and refreshments of cider, wine, and beer.

Their guests from the cape, the seigniory of Sainte-Marie, and from Villier presented their traditional wedding gifts of handmade baskets of grain, dried vegetables and fruits, farm and kitchen implements. The group gradually made its way outdoors on this beautifully warm spring day.

The young Canadians clapped their hands and tapped their feet to the sounds and rhythms of their parents' folk music and dances. They practiced the rapid steps alongside the adults, fully appreciating this music from the old country. Bastien's dancing skills had greatly improved, much to Marguerite's delight. He taught the steps to their sons, while she demonstrated to their daughters.

The bride and groom prepared to leave before dark, in order to safely cross the river to their home at Villier. Merchant Jean Lemoine, a friend and guest at the reception, had already offered to ferry them across on his small river shallop. Everyone joined in loading the bride's belongings and the couple's wedding gifts on the river vessel, and saw them off at dusk.

"My only worry is that they'll be living across the river," Marguerite confided. "There are so few habitants there right now—What if they should be attacked?"

"They have those new redoubts armed with small cannon. They'll manage just as we did, Marguerite. Besides, the militias at the cape and at Trois-Rivières would waste no time going to their defense with their armed barks."

"At least they'll be living near each other, and their children will grow up together—But we won't see as much of them, will we?"

He held her in a comforting hug. "As long as we own that concession next to Aubin's, I'll probably see them more often than you will, but they'll be attending Mass at Sainte-Madeleine every Sunday, and we'll see them then. You can invite them over for Sunday dinner as often as you like, and that can become an even more special day for all of us."

By early May of that year, Louis XIV wrote a letter of recall for both Governor-General Frontenac and Intendant Duchesneau, whose constant bickering had generated endless petty reports to Colbert and the king. Frontenac had quarreled with several members of the Sovereign Council of Québec, having banished from the capital to their country houses: Messieurs de Tilly to Beauport, d'Auteuil to Sillery, and de Villeray to Île-d'Orléans.

He had jailed First Councilor D'Amours for two months, had physically assaulted and imprisoned Intendant Duchesneau's adolescent son. He had also allowed coureurs and *seigneurs* to trade liquor for furs with the natives, and furs with the New England merchants in exchange for silver coins.

King Louis XIV officially opened his Château de Versailles that summer, thus introducing an unprecedented level of opulence, culture, and refinement among European palaces. Its grounds occupied over two hundred fifty acres of land, much of which had originally been an extensive swampland; thousands of laborers had died from fever and pneumonia during its reclamation. His royal engineers had specially designed an underground system to carry water from the Seine River to the palace's Grand Canal and gardens. Construction of the nearby city of Versailles had finally been completed to house the twenty-five thousand people required to accommodate all members of the royal court who would live at the new palace.

England's Duke of York appointed Irish Colonel Thomas Dongan to the governorship of the province of New York. Upon his arrival in North America, Dongan immediately supported the Iroquois claims of sovereignty over the western territory. The governor challenged French claims to, and maintained English trade rights over, territory north of the Great Lakes and in the Mississippi valley. Yet his assertions were not sanctioned by the English government; Britain was now at peace with France.

Dongan wrote to the Duke of York: "'Tis a hard thing that all countries a Frenchman walks over in America must belong to Canada."

Late in the evening of August 4, 1682, fire swept through the capital of Québec; nuns at *l'hôtel-Dieu* reported that the lower town was lit as brightly as at noontime. The fire flared up in one of the private homes. Its blaze quickly spread to the neighboring wooden structures and leaped across the narrow street to the Jesuit storehouse. The summer season had been unusually dry; local settlers resorted to the use of kettles and pails of water to fight the flames. Local men attempted to tear off roofs and pull down houses, but the heat of the fire drove them from their work. By four o'clock the following morning, over fifty homes and warehouses had burned to the ground, and more than half of Canada's stored goods had been incinerated.

Later that month, Radisson and Des Groseilliers left Île Percée on behalf of *la Compagnie du Nord*, leading two ships to the outlet of the Hayes River which flowed into the southwestern part of Hudson Bay.

A week later, Jesuit Father Lamberville warned French authorities: "The Iroquois are ready to attack Canada at the slightest provocation."

Early that September, Governor-General Joseph-Antoine Le Fèbvre de La Barre and Intendant Jacques De Meulles *sieur* de la Source arrived at Québec following a seventy-eight-day crossing. They carried royal orders to Frontenac and Jacques Duchesneau, directing them to be aboard the next ship to sail for La Rochelle.

La Barre arrived at the burnt-out lower town of Québec, and saw that only merchant Aubert de la Chesnaye's house had survived the conflagration. The new governor lodged in the chateau, but since all other buildings of the upper town were overflowing with people made homeless by the fire, Intendant De Meulles, his wife, and daughters found shelter in a house located in the neighboring woods.

Radisson and Des Groseilliers reached the Hayes River that September, and succeeded in capturing Fort Nelson from the English. They seized the Boston ship *Bachelor's Delight* from young Captain Ben Gillam, whom they caught poaching in the bay. Soon after, the British ship *Prince Rupert* arrived with Hudson Bay Governor Bridgar and Ben's father Zachariah Gillam, who never disclosed the identity of the two coureurs to the governor, in his effort to protect his son.

A few days later, fourteen crewmen and Zachariah Gillam drowned when storm-driven ice floes sank the *Prince Rupert*. Through much luck and bravado, Radisson captured the remaining Englishmen and took possession of a great quantity of valuable beaver furs.

At the end of the month, Father Lamberville wrote to Frontenac, whom he assumed was still governor of Nouvelle

France: "The upper Iroquois (Senecas) have no fear of the French. They make war against our allies, whom they capture and convert into Iroquois warriors; and they boast that after growing rich by our plunder, and gaining strength by adopting our allies into their ranks, the Five Nations will attack Canada, and overwhelm it in a single campaign." He added that within the previous two years, the Senecas had reinforced themselves by more than nine hundred captive warriors whom they had adopted as their own.

Immediately after Frontenac's departure, sixty-year old soldier-lawyer La Barre wrote to the king: "The Iroquois have twenty-six hundred warriors. I will attack them with twelve hundred men. They know me before seeing me, for they have been told by the English how roughly I handled them in the West Indies."

On October 20th, Radisson and Des Groseilliers arrived triumphantly at Québec aboard Ben Gillam's ship, *Bachelor's Delight*. But while it was generally believed that Frontenac had unofficially approved of the *Compagnie du Nord*'s venture, newly-arrived Governor La Barre was embarrassed and outraged by its success, because France was then at peace with England.

La Barre immediately restored the ship to its owner, Benjamin Gillam, then released Hudson Bay Governor John Bridgar and allowed him to return to England by way of Boston. Since Radisson and his brother-in-law attempted to evade the 25 percent tax on their impressive cargo of furs, La Barre seized the lot, and ordered both of them to report to Colbert and the king.

The two adventurers returned to the cape and Trois-Rivières where they reunited with their families and brooded through the winter. The story of their misfortune quickly spread through the settlements, generating sympathy and outrage among the settlers.

Bastien discussed this matter with Nicolas Perrot and asked him what he thought about the changes in administration.

"It's my practice to get along with whoever is in power, Bastien, but I sense a change of direction coming from Québec. You see, there are two opposing parties among the fur merchants. Now that La Salle has opened up the Illinois fur country and has claimed the Mississippi River outlet to the Gulf of Mexico, this threatens the importance of the traditional western trade routes."

"But La Salle was granted authority by the king to accomplish these things."

"Maybe so, but these new claims still threaten Montréal's control of the fur trade."

"You know more about these things than I do," Bastien admitted. "Are we likely to fight a war over this?"

"Not likely over this, but a formidable alliance between the western Iroquois, the Dutch and the English of New York has been growing over the past several years. The Five Nations have definitely become stronger and more aggressive since they began trading furs at Albany for guns and ammunition. I think that the movement of French traders and forts into that area south and west of lakes Michigan and Superior has stirred them up. The Senecas, Dutch and English are beginning to challenge our control of the Great Lakes fur regions."

"Does that account for the rumors of a growing threat from the Iroquois?"

Perrot turned away and said nothing as he considered how much he dared to share with this man.

Bastien viewed these developments as a potential menace to his own family's security; if these rumors were true, the militia would likely be called upon for reasons other than self-defense. He already suspected that France had become too involved elsewhere to offer meaningful support to its North American colonies.

Perrot finally told him: "I recently attended an assembly which was called by the new governor-general at Québec. He was warned that the western Iroquois must be destroyed at once, because they're threatening to conquer and destroy our native allies, thus ruining our trade. The Council agreed that Fort Frontenac should be strengthened and its settlers armed, that Québec must petition the King for reinforcements. I'm sure you realize that Nouvelle France can't afford to lose the beaver fur trade—it's our major export."

LA BARRE

Fifteen

Winter 1682-83

Governor La Barre's advisory assembly at Québec led him into an alliance with Frontenac's former adversaries. This group spent that winter developing a strategy to steadily minimize Cavalier de La Salle's achievements in the Illinois and Mississippi areas which threatened to divert the export of furs from Montréal and the Saint Lawrence River to a new warm-weather, year-round port based in the Gulf of Mexico. Montréal merchants allied to the governor repeatedly obstructed the explorer's efforts to obtain trade goods and to recruit volunteer reinforcements for his new Fort Saint-Louis in the Illinois territory.

Bastien and Marguerite welcomed a second grandchild into their extending family when Marie-Renée Cottenoire was born to Marie and Antoine in mid-February 1683.

Early that spring, when Québec authorities received a warning that the westernmost Iroquois were moving to attack the Hurons and Ottawas of the Great Lakes, and the Illinois to the south, La Barre immediately sent reinforcements to protect trade goods at Michillimackinac. A short while later, he sent out a flotilla of seven canoes and fourteen men with 16,000-livres worth of merchandise to trade with the Mississippi tribes near the lakes.

The governor seized Fort Frontenac on the grounds that La Salle had abandoned it and had not lived up to the king's conditions. He then sent Chevalier de Baugis to take over La Salle's Fort Saint-Louis. His letters to the king belittled the explorer's accomplishments and the value of his having discovered the Mississippi River outlet into the Gulf of Mexico.

Rumors spread through the settlements that the Iroquois and the English of New York had begun to challenge French claims to the western territories. The older settlers who had lived through the Mohawk campaigns of the 1660's grew concerned for the future safety of their families; they knew that such a development would pose a threat to their security.

Bastien counseled his daughters and their husbands to reserve extra food supplies against any future emergency. He and Marguerite planned to hold back extra grain, and dry extra meat, fish, vegetables and fruit. They also began to prepare a large supply of pemmican which they knew could be safely stored over a period of several years.

When Louis Lefebvre died and was buried in early May, Bastien's family mourned the loss of a longtime friend and neighbor; Louis had shared many early settlement experiences with Bastien who immediately offered his help to widow Catherine Ferré, and her yet unmarried son Jacques.

The situation in the Great Lakes area continued to deteriorate. Governor La Barre considered launching a preemptive attack against the Senecas but had limited military resources at his disposal. He dispatched a small vessel to La Rochelle with urgent requests that the king send six hundred soldiers, arms and munitions to the colony.

He sent Charles Le Moyne of Montréal as envoy to Onondaga. Le Moyne later returned to Montréal with a deputation of over forty Iroquois chiefs who agreed to meet with La Barre.

The governor held the grand council at the new church of Bonsecours, and distributed presents worth 6,000 livres to his guests. He urged them not to attack the tribes of the lakes, nor to plunder any of the French traders who carried passports from him. They agreed. When he asked why they made war on the Illinois, they answered: "Because they deserve to die."

Their icy reply startled him.

The other chiefs complained that La Salle had given guns, powder, and lead to the Illinois to use against them. La Barre agreed that La Salle should be punished.

Confident that the Iroquois threat to Michillimackinac had been diverted for a while longer, the governor, and merchant Charles Aubert de La Chesnaye sent another thirty men and one hundred trading canoes to that post. Other merchants accused them of diverting furs from Montréal, and of secretly selling them to the Dutch and English of New York, thus avoiding the 25 percent duties at Québec, and collecting payment in English silver coins instead of the unreliable French bills of exchange.

That September, French Minister of the Marine Jean-Baptiste Colbert died and was succeeded by his son Marquis de Seignelay. His death marked the closing of official French efforts to broaden the Canadian economy and strengthen its population, common goals that Colbert and Intendant Talon had worked so hard to implement.

Over the previous eleven years, French Minister of War marquis de Louvois had gradually eroded Colbert's influence over Louis XIV's decisions. While Colbert's mercantile policies had so painstakingly built up the French treasury, and had pushed for the development of a royal navy to protect and defend French overseas colonies, Louvois had diverted these treasury funds toward the development of the most powerful military force in Europe. His martial influence had inspired, encouraged, and financed Louis XIV's increasingly aggressive European policies.

When Radisson and Des Groseilliers reached France shortly after Colbert's death, a furious Louis XIV chastised them for the fiasco over Hudson Bay. This royal treatment led to forty-seven-year old Radisson's permanent return to London, and his sixty-five-year old brother-in-law Des Groseilliers' retirement to his farm at Cap-de-la-Madeleine.

Late in December 1683, Jesuit Father Jacques Bigot wrote of dedicating to Saint-François-de-Sales a new 36-square mile Abenaki mission on the Chaudière River. This reservation soon drew converts from Acadia with the aid of Monsieur de Saint-Castin, who was greatly annoyed by the recently established

English trading post at Pentagouet, on land that he claimed to be his own. The two Fathers Bigot ministered to a mixture of Abenakis, Algonquins, Sokokis, and Gaspesians, some of whom had fled their homelands as a result of King Philip's War.

On May 8, 1684, a group of two hundred Senecas and Cayugas stopped and seized La Barre's seven trading canoes fully loaded with furs. When the traders showed their permits, which were all signed and sealed by the governor, the Iroquois tore them up and threw them aside, declaring that this was their land, that they had the right to confiscate any trade goods carried by the French and to kill them if they resisted. The warriors seized the furs, and released the voyageurs at Fort Saint-Louis-des-Illinois, without weapons, food, or canoes. Three weeks later, these hapless traders reached Québec and reported the incident to Governor La Barre.

Meanwhile, their Iroquois captors had returned to attack Fort Saint-Louis, but had failed in their siege; Chevalier de Baugis and Henri de Tonti had jointly held their positions and repelled the attack.

Troop ships arrived from France with one hundred fifty soldiers, one hundred twenty of whom were battle-worn veterans of the Dutch wars, many of whom already suffered from a virulent strain of influenza. French Intendant Rochefort had sent no clothing, food provisions nor any funds to support the needs of these soldiers. Of the one thousand muskets promised, seven hundred forty were unusable, and rather than sending four light copper cannons, Rochefort had sent iron cannons which were too heavy for the birch canoes. Six hundred of the one thousand swords delivered to Nouvelle France were broken.

La Barre thus realized that France would not help him; that he must act alone. His official orders were to avoid war if possible, but if need be, to crush the Iroquois swiftly and decisively.

When Captain Rivard announced a call for militia volunteers to join Governor La Barre's upcoming military expedition, young men responded enthusiastically, their parents negatively.

Marguerite became alarmed. "Why should we attack the Iroquois in their homeland when they've done us no harm? Our homes aren't threatened."

Bastien shared her concern. Could it be that after fifteen years of peace, the population and the authorities no longer remembered what it was like to be at war with the Five Nations? He knew that if one tribe was attacked, the others would rally together to brutally retaliate against the attacker.

War fever spread through the community. Louis, who had recently turned sixteen and become a proud member of the militia, asked his father for permission to volunteer.

Aubin and Antoine both understood this growing challenge to French control of the western fur trade. When they talked of joining the campaign, both Madeleine and Marie resisted the idea out of fear for the future, and the two couples finally agreed to seek Bastien's advice.

The two young women tearfully embraced their parents.

"Now, now, Madeleine," Bastien gently chided. "What will the children think, seeing you like this?"

"Oh, *Maman*," Marie whispered, "how could we manage without them?"

Bastien invited them all to sit down, and when quiet had been restored, he basically repeated what he had told Marguerite upon leaving her to join the Carignan campaign, to accompany Father Albanel to Hudson Bay, and again later to follow Frontenac to Cataracoui. "Antoine and Aubin have no choice; they're experienced voyageurs. We'll all have to make the best of it and put our trust in God."

Marguerite reluctantly agreed with him. "You'll manage as we did when your papa was called to leave us—and we'll be here to help you. That's what families do; they help each other."

Bastien continued speaking to his daughters: "We understand your concern, but you can move into the bunkhouse with your children, and I'll take care of the fields with the help of your brothers. You might have to join us at harvest time, but we'll work out a way so you can take turns working with us."

Marguerite spoke up again: "Your husbands should carry emergency supplies of pemmican and corn in case they run out of food. You and I will prepare those for them; we can draw from our supplies of dried meat, currants and apples. I may not have enough rendered fat on hand, but if the men can hunt for deer, we can dry some of its meat and use fresh bone marrow."

Empowered by this new sense of direction, the young women gradually regained their composure, and apologized for their panic. Their children hugged them, and their six-year old sister asked: "Can I help?"

"Of course you can!" Marguerite encouraged her.

Bastien was confident that he could maintain the family properties with young Sébastien who was now fourteen, and to some extent with ten-year old François, but his concern for Louis grew daily; he knew from experience that his oldest son was still too young and untrained to go to war.

He shared this opinion with Nicolas Perrot, who told him: "I've just received a trade permit, and a commission from Governor La Barre to recruit our western allies. Would Louis be prepared to accompany me?"

Bastien felt a glimmer of hope. In a voice hoarse with emotion, he replied gratefully: "Yes, I believe he's ready to voyage."

Louis was thrilled to hear this, but the two men cautioned him that such a journey would be much longer and more difficult than the hunting trips he had experienced with his native friends. "You'll need to prove yourself to me before I accept you as a traveling partner," Perrot told him soberly.

"How can I do that?" the young man asked.

"I plan to do some hunting for my family before I leave. With your father's permission, I'd like to take you canoeing and portaging up the Saint-Maurice River over the next two days."

Bastien nodded his approval.

"Your father tells me that you understand and speak the Algonquin language."

"Yes, *Sieur*, but I understand it more easily than I can speak it."

"Then during this test, we'll speak only in Algonquin."

Louis smiled confidently.

Perrot explained: "The natives that I'll visit and trade with speak various Algonquin patois. If you know one, you should be able to understand the others."

He turned to Bastien. "I'll be leaving for Michillimackinac in about a week. If I'm to try him out, Louis should be here at dawn tomorrow. Can you manage that?"

"We certainly can," Bastien replied with confidence.

Their trial trip proved successful. Therefore, Perrot told Bastien that for his voyage west, he planned to travel lightly and quickly, and would supply Louis' basic provisions. Nevertheless, Bastien outfitted Louis with his old leather backpack in which he inserted the travel kit that Red Dawn had given him before his voyage to Hudson Bay. To this he added a hatchet, knife, small whetstone, fishing line and hooks, tin plate, cup, and spoon.

He fashioned a portage collar for his son. This was a three-inch wide leather strap that fit against a voyageur's forehead, and smaller straps extending long enough to bind around the packages of cargo he would carry overland on his back past impassable river rapids and falls. Bastien demonstrated the proper method of using this device, and advised him to pad his back against his initial loads to avoid the formation of painful boils and blisters during his first carries.

Marguerite packed a supply of pemmican, and made sure that Louis had a blanket and proper clothing: extra pants, shirt, and socks, an old pair of soft moccasins to wear in the canoe, and a more rugged pair for portaging past the rapids. Louis learned how to make *banique*, a type of bread which the northern natives had taught his father to bake on the trail. Bastien bought him his first musket and ammunition, but Louis insisted that he would also take along his bow and arrow.

Perrot and his party left for Michillimackinac at the end of May. His native guide Grey Cloud frowned when he first sighted this young Frenchman who was to accompany them. The Algonquin had often traveled with Perrot on these voyages to the Great Lakes, and he dreaded the extra burden of having to compensate for the lack of strength and experience he expected from this white youth.

Nicolas Perrot noticed his reaction, but said nothing as he laid his poles in the bottom of the canoe and evenly spread the weight of their few personal belongings and provisions on top of these.

They paddled to Montréal where they picked up their basic supplies, then headed toward the Ottawa River, facing their first portage at the Lachine Rapids. Their limited supplies were heavy, but Louis quickly learned to lift and handle his share of the load; he had already carried this canoe and poled the rapids. He gained in strength every day.

Louis sensed the guide's wariness, and it troubled him. At their first camping site, he spoke to Grey Cloud in his native tongue, and offered to hunt with him. The Algonquin turned to Perrot, who nodded in agreement; the native uttered a barely perceptible grunt in response.

Grey Cloud started out with his musket; Louis carried his bow and arrows. Any attempt at conversation was met with a chilly silence from the native as they walked quietly through the forest.

Louis pointed to the signs of two wild hares. Grey Cloud motioned him on. They reached a small watering hole and saw abundant signs of small animals; the Algonquin disregarded these and picked up the trail of larger game. Louis followed and focused on stalking their prey as the prints grew fresher. All seemed too quiet; Grey Cloud turned to search for Louis and was startled to find him following so close behind him.

The youth moved as stealthily as his guide, until he fired two arrows to the side of the trail. Grey Cloud glared at him. Louis walked over to retrieve his arrows from the two fat hares he had spotted traveling side-by-side in the brush. He quickly and deftly gutted them with his knife, tied their hind legs together with fish line, and strung them up from a branch high above the trail before continuing on. The Algonquin grunted again, making light of Louis' trophies.

They heard a cracking sound up ahead and froze in their tracks. Grey Cloud signaled Louis to maintain his position and moved silently ahead to spot the animal. A branch partially blocked his line of sight to the small deer, and as he slowly cocked his musket, the doe scampered away. He turned quickly and discovered that Louis had not moved.

Since the light had begun to fade, they turned to make their way back to camp, picking up the two hares along the way. Grey Cloud announced that he would prepare the food that evening.

During the meal, the Algonquin asked Louis where he had learned to hunt with bow and arrow.

Louis replied: "Chief Red Dawn taught me along with his grandsons."

"I know him well; he was my father's friend," said the native.

"He is also my father's friend," Louis told him.

"Then your father must be a great man."

Louis' cheeks grew red, and he nodded.

Perrot interjected: "His father voyaged to the northern sea with Father Albanel. They survived a bitter winter together during that voyage."

Grey Cloud frowned. "I have heard of that journey, and of that man," he admitted.

They traveled well over 1000 miles through the primitive forest, starting with Samuel de Champlain's original route to Lake Huron: the Ottawa River and the Olmstead cut-off to Lac-des-Allumettes, then the Mattawa River to Lake Nipissing. This was where they ceremoniously threw away the setting poles they had used to push their way against swift currents encountered along the way. The western flow of the French River now carried them to Georgian Bay where they paddled through the Inner Passage to Lake Huron.

Louis found that the deeper they reached into the virgin forest, the quieter and more beautiful everything seemed, and the more comfortable he felt within this environment. He finally understood Aubin's comments upon his return from Michillimackinac, and he recalled his father's nod of agreement with Aubin's description of his voyage through the wilderness. He learned to cook their meals which consisted mostly of corn, small game, and *banique*. He also learned to navigate the rapids, to carry and patch the canoe.

They continued their journey by paddling across Lake Huron to reach their final destination. Crossing this great lake proved to be the most difficult part of the journey; they struggled repeatedly through sudden wind squalls. They set up camp on the lake shore at night, and slept under their overturned canoe, with little protection from wind and rain. Chill gusts invariably blew in from across the lake in the early morning hours in spite of the summer months.

Upon their arrival at Michillimackinac, Perrot discovered that La Durantaye and Du Luth had failed to recruit the tribes of the Upper Lakes to join the French campaign against the Iroquois. Only the Huron warriors had volunteered, although they, along with the Ottawas, Ojibwas, Pottawatamies, and Foxes already knew that their beaver skins were worth twice as much in Albany than in Montréal.

Nicolas Perrot not only spoke the several Algonquin patois, he understood the Algonquin mind-set; he could interpret their meanings not only through their words, but also through an intuitive understanding of their culture, body language and thought processes. They knew this, and they trusted him. He managed to turn things around and recruited five hundred warriors from among the various tribes.

Louis was greatly impressed by his mentor's accomplishment. He could see that these Upper Algonquins were quite different from those he had come to know at the local missions. The many variations of the common language he heard spoken by the different tribes fascinated him, and he soon learned to recognize their affiliations by speech as well as by appearance.

His presence attracted much attention among the native warriors who sensed that this young man was greatly favored by Perrot. The Ottawas understood that he knew their language, and some attempted to communicate with him. He welcomed this, but became embarrassed when they discovered his innocence with women. Their remarks made him uncomfortable; he blushed, and this truly amused them. Grey Cloud finally noticed the problem and came to his rescue. He chastised the Upper Algonquins for treating a Christian man in such a manner, and haughtily led him away from them.

The two area commanders, Du Luth and La Durantaye led the force of five hundred warriors and one hundred coureurs toward the scheduled rendezvous of military and allied forces at Niagara. This wild, undisciplined volunteer army filled a third as many canoes.

They stopped along the way to hunt on the shore of Lake Michigan, where a Frenchman accidentally shot himself in the foot with his own gun. The frightened natives thought this to be a bad sign. Nicolas Perrot spent the next few days working to overcome their fears and superstitions.

When they stopped for another hunt in the strait of Detroit, one of the natives inadvertantly wounded his brother while shooting at a deer. His tribe threatened to wound the French, blaming them for the accident. Again, Perrot prevailed.

They reached the long point of Lake Erie, where one hundred *Loups* threatened to desert the mission. Perrot challenged their courage and manhood; they became determined to prove him wrong.

When the Ottawas refused to continue this long journey, Perrot persuaded them to go as far as Niagara where he promised that La Durantaye's three vessels would deliver a present of guns for them. They portaged their canoes past the mighty falls, and paddled to the mouth of the river, where they waited for the delivery of muskets, powder, and shot.

Finally, one ship appeared, without cargo, but with a letter from Governor La Barre.

Sixteen

D uring the previous two years, furs from Michillimakinac had reached New York, whose governor Colonel Thomas Dongan encouraged poaching of the French western fur country. The Iroquois, Dutch, and English traders had already moved into the lower Great Lakes region, and openly dealt with the lake tribes. Reports reached France from merchant customhouses, the Intendant, and several other quarters that Governor La Barre and merchant La Chesnaye regularly delivered furs to Albany under the pretext of official communications with the governor of New York.

Frustrated at every turn by La Barre's machinations against him, La Salle had sailed to France to plead his case before the king for the restoration of his rights to Cataracoui, which La Barre had taken away from him. Convinced by the explorer's arguments in favor of French colonization of the outlet area of the Mississippi River, Louis XIV responded by commissioning La Salle to command all territories between Fort Saint-Louis-des-Illinois and the Gulf of Mexico. The king further wrote to La Barre: "My intention is that you immediately undo the injury you've done to La Salle and order the return of all his property which properly belongs to him. I am certain that La Salle did not abandon that fort as you had previously reported to me."

Governor La Barre now focused on the aggressive intent of the Senecas and Cayugas who had looted his own trading convoy and had besieged Fort Saint-Louis-des-Illinois the previous year.

In early June, the governor of Nouvelle France wrote to his king that he planned to attack the Senecas in the middle of August, with or without French help.

Two weeks later, he wrote to Governor Dongan of New York, alerting him that he planned to chastise the Senecas and Cayugas, and he requested that the Dutch and English not supply them with muskets and ammunition.

During several previous years, the Oneidas, Onondagas, and Cayugas had attacked Maryland and Virginia, plundering and killing English settlers. Governor of Virginia Lord Howard of Effingham traveled once again to negotiate and formalize a friendship treaty with the Iroquois nations during their meeting at Albany. Dongan addressed the confederacy, and gave warning of the French governor's invasion plans, thus drawing them into a protective alliance with the English against the French. However, their consent to that agreement was qualified by statements from the Onondaga and Cayuga chiefs that they remained "a free people, although united to the English."

On June 24th, Dongan replied to La Barre that the English had sovereignty over the Five Nations and thus possessed the whole country south of the Great Lakes. He urged the French not to invade English territory, claiming that the Iroquois were subjects of England and therefore were under its protection. He added that the Senecas were ready to pay for damages caused to French canoes and coureurs.

Nevertheless, Governor La Barre prepared for his campaign by first sending an embassy to the Mohawks, Oneidas and Onondagas, to reassure them that the French would go to war only against the Senecas.

Another two weeks later, the Québec governor wrote to the French Minister of the Marine, informing him that he was about to advance on the enemy with seven hundred Canadians, one hundred thirty regulars, and two hundred native converts; and that Du Luth and La Durantaye would lead additional native allies and French coureurs to join him at Niagara. He stated: "When we are united, we will perish or we will destroy the enemy."

That same day, he notified the king: "My purpose is to exterminate the Senecas, since there is no hope of peace with them, except when they are driven to it by force. I pray you do not abandon me; and be assured that I shall do my duty at the head of your faithful colonists."

The following day, Intendant De Meulles wrote to the Minister of Marine that on July 10th, the governor had left Québec with two hundred men, and merchant La Chesnaye.

During the next five days, Bastien's family prepared for the upcoming campaign. Marguerite taught her daughters how to prepare and package trail food for their husbands, while Bastien helped his sons-in-law assemble the rest of their supplies and equipment for the campaign.

"Where did you learn to make this pemmican?" Madeleine asked.

"Your godmother was chief cook at the Jesuit manor when I first arrived at Cap-de-la-Madeleine," Marguerite replied. "An Algonquin woman had taught her how to prepare it for the missionary priests."

"I barely remember my godmother."

"Madeleine Eprinchard could be intimidating, but she became my first friend in Nouvelle France. She was like a mother to me when I arrived, and helped me prepare for the wedding. She was very fond of you."

"Is this one of those bad times that Papa told us about when we saw the great comet?" asked Marie.

"He's been here longer than any of us, *cherie*—He lived through the Mohawk raids."

"Well, I'm glad we followed his advice and had enough dried meat and berries to make this," said Madeleine. "Will we have enough fat?"

"I think there should be enough for both you and Marie," she replied while she demonstrated how to pound and grind the deer meat between washed stones. "Did you bring the nuts and honey?"

They both showed her what they had.

"Well then, while you finish grinding these dry ingredients, I'll prepare the marrow."

Marguerite moved that messy work outside. The men had butchered two newly killed deer, and had salvaged the leg bones which she had already stripped of meat and excess fat; now she cracked and broke the shafts between two stones to expose their rich marrow. She placed these in an iron pot, covered them with water, set them to simmer all afternoon, and left the liquid to cool overnight. She told her daughters that if this supply of marrow grease proved to be insufficient, they could add rendered tallow from her supply of lard.

The following day, they mixed the thoroughly grounded meat, ground dried currants and nuts with the warmed marrow grease. Once this mixture was well blended, they added a bit of honey and enough melted tallow to achieve an even consistency.

Marguerite packaged the pemmican into two separate hide containers for each man, sewed these shut, then, before they had a chance to harden, taught Madeleine and Marie to pound each pack to about a three-inch thickness. Finally, they sealed these with hot tallow, and left them to cool in the root cellar.

On July 15th, the Québec contingent arrived at Trois-Rivières, and the two young mothers moved into Bastien's bunkhouse with their daughters, five-year old Madeleine Maudoux, and seventeen-month old Marie-Renée Cottenoire.

Early the following morning, Aubin and Antoine fitted the pemmican into their knapsacks along with small bags of ground corn. Bastien reminded them that this emergency food supply would remain edible over a period of four months, as long as they kept it dry and away from direct heat and sun. Both men already had their voyaging equipment and supplies; Bastien merely helped them to assemble these together, and to load them into Antoine's canoe.

The families at the cape sadly and anxiously watched as their men paddled away toward their military rendezvous.

From Montréal, Governor La Barre sent an advance contingent to Cataracoui to protect his marching army, clear the way of trees and brush, reinforce the fort, and receive the advance convoys of food and munitions. La Barre did not follow until July 30th; by then, his force had grown into an army of seven hundred militiamen, three hundred seventy-eight native allies, and one hundred thirty regulars who were still weak from the sickness they had contracted during and after their ocean voyage.

This part of the journey proved to be extremely difficult to accomplish because of the series of rapids and falls that they encountered. Where poling proved to be impossible, the militiamen portaged all the supplies, equipment, and canoes, but they also dragged or pushed the heavier, more awkward military flat boats close along the bank, struggling against the strong rapids that made up this ascending section of the Saint Lawrence River. Since the French soldiers lacked the strength and experience to accomplish this, the Canadians did the heavier work among the rocks and foam, in water often reaching up to their armpits.

Aubin and Antoine were already exhausted, and were plagued by tiny gnats and mosquitos both day and night which made it very difficult for them to rest.

La Barre's forces hauled for a week before they reached Long Sault and spent another several days portaging river craft and cargo up this long, steep incline. A few days after clearing this last rapid, they finally reached calmer waters. Due to the condition of his troops, the governor called a day's rest before moving on.

They eventually traveled through the Thousand Islands area, where their fleet of canoes and flatboats wended its way through a long series of rocky islets. When they sighted the open waters of Lake Ontario, the Canadians broke into a cheer.

On August 9th, they entered the harbor of Cataracoui and landed close to the fort's palisades. When La Barre chose a nearby plain for the army's encampment, Antoine persuaded Captain Rivard to choose the slightly elevated fringes of that low, damp area to set up camp for the cape and Villier contingents.

Soldiers set up their tents, Canadians and their native allies constructed their huts and sheds of bark. Most of the Abenakis raised the dome-shaped, woven mat wigwams that they traditionally favored during the warm summer months. The several hundred native allies included the Algonquins from Sillery, Abenakis from Sillery and Villier, Hurons from Lorette, and Christian Iroquois from the Jesuit mission at Sault Saint-Louis near Montréal.

A "malarious fever" continued to afflict many of the French

regulars and spread through the camp. This highly virulent influenza epidemic killed many and weakened many more of the men, including La Barre.

Food provisions ran out by mid-August; men grew hungry and miserable. August soon turned to September, while the sickness continued to spread. Governor La Barre finally and reluctantly admitted that since his army was in no condition to fight, he would have to negotiate from weakness. He sent Charles Le Moyne to accept an Onondaga offer to mediate between the French and the Senecas, while he evacuated the sickest men homeward in an effort to obscure his tenuous position.

The Onondaga chief agreed to participate, but insisted that the parley must be held on his side of the lake, across the mouth of the Salmon River, at a site which the French would always refer to as *La Famine,* but which the natives knew as *Keyouanonague.*

On September 3rd, Le Moyne arrived with Onondaga spokesman Otréouati and thirteen Iroquois deputies. La Barre greeted them, exchanged presents with his guests and offered them a feast of bread, wine, and salmon trout before they retired for the night.

The Council began the following day with Jesuit Father Bruyas acting as interpreter between the two parties. The Onondaga chiefs stated that they could not understand why the French planned to attack the Senecas who had already offered to make restitution.

La Barre sat in an armchair, facing a scene only slightly reminiscent of Frontenac's first council with the Iroquois at Cataracoui. In diplomatic language, he challenged their belligerence. He listed their offenses against his king, and warned that if they did not make reparations, peace could not be established between them. If there were no peace, his king had ordered him to declare war against them.

Also speaking in diplomatic language, the great Onondaga orator, Otréouati, derided the French governor's original intentions to make war, and the apparent weakness of his troops. He boasted that the Iroquois had introduced the English into their Great Lakes area, just as the Algonquins had led the French to the villages of the Five Nations to engage in trade that the English claimed as their own. He stressed the following points in the name of the Five Nations: they were born free and remained free agents dependent neither on the French nor the English; they attacked the Illinois because they hunted for beaver on Iroquois lands, armed with French muskets and shot; the original Iroquois agreement with the French at Cataracoui was that a trading, not military, fort be built; the Iroquois would keep the peace as long as the French or the English did not attack them in their country which the Great spirit had given them.

The session closed and La Barre retreated to his tent. Meanwhile, Otréouati entertained some of the French at a feast which he personally opened with a dance.

The two parties discussed peace terms in the afternoon, and defined them that evening. La Barre promised not to attack the Senecas, while Otréouati consented that the Iroquois should make amends for the pillaging of La Barre's traders. The chief declared that the Iroquois would fight the Illinois to the death, and La Barre did not protest. The sachem demanded that the council fire be moved permanently to La Famine on Iroquois territory. La Barre agreed and announced that he would leave with his troops the following morning.

That night, he sent a messenger to Niagara.

The following morning, the French encampment remained filled with sick soldiers, militiamen, and allied warriors when the governor embarked and left in advance of his troops. The able-bodied Canadians and natives placed the shivering disabled men onboard the flatboats and canoes, and the entire force, scattered and disorganized, floated down the river to Montréal.

Upon his arrival at Québec, La Barre found a letter from the king, which was dated July 31st, the day after the governor had left Montréal for Cataracoui. La Barre read: "I have written my ambassador to England, Monsieur Barillon, to work to withdraw the orders of the Duke of York in order to prevent the Boston commander from assisting the savages with troops, arms, or munitions and I believe that this will be expedited as soon as my message is delivered. Since it would benefit France to lessen the number of Iroquois and since these savages are strong and robust, they would be of valuable service on my galleons; therefore, attempt to capture as many prisoners of war as you can and deliver them to France."

To the great relief of their families, Louis and Nicolas Perrot arrived home safely, and in time for the September grain harvest.

"Were there any problems during your journey?" Bastien immediately asked his son.

Louis hesitated as he considered where to begin his report.

"Sounds like an uneventful voyage!"

"Papa, there's so much to tell—What would you like to know?"

"Were you in any danger?"

"No."

"Did you ever run out of food?"

Louis' face lit up with a smile. "Of course not."

"Did you learn anything?"

"A lot."

"Tell me about that."

"I learned how quiet and beautiful the forest can be. That not all the Algonquins speak exactly the same, but they all understand each other. That Nicolas Perrot is an important man."

Bastien nodded at every statement.

"And so are you!" Louis added.

"Why do you say that?"

Louis explained his initial relationship with Grey Cloud, and how he eventually managed to turn that around.

Bastien smiled proudly at his son. "He may have heard about me, and his father may also have been a friend of Red Dawn, but your skill with the bow and arrow is what won him over."

Louis shrugged his shoulders, then continued: "Monsieur Perrot is greatly respected by our western allies. Messieurs Du Luth and La Durantaye had not been able to gain their cooperation, except for some of the Hurons, but once Monsieur Perrot talked with the other tribal chiefs, we had a whole army of volunteer warriors! You should have seen that line of canoes working its way to Niagara!"

Bastien shared his son's enthusiasm as he pictured that scene in his mind. "Why do you think he succeeded where they had not?"

Louis thought this over carefully. "I don't know, Papa, except that he seemed like a different person while he talked with them. You could see that they completely understood each other."

"Were there any problems on your way to Niagara?"

"Monsieur Perrot had to persuade some of the tribes not to turn back, and always succeeded." He hesitated.

"What is it, Louis?"

"We finally reached Niagara, and expected to receive a supply of muskets and ammunition as a reward to the natives, but all that arrived was a message from the governor."

"What did it say?"

"That he had made peace with the Iroquois, that he didn't need the warriors and the coureurs after all, that they should all turn around and go home."

Louis' expression tugged at Bastien's heart, in spite of his relief that his son had not been required to fight the Iroquois.

Louis continued, his voice tense with emotion: "Papa, so many of those warriors had traveled six weeks or more to strike a powerful blow against the Senecas. They turned away from us with disgust, anger, and a loss of respect for our governor and for all of us."

Louis had sensed their mood, and had shared their disillusionment. He had been shaken by how quickly the tide had turned. Du Luth and La Durantaye had shown immediate and obvious outrage at the sudden cancellation of the campaign, for they knew effect this message would have on the allegiance of the lake tribes.

Nicolas Perrot had expressed his sorrow, given presents, and bid farewell to his native friends. Then he had prepared his party for the journey home. Grey Cloud's mood had matched his name during their long voyage back to the Saint Lawrence River valley. Louis' disappointment had turned to disillusionment, and eventually to a sense of foreboding.

Seventeen

In late September, Abenaki casualties from La Famine began to arrive at the Jesuit missions. At Saint-François-de-Sales, only one or two of those who had participated in the military campaign had escaped the epidemic; their Abenaki chief died within twelve hours after his arrival. The nearby communities at côte Saint-Ignace and at Saint-Michel also suffered from the epidemic. Abenaki warriors who returned to the Bécancour mission introduced the infectious disease to the southern shore of the Trois-Rivières area.

Soon afterward, Aubin and Antoine returned safely, in time to help Bastien with the remainder of the grain harvest on the south shore, and to manage their own food storage. They also had much news to share with their father-in-law.

Again, Bastien's first question to them was: "Were there any problems during your voyage?"

Both men had obviously lost weight, and appeared to be exhausted. They turned to each other in silence, then Antoine replied with unmistakable anger in his voice: "That was the most badly managed expedition I've ever heard of!"

Bastien waited patiently to hear more.

Aubin continued with less fury. "The French regulars should have been in hospital, but instead were required to go on this expedition. They were too weak to carry their own supplies, let alone haul their flatboats against the rapids—our militia had to carry our own load and theirs."

Antoine added: "The governor chose a low-lying, damp field for the encampment. The soldiers' sickness soon spread to most of the troops, including La Barre. This went on for several miserable weeks."

Bastien was relieved that Marguerite was not present to hear this. His own anger began to rise. "Did it affect you?"

"No," Aubin replied, "Antoine was smart enough to set us up on the edge of the encampment, which was higher and drier than the rest of the camping site. This location also made it easier for us to catch small game, because it was closer to the edge of the woods."

"The food supplies ran out at least a month before we left for home." Antoine added. "We were among the lucky ones who could forage for food. The corn and pemmican we carried kept us healthy."

"What happened at the negotiations?"

"The Iroquois won that battle without a fight," Antoine replied in a tight voice. "They were insolent to the governor. He retreated into his tent; everyone could hear his fury while the Iroquois spokesman danced among his people."

"The governor left early and alone the following morning, and abandoned us to take care of the sick and find our way back as best we could," Aubin explained.

Bastien shared their feelings of betrayal. "Then all I've heard about that man is true," he muttered. And he thanked God for having spared his oldest son from that campaign.

He immediately set the family to gathering whatever fruit and nuts they could find in the forest. He went hunting for meat with his sons and sons-in-law. The women set up drying racks. This time, they would produce a supply of pemmican for the entire family, and waste nothing.

Shortly after this effort got underway, Aubin and Antoine became ill with the flu, apparently as a result of their efforts to transport and care for the sick on their way back from La Famine. Bastien moved them into the empty bunkhouse, and allowed no one else to go near them while he personally nursed them back to health with his herbal medicines. During this time, Louis and Sébastien ran errands and took over their father's responsibilities, while the women concentrated their efforts toward bringing in the vegetable harvest and processing the ingredients for the pemmican.

Two weeks later, just as his sons-in-law had mostly regained their strength, Bastien, in turn, developed the now familiar high fever, chills, and deep cough. Antoine offered to take care of him in the bunkhouse while the families continued to complete the vegetable, fruit, and nut harvests, and build up their food supplies. Aubin, Louis and Sébastien maintained communication back and forth between the three houses and the bunkhouse, while building up supplies of firewood, food and water at all locations.

The treaty made at La Famine was greeted with anger throughout the colony. While those who could, tilled and sowed their winter grain fields, it became obvious that the population would suffer from shortages of food and fuel throughout the following winter and summer.

On October 10th, the Intendant informed the French Minister that La Barre's excuses were false, and that everyone had lost respect for him. De Meulles reported that the governor had badly mismanaged the campaign, had been responsible for the spread of sickness among his troops, and that he had been shamefully intimidated by the Iroquois, so that after the council at La Famine, he had lost any semblance of leadership and abandoned his disabled forces in the field.

De Meulles also related to the king that since the return of the French forces, the military officers scorned the governor. He added that the people had come close to rebelling against him, but that he, De Meulles, had managed to calm them.

Canada had lost the respect not only of its enemies, but also of its allies. There rose great concern among Canadian officials and merchants that their native trading partners might now finally spurn the French alliance, welcome the Albany traders, and make peace at any price with the Iroquois. The Canadian fur trade was more deeply jeopardized now than before La Barre's campaign.

Upon reading these reports, Louis XIV wrote to Intendant De Meulles: "I'm very dissatisfied with the treaty agreed to between

La Barre and the Iroquois. His abandonment of the Illinois has greatly displeased me and has convinced me that I must recall him."

The next ship from France delivered the king's letter to Governor La Barre.

There followed a very difficult winter for the population of Nouvelle France. The flu epidemic spread throughout the Saint Lawrence River valley settlements, creating a shortage of available manpower for the fall sowing of grain crops and the collection of firewood; the weather turned bitterly cold; snow depth was greater than in the previous few years.

1685

English King Charles II died on February 6th. Since he had no sons, his brother, the Duke of York, succeeded him to the British throne as King James II. The British Parliament and the military soon rebelled against his obvious intention to restore Catholicism in England.

King Louis XIV had always regarded the Acadian fisheries and the Canadian fur trade as inexhaustible sources of wealth for the mother country, and had easily taken these natural resources for granted during Colbert's efficient ministry of colonial affairs. Now Canada's value to the French crown faced two major threats: the rapid expansion of the New England population and its fishing fleet, coupled with the steady encroachment of English traders into the northern and western fur countries from Hudson Bay and New York.

Although the Iroquois had become Canada's main protagonists along its southern frontiers, there was no doubt in the minds of the people at Versailles that these warriors acted as convenient surrogates for the English colonies in their battle to take over the North American beaver fur trade. Meanwhile, the French Acadians complained that *bostonnais* privateer ships raised havoc along their coasts, and threatened their fishing harvests.

Intendant De Meulles' most immediate concern was for the financial support of the troops who had arrived in Canada the previous year.

France minted special Canadian coins in the form of fifteen-sols-silver, and five-sols-copper pieces which were usually delivered to Québec in the spring to provision the French troops who were stationed in the colony. This currency would then be used in colonial payment for French goods. When this monetary shipment failed to arrive in the spring of 1685, the colonists refused to deal on credit, because La Barre's call-up of the militia and the effects of the epidemic that followed the campaign had greatly depressed the summer and fall harvests that previous year. The colonial barter system traditionally used wheat and moose skins as legal tender, sometimes beaver skins, wildcat skins, and even liquor, but these proved insufficient to meet the existing needs.

In an attempt to solve this problem, Intendant De Meulles devised a system of currency based on the use of playing cards which were plentiful in Québec. He accorded several different values and affixed his seal to these, then released them in legal payment for goods purchased for the troops. When the currency shipments finally arrived in the autumn of that year, this card money was exchanged for the special colonial coinage.

Early that spring, La Barre named Nicolas Perrot commander-in-chief of the Green Bay territory which Daumont de Saint-Lusson had claimed for France fourteen years earlier. At his home at Villier (now Bécancour), Perrot signed a procuration granting his wife power of attorney over their legal affairs, and prepared to leave the management of his farm in the hands of his faithful servant, Jean Boutilly.

Since Bastien was working with his sons at Bécancour during this time, he walked over to Perrot's farm to bid him bon voyage.

"Will you be gone long?" Bastien inquired.

"I don't know," Perrot replied. "I expect that the new governor will arrive at Québec before I reach De Père—he might have other plans regarding Green Bay."

"Well, if your wife or Jean should need help of any kind, they must let us know. We'll do what we can "

"I appreciate that. It seems that I've managed to spend so little time with my family over the years. My wife has been very patient."

"Isn't it more dangerous now for you to travel out west?"

"I have many good friends among the natives, Bastien. I'm not concerned."

"It's a totally different life out there, isn't it?"

"They live life one day at a time, one year at a time, and don't seem to worry very much about the future "

"Do you miss it when you come back home?"

"Did you?"

"I still do, once in a while, but I greatly prefer the comfort of my home and family. Of course, you've had more experience in the wilderness than I've had. "

"Yes, and I must say that your Louis has a natural ability to cope with it."

"I'll remember that," Bastien responded.

In mid-May 1685, Nicolas Perrot left Montréal by way of the Ottawa River to journey with a group of twenty men to the junction of the Wisconsin and Mississippi rivers. He would ascend the mighty river to the edge of Sioux territory to build Fort Saint-Antoine, then continue on to his final destination, a Jesuit mission located at the southern tip of Green Bay, at the Fox River rapids.

Louis XIV's next choice for Governor-General of the French Dominions of North America was an experienced officer, Jacques-René de Brisay, marquis de Denonville, whose honesty and loyalty had earned the king's respect. His orders were to humble the Iroquois, circumvent Governor Dongan's schemes, and restore the peace and security of the colony.

Early that June, Governor Denonville left France with his pregnant wife, two young daughters, and Bishop Laval's replacement, Vicar-general Monseigneur Jean-Baptiste de La Croix-Chevrières de Saint-Vallier.

The governor sailed from La Rochelle with eight hundred soldiers who were assigned in equal numbers to two of the king's ships, and suffered from overcrowding in the areas between decks during the entire crossing. One hundred and fifty of those army regulars died from fever and scurvy while en route to Nouvelle France.

Shortly after their arrival at Québec on the first day of August, the local hospital was once more overwhelmed by the sick. Sister

Superior recorded: "Not only our halls, but our church, our lofts, our hen-yard, and every corner of the hospital where we could make room, are filled with them. We set up tents in the yard. We work doubly hard to serve them." Over three hundred soldiers suffered from high fevers, delirium, and severe cases of scurvy. The women's ward was filled with military officers. Twenty of the soldiers died soon after their arrival. During the next several weeks, the survivors remained too weak to fulfill their military service. The sickness spread through the convent, and the settlement of Québec. Denonville reported to the French Minister that one third of those hospitalized had died from the pulmonary infection.

Denonville consulted with civil and religious representatives about the problems facing Nouvelle France, and traveled to Cataracoui in order to broaden his understanding of conditions in the outlaying areas. He learned that the Iroquois openly threatened to wage war on the Canadian colony; that the English of New York claimed all territory south of the Great Lakes; that the flight of young coureurs into the western fur country caused grave problems at the outer missionary posts, where outlawed French adventurers ran wild and corrupted native societies through their brandy and debauchery. His early assessment of the colony's situation led him to write to Minister of Marine Seignelay: "If we have war, nothing can save this country but a miracle of God."

At about this time, there were 160,000 English, and 10,725 French settlers in North America.

In early August, Jean Lemoine, seigneur de Sainte-Marie (at Champlain) granted a concession on the north shore to Bastien's son-in-law, Antoine Cottenoire.

A week later, the people of Nouvelle France rejoiced as Joseph-Antoine Le Fèbvre de La Barre sailed away from Québec.

Bastien and his extended family shared a meal that Sunday. While the women set the food dishes on the table, young Sébastien asked: "Will things be better now, Papa?"

His father hushed him, waited for his wife and daughters to be seated, then led the family in prayers before the meal. "Heavenly Father, we thank you for this food that we have before us, for the health you have given us, and for the children and grandchildren that you have bestowed upon us. Bless this meal which we are about to share—And grant us peace."

Then Bastien answered his son's question. "I honestly don't know, *mon gars*. We can only hope and pray that our new governor has the strength and wisdom to help us out of our troubles."

He turned to Antoine and congratulated him. "You've been granted a good piece of land. Have you made any plans for it yet?"

"Not yet. I sense the rumblings of another campaign, Bastien. We're comfortable where we are now; our crops grow well on the south shore. I might clear some of the forest on the new lot, but I'll put off the rest of the work until things quiet down at Québec."

The children continued their chatter while the adults reacted to Antoine's reply.

Bastien glanced toward Marguerite. They had enjoyed many good years together, but he remembered her dread of Mohawk attacks during her first years in Nouvelle France. He saw the resurgence of that old fear in her eyes. She was still the beautiful woman he had married, but he knew that she had lost much of her energy during the last few years. When had it begun? Was it after the birth of their sixth child? Or when they both feared that their oldest son Louis would be called to war against the Senecas? Perhaps it had started with the marriage of their two daughters.

He heard Madeleine ask her husband: "Does that mean that you might have to leave us again?"

Aubin replied: "If we do have to leave with the militia, at least Antoine and I are more experienced now. It certainly couldn't be as bad as the last campaign."

Antoine nodded. "Governor Denonville was a colonel in the king's dragoons; he must be an experienced military leader."

This was true, of course, thought Bastien, but leadership also required strength of character. He knew nothing about this man Denonville.

Marguerite looked around her, concerned that everyone should have a fair share of the food she had prepared. She saw her family's obvious enjoyment, and relaxed, but Bastien seemed to be deep in thought, as he tended to be whenever he grew concerned about his family. Their eyes met and she smiled at him.

He warmly matched that smile. Her mood had changed; perhaps he had been wrong to worry about her.

Antoine reached into his pocket and took out what looked like several playing cards. "Have you all seen our new colonial currency?" he asked.

DENONVILLE

Eighteen

Autumn 1685

Governor-General Denonville shrewdly recognized that the fur trade was the lifeblood of the colony, but that in its pursuit of that trade, Nouvelle France had vastly overextended its territorial claims beyond its capacity to defend itself. Although the new English king had counseled his Irish colonial governor not to offend the French authorities of Canada, Governor Dongan of New York continued to arm the Iroquois through their fur trade and encourage Dutch and English traders to poach furs in territories claimed by Nouvelle France.

Denonville also understood that his immediate problem was to prevent the loss of their western allies to the increasing Iroquois aggression and the seduction of less expensive English trade goods. He knew that the native societies around the Great Lakes area had been steadily corrupted by an increasing number of outlawed coureurs de bois, and had grown disaffected and contemptuous toward the French since La Barre's failed campaign. Despite the constant threat of Iroquois attack on the two outermost and most vulnerable western tribes, the traditional dislike between the Miami and Illinois was so strong that Henri de Tonti constantly struggled to maintain their joint aggressive focus toward their common enemy rather than against each other.

The French governor lacked the military resources to launch a campaign against the Iroquois or the English, but he knew that Nouvelle France must somehow regain the trust and respect of its western allies.

That autumn, the governor assigned Olivier Morel de La Durantaye to replace Nicolas Perrot as commandant at Michillimackinac and over all Frenchmen located in the Great Lakes area, thereby placing the western territory under the leadership of a veteran Carignan officer and garrison. While begging for reinforcements from France and hoping for their arrival early the following summer, Denonville considered several other alternatives.

He dispatched Intendant De Meulles to assess the condition of the Acadian settlements, which had been long neglected by France and by his predecessors. In October, the intendant traveled aboard a fishing bark to tour the French colony which collected and processed the second largest French export from North America—North Atlantic cod to satisfy the demands of the Catholic European market.

On October 22, 1685, King Louis XIV revoked the Edict of Nantes which had legally protected the rights of French Protestants since 1598. Although the political privileges granted by Henri IV had ended in 1629, the present French king and his father, Louis XIII, had gradually eroded the edict's remaining protections, until this new decree eliminated them altogether.

Louis XIV's proclamation quickly led to the social and political persecution of the Huguenots, and initiated the flight of close to a million French bourgeois, a highly skilled, productive, and wealthy segment of the French population. If they had been allowed to emigrate to western Canada, they could have strengthened the colony and energized its economy; instead, they fled to England and its colonies. Enforcement of the king's revocation also increased British and German hostility toward the French monarch and Catholics in general, including newly crowned King James II of England, who had long been influenced and financially supported by Louis XIV.

Meanwhile in North America, some Huron chiefs betrayed their allies, allowing the Iroquois to capture several Hurons and Ottawas to hold hostage against their nations' traditional alliances with the French. Denonville strongly suspected that the governor of New York had encouraged this.

Dongan had already concluded that France planned to control the center of the North American continent, thereby blocking English expansion toward the west. Yet he stood alone against Louis XIV's apparent strategy, without the support of his own settlers, other English colonies, or King James II who had appointed him.

1686

At the end of January, Denonville focused his attention on the French renegade coureurs who now served as middlemen between Albany and the Great Lakes natives. He ordered Du Luth, and the lieutenant-governors of Nouvelle France to chase down the culprits, confiscate their trade goods and furs, and shoot them if they resisted.

Conscious of La Barre's blunder of having alerted the English and the Iroquois to his invasion plans, the Québec governor planned his own strategy against the Senecas with such great secrecy that the general population of Nouvelle France and the Jesuit missionaries who lived among the Five Nations remained totally unaware of his upcoming campaign.

A month later, Bastien's and Jacques Vaudry's families walked home together following Sunday Mass. The air was cold and brisk in spite of the bright sunshine; the snow crunched under their feet as they made their way east along the shore road. The younger children ran ahead of the others and played tag with each other, while the adolescents exchanged nonsensical jokes. Marguerite and her longtime friend, Jeanne, caught up with each other's news, while their husbands followed close behind.

"Bastien, *mon vieux*, do you remember the first few years that we walked home together after Mass?"

"That was such a long time ago," Bastien replied. "There weren't as many houses then. We'd walk through the woods for a good part of the way before we reached home, and we kept our muskets primed and loaded."

"We cleared a lot of giant trees during those first few winters."

"And we hewed a lot of lumber."

"And chopped a lot of firewood."

They both laughed over it. "It still takes a lot of firewood to get through the winter," Bastien quipped.

"Then we had twenty years of peace." Jacques continued.

"Our children don't know what it was like to fight the Iroquois."

"Let's hope and pray that they never will."

"Do you still make your own pottery?" Marguerite asked her longtime friend.

"I've only done three pieces, but I still use them every day," Jeanne replied.

"Blue Bird was a good teacher—so was Red Dawn. Bastien still tans his own leather, you know, and he's taught our sons to do so."

"The natives helped us in so many ways."

Marguerite's tension resurfaced. "I've always wondered why the Iroquois hate us so."

"My parents once told me that it began when the early French traders exchanged metal tools for furs with the Hurons and the Algonquins. They quickly became our allies, but they also turned out to be the traditional enemies of the Iroquois."

"Didn't we also trade with the Iroquois?"

"They also wished to trade furs for our metal tools, but they soon insisted on trading furs for firearms. The French authorities refused."

They walked in silence for a while, laughing at their children who ran ahead of them and playfully threw soft-packed snowballs at each other. Then Jeanne added: "My father also explained that when our first explorers sailed up the Saint Lawrence River, they found large Mohawk communities at Québec and Montréal. Those summer settlements were gone by the time Samuel de Champlain arrived, yet the land remained clear and fertile. The natives spoke of a mysterious disease that had killed large numbers of the Iroquois people, and they related it to the arrival of the first European explorers."

When they reached Bastien's house, he and Marguerite invited their friends to come in out of the cold and share dinner with them. While the younger children warmed themselves by the fire and the older children played cards, Jeanne and Marguerite added more vegetables to the simmering stew, and the adults continued their conversation.

"We've seen a lot of changes since we first built our homes together," Bastien reminded them.

"But you always stayed here, on your original concession," Jacques added.

"I decided long ago to spend the rest of my life here, Jacques. I could never have moved as often as you and Jeanne have. I was ready to settle down permanently when I first arrived in Canada."

"We'll be moving again soon," Jeanne announced.

"Where to?" Marguerite asked.

"Upriver to Louiseville, at Rivière-du-Loup."

"It's a beautiful area on the north shore of Lac Saint-Pierre, just beyond Trois-Rivières," Jacques explained. "We can live there while I work the land and care for the animals at *Sieur* Lechasseur's *seigneurie*."

"Do you plan to sell your present concession?" Bastien asked.

"We've given that a lot of thought. Jeanne and I would like to keep it as an investment and lease it out. In that case, we need someone we can trust to maintain the property for us."

"Do you have someone in mind?"

"Would you be interested in signing a lifetime lease contract with us?"

Marguerite and Bastien were both taken by surprise. Such a commitment would remain in effect during their own lifetime.

Bastien finally spoke up. "That's quite an obligation to take on at this time, Jacques. We're pleased that you'd trust us to do this for you, but I'm sure you'll understand that we can't give you an immediate answer."

"I know, Bastien. We plan to move in about two weeks. Think it over, and tell us your decision before then. You know, you've been like a brother to me."

"And you've been like a sister to me, Marguerite," Jeanne added.

On March 10, 1686, the Vaudrys signed a lifetime lease contract, granting Bastien long-term use of their second concession located three lots away from his own, in exchange for a yearly rent payable in wheat.

Two weeks later, Chevalier de Troyes of Montréal led an

expedition overland to Hudson Bay, with orders to build forts and seize renegade coureurs and others who harassed the licensed French traders who operated in that area. Troyes left Montréal at the end of March, and headed up the Ottawa River to James Bay with thirty French soldiers, seventy Canadians, Jesuit chaplain Father Silvy, several experienced guides, and three adventurous sons of Charles Le Moyne: Iberville, Sainte-Hélène and Maricourt.

Monsignor Saint-Vallier, who had recently assumed administrative responsibility for the Catholic Church in French North America, left for Acadia. Accompanied by two other priests and a small escort, he traveled overland by rivers and lakes before the spring thaw.

That spring, Nicolas Perrot received the news that La Durantaye would relieve him of his command at Michillimackinac, and that he would then be reassigned to Green Bay in order to recruit a force of allied warriors and Frenchmen to join Denonville's campaign against the Senecas. The governor also planned to restore or build, and man military forts at Niagara, Toronto on Lake Erie, and Detroit at the outlet of Lake Huron, on the west side of the strait.

In early June, Denonville ordered Du Luth, then located at Michillimackinac, to fortify and occupy with fifty coureurs the French trading fort at Detroit, thereby militarizing the trading post and strengthening its defense.

La Durantaye reached Michillimackinac at the end of June. Nicolas Perrot left soon after for Green Bay to construct Fort Saint-Antoine on Lac Pépin, and to initiate trade with the Sioux and other local tribes.

Intendant De Meulles returned by bark from Acadia that September, accompanied by Monsignor Saint-Vallier and his party. Two weeks later, De Meulles presided over a meeting of the Sovereign Council during which it accepted the appointment of Jean Bochart-Noray, chevalier de Champigny, Noroy & Werneuil, King's Counselor, as colonial Intendant of Justice, Police, and Finance at Québec.

The following October, Chevalier de Troyes returned victorious from Hudson Bay, with fifty thousand prime beaver pelts and

75,000 pounds sterling, having left Pierre Le Moyne d'Iberville and part of his original force in command of three captured English forts. All British captives had been permitted to sail back to England, including Governor Bridgar, who had previously lost Hudson Bay to Radisson and Des Groseilliers four years earlier.

The populations of the Trois-Rivières area communities displayed a mixed reaction to the news. Bastien and his friends knew only too well how quickly such daring accomplishments could be negated by Versailles and its Québec representatives.

That autumn, Denonville sent word to Tonti who commanded the Illinois, and La Durantaye at Michillimackinac, to muster as many coureurs and allies as they could to join his forces the following July at Niagara.

Early in November, Jesuit Father Lamberville, who had ministered among the Onondaga Iroquois for over eighteen years, sent a letter to Chevalier de Callières, governor at Montréal. His message stated that Governor Dongan of New York had assembled the leaders of the Five Nations at his place of residence at *Manatte*, and forbade them to go to Fort Frontenac to trade with the French. He ordered them to deliver to him all of their Huron and Ottawa prisoners so that he might gain the allegiance of those tribes. Dongan further ordered that the Iroquois escort thirty Englishmen and their renegade Canadian guides whom he would send to seize Michillimackinac, the Great Lakes, rivers and adjoining land. He announced that he would recall the Mohawk Christians, longtime residents at Sault Saint-Louis near the island of Montréal, promising them other land and an English Jesuit to govern them. Furthermore, the New York governor called upon the Iroquois nations to expel all French Jesuits who lived among them, and declared that none other than his missionaries must be accepted among them. He promised to protect them against any attack by Denonville, and ordered that the Iroquois plunder all Frenchmen who visited them; that they bind and bring them to him.

Two weeks later, following the English uproar over the loss of three Hudson Bay Company stations, the English and French monarchs signed a neutrality pact in an attempt to settle their North American colonial problems. Louis XIV had already sent troops, money, and munitions to attack the Iroquois towns.

Governor Dongan continued to arm the well-disciplined warriors, whom he claimed to have accepted English protection as loyal subjects of the King. The Five Nations now had the strongest organized military force on the continent.

In mid-December 1686, Jacques Vaudry signed a three-year lease of the seignorial land and livestock belonging to *Sieur* Lechasseur at Louiseville. The contract stipulated that Jacques and Jeanne must pay yearly, half of their grain harvest and twelve pounds of butter for each cow provided by their contract.

1687

On January 10th, Lieutenant-General at Trois-Rivières Jean Lechasseur presided over a court case in which Jacques Massé accused Guillaume Barette or his son of shooting and killing his dog, and then dropping his musket alongside the road. Guillaume Barette protested the charges and demanded to have his gun back. His musket was returned, but he was forbidden to leave it near his neighbors' homes.

A month later, Antoine Cottenoire sold 50-livres worth of beaver fur to Jean Lemoine, allowing him to make the first of three yearly cash payments to Pierre Guillet for his concession at Bécancour.

During these first months of 1687, militia captains supervised the production of a large supply of hewed boards ordered by Governor Denonville for use by his military.

The Québec governor wrote to Jesuit Father Lamberville, directing him to urge the Iroquois chiefs at Onondaga to meet with him at council at Fort Frontenac. The missionary trusted the governor, but many of his converts did not; renegade coureurs had already carried rumors of an impending French military campaign, first to Albany, then to the Iroquois villages. The Five Nations called a war council, at which Governor Dongan convinced the chiefs to submit to his leadership. He subsequently increased their supply of arms and ammunition and ordered them to recall their powerful war parties from the Illinois country.

Correspondence between the two governors had already turned from French to English, from diplomatic to sarcastic and accusatory.

That April, Denonville officially mustered the colonial militia to "accompany him to Cataracoui for a peace council." The militiamen grumbled, having suffered greatly as a result of La Barre's failures.

Denonville issued a proclamation; Saint-Vallier declared a pastoral mandate. Priests throughout the parishes and missions exhorted the settlers and native converts to answer and support the new governor's call.

The Church mandate and civil proclamation, repeatedly announced during and after Sunday Mass, became the main topics of conversation at family dinner tables throughout the colony.

"Another 'peace council' at Cataracoui..." Bastien began.

Aubin categorized it as "nothing new".

"It would explain why we had to provide so much hewed lumber this past winter," Antoine suggested.

Louis listened quietly, and finally said: "The governor's need for so many canoes and eight hundred militiamen will surely draw most farmers away from their fields again."

Marguerite and her daughters looked up from their food preparation.

"We'll have to get as much work done as we can before you leave," Bastien continued. The men strongly suspected that such a large force must necessarily mean a military campaign rather than peace negotiations. Bastien fully expected that he would be allowed to stay home this time to tend the fields.

Young Sébastien asked: "Won't the seed rot in the ground if we sow too early?"

"That depends on the weather," his father replied. "If we can get the fields plowed and harrowed before you leave, I'm sure that François and I can accomplish the rest."

"But you have this farm, Vaudry's lease, and the concession across the river," Marguerite protested.

"François and I can do it," he said firmly.

Aubin spoke up. "I'll sign another procuration for Madeleine, but I worry about how she can manage the farm."

Madeleine spoke to her father: "I know it's a lot to ask of you, but if you could sow enough grain on our land to meet our basic needs until Aubin gets back, I'd be happy to lease our farm to you for the next two years."

Bastien's eyes softened, as did Marguerite's. "We'll see what we can do," he replied, then turned to Aubin. "You'd still have to get that field plowed and harrowed before you leave."

Aubin nodded.

Marie exchanged brief eye contact with Antoine. They both sympathized with Madeleine, but Marie knew that their engagé could manage the farm, as he always did during Antoine's trading voyages, and that her husband routinely signed a procuration granting her power of attorney during his many absences.

Marguerite asked her two daughters if they would consider staying in the bunkhouse for the duration of the campaign. They both declined.

Bastien addressed his two older sons: "Louis, you've journeyed before, so you must stay close to Sébastien and help him on his first expedition. You'll use our canoe, so you'll be its leader, but you'll need a third person to join your crew. Do you have someone in mind?"

"François Vaudry is older than I am, but I think he'd join us. I'll ask him later today."

Everyone approved of his choice.

Antoine offered Bastien the use of his wooden bateau to navigate across the river between farms. Then he invited Aubin to travel with him in his canoe.

"It will be like old times, *mon ami*. Let's hope that this has a happier ending than La Barre's expedition."

"I thought we might invite Jacques Lefebvre to join us. This would be his first campaign, and he seems like a reliable young man," Antoine continued.

"Good choice. I'm sure that Louis will be relieved to have his son travel with us."

Within the next few days, the family learned that Michel Arsonneau would share a canoe with brothers Jean and Nicolas Leblanc, and the three Barette brothers, Laurent, Jacques, and Jean, would travel together in Guillaume's canoe. Nicolas Rivard the younger, Jean Joliet, and an Abenaki guide from the Bécancour mission would lead the cape contingent.

On the first of May, Madeleine and her husband, Aubin, leased to Bastien for two years, their land at Bécancour for a yearly payment of one *minot* of grain per arpent sowed.

The women at the cape had heard of Marguerite's pemmican; now they sought her guidance in its production. By the time the men had accomplished the spring sowing, their wives had prepared their extra food provisions, and the herbal medicines that Bastien had also recommended.

Nineteen

Late spring 1687

Even as he left Québec on May 22nd, Denonville continued to maintain that he would conduct peace negotiations with the Senecas at Fort Frontenac. He arrived three days later at Trois-Rivières, where the local militias stood ready for departure.

The combined force left the following morning. While fathers gave their blessings, and mothers bade farewell to their young sons, it became apparent that the militia was now primarily manned by recruits from the first Canadian-born generation.

Four days later at Montréal, these troops from Québec and Trois-Rivières merged into a military force of eight hundred regulars, eight hundred militiamen, one hundred Canadian voyageurs, one hundred Canadian advance guard, and three hundred allied Iroquois, Algonquin, Abenaki, and Huron warriors. Four hundred canoes and bateaux stood ready to transport these men and their provisions to Cataracoui and beyond. The army's campsite extended along the riverfront from the fortified settlement of Montréal all the way to Lachine.

Sébastien and François Vaudry had already gained respect for Louis' camping and canoeing skills.

"You actually enjoy this, don't you, Louis?" François observed.

Sébastien smiled as he helped them set up for the night. "We know he does! Louis loves the forest. But give me a roof over my head any time! I haven't had a good night's sleep since we left home—Have you?"

François replied: "I've been too busy scratching my mosquito bites to fall asleep! How do you manage it, Louis?"

"I guess I'm just more mean than they are—Would you two like to walk through Montréal and look for an auberge where we can order a cup of wine or a beer? That might help to keep the mosquitoes away," he added with mischief in his eyes.

After a spartan meal, they joined their neighbors on a tour of the greatly overcrowded community and became more enthusiastic about taking part in such a large military expedition.

Meanwhile at Québec, eight hundred soldiers arrived from France under the command of Philippe de Rigaud Chevalier de Vaudreuil. Although it was too late to outfit and move those troops upriver, Vaudreuil and some of his officers caught up with Denonville at Montréal.

The military commandant at Québec billeted these newly-arrrived regulars throughout the settlements to provide protection and assistance for the remaining farmers. Four of the highly disciplined soldiers moved into Bastien's bunkhouse with orders to help him with farming and hunting chores in exchange for their room and board.

On June 11th, separate troop contingents began to leave Montréal at intervals. They faced persistent rain and contrary winds, requiring additional portages past swollen rapids for the next forty leagues of the upper Saint Lawrence River. Two men drowned as they struggled to tow the heavily loaded bateaux against the current.

Denonville cautioned his troops to move quietly in order not to betray their presence to the enemy. The two hundred bateaux that carried their military supplies and equipment moved sluggishly against the current; the more experienced Canadians and native allies took over most of this burden. They pushed on under miserable conditions, working through long days of exhaustive labor, plagued by the ubiquitous black flies during the day, and mosquitoes at night as they attempted to sleep under their overturned canoes

A week into the expedition, they reached Pointe Beaudet, where they met a band of ten Iroquois, including four women and two young boys. In order to maintain the secrecy of their movement upriver, Denonville ordered their immediate capture, and their transfer to Montréal the following day. These were the first Iroquois that the young Canadians from the cape had ever seen. They appeared harmless to Louis; not at all what he expected.

Denonville caught up with Intendant Champigny at Cataracoui on the last day of June. This official had arrived some days before and had immediately complied with the governor's instructions to avoid alerting the enemy by any means at his disposal. The intendant now turned over to the governor fifty-one local Iroquois men and one hundred fifty women and children he had captured through deception. Since their arrest, these native men had stood outdoors in the central yard, bound to wooden posts by the neck and ankles, with arms tied behind their backs. Their wives had been allowed to feed them as best they could, while other natives freely harassed them.

Louis recognized some of these captives from his previous stay at Cataracoui with Nicolas Perrot. He knew them to be peaceful Mohawks who lived nearby on the northern shore of Lake Ontario and traded their fish and game at the fort. His anger flared at their obvious mistreatment.

Antoine quickly grabbed Louis by the arm and pulled him away from the scene.

"But they're not any danger to us!" Louis protested.

"That's not for you to decide. If you value your own neck, you'll keep quiet," Antoine emphatically warned him. "This is neither the time nor the place to fight this!"

"It's so unjust!" Louis fought back the tears.

Antoine pulled him deeper into the woods, grabbed him by both arms and looked him squarely in the eyes. "Be quiet! Get a hold of yourself or you'll endanger all of us!"

Louis finally managed to conceal his anger by avoiding the fort.

From then on, Aubin and Antoine kept close watch over their two brothers-in-law, making sure that they maintained their camp on high, dry ground, and kept out of trouble.

The following day, François Dauphin de La Forest reported that La Durantaye had captured sixty Englishmen who had been sent by Dongan to trade with the natives at Michillimackinac. He also delivered the welcome news that one hundred eighty coureurs and four hundred allied warriors awaited orders at Niagara. These additional troops had been recruited by Tonti at Fort Saint-Louis-des-Illinois, by Du Luth from among the Sioux near Detroit, by La Forest and La Durantaye from the Hurons and Algonquins around the upper lakes and Michillimackinac, and by Nicolas Perrot from the Mississippi and Lake Michigan areas. While Denonville and his officers celebrated the news, Louis looked forward to seeing Perrot and perhaps Grey Cloud again.

Denonville immediately sent instructions to La Durantaye to deliver the English prisoners to Fort Frontenac, and to lead his reinforcements to rendezvous with the main force at Irondequoit Bay no later than July 10th.

The governor waited four days for favorable weather before crossing Lake Ontario to reach its south shore.

This part of their journey proved uneventful, but as they drew closer to Seneca country, Louis, Antoine, and Aubin became extra watchful and wary, for this was new and unknown territory for them.

The French forces encountered rough weather during the next six days while the long line of canoes and bateaux moved westward along the south shore to Irondequoit Bay.

From a distance, the French finally sighted the fleet of canoes, filled with coureurs and western allies who had already traveled as much as 1000 miles from the western lakes area. They also saw a second large group arriving separately from north of Michillimackinac. These upper Algonquin tribes had at first refused to follow La Durantaye, but had changed their minds, and had journeyed through Lake Huron to join the allied force at Niagara.

On the designated date, all parties rendezvoused successfully at Irondequoit, only ten leagues from the Seneca villages. Although the French had expected Iroquois resistance, they encountered none, yet Louis and Antoine remained vigilant.

This was the largest army ever assembled in North America up until that time; the logistics had seemed impossible to achieve.

It now consisted of three thousand men, and was led by Governor-General Denonville of Québec, Lieutenant-Governor Louis Hector de Callières-Bonnevue of Montréal, and Philippe de Rigaud Chevalier de Vaudreuil, commander of the French regiment that had recently arrived from France.

From the edge of the woods, three young Seneca scouts called out and asked their intentions. The Christian Mohawks hollered back: "To fight you!" and fired at them.

The scouts retreated to warn their people. Their ablest warriors were away, which weakened their defensive capability. The village elders reacted to this ominous threat by sending off their women and children, burning their major village, and organizing their remaining troops for the pending attack.

Meanwhile, the French forces quickly cleared the land, prepared two thousand wooden posts, and dug trenches for the construction of a strong palisade to enclose and protect the boats and canoes that ensured the army's only line of retreat.

Louis, Sébastien, François, Aubin, and Antoine were already experienced at hewing and shaping logs, as were many of the others. This spared them from having to dig the trench through the tree-root ridden soil.

While the French forces worked with primed muskets always at arm's reach, another small group of Senecas appeared on a nearby hill and shouted to them that they were wasting their time in building palisades. They taunted the French as they worked: "Come fight us, you won't need a fort. Come to your death; we're hungry for white flesh."

Sébastien shuddered and grew pale. The French commanders urged their soldiers and militiamen to continue their work.

The Senecas fired two shots which landed at the tail end of the row of bateaux and caused no damage. They invited the invaders to advance their troops, told them that their people looked forward to fighting the French. They yelled loudly, discharged their guns from beyond range, then fled.

During this time at Irondequoit, a war council declared their Canadian prisoner Marion Lafontaine guilty of having guided the English toward Michillimackinac, and sentenced him to be executed at dawn by a military firing squad.

Sébastien was appalled by this. "How can anyone spend his

life in the army, killing people?" he asked Antoine.

"There are times when a man's actions can either save or endanger his country. Let's hope and pray that those who called for this execution were justified in doing so."

While they labored side by side with the coureurs to construct the fort, the militiamen learned about the reputation of the Senecas. This westernmost Iroquois nation was the largest and the most belligerent of the five; their warriors were more fierce than those of the Mohawks; more Frenchmen and their native allies had been burnt to death in their main village than in any other Iroquois village. The coureurs described scenes of strange orgies, cannibalism, and witchcraft. They strongly believed that the defeat of the Senecas would bring peace with the other four nations. And they soberly warned the young men from the cape: "Be extra watchful from now on; you don't want to be captured by them."

Antoine and Louis were determined that their group should stay close together at all times, weapons at the ready, and not stray away from the main force.

At noon of July 12th, Denonville assigned four hundred men under officer François Chorel *Sieur* de Saint-Romain dit d'Orvilliers to remain on-site to complete the fort and protect the boats.

The officers rationed out ten biscuits for each man to carry in his own backpack, and Denonville's army began its overland march toward the Seneca villages which were located south of Irondequoit Bay. Christian Mohawks led them down a wide, blazed trail toward the largest Seneca town. They covered three leagues through open forests of oak before they set up camp for the night.

The French moved out quickly at first light the following day. Soldiers who wore body armor especially suffered from the sweltering morning heat. They marched through waist-high grass in a narrow marshy area that teemed with mosquitoes, passed through two narrow gorges, then faced another which was located a quarter-league away from the Seneca villages.

They entered that final narrow passage at mid-afternoon. Dense forests covered the hills on either side. La Durantaye, Tonti and

Du Luth led the column, each with his own band of coureurs. The Iroquois converts from Sault Saint-Louis and Montréal stalked along their left. To their right, Nicolas Perrot and two other French voyageurs led their western allies. This entire vanguard of over eight hundred men was under the command of Governor Callières of Montréal.

Governor Denonville led the main body, which consisted of four battalions of regulars alternating with battalions of Canadians. The cape militiamen marched as a group with the third of four Canadian contingents. Some soldiers wore light armor, while the habitants and voyageurs wore plain coarse linen or buckskin. Denonville marched in his shirt sleeves, accompanied by Chevalier de Vaudreuil, and several Canadian *seigneurs*. Everyone constantly suffered from the voracious mosquitoes.

The rear guard consisted of specially skilled Montréal rangers and native allies.

Advance scouts ran back to report to Governor Callières that they had reached the Seneca clearings and had seen women working in the cornfields—a sign of normal activity in an inhabited village.

Callières led the French vanguard, charging forward toward the clearing. They passed a ridge of thick forest to their right, which was covered with a heavy growth of beech trees. Separated from their main body, Callières and his men reached the end of the gorge.

From dense woods on the left and at the front, and a great marsh to their right, covered with alder thickets and grass, there rose shrill war whoops and heavy, rapid weapons fire. Great numbers of naked, painted, screeching warriors armed with knives, bludgeons, and hatchets sprang from the undergrowth on all sides and rushed against the forward French contingent. The sounds of attack echoed loudly against the walls of the gorge, causing instant confusion among the French.

Callières quickly ordered his men forward to charge into the enemy. His troops instantly followed his lead.

A simultaneous burst of yells and musket shots occurred at the rear of the vanguard, where another several hundred Senecas suddenly emerged from that heavy growth of beech trees on the right ridge of the gorge. Sword in hand, Governor Denonville ordered his drummers to beat the charge as he ran toward the sounds of ambush, throwing forward his front battalions with the full support of his officers and directing a heavy volley of fire at the enemy. The Christian Iroquois, led by the "Great Mohawk" Ryn, ran from tree to tree and exchanged shots with their non-Christian brothers.

Confronted by what now appeared to be an endless military force, the Iroquois warriors fled after heavy loss, carrying away many of their dead and all of their wounded.

This section of the forest was so dense that the advancing battalions could see neither the enemy nor each other. Judging by the numbers of the vanguard, the Senecas had taken it to be the entire army and had attacked with all of their warriors. Then Denonville had joined into the battle with another sixteen hundred men.

Both sides had been taken by surprise, but the French had the larger and more disciplined force, and so they succeeded in routing the Iroquois.

Denonville did not pursue the enemy into the dense, unfamiliar forest, since his troops were exhausted from the forced march over rough terrain, in very hot weather. He also did not want to be ambushed while out of military formation. Their native allies spoke so many different languages that they might have mistakenly fired upon each other.

Five militiamen, one soldier, and five allies had died during the ambush. The French army encamped on the spot, cared for its twenty wounded, then evacuated them to the fort at Irondequoit from where they could be moved to Cataracoui. A few days later, they would learn from a slave who had escaped from the Senecas, that fifty Iroquois had been killed, sixty mortally wounded, others less seriously; the young Seneca forces had been thrown into confusion.

The western allies butchered and feasted on twenty-five of their dead enemies that night. Louis and Sébastien stumbled into the area, and were physically sickened by the sight. Was this the way all natives dealt with the bodies of their enemies?

Heavy rain fell the following day. Denonville moved out of the woods at noon, and marched his troops in formation to the first village, a half-league away. They moved through a marsh covered with alders and tall grass, and soon emerged to view the empty "Babylon of the Senecas", the site of torture and burning of their many captive victims. Its burnt huts were of bark and sat at the top of a hill. The Senecas had torched their major town of Gannagaro, but the fire had spared several huge bark containers that contained corn from the previous season. Large fields surrounded the site and were covered with bountiful crops of maize and yellow pumpkin vines which were ripening in the July sun. A great number of hogs ran free in the clearings.

During the following nine days, Denonville exhorted his men to destroy whatever food their enemy had left behind. The soldiers killed the hogs, burned the stored corn, and hacked down the ripening maize and pumpkin vines with their swords. Then they advanced to an abandoned Seneca fort on a hill a half-league away; its heavily constructed palisades fortified a highly strategic position where the Seneca warriors had obviously intended to defend themselves. The French set fire to the food storage and the fort.

Four leagues farther on, they discovered three more villages which their native allies had plundered of whatever had been left behind. Again, they leveled these structures and laid all their fields to waste. The amount of corn destroyed was estimated at 400 thousand *minots*.

Burdened with whatever possessions they could carry, the Senecas had fled eastward to seek sanctuary among their confederates. Denonville did not pursue them. His men were sick from their feasting on green corn and fresh pork; his allies were deserting him.

The governor and his advisors were convinced that the Senecas would be unable to replenish their food supply for another fourteen months, and that they would be forced to move into the woods to live off wild game and fish in order to survive.

On July 24th, the French withdrew all their forces to Irondequoit Bay. Six days later, they moved westward to Niagara where they rebuilt La Salle's fort which had fallen into disrepair. Denonville ordered that the new structure be built on a point of land where the waters of Lake Erie were discharged by the

Niagara River into Lake Ontario. This site was estimated to be eighty leagues from Cataracoui, over one hundred forty from Montréal, and thirty from the Seneca villages.

Denonville left Chevalier de Troyes and one hundred soldiers to guard this junction between the two great lakes. Then he embarked with the rest of his army and militia to recross Lake Ontario, and travel down the upper Saint Lawrence River on their way back to Montréal.

Twenty

Mid-July 1687

When Denonville's troops undertook the destruction of standing food crops, the western allied warriors left the deserted Seneca homeland, and Nicolas Perrot headed back to Green Bay with them.

Unlike many of their western cousins and the Senecas of that time, the Abenaki and eastern Algonquin converts did not practice cannibalism, nor did they take pleasure in destroying ripening corn, so they had left even earlier than the Ottawas. Shortly after these allied warriors returned to the missions at Sillery and Bécancour, smallpox and measles epidemics flared up among the native populations of those areas. One hundred and thirty converts died at Sillery, and scores of native residents at Bécancour developed an epidemic fever that eventually spread to the French population.

When the Miamis arrived at their villages near Chicago, they discovered that the Senecas had destroyed their homes and taken away their women and children. The Miamis immediately left in pursuit of their enemy, and followed a grim trail of half-eaten children until they caught up to and killed most of the raiders.

During his return trip to Montréal, Chevalier de Vaudreuil encountered enemy Iroquois about six leagues from Cataracoui; he and his men survived an ambush along the north shore of Lake Ontario and lost nine of their own.

Nicolas Perrot returned to Montréal before mid-August 1687, having failed to reclaim the furs that he had been forced to leave behind at the mission of Saint-François-Xavier at De Per (Wisconsin). Upon his arrival at the mission, he had learned that his 40,000-livres worth of prime beaver pelts had been lost in a fire that had consumed all buildings at that site. This was his third major loss.

When Louis and Sébastien returned home in mid-August, they learned that nine-year old Jacques Massé had died that day of the fever, and that his mother had prematurely given birth to another son. Bastien and Marguerite were not at home to greet their own sons, having gone to the Massé home to offer aid and comfort to their friends.

Jacques and Catherine were relieved to see the couple. He obviously anguished over what had happened that day. His oldest son was gone; the baby was fragile; Catherine was overwhelmed and depressed. The girls did the best they could, but they too were obviously shaken emotionally.

Bastien invited Jacques to walk through the fields with him and listened while his grieving friend vented his anger and challenged the justice of his young son's death.

Upon her arrival, Marguerite had immediately picked up the infant and checked him thoroughly. Although underweight, the boy appeared normal and healthy.

Catherine seemed unusually listless.

"Are you all right?" Marguerite asked. "Can I do anything for you?"

"The girls have taken care of me, but I can't stop weeping."

"That's to be expected, considering what you've been through."

"Will the baby be all right?"

"You'll have to keep him warm, and nurse him more often since he can only eat a little at a time. But he'll be fine."

Marguerite lay the boy on his mother's chest, and looked toward young Jacques' shrouded body which lay on the table. "Should I prepare him for burial?" she asked gently.

Catherine barely shook her head. "Jacques took care of that— He seemed very angry—as though he might be blaming me..."

"Oh no! Of course not, Catherine! You mustn't think that. Men show their pain differently than we do, that's all." She quickly changed the subject: "If you'll tell me where the cradle and baby clothes are, I'll set those up for you."

The older daughter Simonne immediately climbed to the loft and brought down the wooden cradle, while her sister Anne opened the nearby wooden chest to take out the cradle linen.

Baby Jean-Baptiste had fallen asleep after a short feeding. Marguerite gently bathed, dried, and swaddled him before returning him to nestle against the warmth of his mother's body. Once she made up and set the cradle close by his mother's bed, Catherine breathed a sigh of relief and fell asleep.

Marguerite and the girls assessed the family's available food, fuel, and laundry needs. "I brought some fresh bread," she told them. "Bastien has some fresh meat and wine for you. A cup of wine might help all of you."

They quietly prepared a pot of soup for Catherine and stew for the family. They collected dirty clothes and linen, and set those to soak in a wooden tub filled with soapy water while they continued to straighten out the house.

Jacques had begun to relax, but remained deeply saddened and exhausted from the emotional events of the day. "I thought that by leaving France, I could escape the cycle of war, famine, and disease I'd known all my life," he confided. "This is a second pestilence, following another war campaign on behalf of the fur trade, in which most of us have never engaged. All within three years. We might have been better off had I stayed in France..."

"In that case, you'd never have met and married Catherine, and you wouldn't have the family you have now—Besides, nothing much seems to have changed in France, *mon vieux*," Bastien reminded him.

As Jacques continued to weigh the consequences of his decision, Bastien prayed for him and Catherine—for all of Nouvelle France—because from what he had heard, Denonville's mighty army had shaken, but not defeated the Senecas. He feared that the governor might have reunited the Five Nations against the French and their allies, and he dreaded what the future might hold in store for his family and his friends.

He in turn confided: "Jacques, I came to Nouvelle France after serving my family's military corvée when I was no older than my oldest sons. I had finally come home only to find that both of my parents had died from famine and sickness. Life in Canada held the hope for a brighter future—I've had no regrets. The trials have been great, but Marguerite and I both believe that the rewards have been greater. We've always put our trust in God."

Their conversation took a philosophical turn about life in general; Jacques' dark mood gradually abated.

Bastien finally offered: "I can build a pine box for him, if you wish."

Jacques winced. "That's something a father must do for his son, Bastien, but you can help if you like."

The following morning, Bastien, Michel Rochereau, and Catherine's father, Pierre Guillet loaded the casket onto Jacques' oxcart and escorted his son's body to funeral rites and burial at the church of Sainte-Madeleine.

Reports from the western forts revealed that Le Moyne d'Iberville's exploits at Hudson Bay, and the capture of English traders on the Great Lakes had restored some respect for the French, and had prevented the imminent defection of their western allies.

Although Governor Denonville and his advisors considered his campaign to have been a great success, his letters to Minister of Marine Seignelay expressed great concern for the safety of the outlying Canadian villages. "All persons agree that, in the present condition of the country, five hundred Iroquois with European support could devastate Canada in three-months time, regardless of all precautions taken or the forces that the French have to oppose them, because of the enemy's guerilla tactics, and his ability to live off the land." He added: "It is well-known that had we not marched against the Tsonnontouans (Senecas), and had not humiliated them, our Ottawa and Huron allies would have turned to them for trade and protection."

Late that August, Mohawks captured several colonists at Chambly. A week later, they attacked a farmhouse at the northern end of Montréal Island, but the French settlers managed to repel them with heavy musket fire from behind their palisades. The warriors moved on to burn several other houses, and barns full of wheat; they ravaged the outer frontier settlements with impunity. French fields could not be safely harvested, nor tilled.

That September, Denonville sent to France thirty-six of the Iroquois men whom he had ordered captured in the vicinity of Cataracoui "to maintain the secrecy of his troop movements". These were to serve as slaves in the king's Mediterranean galleys. Another fifteen Iroquois males and more than one hundred twenty women and children remained captive at Fort Frontenac.

New York Governor Dongan reacted with fury when he heard that the French had invaded the Seneca villages, seized his English traders on the lakes, and built a fort at Niagara. He summoned delegate chiefs from the Iroquois nations to Albany, blamed them for having held councils with the French without his permission, and forbade them to do so again. He declared that the Ottawas and other remote tribes were British subjects, that they should unite with the Iroquois to expel the French from the West, and that they should bring all their beaver skins to Albany. He counseled them not to receive any French Jesuits into their towns, and told them that they should recall home all of their countrymen from the Canadian missions and from their campaign against the Illinois and Miamis.

The Iroquois chiefs agreed to submit to his leadership and vowed to fight the French to the death.

Governor Dongan wrote to Denonville, demanding the immediate release of the Dutch and English traders whom the French had captured on the lakes. Denonville refused on the grounds that the New York governor had broken their kings' treaty of neutrality by arming the savages. Dongan accused the French governor of invading British territory with French troops, and claimed that he had not armed and united the Iroquois until August 6, 1687, following the French attack on the Senecas, and had done so in defense of English territory. He reiterated his demand that Denonville return all Christian and captive Iroquois, who were subjects of the English king and were improperly detained by the French. He ridiculed French claims to the western country on the basis of its missionary occupation: "Pardon me if I say it is a mistake, except you will affirm that a few loose fellows rambling amongst Indians to keep themselves from starving gives the French a right to the Country." And in regards to the French claim based on geographical divisions: "Your reason is that some rivers or rivulets of this country run out into the great river of Canada. Oh just God! What new, far-fetched, and unheard-of pretense is this for a title to a country?"

On November 11th, King James II finally authorized Governor Dongan to protect his Iroquois with force of arms if necessary.

Upon hearing rumors that the French planned to attack and destroy Albany, Dongan fortified New York's largest trading center, and assigned a garrison of infantry, light cavalry and Iroquois to defend it. His letters to the Earl of Sunderland, Chief Secretary of State in London, argued that he must build forts in the Great Lakes area, or lose the country, beaver trade, and the Iroquois alliance.

Twelve days later, word quickly spread through the parish community of Cap-de-la-Madeleine that Jacques Massé had died of epidemic fever at age forty-seven. His thirty-one-year old widow Catherine was left with seven children; her youngest, who had been born prematurely, was barely two months old.

Bastien and Marguerite both reacted with disbelief at the amount of grief and misfortune that had befallen this family in such a short period of time.

"So many young children left without a father!" Marguerite whispered. "We must do all we can for her, Bastien."

He agreed and immediately walked out into a frigid northwesterly wind to see what he could do.

When he arrived at the Massé home, Pierre Guillet had already prepared his son-in-law's body for burial. Catherine and the children wept quietly over the body, whispering prayers for the dead. Bastien joined them as they recited the rosary.

"Marguerite and I wish to extend our deepest sympathy, Catherine. She deeply regrets that she can't come to you at this time, but the weather is so cold, and she hasn't been well lately."

He turned to Pierre and asked what he could do for them.

"Perhaps you could help me prepare the pine box?"

While they worked together in the barn, using Jacques' tools in his well-furnished workshop, Bastien asked: "How will Catherine manage alone with so many young children?"

"I'm afraid it's going to be difficult for her, Bastien. She's already suffered a lot these past few months—Jacques never truly recovered from his son's death. And although Simonne and Anne are old enough to help her with the children and the housework, Louis is only eleven, not yet strong enough to be of any help in the fields and woods. Then there's Jean-Baptiste who is still quite frail. Her three other daughters are too young to help in any way."

Bastien considered this, then told him: "I have three sturdy sons, and as long as they aren't called to service with the militia, I'm sure they won't mind helping with the farmwork."

Pierre's eyes visibly moistened. "Although I live close by and will give her as much moral support as I can, I just can't work the fields anymore, and it's so difficult right now to find an engagé—You've put my mind at ease."

They had finished building the casket and were about to bring it into the house when Pierre placed his hand on Bastien's shoulder and said: "Thank you again. Now if you'll help me place Jacques' body into the funerary box, you will have made an old man's duty a lot lighter."

Bastien, Louis, and Sébastien promised Catherine that they would provide her with firewood and meat throughout the winter.

Shortly after the winter holidays, the family rallied around Marguerite who continued to weaken until she became bed-ridden. Her older sons hunted fresh meat daily; Madeleine, Marie and their children moved back to the family homestead so that they could be by their mother's bedside, to provide the soup and bake the bread that they hoped would strengthen her. All of the boys moved into the bunkhouse to allow more room for their older sisters and the grandchildren. Young Catherine watched over her nieces while her sisters Madeleine and Marie cared for their mother and did the housework.

Bastien treated Marguerite with herbal medicines, but she continued to lose strength.

One morning she finally seemed to rally and spoke softly to each of her children and grandchildren. She told them she greatly loved every one of them, and was so proud of them. While they surrounded her sickbed, she squeezed Bastien's hand and, with a wan smile, told him: "Look at what we've accomplished together." Then she fell asleep.

When she awoke, she asked to be alone with Bastien. Each child kissed her and retreated to the bunkhouse where Louis stirred up the fire to heat the space, and his siblings quietly entertained their nieces. Madeleine and Marie remained very quiet.

A sense of foreboding gripped Bastien. He took Marguerite's hand and whispered softly about how much he loved her. And he felt her grip grow weaker.

Her voice became barely audible. "Bastien, you've been a gentle, caring husband, a strong and loving father—You brought joy into my life, and gave me the family I so longed for when we first met..." She rested.

His eyes began to fill with tears. He held her hand firmly and told her: "I wish I could give you some of my own strength right now—You'll never know how grateful I was that you were willing to wait so many years, and had the courage to join me here in Nouvelle France. I've never known another woman like you, Marguerite—and I never will," he added forcefully.

Her eyes brightened. "You mustn't say that, or believe that, Sébastien—our children will need a mother—Don't mourn too long for me, we've had many good years together—Life will go on for you and the children—You'll need someone to help you..."

Her hand went limp within his; her eyes grew dull. He sobbed.

On Friday, January 27, 1688, upon hearing that fifty-one-year old Marguerite had died, Catherine Guillet traveled with neighbors Guillaume Barette and Michel Rochereau to offer what help they could to the widower and his family.

"She was younger than I," he told them. "She was such a strong woman, I always expected that she would outlive me."

That night, Louis and Sébastien the younger helped their father build another pine box, and watched as Bastien carefully and lovingly carved a periwinkle design into the cover.

Early the following morning, Bastien, Louis, and Sébastien transported Marguerite's casket by ox-sled, over the frozen Saint Lawrence River to the church of Sainte-Madeleine, where Guillaume Barette and Michel Rochereau served as witnesses to her funeral rites and temporary winter burial.

Twenty-one

Winter 1687-88

Nouvelle France's fur trade had literally come to a full stop since 1685, depriving the colony of its major export. Throughout the fall and winter that followed Denonville's campaign, Canada was besieged by famine, poverty, disease, and the Iroquois. Intendant Champigny resorted to drawing food rations from the king's warehouses at Québec, Trois-Rivières and Montréal to keep many from starving both in the cities and in the countryside.

The upper Canadian settlements suffered repeated assaults. Settlers above Trois-Rivières frequently found themselves confined in stockade forts that had been hastily built in every seigniory. Thus, the settlers could not effectively work their farms while Iroquois warriors roamed freely through the deserted settlements or about the forts, setting fire to homes, and barns filled with grain, killing or capturing any Frenchman they happened to come upon.

The epidemic fever took a heavy toll among the population.

In the depth of the Canadian winter, Catherine and her daughters found it impossible to venture beyond their own farm.

Although Bastien's house often filled with family and friends, it remained empty of its usual energy during the first few weeks following Marguerite's death. The fifty-four-year old widower, his three sons, and youngest daughter retreated within themselves, lost in their memories of Marguerite and the life they had shared together. Madeleine stayed with them for the first few days and taught her brothers the simplest methods of providing meals for the family: the preparation of stews, the baking of bread and beans.

By the end of the first week, Bastien assessed his family's situation, and realized that he and his children must learn to function on their own. He encouraged Madeleine to return to her own home and family and asked his sons to transport her across the frozen river. With their help and encouragement, he renewed his cooking and baking skills.

They all realized that Catherine and her children were in a more vulnerable position than they were, so the boys continued to provide firewood and meat for both families, traveling and working together for safety and companionship.

Although most of the Iroquois raids had been to the west of Trois-Rivières toward Montréal, Bastien recalled having been attacked in the woods by a young Mohawk thirty years earlier when he had been distracted and had wandered off from his friend Jacques Vaudry. He repeatedly reminded Louis and Sébastien to stay together, remain armed and alert to any unusual sounds or activity. Louis proved to be especially adept at this.

Catherine often rewarded them with baked goods, butter, and cheese. She also insisted that they bring her any of their clothing that needed mending or washing. Meanwhile, Louis and Sébastien gradually developed comfortable friendships with Catherine's daughters Simonne and Anne.

The boys set up to collect the maple sap at both farms. Catherine and the girls kept the liquid boiling through the nights, while Bastien and his sons took turns at home.

Three weeks later, when the sap stopped flowing and the sweet harvest was processed and stored, Bastien and his boys prepared their tools and equipment for plowing and sowing their fields and Catherine's.

The cape settlers had fared relatively well during these hard times, had turned to their pemmican when their stored foods ran low, and had worked together whenever they ventured into the woods.

Winter ice finally cleared from the Saint Lawrence River in

late spring 1688, and the first ship to arrive at Québec carried a letter from Louis XIV, written in early March of that year. The king informed Governor Denonville that Governor Dongan of New York would be recalled home by King James II. He authorized war against the Iroquois while offering no additional military resources from the home country, and he ordered Denonville to maintain peace with the English colonies. These new orders placed the Québec governor in an impossible position. The English would consider any attack against the Iroquois villages as an act of war, yet if he did not attack preemptively, the enemy warriors had the capacity to devastate the French colony.

Denonville's own recommendation to the king was that France either purchase the New York colony or seize it by land and sea. He quickly dispatched Lieutenant-Governor Callières of Montréal to propose to the king his own plan of attack against Albany and *Manatte*, New York's two largest settlements. One thousand regulars and six hundred Canadian militiamen, already in Nouvelle France, would travel the traditional invasion route by canoe and bateaux through lakes Champlain and Saint-Sacrement to cross the Hudson River, capture Albany, and use its shallops to seize *Manatte*. Simultaneously, two French ships of war would enter the New York harbor to join in the attack. Callières predicted that all of this could be accomplished by the end of October. He argued that such a strategy would deprive the Iroquois of arms and munitions, negate English claims to the western fur territory, and provide Nouvelle France with a year-round seaport.

The winter 1687-88 convinced Denonville that Fort Niagara was too isolated and could not be held. Hemmed in by repeated Iroquois attacks, the garrison had been unable to hunt, fish, or grow their own food, subjecting its soldiers to prolonged famine, scurvy, and disease. Friendly Miamis had arrived in early spring, to discover that the fort had become a house of death; of the twelve soldiers who had survived that winter, none had the strength to bury their dead. The Miamis had cared for the sick and had stayed to protect the remaining garrison until the rivers and lakes had cleared of ice, allowing the arrival of a military relief party from Montréal. Fort Frontenac had fared only slightly better.

Dongan and the Senecas continued to insist that Denonville

release the Iroquois he had captured at Fort Frontenac and surrender Fort Niagara.

The French governor received another letter from his king, who now faced a strong coalition of military powers in Europe. Louis XIV directed Denonville to negotiate an honorable peace with the Iroquois.

Governor Denonville sent a peace embassy of Seneca converts from Fort Frontenac to Onondaga with his promise to return those whom he had captured and sent to the king's galleys. The Five Nations saw this as a sign of French weakness and as an opportunity to act as independent agents, free of allegiance to either of the two European adversaries. Onondaga chief Garakontié defied English orders and agreed to meet with the French for peace talks.

Bastien and his sons were overjoyed to hear of such promising developments.

Since his return to Montréal in mid-August 1687, Nicolas Perrot had completed a series of contractual agreements in an attempt to consolidate his debts and trading status. He had bought out his former trade associates, hired several voyageurs, signed several promissory notes and a contract to purchase Jean Lechasseur's Louiseville seigneury.

On May 20, 1688, Perrot hired François Vaudry as voyageur, offering him 300 livres upon his safe return with a cargo of furs. He asked Vaudry if he knew of any other reliable men who might accompany him. When François recommended his childhood friend Louis, and offered to approach him, Perrot agreed that he would be a good choice.

François had last seen Bastien and his family at Marguerite's funeral Mass. Although he was warmly greeted by the family, their lingering grief still hung heavily over the household.

Bastien was the first to welcome him and ask about his family.

"We're all doing well, although we continue to be wary around Lac Saint-Pierre, as you can well expect."

"Is there anything we can do for you and your family?"

"There's a matter that I need to discuss with you and Louis."

"It sounds serious."

"It could be an unusual opportunity for him."

Bastien called his son over to join them. The two young men exchanged pleasantries, but François saw the subdued sadness in his friend's eyes.

"Would you consider joining me in a trading voyage out west on behalf of Nicolas Perrot?" he asked.

Louis' eyes brightened and his mouth widened into a smile. "When do you leave?"

Bastien knew that this route would take them northwestward by way of the Ottawa River and north of the Great Lakes to Michillimackinac, avoiding the Iroquois country which lay south of the lakes. He also appreciated the value of such an opportunity for his twenty-year old son. "On what terms?" he asked.

In early summer 1688, twelve hundred Iroquois warriors moved toward Fort Frontenac in support of their chiefs, whom they escorted as far as Lac Saint-François, upriver from Montréal. They would wait there for the safe return of the peace embassy.

In mid-June, Nicolas Perrot served as official interpreter during these negotiations. Onondaga chief Garakontié addressed Governor Denonville in confident terms. He claimed that he and his people were subjects of neither the French nor the English, but wished to be friends of both; that his people held their country of the Great Spirit, and had never been conquered in war. He declared that the Iroquois knew the weakness of the French and could have easily exterminated them; that the Five Nations had already formed a plan to burn all the houses and barns of Canada, to kill their cattle, to set fire to their ripe grain. Then, while the French people starved, they would have attacked the forts. The chief took credit for having held back the power of the Iroquois confederacy. He made it clear that he had no more than four days to bring back the results of their parley, and that if he were late, he had no control over what might happen.

The Iroquois delegation appeared ready to make peace only with the French, and promised neutrality on the part of the Onondagas, the Cayugas, and the Oneidas. But the chiefs did not promise to discontinue their attacks on the natives allied to the French. During these talks at Montréal, Denonville received reports that Iroquois warriors at Lac Saint-François had recently killed several native converts, but he did not protest.

Both parties agreed upon a declaration of neutrality which Garakontié and the chiefs in attendance signed with drawings of their representative birds and animals. He promised that other deputies from the confederacy would come later to Montréal and conclude the agreement.

Soon after, Huron chief Kondiaronk, whose people had been allied with the French since Samuel de Champlain's time, arrived at Fort Frontenac and heard of Denonville's acceptance of the Iroquois terms. He knew what had happened to the Illinois after La Barre had turned his back on their defense alliance.

Six days later at La Famine, Kondiaronk and other Hurons from Michillimackinac ambushed the second delegation of Iroquois chiefs while it was on its way to finalize the agreement. Kondiaronk fooled the survivors into believing that his warriors were following orders from Denonville. He claimed that the French governor had misled them into attacking the Iroquois, and that this ambush represented a French betrayal of the peace process. The Hurons patched up the wounded and sent them back to Onondaga to carry this message to Garakontié.

In this attempt to protect his own people from the wrath of the Iroquois, the Huron chief successfully diverted it toward the French, and although Denonville tried valiantly to undo this damaging lie, the Iroquois remained ominously silent from then on.

The French governor had at his disposal fourteen hundred regulars, over three hundred Indian converts, and the militia of the colony, many of whom he stationed at Montréal. He requested eight hundred more French soldiers. The king sent him three hundred.

Denonville considered a double-attack on the Iroquois: fielding one force against the Onondagas and Cayugas, and the other against the Mohawks and the Oneidas. He requested four thousand soldiers to accomplish this plan, which was warmly supported by Bishop Saint-Vallier. However, Minister Seignelay replied: "Raise the militia; the king has no troops to spare at this time."

In mid-August, Denonville begged the king once more to send the Iroquois galley slaves back to Canada. In his letters to Minister Seignelay, the governor expressed his firm belief that there would have been peace had it not been for "the malice of the English and the protection they gave the Iroquois." He also complained that the English intended to establish a trading post in Ohio and had already made three attempts to do so.

Finally, Denonville acceded to Dongan's and the Iroquois' demands. He ordered the destruction of the palisades, and abandonment of his fort at Niagara. He then verified this directive in a letter to the New York governor.

On August 19, 1688 Antoine Cottenoire the younger was born to Marie and her husband. Three days later, young Sébastien and Simonne Massé served as godparents for the boy.

That August, shortly after he returned to his family at Bécancour, Nicolas Perrot received an assignment from Governor Denonville to recruit the Sioux as allies. He left early that autumn with a company of forty Frenchmen who were assigned by the governor to assist him.

A month later, New York and New Jersey were absorbed into the Dominion of New England which now included all of the English North American settlements between Maryland and Canada, except Pennsylvania. These united colonies would be governed by Sir Edmund Andros, who renewed English claims that the Iroquois were English subjects and forbade the French to attack them. He also contested the frontier boundaries between New England and French Acadia and ordered the seizure of the Acadian Fort Saint-Castin at Pentagouet.

The French colony had suffered through a period of great distress; sickness had decimated the French troops; several forts were abandoned for lack of soldiers to protect them. Fourteen hundred of the twelve thousand people who formed the entire population of Nouvelle France had died from the epidemics. Due to sickness and death among the habitants and the constant threat of Iroquois raids, fields had been neglected, leading to food shortages that caused farmers to dip into their stored grain seed for sustenance, thus affecting the size of future crops.

Civil and church officials called for the sharing of food surpluses, since the king's warehouses were running low on grain. Bastien and his neighbors met to discuss the situation and concluded that although their food supplies were lower than usual for this time of year, their standing grain crops appeared to promise a good harvest. If the weather held and they were able to defend their farms against Iroquois attacks, they could store another adequate supply of grain and vegetables for their families. They resolved to reap their crops cooperatively, share among themselves if necessary, but would otherwise disregard the directive.

Meanwhile, Pierre Guillet's concern for the safety of his daughter Catherine and her children continued to grow.

One day, he approached Bastien as he inspected Massé's fields: "I wish I could do more for her, but I'm not as strong as I used to be, and I don't think my wife and I could cope with having that large a family under our own roof."

Bastien had heard this before and knew how the conversation would go. He liked this man and respected him. He also knew that Catherine was used to running her own household; she would not expect her father to take her into his home. This young woman certainly had mastered her responsibilities; her seven children were always neatly dressed, courteous, gentle and kind to each other. Even the little ones were eager to help their mother.

"She needs to find herself another husband, but with so many children..."

"She's a good woman," Bastien reassured him noncommittally.

"Yes, she is," Pierre persisted. "Don't you find it difficult to provide for two separate families? Wouldn't it be more practical to merge them into one?"

Bastien's neck prickled; his face reddened. This was something new; his friend was not usually so direct.

Pierre pressed on. "I worry more and more about Catherine's family, with no man around to offer them protection. Right now, it's dangerous for a woman to live alone with young children."

Bastien had gradually regained his composure. "Have you talked to her about this?" he asked.

"No, I haven't; I know it would upset her if she knew I was talking to you this way. But I'll tell you, Bastien, if you'd consider such an arrangement, I'd gladly help you build a larger home to accommodate everyone."

Bastien felt a mixture of wonder and amazement that this man would offer such a proposal, yet he realized that he had done it out of trust and friendship. Pierre was right, of course, Catherine and her children were more vulnerable to marauders than most of their neighbors.

"That's very generous of you," Bastien replied, "but I'm still mourning the loss of my wife. Catherine and I are helping each other as friends—Marguerite and Catherine were very close."

Pierre's voice softened. "You must admit that your family's living arrangement also suffers from the lack of a housekeeper and cook. Life goes on—your family needs a woman about the house."

This echo of Marguerite's last words startled Bastien.

Pierre continued: "I know and understand what you're going through because I also experienced it after my first wife died—but these are especially difficult times for both your families."

LACHINE

Twenty-two

Bastien lay awake that night, deeply concerned about what he should do. Marguerite had always given him a sense of direction when he faced this important a decision. Had she done so again? He greatly missed her, but lately, he had begun to dwell on the good times that they had shared, and he increasingly found himself enjoying those memories rather than suffering as acutely from his loss. Pierre was right: he and Catherine had managed to help each other through the winter and summer, but in these increasingly difficult times, and facing another winter, perhaps such half-measures would not be enough. She was a lovely woman, but so much younger than he was. What would she think of such a proposal? How would the children react?

Finally, he realized that that would not be a problem; they all enjoyed each other's company. No one, he thought, could ever replace Marguerite in his heart. But now, Catherine...

He considered Pierre's offer to help him build a larger house. He knew the man to be an experienced craftsman who had worked several construction projects with Elie Bourbaust, their community's master carpenter. However, such an undertaking would require a lot of planning—and physical labor. Pierre could advise and direct, but would not have the strength to work with him. Could the boys accomplish this with him?

During the next few months, Bastien's relationship with Catherine slowly and steadily changed; he began to see her more as a woman than strictly as Marguerite's friend. He also found himself talking more freely with her about their children and came to realize that their conversations had gradually become easier, less formal.

Pierre spoke no more about the proposed arrangement, but he could see them growing closer and more comfortable with each other. Their families got together more frequently, especially on Sundays. Their children, who shared similar losses, had already developed close-knit relationships.

That autumn, as the sun began to set much earlier, and the days grew cooler, Bastien found himself alone with the young widow. And he felt ready to speak seriously about the coming season.

"Does the winter isolation bother you?" he asked.

She thought about it and replied: "It never bothered me when Jacques was with us, but now, the evenings seem so long, and there are days when I don't get to speak to another adult unless Papa comes by to visit us—We're always happy to see you or Louis and Sébastien.

"There's always plenty to do. The children are always in need of new clothes, so I keep busy most winter evenings spinning, weaving, or sewing."

"Marguerite would do the same. I miss the clicking sound of her working the cloth."

"She was much better at it than I am. Her web always turned out evenly and perfectly aligned—She seemed to work effortlessly; I always wondered how she could do that."

"She grew up in a convent, you know."

"No, I didn't know. That would explain the quality of her work."

"She enjoyed weaving; it was her way of relaxing at the end of the day."

"I can understand that."

"You're very much like her, you know."

"Am I?"

"Your love of family and children, the way you manage a household, your ability to spin and weave."

"You flatter me."

"I speak the truth."

The intensity in his voice led her to change the subject.

"Does the winter isolation bother you?" she asked.

"It's easier for me, I think. I'm not confined to the house because I must go out to hunt, take care of the livestock, and clear the forest."

"Do you mind spending so much time in the cold?"

"I've always enjoyed working outdoors in the winter."

There was a pause in the conversation, and finally he asked her: "Have you ever considered the possibility of joining our two families under one roof, Catherine?"

There was a longer pause as she studied his profile, and finally she answered truthfully: "Yes, I have, Bastien, but I thought you'd never ask."

They laughed together, and the awkwardness passed.

They began to make plans that very next Sunday, while Pierre and his wife quietly listened and held back any suggestion unless they were asked. Pierre was delighted to see how things had progressed, but he realized how much work lay ahead of them to build a house for a family of thirteen which included offspring spanning ages twenty through infancy.

They all agreed that Catherine and her children should move to Bastien's present house for the winter; that Bastien and the boys would move into the bunkhouse to sleep at night, while Catherine, the girls and young Jean-Baptiste would sleep in the main house. The children of both families were delighted to learn that they would spend the winter together.

The adults fully expected that this arrangement would last through the following summer. One major problem was to provide winter shelter for the additional livestock; Pierre and Bastien agreed that the present stable must be enlarged to accommodate Catherine's animals.

Their first priority was to set up new defensive walls before the beginning of frost and snow. Pierre and Bastien immediately marked the outline of the proposed construction, then Bastien and his two older sons dug trenches for the larger palisades. Meanwhile, François led those of the younger children who were strong enough to collect stones for the cellar walls. He loaded these onto the stone boat, which he then directed the oxen to pull to the construction site. Several of their neighbors joined in this part of the project and helped to raise the palisades and enlarge the animal shelter before the first snowfall in early November.

On November 1, 1688, at the invitation of seven powerful Protestant English lords to unseat his Catholic father-in-law from the British throne, Prince William of Orange sailed from Holland with a fleet of two hundred twenty-five vessels and his professional Dutch army of fifteen thousand men. Additional cargo included a portable bridge, a mobile smithy, a printing press, a mold for new coinage, four tons of tobacco, sixteen hundred hogsheads of beer, ten thousand pairs of boots, a coach and horses.

The English landholders welcomed him two weeks later, when he joined forces with the Earl of Bath and set out for Salisbury in pursuit of James II's army. James retreated to London; then, by mid-December, he fled to exile in France.

On February 22, 1689, the British Parliament declared William and Mary joint monarchs of England. They were cousins; his mother and her grandfather were half-siblings, fathered by King Charles I.

William of Orange had fought against Louis XIV's several invasions of the Netherlands since 1673, and his interests lay primarily in combating French and Spanish continental expansion into strongly Protestant territories. Queen Mary II would concentrate her reign over her faithful English subjects.

That winter, lack of progress in the finalization of the peace agreement with the Iroquois nations troubled the people of Nouvelle France. Nevertheless, the boys helped their father cut down trees and gather lumber for the construction of the new house. Hunting expeditions took them deeper into the woods, and although they remained constantly alert, they felt relatively secure at the cape. Iroquois raids had tapered off as they usually did during the winter, and the few small bands that remained concentrated their hit-and-run attacks farther upriver.

Hunting and food preparation proved to be more efficient as a result of their new living arrangement, enabling Catherine and her daughters to provide hot, nourishing midday meals for both families, while Bastien and his sons could concentrate more time and effort at hewing lumber to Pierre's specifications.

Catherine and her daughter Simonne processed wool fleece that Pierre Guillet had given them, since he raised his own sheep, and his wife Madeleine no longer made her own cloth. Bastien and Pierre had set up Catherine's own spinning wheel and loom in the main room, since she insisted that she was more familiar with these and would prefer them to Marguerite's equipment. The two women carded and spun the wool, then set the warp for weaving enough homespun to meet the clothing needs of both families. Marguerite's equipment had been moved to Madeleine's house at Bécancour so that she and Marie could provide clothing for their own families.

In March of 1689, French ships transported James II, a number of French officers, and a small body of French troops to Ireland in support of his attempt to regain the British throne with an army of loyal Irish supporters. His troops laid siege on Londonderry the following month.

The French king had finally accepted Governor Callières' plan to attack New York by land and sea, but he had greatly complicated and weakened the Canadian strategy by adding his own modifications.

On April 11th, William and Mary were officially crowned joint English monarchs; the claim of divine or hereditary right to the crown of Britain, independent of law, was formally brought to an end, and Protestantism was officially restored to the British Empire. William III was now king of England, Scotland, Wales, and the Netherlands.

France was already at war with the Hapsburg Empire, Spain, and the Netherlands when Great Britain joined their League of Augsburg in May of 1689. Word soon reached New England, and the Iroquois, that the English and French armies were again fighting each other across the sea. The English colonial population already greatly outnumbered the French settlers in North America: 200,000 to 12,000.

Louis XIV now granted Denonville's request to return to France for health reasons, and reassigned sixty-seven-year old Louis de Buade, comte de Palluau et de Frontenac to replace him as governor-general of Québec and Acadia.

In the meantime, the French in North America remained

isolated from the rest of the world, since the first ships due to deliver vital supplies and official letters to Québec failed to arrive. Therefore, Denonville remained totally uninformed about events in Europe, and knew nothing of the king's decision regarding the invasion of New York. Nouvelle France continued to experience that long silence maintained by the Iroquois league.

Out west, Nicolas Perrot had built Fort Saint-Nicolas at the junction of the Wisconsin and Mississippi rivers. On May 8, 1689, with the consent of his western native allies, the explorer formally claimed French possession of the Green Bay territory, including all rivers and lakes which emptied into the bay. He then headed back to Montréal with a large cargo of furs.

At the end of May, Bastien leased a pew in the east row of the the church of Sainte-Madeleine to accommodate Catherine and their daughters.

Louis returned from his successful voyage to Michillimackinac in late spring 1689 and was surprised to see so many changes: the ambitious construction project, and the new living arrangements with Catherine and her family. Following the celebration of his homecoming, his father and brothers led him through an inspection of the completed palisades, the new stable, and the footprint of the new house.

In the following weeks, Catherine, Simonne, and Anne worked with Louis and François during the bird migrations and fish runs, to collect, clean and dry food for storage, while Sébastien and Bastien continued to hew the lumber to Pierre's specifications.

Between tilling the fields, sowing, and harvesting their crops, Bastien and his sons worked at the construction site throughout the spring and summer, digging the larger cellar, building its stone wall and hearth foundations, and erecting the skeletal structure of the new house. Pierre continued to supervise and guide the project, and provided his lifting equipment and ox teams.

The children were already bonding together as a family. The girls shared chores in the house, garden, and barn under Catherine's supervision, while Bastien directed the boys in the fields and at the construction site. Evening leisure activities drew the two groups even closer together.

Louis and Simonne especially shared much of the responsibility for their younger siblings. As the summer wore on, the adults warmly approved of the growing friendship between the two young adults.

"Do you ever think of what it would be like to have a home of your own?" Louis asked her one evening.

"I'd miss my family," she replied seriously.

"So would I, I guess, but I'd choose to live close to them."

"Didn't you miss them while you were away?"

"Only at night when I had time to think about it. We were always so busy during the day—we had to concentrate on our every move."

"Whom did you miss the most?"

"Papa, I think—He's always been such a hero to me. But on this last voyage, I thought about you quite a lot."

Simonne gazed intently into his eyes, knowing that she had also spent much of her time thinking and worrying about him while he was gone. His admission came as a pleasant surprise to her. "I missed you too, Louis," she confessed.

They both smiled warmly as they considered the significance of these admissions.

"Would you consider marrying me?" he asked.

"I've thought of little else this past year."

Louis breathed a sigh of relief; this had happened much more easily than he had expected. He took her hands and drew her to him. They stood at the top of the bluff overlooking the river on that moonlit night and shared their first kiss in the shadow of a great oak tree. It seemed so natural and comforting for them to be in each other's arms.

Then he kissed her more intensely, and she drew back to catch her breath. "I didn't expect this to happen tonight."

"Nor did I, but I'm certainly glad that it did."

She smiled again at his frankness. "When do you think we can marry?"

Louis considered this and told her: "I'll need to talk to my father and your grandfather, because neither of us has reached the age of majority yet. I must be ready to provide a home for us and comfortably support you and a family."

"And I must work on a trousseau, that will take at least a year."

Bastien favored the engagement, and so did Pierre, whose thoughts ranged well beyond these two matches between the two families.

"I'm very pleased that you would ask my permission, Louis," the carpenter replied.

"What are your plans?" Bastien asked.

"Simonne and I both realize that it will take at least a year before I can provide for a wife and family—I'd need to make another voyage out west so that I can afford to buy an existing farm. We hope to settle close to the two families; the new concessions are located farther out each year."

"Are you looking to settle on the south shore?" Pierre asked.

"We'd both prefer to stay on this side of the river, near here."

Pierre told him: "I certainly would welcome that. You have my blessing. And I'm certain that both families will be happy for both of you."

News of England's declaration of war against France did not reach Québec until mid-summer. Meanwhile, Abenaki warriors continued to raid the newer English frontier settlements along the Kennebec River, on what had been their ancestral lands for countless generations.

Count Frontenac finally sailed from La Rochelle on July 23, 1689, with two French ships of war which Louis XIV provided for the proposed French military expedition against the English of New York. Strong headwinds delayed their arrival at Québec.

Lachine, early August 1689

Under cover of a violent hailstorm, fifteen hundred Iroquois warriors crossed Lac Saint-Louis, upriver from Montréal, and landed quietly on the southern shore of that island. They avoided the forts and dispersed into smaller bands across three leagues, to lie in wait around the farms of Lachine.

Quite unexpectedly, at early morning light of August 5th, piercing screams of *"Cassee kouee!"* filled the air and woke the French settlers from their sleep. The warriors shattered windows and doors, burst into the farmhouses, and overwhelmed the habitants and their families. They burned homes and barns, butchered parents and grandparents, and threw French babies and children into the fires. Their onslaught immediately and totally terrorized the entire French population.

Three garrisoned forts were located nearby. At early morning light, another two hundred French regulars, encamped only three miles away, heard a warning cannon-shot from one of the forts, an immediate call to action. They saw a man who had escaped from the brutal scene and was running to alert Montréal, another six miles away. Several more escapees appeared, chased by a group of Iroquois who, upon seeing the soldiers, turned away to pillage nearby houses. The regulars were joined by Officer Subercase who returned from Montréal in time to lead them and one hundred settler-volunteers toward the site of the massacre.

The village area presented a grisly scene: the corpses of its burnt and tortured inhabitants lay grotesquely scattered amid the town's smoldering ashes. Two hundred settlers had perished in the fires; ninety more had been captured and led away to be tortured and devoured at Châteauguay, within sight of Lachine. Very few habitants had managed to escape the slaughter.

Subercase learned that the Iroquois had set up camp a half-league away, and that most of them were hopelessly drunk from the brandy they had looted from the settlement. The young officer prepared to lead his ever-growing and eager force, but Chevalier de Vaudreuil arrived from Montréal in time to order him to halt and give up command of his five hundred regulars and militia. Subercase did so under protest, arguing that the governor could not possibly know of the extent of this disaster.

While Governor-General Denonville, his wife, and daughters remained within that strongly fortified settlement, his orders to all French troops were to hold defensive positions. Thus, the military governor withheld any hope of rescue for the unfortunate captives.

The Iroquois paddled their canoes in view of the forts, flaunted their French prisoners, and shouted: "*Onontio!* You deceived us! Now we have deceived you!"

The warriors held the open countryside, burned over fifty farms, pillaged, and scalped French settlers within more than 20 miles. Then they retreated across Lac Saint-Louis with their hostages to set up stakes and torture fires for their victims within sight of the people of Montréal, who cringed in terror from behind that settlement's palisades. Later on, the majority of the warriors left with their remaining captives, while others stayed behind to spread terror throughout the upper parts of the colony.

Garakontié had finally unleashed the power of the Five Nations. Five hundred French soldiers would have routed them, but Denonville failed to mobilize his troops.

Twenty-three

The Iroquois campaign seriously threatened Montréal, yet nearby Boucherville remained untouched. Trois-Rivières was attacked again. At the cape, as everywhere else in Nouvelle France, the settlers felt helpless panic. Where were the French soldiers who had been sent to Canada to defend them? Where was the militia?

Bastien remembered how he and his fellow habitants had been trained to respond to this same threat so many years ago, but he was older now and looked to Louis to instruct his brothers in the Algonquin methods of self-defense. He considered the cape's present fortifications and was reassured that his own palisades would be strong enough to withstand any attack, as long as his sons could help him defend the family compound. He worried about his daughters on the south shore, but he knew that the seignory had built strong redoubts within easy reach of that small population.

Bastien insisted that no one go beyond the palisades without his permission. He considered the safety of their ripening grain crop and decided that they could harvest it only if they worked together with their neighbors. The edge of the forest had receded away from the farm buildings since the end of the Mohawk attacks twenty-five years earlier; this lent increased security. Their hunt for meat would be difficult and so would the fall eel harvest which usually fed them through the winter until February. They had a cache of pemmican, but needed to add to it.

He was grateful that they had managed to prepare enough lumber for construction; that project would distract the family if they were forced to isolate themselves and their livestock within their palisades. The timber framing was now completed; they were in the process of splitting boards for the shell, the floors, and the inside partitions of the new house.

While the Iroquois continued to run freely throughout the countryside, Nicolas Perrot returned to Montréal in mid-August, shortly after the terrible events at Lachine. He was shocked to find Governor Denonville well-established within the safety of that community's fortifications, shut off from any communication with France.

The explorer hired another group of voyageurs who signed his contracts at Ville-Marie on August 28, 1689, in the presence of notary Jean Cusson. Bastien's son Louis, and Louis Duquet agreed to trade with the Ottawas on behalf of Perrot and promised to return by August of the following year. Perrot would furnish their food and provisions, canoe and whatever else they would need during the journey. In addition, he would pay each of them 600-livres worth of beaver fur upon their successful delivery of the pelts to Montréal.

Three days later, Louis Duquet delivered to Perrot 400-livres worth of beaver fur from *Sieur* Amiot of Québec. That same day, Perrot signed contractual obligations to Louis Duquet for 428-livres worth of beaver fur, and to Bastien's son for 782-livres worth of the same.

On September 29th, Bastien signed a promissory note to Pierre Le Boulanger in the amount of 1829 livres, 2 sols, 2 deniers.

Lieutenant-Governor of Montréal Callières and Count de Frontenac reached Québec in mid-October, three months too late in the season to launch the planned attack against New York. However, the newly reappointed governor-general of Nouvelle France arrived with thirteen Iroquois survivors of the king's galleys, one of whom was a highly respected Cayuga chief who had become his loyal friend during the eighty-one-day crossing.

The two governors quickly assessed the reports of the Lachine massacre and immediately traveled to Montréal, where they found Denonville still safely sheltered with his wife and three daughters, while terror and depression continued to grip the rest of the colony. The Iroquois attacks had abated; local officials suggested that the warriors must be returning to their home villages, having already reduced the surrounding countryside to a burnt out wasteland extending eight miles in every direction.

Governor Frontenac heard reports that two hundred French settlers had been massacred, some roasted and eaten; that pregnant women had their bellies cut open, their babies snatched from their wombs; and that one hundred twenty men, women, and children had been taken prisoner. What he saw and heard deeply saddened and angered him, but he became furious when he learned that Denonville had satisfied Iroquois and English demands by ordering the destruction of Fort Frontenac.

Callières took command of the local troops and defenses. He now assigned soldiers to the fourteen-foot redoubts he had ordered built as centers of sanctuary from attack in each seignory, and he organized expeditions to pursue any Iroquois remaining in the area.

A month later, a band of Mohawks attacked less than thirty miles southwest of Trois-Rivières, at Saint-François-du-Lac, where they burnt down the church and killed at least two French settlers. Another one hundred fifty warriors trudged through the snow to ravage the settlements of Lachenaie near the northeastern tip of Montréal Island and of Île-de-Jésus, an island west of Montréal, with much the same fury as at Lachine. This renewed carnage occurred at a time when most of the population had been heartened by Frontenac's arrival and had come to believe that the danger had passed. These new attacks further increased the level of terror and despair among the French population.

The settlers and officials of Nouvelle France were convinced that the English colonies had armed and incited the Five Nations against them; these were, after all, English muskets, powder and shot, hatchets, and scalping knives that the emboldened warriors of the Five Nations had used in their attacks against the French habitants.

Although Frontenac learned later that his own fort at Cataracoui had been mostly destroyed, and that its remains had fallen into the hands of the Iroquois, he called the chiefs of the

Five Nations to council at that location, but failed in his several attempts in spite of the Cayuga chief's assistance. The Iroquois now held the French in total contempt because of their simmering anger over Denonville's betrayals at Cataracoui and at La Famine.

The new governor-general received reports from La Durantaye and Jesuit Father Carheil at Michillimackinac that their western alliance was falling apart. The western Hurons and Algonquins had lost confidence in their traditional defensive agreements with the French. They knew that Denonville had nearly signed a treaty at Montréal which would have exposed his western allies to Iroquoian carnage. The French governor's failure to defend Lachine and punish the Iroquois for their actions had caused further disillusionment. They now leaned toward joining a triple alliance with the Iroquois and the English as their best chance for survival.

Winter of 1689-90

Frontenac considered the strengths and vulnerabilities of Nouvelle France, and saw that although Québec held a commanding position facing the Saint Lawrence River, its inland fortifications were weak. He ordered his soldiers and settlers to collect and hew heavy timber from the surrounding forests, so that they could raise strong palisades early the following spring to guard that part of the capital's approaches.

Throughout the winter and spring, Frontenac also stationed several detachments of soldiers at the stockade forts Denonville had built in all parishes upriver from Trois-Rivières. He ordered these regulars to maintain strong scouting parties throughout that area, and to guard the farmers while they worked their fields. In spite of these extra measures, Iroquois parties still managed to pillage, brutalize and terrorize the habitants in some of the districts, thus jeopardizing the colony's food supply.

Faced with the urgent need to reclaim his allies, regain the respect of his enemies, and strengthen the resolve of the Canadian population, the governor devised a bold offensive strategy against the English.

Although the colony was short of resources, and most recent population counts estimated 15,000 French habitants compared to 200,000 English settlers, Frontenac raised three volunteer forces from among the coureurs and native converts of the Montréal, Trois-Rivières, and Québec areas. He planned to unleash these forces to strike simultaneously along the frontiers of New York and northern New England. In the depth of winter, his recruits would march on *raquettes* over the deep snow of the virgin forest and across frozen lakes and rivers, while pulling their minimal provisions and supplies on native travois. They would surprise the English "who had stirred up the Iroquois against the Canadian habitants, prompting them to torture French prisoners."

François Hertel, who had been captured and held by the Mohawks as a young man, left Trois-Rivières on January 28th to lead twenty-four French volunteers and twenty Abenakis of the Sokoki band toward Salmon Falls in northern New England.

On that same day, Canadian officers Courtemanche and Portneuf and left Québec with fifty Frenchmen and sixty Abenakis to lead them toward Casco Bay, which was also located in northern New England.

A few days later, d'Ailleboust de Mantet and the Le Moyne brothers left Montréal to deliver a surprise blow against New York's frontier fort at Schenectady. They led a force of two hundred ten, which included ninety-six Iroquois converts from two missions near Montréal.

Bastien's and Catherine's families worked inside the new house throughout the winter months. Sébastien and François thus learned some of the basic building skills their father had mastered during the construction of his first home. Pierre Guillet continued to supervise and advise on a weekly basis, usually while he and his wife visited his daughter and grandchildren on their way home after Sunday Mass.

When François reached the age of sixteen on the first day of February, his father accompanied him to Captain Nicolas Rivard's home where he signed up for the local militia.

"My niece Catherine has told me good things about you, young man," said Rivard. "We're glad to have you; we need as many as can join us now that the Mohawks are on the warpath again."

He turned to Bastien: "I want to thank you for what you've done to protect my niece and her children. We look forward to welcoming you into the family. I saw your palisades, and found them impressive. They look strong enough to shelter half the settlement!"

Bastien caught the humor in his voice. "They'd have to be, to protect our combined families."

Three days later, young Sébastien and Anne Massé served as godparents to Marie-Anne Dehaye, Catherine Guillet's niece.

That same week, François was collecting fuel from the woodpile when he recognized Jean Cusson and Pierre Guillet approaching from Champlain on an ox-drawn sledge. François waved to them but received no reply; both men bore grim expressions. He ran into the house to call his father.

Bastien reacted quickly to his concern and understood when he saw how slowly and deliberately they moved toward them. They ran ahead to meet the sledge.

"We carry bad news," Pierre told them as gently as he could.

When Bastien looked into the cart and pulled back the fur covering, he was shocked to see Aubin Maudoux' prostrate body. He was apparently unconscious, his head heavily bandaged. Bastien caught his breath as he instinctively and lightly put his hand on the young man's chest. "What happened to him?" he asked.

"There was an incident where he was working at Batiscan," Jean Cusson replied.

Bastien immediately scanned the area. "Mohawks?"

"No," Pierre reassured him, "He was struck by an officer of the *Troupes de la Marine.*"

A cold prickling sensation crept across the nape of Bastien's neck. "But why?" he asked. Receiving no answer other than a slight shake of the head, he quickly decided: "Let's take him into the bunkhouse; I don't want the little ones to see him like this."

While the three men smoothly transferred Aubin onto one of the bunks, François stirred up a warm fire in the hearth and went to the main house to get Catherine, his older brother, hot water and clean cloths.

"Has he been seen by the doctor?" Bastien asked.

Cusson replied: "Yes. The physician gave us these extra dressings and told us to change them whenever the blood shows through. We had to travel slowly to avoid shaking him."

"How serious is his injury?"

"Enough to knock him senseless, but the physician told us that we won't really know until he wakes up. The first blow was from an axe-handle, the second from the flat side of a sword."

Bastien's outrage erupted just as Catherine entered with the supplies. She had never witnessed his impassioned anger. He saw the confusion and fear in her eyes and left the bunkhouse. She saw Aubin and, with her father's help, she immediately set about making the wounded man as comfortable as she could. He remained unconscious throughout their ministrations.

Meanwhile, the boys had followed their father outdoors and remained shaken by Bastien's fury. They watched helplessly as he continued to stomp through the snow. Sébastien decided to take charge. He reminded Bastien that Madeleine must be told, that he himself would walk on snowshoes across the frozen Saint Lawrence River to speak to her and bring her back with him; he knew that his other sister Marie would take care of the little one. Bastien nodded and seemed to quiet down a bit.

"I'm sorry," he had to admit. "I saw so many incidents like this before coming to Canada—I thought that life would be different here as an habitant—You're right, of course, Sébastien; you must tell Madeleine. Let's hope and pray that Aubin will completely recover from this."

He rarely spoke of his life in France. His statements puzzled both of his sons, but he seemed to have regained much of his composure. The older son left and François reentered the bunkhouse to offer his help.

When Antoine Cottenoire delivered Madeleine and Sébastien across the ice by ox-drawn sledge, Jean Cusson related the details of the incident as he had heard them from witnesses at Batiscan. While Aubin was privately employed and housed in that community, he had been present at the local pub when the young wife of *Troupes de la Marine* officer Jacques-François de Bourgchemin entered that local establishment. Shortly after her arrival, two customers, one of whom was a soldier, rose to settle their tab before leaving. A disagreement developed between the owner and the two young men over the amount owed. The eighteen-year old woman spoke up in favor of the owner. This irritated the men; the soldier and Aubin were among several patrons who protested her interference.

The following morning, Aubin was seated on a wooden stool in front of his employer's hearth, shaving and sanding an axe handle, when officer Bourgchemin stormed into the house and demanded to know the whereabouts of the soldier. Aubin denied knowing where he was and continued working. The officer picked up another axe handle and swung it with all his strength at Aubin's right forehead, catching him completely by surprise. Aubin fell, his head landing against the opening corner of the fireplace. He was visibly dazed and covered with blood as he got up, only to suffer further injury by a second blow to the head from the flat of Bourgchemin's sword. One witness told Cusson that when he reported the brutal incident to military authorities, he was brusquely warned in Bourgchemin's presence that he must leave or else he would be thrown in jail.

The settlers knew that the French military officers stationed and billeted among the Canadian population were members of the lesser nobility of France who had grown accustomed to treating peasants in such a manner, but such behavior against the Canadian habitants could not be condoned by the colonial authorities.

Although Bastien had never been in court before, he lodged a complaint before the judge of civil and criminal affairs at Trois-Rivières. Speaking passionately on behalf of his son-in-law who remained incapacitated from his injuries, he demanded that justice be served against the officer responsible for this brutal, unprovoked attack. He offered several voluntary witnesses to the incident and argued that the king had sent his officers and soldiers to Nouvelle France to protect, not to abuse, its population.

Officer Bourgchemin had been summoned to appear, but he had not. The court ruled against him, and he later settled the matter by offering his victim 200 livres to cover damages. Aubin accepted his offer and dropped the charges.

Early that April, the first reports of French reprisal against Schenectady reached Canada and renewed hope among the French population that all was not lost.

A few weeks later, Frontenac dispatched Captain Louvigny with one hundred forty-three Canadians, thirty soldiers, and six native guides to Michillimackinac. Nicolas Perrot traveled with them and carried a message from the governor which he was instructed to translate for the western allies.

Following the attack on Schenectady, three French captives revealed to their Dutch captors that Frontenac planned to seize Albany in the spring. On February 15, 1690, civil leaders Peter Schuyler and Van Rensselaer, fully realizing the vulnerability of New York, appealed to the governor and council of Massachusetts to prepare a naval attack against Québec in the spring. Mindful of the French capacity to invade both the westernmost and the easternmost "houses" of the Five Nations, the Mohawks offered to join with the English in an overland campaign against Montréal.

Meanwhile, the daring and brutal winter raids against the outer settlements of New Hampshire and Maine had horrified the northern New Englanders whose frontier defenses had fallen into disrepair. News of England's Glorious Revolution and William III's declaration of war against continental France had led them to free the New England alliance from Andros' autocratic governance and to dismantle the defensive forts and garrisons that he had set up and garrisoned with English regulars. After all, they had argued, Catholic James II had appointed Andros, not Protestant King William III.

Twenty-four

Over the previous decades, the trade of English rum had corrupted native family and tribal structures along the southern Acadian frontier. In conflict with aboriginal land claims, a rapidly expanding English population had extended its settlements into the traditional Abenaki homeland that had buffered the territorial boundaries between French Acadia and New England. Consequently, over six hundred members of these displaced native populations had voluntarily migrated toward the Canadian and Acadian Jesuit missions where their villages were reorganized, and liquor was prohibited.

Port-Royal had become a harbor for French cruisers and a source of munitions and supplies which the Abenakis used in their attempts to reclaim their tribal territory during the late 1680's. Several other Acadian harbors and inlets also served as bases for French privateers who profited from their attacks against English merchant and fishing vessels.

Driven to action by a history of Abenaki raids on their New England frontier and outposts, French seizure of English vessels off the Acadian coast, and Frontenac's winter thrusts, New England shipping interests resolved to attack and seize Port-Royal. The merchants of Salem and Boston financed a fleet and placed it under the command of Sir William Phips, armed its seven ships with seventy-eight cannon, and provided a force of seven hundred thirty-six, which included four hundred forty-six militiamen.

Phips left Nantasket at the end of April 1690. By mid-May, his colonial fleet arrived off Digby Gut, and proceeded into the basin of Port-Royal to attack its French garrison of eighty men.

The fort's palisades had not been completed, and its cannons remained unmounted. Faced by superior forces, French Governor Meneval did not put up a fight but managed to negotiate terms that were favorable to the French. The two opposing officers agreed that: the resident governor and his soldiers would leave the fort with arms and baggage and be sent to Québec by sea; the habitants would peacefully retain their property, and the females would not be molested; the French settlers would not be interfered with in their religion, and the church would not be desecrated.

During the twelve days that followed the French surrender, Phips allowed the New Englanders to pillage the community, loot the fort and warehouse, remove the twenty-two pieces of cannon and level the partial fortification.

Sir William called the Acadian habitants together and ordered them to take an oath of allegiance to William and Mary of England, which most of the settlers did; those who refused lost all their property. He took captive the community's two priests, Governor Meneval, and fifty-eight soldiers. Then he organized a provisional government by personally selecting certain French Acadians as members of the governing council.

While his troops looted and desecrated the church, he seized the money, silverware, and personal effects of the French governor before leaving Port-Royal.

Captain Alden had already taken possession of Saint-Castin's post at Pentagouet; now Phips ordered him to seize La Hève, Chedabouctou and other stations on the southeastern coast of Acadia. Sir William proceeded to destroy the French settlements at the head of the Bay of Fundy: Grand Pré, Beaubassin, and Cobequid. His fleet returned triumphantly to Boston on May 30th.

Early that May, Pierre Guillet officially ceded his land at Bécancour to Antoine Cottenoire upon receipt of his final payment. Pierre and his wife had already retreated to his original concession in Champlain.

That same week, the Mohawks and the English prepared a combined attack on Canada. The several colonial governments welcomed the Iroquois warriors, and a great crusade against the papists rose from Puritan New England.

New York pledged to provide four hundred men; Plymouth, Massachusetts, and Connecticut promised to raise a force of three hundred fifty-five; the Five Nations had already indicated that they would join the English forces with nearly all of their warriors. They all agreed to rendezvous at Albany, and although there were difficulties in the selection of a commander, they finally appointed Fitz-John Winthrop of Connecticut.

The English plan called for Massachusetts and the other northern colonies to attack Québec by sea which would be expensive. Massachusetts hesitated because its men and ships had not yet returned from Acadia.

Upon his arrival from Port-Royal at the end of May, Sir William Phips enthusiastically agreed to lead the thrust against Québec. Massachusetts Governor Bradstreet had asked for a supply of arms and ammunition from England and was refused because Britain was still at war against the French-backed Jacobites in Ireland.

The English colonists spent the next two months assembling and provisioning another, larger fleet. The flagship *Six Friends*, had previously served the English in the West Indies and carried forty-four guns. In addition, they pressed into service thirty-two trading and fishing vessels. Among the twenty-two hundred militiamen and sailors, some were recruited, others impressed.

Late June 1690

Now that Aubin Maudoux had recovered from his head injury, Pierre leased his own forty-five arpents of cleared farmland to him for thirty-six *minots* of wheat per year.

Less than a week later, Des Groseilliers' son-in-law, Jean Jalot, and nine other settlers from Cap-de-la-Madeleine were killed by the Mohawks upriver near the coulé de Jean Grou. They were hastily buried on-site.

Early in July, Captain Rivard's civil announcements informed the parishioners of Sainte-Madeleine that the English and their Iroquois allies planned to attack Montréal. He also relayed Governor Frontenac's call for militia volunteers to join forces with the French regulars whom he would lead to defend that frontier community.

Aubin, Madeleine, Marguerite and their children shared the noon meal with the family that Sunday, and while the women prepared dinner, the men gravely discussed this new development.

Aubin had no reservations about volunteering.

"But are you strong enough?" Madeleine asked anxiously.

"Of course, I am—I've been doing my regular chores."

Marguerite offered news about her husband: "Antoine is already at Montréal on business. I hope he leaves before the English get there."

"I'm sure he will," Bastien reassured her, "News of this must have reached Montréal by now."

Sébastien sought his father's counsel. "Is this any different from the previous campaigns?"

"*Oui, mon gars*. The militia was originally formed for self-defense. We have to put an end to these Iroquois attacks, especially now that the English are joining with them."

"Will you be volunteering?" Aubin asked.

Bastien replied: "I must stay here with the women and children. But you and Sébastien are free to volunteer if you wish."

"Can I join too, Papa?" François asked.

Despite his sixteen-year old son's eagerness, Bastien replied: "It would be best if you stayed here to help me with the summer harvest and to defend these palisades, if it comes to that."

"If Louis were here, he'd go," the young man added.

"Yes, he would, but in his absence, Sébastien will represent the family. You know that I can't accomplish the harvest by myself, and it's been difficult enough to keep our crops growing. We need all the grain we can gather."

Sébastien and Aubin recalled the warnings that they had received from the coureurs at Irondequoit Bay regarding the fierceness of the Seneca warriors.

Twenty-year old Sébastien eyed his father. "I've never fought the Iroquois—Are they as cruel as they say?"

Bastien sensed his apprehension and understood. "War is always cruel, and Canadian militiamen have usually fought to the death rather than be captured by the Mohawks."

He added: "Captain Rivard will equip and train you in hand-to-hand combat skills, just as I was trained by Red Dawn."

Sébastien's eyes widened.

"There comes a time in a man's life when he must stand up and fight, *mon gars*. This governor knows what he's doing," his father assured him. "You can trust his judgement in military matters, and you must trust in God."

At the end of July, as Frontenac and Intendant Champigny led the French forces toward Montréal, the cape volunteers saw the effects of the pillaging and burning that the Mohawks had wrought on both sides of the Saint Lawrence River; they were outraged by the extent of the devastation.

While they worked to further strengthen Montréal's defenses, a messenger reported from Lachine that Lac Saint-Louis was covered with canoes. The governor ordered that the fort's cannon be fired to summon the army and militia to arms.

Sébastien and Aubin were startled by the cannon boom and the sudden urgent activity that surrounded them. They quickly prepared for battle.

Then a second messenger announced that the canoes were those of friendly Indians from Michillimackinac who were coming to trade their furs at Montréal—the first such native flotilla to arrive in several years.

The young militiamen witnessed the appearance of five hundred Hurons, Ottawas, Ojibwas, Potawatomis, Crees, and Nipissings aboard one hundred ten canoes filled with a fabulous cargo of prime beaver pelts. Their tribal leaders announced that they wished to reunite with their *Onontio* Frontenac, whose words of wisdom they sought to hear. The Hurons exhorted the governor to fight against the Iroquois until they begged for a truce, and they promised to fight alongside him until that was achieved.

Antoine had just returned home to his family when word of these events reached the Trois-Rivières area. He immediately picked up over a 1000-livres worth of merchandise from merchant Pierre Le Boulanger and left with Aubin to join in the fur trade.

By the time he reached Montréal, a second flotilla had arrived. Led by La Durantaye, commander at Michillimackinac, its fifty-five canoes were manned by French traders and filled with an additional cargo of prized winter furs. Nicolas Perrot and Louis were among this group; Bastien's son thus met his contract date of delivery and was happy to reunite with Antoine and Aubin.

They arrived home a week later, each towing a second canoe neatly loaded with his furs, thus setting off another festive celebration. Antoine's trading at Montréal had been highly profitable; Aubin had gone along to help him. Louis' voyage had recouped his investment seven times over; Nicolas Perrot had redeemed his debt to him and paid his wage as promised. The family marveled at the wealth the two men had acquired.

The boys helped to unload, carry, and place Louis' fur packs in the new cellar, while Antoine and Aubin headed across the river.

Bastien looked on with fatherly pride. "It was well worth your time and effort, *mon gars*! I thank God that you had a safe voyage—The Mohawks have been very active around here."

Louis hugged him warmly, fully realizing that his father's remarks expressed genuine respect for him as a man.

Once his furs were safely stored, the family sat down to a special meal of roast chicken, fresh corn on the cob, baguettes, and blueberries with cream.

Sébastien spoke up immediately after the prayer. "Papa, the countryside between Lac Saint-Pierre and Montréal is completely pillaged and burned on both sides of the river."

Bastien understood his anger. "I thought as much, *mon gars*; we can expect difficult times ahead. You must all remember that the most important things in life are the love and mutual help of family and friends, food on the table, a roof over your head, a warm fire in the winter, comfortable clothing, and the tools to provide them from the forest and the land."

Catherine studied his face as he shared this advice with his sons and was grateful that her children had also heard it. She knew that those words had come from his heart, that they had been, and always would be his main priorities in life.

Louis described for his father the problems that he had encountered at Michillimackinac. "The voyage west proved to be uneventful; we managed to avoid the Iroquois on our way out. But as we approached the fort, we found the Hurons and Ottawas to be sullen and spiteful. They repeatedly argued that the English and Dutch traded more generously for their furs.

"The French clerks at the fort told us that the Iroquois had been playing on the natives' fears, pointing out to them that our last two governors would have abandoned our traditional alliances. So when we arrived at Michillimackinac, our allies had little respect for us, claiming that the French were weak, and that their alliances with us were worthless."

"Did they threaten you?"

"Not really, because I could speak to them in their own language, and they respect that. But we felt uncomfortable in their presence, and we tried not to show it.

"When I spoke to the Jesuit missionaries, they expressed great concern about this definite change in attitude. They sensed that increased contacts with the Iroquois were steadily persuading the lake tribes to switch their loyalty to the Five Nations, the Dutch, and English of Albany."

Bastien drew deeply from his pipe. "We would lose the fur trade, and we'd be even weaker against our enemies."

"Yes! Nouvelle France has already suffered from a slowdown in the flow of furs. It's badly affected our ability to buy the essential supplies we need from France—and the English settlers greatly outnumber us now."

"But surely the western natives know that Frontenac won't abandon them; they always respected his wisdom and strength as a warrior."

Louis shrugged his shoulders and continued: "We managed to do some trading because the missionaries spoke in our favor, but the Hurons and Ottawas only offered us furs that were of poor quality.

"Then Captain Louvigny and Nicolas Perrot arrived with a large detachment of men. They had fought and defeated a group of Iroquois warriors along the way, and they displayed one captive and a long string of scalps. The upper Hurons and Algonquins fought over who should have power over the Iroquois prisoner.

"During their assembly, Monsieur Perrot translated a letter from Governor Frontenac. Many of the natives didn't know or remember this governor, but those who did, recalled the respect he had earned among all the native tribes as their *Onontio*.

"Then Monsieur Perrot announced that the French had destroyed Schenectady.

"They were definitely impressed by all of these news; so much so, that the chiefs called their tribal meetings and decided to come to Montréal to meet with the governor. Those who couldn't make the voyage traded briskly with us, while others came from farther away to join the trading fleet of over one hundred canoes!

"The cannon sounded as we approached Montréal; Frontenac and his troops apparently thought this was part of an invasion, but it turned out to be a great cause for celebration!

"You should have seen the governor's reunion with them! I always admired Perrot's way with the natives, but Frontenac is truly a master. We saw him dancing and whooping wildly among them, raising their confidence and determination that they could gain the respect of the Iroquois. They offered their allegiance to him without reservations."

Bastien waited to hear more, but Louis had finished; he did not want to frighten the children.

"I wish I could have been there to see all of that," Bastien mused.

"You can well imagine how relieved we were to see Monsieur Perrot."

Bastien nodded. "The largest trading fleet of canoes I ever saw was during my indenture when Radisson and Des Groseilliers arrived at Trois-Rivières at the end of their first voyage together—I'm glad to hear that you had no major problems and that things turned out so well for you. You've realized quite a profit on your investment."

Louis promised him: "I plan to settle my account with Le Boulanger tomorrow morning." He turned to Simonne who sat by his side. "Then I'll look for land, hopefully with a house, so that Simonne and I can marry."

"Wonderful!" she said, as she covered his hand with hers and smiled.

The children laughed, while Bastien and Catherine looked knowingly and approvingly at each other from across the length of the table.

Louis voiced his approval of the strong palisades and asked about progress on the new house.

Bastien told him: "I must warn you that Jean Jalot and nine other men from the cape were ambushed and killed by the Mohawks about a month ago."

Louis unconsciously tightened his brow and strengthened his hold on Simonne's hand. "Then we must find ourselves a secure property, with strong palisades."

"As for the house," Bastien continued, "we're making progress. Sébastien and François have both worked hard to help me."

"We've learned a lot!" Sébastien interjected, and his younger brother nodded in agreement.

"I'm sorry I couldn't be here to do my share," Louis told them, "but I'll make up for it now that I'm home. Simonne and I hope to see that project completed and our families settled before we marry."

Catherine spoke up. "My father sold several of his properties this past year, but he still holds a particular one at côte Saint-Marc that he wants you to see."

"I'll speak to him tomorrow," Louis promised. Then he turned to the rest of the family and questioned everyone about their activities during his absence.

Later that afternoon, he and Simonne toured the new house and discussed their plans for the future.

"If all goes well," he told her, "we could marry early next year. What do you think?"

"That would be perfect! I need more time to finish my trousseau, and I'd like to help *Maman* move some of her own things to the new house; that will take a while longer."

"Will she sell the old farm?"

"I don't think so, *Pepère* told her that she should lease it out."

Once the younger boys had fallen asleep that evening, Bastien and François heard the rest of Louis' story. He described the first day of trade at Montréal, when another Iroquois convert arrived from Albany to announce having seen massive war preparations on Lac Saint-Sacrement. Governor Frontenac dispatched Chevalier de Clermont to scout as far as the southern end of Lac Champlain and soon received a report that some of the enemy were already on the Richelieu River.

The governor moved his twelve hundred men east, across the river to Laprairie, where he planned to challenge the Iroquois and the English forces, but none appeared. After three days of trading and waiting at Laprairie, the western allies grew restless and prepared to go home. Frontenac presented gifts to them, garrisoned a small force, and moved back across the river to station his troops throughout the Montréal area to protect and assist the habitants during their upcoming grain harvest.

Louis, Sébastien, Aubin, and Antoine left for Trois-Rivières toward the end of the evacuation, and as they coasted downriver with the current and approached the northern end of Montréal Island, they heard the unmistakable echo of a cannon boom from the direction of Laprairie.

The first report from Lac Saint-Sacrement had been of the New York-Connecticut units heading north toward Montréal, but these troops stopped at the southern end of Lake Champlain. Shortages of provisions and canoes, the failure of the western Iroquois tribes to arrive, the spread of dysentery and smallpox among the militia and warriors, ensuing quarrels between the English and Iroquois leaders and among their men, all contributed to the unanimous decision to disband and go home. But first, Commander Winthrop allowed Captain Schuyler of New York to launch a small-scale thrust into Canada with about thirty English volunteers, and one hundred twenty Mohawks.

This was the group that the second messenger had seen descending the Richelieu. Once Governor Frontenac had moved the major part of his force back to Montréal, and while the remaining soldiers and habitants were harvesting the wheat fields at Laprairie, this smaller English-led force raided that settlement, capturing twenty-five, including women, killing the livestock, burning houses, barns, and haystacks.

Frontenac remained at Montréal, monitoring and fending off several attacks in that area. On October 10th, he received an urgent message from the capital reporting that a large fleet had sailed from Boston to attack Québec. Although he was skeptical about the news, he immediately set off downriver with two hundred men.

The following day, he encountered another messenger who alerted him to several reports that the English fleet had already been seen moving up the Saint Lawrence near Tadoussac. He sent word to Governor Callières of Montréal, ordering him to move all of his forces to the capital as quickly as possible.

Frontenac's own men paddled past Trois-Rivières at top speed and arrived at Québec on October 14th. Leaving nothing to chance, he hastened to reinforce and organize the capital's defenses against the pending naval attack.

The French knew that if the fortress of Québec fell to the enemy, all of Nouvelle France would be lost. Bad weather and repeated strategy meetings delayed the New England fleet's movement upriver, allowing Frontenac two more precious days to strengthen the capital's defenses against a possible landing.

Bishop Saint-Vallier sent out a pastoral letter to all parishes, exhorting the settlers to defend the capital against the English naval invasion. Volunteer reinforcements steadily arrived from throughout the valley settlements, including Antoine, Louis, and Sébastien.

The night before Phips' fleet appeared before Québec, twenty-seven hundred regulars and militiamen manned the capital's barricades.

DOUBLE WEDDING

Twenty-five

Within two and half months after his arrival from Port-Royal, Phips had undertaken a second major military adventure against the French colonies. This ambitious schedule had caused him to leave Boston late in the season, with little time to conduct an extended siege before the onset of the Canadian winter. The English fleet had sailed at mid-August with a force of twenty-three hundred mostly inexperienced militia farmers, tradesmen, and townspeople, and enough provisions to last four months, but with a limited supply of ammunition, and no experienced pilot to navigate the Saint Lawrence River. Admiral William Phips had led his fleet toward Québec with full confidence that an army of two thousand native allies and some four thousand English settlers would travel overland to successfully attack Montréal, then join forces with him at Québec.

The English militia had already raided Île-Percée before the fleet made its way around the Gaspée peninsula, entered the Saint Lawrence River, and easily captured three French barks. Phips then relied on his captives' sometimes misleading information to navigate the mighty waterway towards the capital of Nouvelle France.

At morning light of October 16th, Louis and Sébastien saw seagoing vessels for the first time in their lives, as they watched thirty-four New England ships glide into the anchorage below.

The invasion fleet consisted of several large ships, including the flagship *Six Friends* with forty-four guns, the *John and Thomas* with twenty-six, and other vessels of various size, including fishing craft. Flush from his easy victory in Acadia, the English admiral sent an emissary to deliver to the French governor his tersely written orders for the surrender of the fortress of Québec.

As soon as the young officer landed, he was securely blindfolded and deliberately led to Frontenac's headquarters by way of a long, circuitous route, through small groups of settlers and soldiers who deliberately gave him the impression that soldiers and habitants crowded the town, that they had enthusiastically and energetically prepared for battle. His senses convinced him that the entire Canadian population had mobilized and assembled at Québec to repel the invasion.

Governor Frontenac and his officers wore their finest satin, silk and lace to receive the young Englishman who was finally relieved of his blindfold. He delivered Phips' message and informed the governor that the admiral required a reply within the hour. Frontenac had the document translated and immediately replied that God would not favor traitors to religion and to their legitimate king (Catholic James II), that the mouths of French cannons and muskets would answer English demands.

The Governor's response reverberated throughout the capital and the other settlements, and was accompanied by a rumor that its delivery to the Admiral was emphasized by a cannon shot that took down the flagship's standard. Once more, Count Frontenac had energized the French population.

On October 18th, Antoine, Louis, and Sébastien were stationed among the cape and Montréal militiamen who guarded the northeastern defenses of the fortress, when the four largest New England vessels began their cannonade against Québec. Sixty-eight-pound cannonballs flew over the walls and destroyed the buildings of the upper and lower towns. The repeated sounds of cannon were deafening and alarming. None of the cape militiamen had ever experienced this type of warfare.

Nicolas Rivard and one of the Le Moyne brothers passed among them and gave instructions to settle in and wait, but to remain alert and keep watch over the side. Both warned that this cannon fire was obviously meant to cover a military landing, most likely against their section of the fortifications.

At dusk, Antoine and his brothers-in-law could see rowboats heading toward the northern riverbank and unloading fourteen hundred English colonials between Beauport and Québec.

"They're landing across Rivière Saint-Charles," Antoine announced.

Louis peeked over the side. "They're also unloading and hauling several cannon; they must intend to fire them against our section."

"They'll have to fire up at us. How much harm can that do?" Sébastien asked.

"It depends on how close they can get to these walls," Rivard replied, having overheard them. "We have to make sure that they don't get across the river."

While the English colonists approached the waterway, Rivard and Le Moyne judged their five cannons to be heavy and awkward to transport. They ordered the French militia to fire a heavy fusillade as the Englishmen began to haul them across by boat.

The New Englanders remained three days at that site, unable to cross the river with their cannons. They ventured away from Québec to burn local farms, carry off some cattle, kill two Frenchmen, and wound a dozen others through various skirmishes. Their cannons remained out of range of the capital's walls, and French cannon fire from the upper town prevented English delivery of badly needed supplies to their landing force.

During those same three days, Phips' four largest armed vessels fired fifteen hundred cannonballs against Québec's upper and lower towns in support of its troops. This punishing barrage ceased when the fleet's supply of ammunition ran out.

Meanwhile, French artillery directed eighteen-pound balls from a greater height and damaged the four largest English vessels. The Admiral's ship lost its flag, its mainmast and mizzenmast were broken, its cabin pierced, and its stern-gallery shattered.

On the 23rd, the admiral recovered his men from the landing area and withdrew his badly damaged ships from French cannon range. He attempted to land on Île d'Orléans but failed, and so he remained offshore, patching up his fleet as ice formed at night on the river and on the New England vessels.

Two days later, the admiral called for a prisoner exchange. He released the prisoners from Port-Royal whom he had brought from Boston to guide his fleet toward Québec, and the French crewmen whose vessels he had captured upon entering the Saint Lawrence River. Once this exchange was accomplished and his ships repaired, Phips turned his ships downriver and headed back to Boston. Close to one hundred of his men had been killed and a great many more wounded during and after the landing. He had lost three shallops during the siege, and a bark sank during foul weather before they reached the Atlantic.

Following their release, the French captives reported to the Governor Frontenac that the Boston merchants who financed Phip's expedition, and the officers who led it, had been so confident of victory that they had argued in court over the fair division of the spoils, especially in regards to six silver chandeliers belonging to the Jesuit church.

While Louis was away with the militia, Bastien completed a transaction on his behalf, purchasing from Pierre Guillet the two parcels of land with buildings that he had set aside for Louis and Simonne. The two concessions were at côte Saint-Marc. One measured four arpents of river frontage by forty deep, bordering Marie Boucher's land to the southwest, and René Blanchet's land to the northeast; the other consisted of two adjoining parcels of land, each of two arpents frontage by forty deep, bordering widow Massé's land to the southwest, and Pierre Guillet's land to the northeast. Pierre was delighted to know that his granddaughter Simonne would be living next door to him.

Winter 1690-91

Canada seemed relatively quiet that winter. The Iroquois had retreated to their home villages. New England struggled to recover from the ravages of King Philip's War, its overthrow of Governor Andros, and its loss of manpower and investment in its naval campaign against Québec. The militiamen of New York and Connecticut, and the warriors of the western Iroquois nations had carried home the dysentery and smallpox that had plagued them during their overland expedition to Lake Champlain.

As for Nouvelle France, its capital lay in ruins, half of its fields had been left untilled. Although four supply ships had reached Québec before ice blocked the rivers, twice as many vessels had been seized by the several armed English privateer vessels that blockaded the Gulf of Saint Lawrence.

In Europe, William III of England concentrated his military and naval resources against the continental forces of Louis XIV, much as the French king did against those of the British monarch. Such policies meant that the North American colonies would have to survive on their own for the time being. To this end, New York continued to arm and incite the Iroquois and the Mohicans against the French, while the Canadians armed and incited their Acadian Abenaki and western allies against New England and the Iroquois.

The French colonial government continued to construct stockade forts to house its troops in the individual parishes. French soldiers were gradually reassigned to these while the population struggled to feed itself. The presence of these small local garrisons provided extra security to those living on either shore of the Saint Lawrence River, and their additional muskets assisted in the winter hunt for moose and elk.

Bastien and Catherine had moved her family's grain and livestock to his farm, but he had kept these separate from his own. Now they jointly took stock of what they had and determined that if they carefully managed their resources, their supplies would see them through the winter and beyond. They began by rationing their flour.

Their families lived more economically together than they would have had they remained apart. Louis taught everyone to set traps for the smaller animals of the forest, and the older boys and girls learned to clean and skin whatever the hunters provided.

The new clay fireplace and chimney had its first firing under Bastien's and Catherine's watchful eyes. Louis helped to finish the inside of the main house, while Bastien taught his sons the skills that they would use one day to provide basic, simple furnishings for their own homes.

One evening in early December, while they were all gathered by the fire in the old house, Bastien enjoyed one of those happy occasions when everyone was present, and found himself contrasting this scene with that of his lonely arrival at Québec so many years ago.

"This is the first Noël that we can all attend Midnight Mass together!" he declared.

Catherine agreed, and the children began to plan for that very special night. They discussed the menu and drew lots to learn whose gift each would make. The older children offered to help their younger siblings with their projects, but would let them plan them on their own.

On a cold, clear Christmas Eve, Pierre Guillet and his wife Madeleine Delaunay arrived early with *tourtières* of deer and pork, wine for the adults, and various herbal teas for the children. Catherine roasted one of her turkeys while her daughters prepared a mixture of various root vegetables for the after-midnight feast. The pleasant aroma of baked bread and desserts filled the new house. The youngest children, Catherine's Louise and Jean-Baptiste, slept upstairs in the loft while the boys brought in evergreen branches and clusters of colored berries which the girls placed around the room, adding color and additional fragrance to the festivities.

The adults filled the sleeping children's sabots with sweets provided by Pierre and Madeleine, and small presents: two tiny animal carvings by Bastien for the boy and bits of ribbon and lace that Catherine provided for her daughter.

Everyone agreed that the night would be too cold for the little ones to ride to and from church in the sledges, so Pierre volunteered to stay with the sleeping children while the rest of the family attended Midnight Mass. His wife Madeleine offered to stay with him to make sure that everything would be ready for the family's arrival.

Bastien and Louis covered their passengers with furs as they prepared to drive both ox-drawn sledges to the village church. The night air remained cold and clear, there was no wind, and a full moon brightly lit their way. Catherine rode with Bastien, and Simonne sat next to Louis. Amid the singing of traditional Christmas carols, no one noticed that Sébastien and Anne Massé sat next to each other and spoke softly all the way to church that night.

After the holidays, everyone worked together to help Louis and Simonne prepare their future home. In mid-January, family and friends gathered at the new house to witness the signing of their marriage contract. She would bring 100-livres worth of personal property to the union, while he would commit 1000-livres worth of real property, the land and house that he had purchased from Pierre Guillet. Notary Jean Cusson prepared the agreement. Adult relatives and friends of both families signed or made their marks as witnesses to the young couple's mutual commitments.

Early the following April, Governor Frontenac received a report from Jesuit Father Bruyas at Sault Saint-Louis near Montréal that one hundred forty Mohawks and Dutchmen had captured twelve converts near the mission, freed them, and sent three of their own chiefs to petition the *Onontio* to end the conflict. They claimed that their people had borne the greater burden in this war against the French. And they warned that an army of eight hundred of their brothers were preparing to attack the French and capture as many settlers as they could from between Trois-Rivières and Montréal.

The Mohawk delegates sought to arrange a summer meeting with Governor Frontenac. Father Bruyas had advised them to prove their goodwill by stopping all attacks against the French and their native allies, and by calling upon the Mohicans to join in the cease-fire. He had also initiated a prisoner exchange. The Mohawks claimed that although their own warriors asked for peace, they had not yet discussed this with their elders. They left two of their own people to carry Frontenac's reply to the Mohawk villages once he set the time and place for peace talks. The priest assured the governor that the Iroquois converts and the French of Montréal considered this to be an honest and sincere offer.

On April 5th, an official inventory of Bastien and Marguerite's property was appraised by Claude Herlin and Guillaume Barette. Their list included the estimated values of eighteen *minots* of wheat and ten of oats; five "horned beasts", one pair of pigs, fifteen chickens, and one rooster. Most importantly, Bastien's concession of two arpents frontage by forty deep showed eighteen square arpents of cleared and tillable land. One new house measured thirty-seven feet long by sixteen wide, with a clay chimney, and two rooms at each end. One older house measured twenty-five feet by sixteen. One barn measured fifty feet by twenty-four. One new twenty-five-foot long stable, and one fully equipped plow were also listed along with all personal, household, and farm equipment. His assets amounted to 2321 livres, 15 sols; his debts totaled 639 livres, 14 sols, all but 19 livres of which he owed to merchant Pierre Le Boulanger. His son Louis lent him 400 livres toward payment of that debt.

The following week, widow Marie Boucher leased to Aubin Maudoux two lots along the Trois-Rivières canal for three years. The agreement required that he pay her forty *minots* of wheat and ten of peas for each of those three years.

On the 26th of April, Bastien and Guillaume Barette made an official appraisal of the Massé property, as was required by law. Jacques Massé's heirs held a piece of land two arpents by forty, twenty square arpents of which were cleared and tillable. The property also included one wooden house measuring twenty-five feet by sixteen, with thatched roof, wooden floor, and a partitioned loft dividing that space into two rooms. A thatched barn measured forty feet by eighteen and was palisaded with the house. A stable measuring twenty feet by fourteen was thatched and palisaded. A laundry building, thirteen feet by eleven, was thatched and palisaded. Livestock included three bulls, four cows and one heifer, three male pigs and two sows, twelve chickens, one rooster, and two female turkeys. Grain storage included fourteen *minots* of wheat, ten of grey peas, and three of oats. The Massé estate showed assets of 2377 livres, and debts of 372 livres, 19 sols.

The following day, Bastien and Catherine signed their own marriage contract in the presence of Pierre Guillet, Antoine Cottenoire, François, and Sébastien. The agreement declared that the children of both spouses would be raised with equal devotion by both parents, as long as the children contributed their fair share of effort and work for the welfare of the combined family. The rights of the remaining minor children would be safeguarded and overseen by their legal guardians: Catherine's father Pierre Guillet and Bastien's oldest son Louis. Bastien had three sons and one daughter yet unmarried and living at home. Catherine had five daughters and two sons remaining with her.

Three days later, as required by law for the protection of his children by his first wife, Bastien testified before royal procurator

Elie Bourbaust, that his inventory was honest and true.

The following week, Catherine testified at Trois-Rivières before Lieutenant-Governor Jean Lechasseur that her inventory was honest and true.

On Monday morning, May 14, 1691, a double wedding took place at the village church of Sainte-Madeleine. Bastien and Catherine preceded Louis and Simonne down the aisle to where pastor Paul Vachon and an altar servant waited to receive both couples. Abbé Vachon led them in their exchange of wedding vows, blessed their rings, said Mass, then distributed Communion to the brides and grooms, and to all the family members and friends who were present. At the end of the liturgy, he blessed the four newlyweds, and solemnly reminded them of their nuptial obligations to their respective spouses.

Bastien, Pierre Guillet, and Antoine Cottenoire served as witnesses to Louis and Simonne's wedding; Pierre Guillet, Antoine Cottenoire, Sébastien, and François served in the same capacity for Bastien and Catherine's ceremony.

Afterward, the wedding parties made their way to the new house, where Bastien's two married daughters, Catherine's sisters and daughters set out food and refreshments for the reception.

Bastien and Catherine circulated among their guests, while the fiddler played his usual lively music, encouraging the younger couple to try out their dancing skills with the gigue, gavotte, and quadrille. Several of the men took turns at keeping rhythm with the wooden spoons. Aubin surprised everyone by reaching into his pocket and retrieving a small wooden flute which he began to play in accompaniment to the fiddle. Although the rest of the family was amazed to hear him play, Madeleine had discovered this skill of his on their wedding night. He very rarely performed, but he apparently considered this to be a very special occasion. The little ones clustered about him, fascinated and delighted by the beautiful sounds emanating from so small an instrument.

Louis and Simonne prepared to leave the party before dusk, to travel east to their new home at côte Saint-Marc. But before they left, Pierre proposed a toast to their future: "May you have many children," met with loud applause. "May you share a long and happy life together," met with longer applause. "May you prosper."

The fiddler took up his cue and played a romantic tune as he accompanied them to Louis' new oxcart which was already loaded with their wedding gifts.

Most of the guests bid farewell to their hosts and left soon after the young couple, since no one wished to be out on the river road after dark. Pierre and his wife Madeleine lingered on for a little while longer.

"I'm sure you realize how happy we are to see you two married," Pierre told them with great emotion. "My mind is now at peace over the welfare of my grandchildren."

Catherine hugged him. "I'm sure you had this in mind for us long before we thought of it, Papa."

Bastien chuckled. "I know he did, Catherine. But it might have been impossible to accomplish without his offer to help me build this house. I must thank you again, Pierre."

"We wish you both much happiness," Madeleine offered. "Enjoy your first night together, alone in this new home of yours—It will probably be the quietest this house will ever offer you!"

She scanned the room, saw that all was as it should be for the newlyweds, took her husband's arm and nudged him toward the door. Guillaume and his family waited outside to take them home.

Once they had left, Bastien closed and locked the door. He turned toward this woman whom he had grown to love, admire, and respect during the past three years. She moved toward him and settled peacefully into his arms. They stood there for a long while, enjoying the moment.

"Would you like some brandy?" he asked.

"Will you have some?"

"Just a little on this very special occasion."

"Then I'll join you."

As he turned and moved to pour the drinks into two small cups, she slipped into one of the corner rooms.

She reappeared a short while later in a fine white linen gown, her blond hair released to her shoulders, her hazel eyes shining in the candlelight. She looks so young, he thought, and so beautiful.

They sat together on the edge of the bed, sipping their drinks as he took off his shoes, unbuttoned his shirt, and relaxed.

"No more lonely nights," she almost whispered.

There had always been this frankness between them. He took her hand and kissed it gently—it felt so delicate compared to his—yet he had seen the strength those hands had mustered in accomplishing some very difficult chores.

She finished her brandy and slipped under the covers. He soon joined her, and they quite easily moved into each other's arms in search of that closeness, comfort and peace that they had both lost three years earlier.

Farther down the river, at côte Saint-Marc, Louis and Simonne had already experienced a new-found passion for each other. They lay in each other's arms and talked through the night about what their lives would be like from now on.

"I'm so glad we could share the nuptial blessing with our parents—It was that much more special, don't you think?" she asked.

"Yes—There was a time when I thought Papa would never get over the loss of my mother—Your grandfather is a very wise man; he saw their marriage as a possibility long before anyone else did. I think *Maman* must be very happy for both of them."

"Do you believe that she's aware of what happened today?"

"I felt her presence, and that was comforting."

She dwelt on this for a while and admitted: "I seemed to feel Papa's presence too—but I thought it was because I missed him so much on my wedding day—I hope you're right."

Twenty-six

Québec had begun to import much of the colony's flour from France. Lack of wind slowed the ocean crossings; money became scarce; odd items were melted into bullets. Mohawk raids continued to hamper work in the fields; women and children learned to fight alongside the men.

During the two years since the Lachine massacre, the Canadians had gradually adopted the Iroquois guerilla tactics of attack which the French called *la petite guerre*. South of Acadia, French and Abenaki retaliation had destroyed several English fortified settlements, yet had left Wells, York, and Kittery untouched. However, Phips' easy takeover of Port-Royal, and one punishing English land expedition against the Abenakis' own villages caused these natives to reconsider their attitude toward the New Englanders. Several chiefs signed a truce with the *bostonnais* and promised to talk peace with them in the near future.

The French feared the loss of their native buffer against English encroachment into Acadian territory and overland access into the Saint Lawrence River valley. King Louis XIV sent a Cape Breton squadron to counteract the English privateer blockade that followed Phips' assault on Québec, and he assigned Canadian *Sieur* de Villebon as governor of Acadia with orders to regain the loyalty of the Abenaki warriors.

Upon his arrival at Port-Royal in mid-June 1691, Villebon saw no sign of English presence but he found the town plundered, its fort, church and other buildings in ruins, and Governor Meneval still imprisoned in Boston.

The new military governor easily reclaimed possession of the area, but chose to locate his own fort across the Bay of Fundy at Jemseg, part way up Rivière Saint-Jean.

1692

Early in February, Abenaki warriors from the Penobscot and Kennebec river areas left Acadia and snow-shoed across the winter frontier toward New England. Four weeks later, they reached their destination at the village of York, attacked its residents and livestock, and left the settlement in ashes.

In mid-February, François and Anne Massé served as godparents for their half-sister Jeanne, who was born to Bastien and Catherine. Two days later, Bastien and Catherine served as godparents for Madeleine who was born to Louis and Simonne.

Pierre Guillet and his wife Madeleine joined the family as they gathered together at Bastien's house not only to welcome the two newest babies, but also to celebrate Sébastien's and Antoine's news that Pierre Robineau de Villier, seigneur de Bécancour had granted them adjoining concessions. Both of these lots were of four arpents frontage along the Saint Lawrence River, and extended to one arpent away from Lac Saint-Paul. Sébastien and his sister Marie would be next-door neighbors on the south shore.

The older members of the family smiled knowingly at each other. It had been evident for some time now that Sébastien and Catherine's daughter Anne were spending much of their free time together.

Bastien told his son: "I'll be sorry to see you leave the north shore, *mon gars*, but we all know that your crops will grow better across the river—and you'll be living close to your sisters."

François and sixteen-year old Louis Massé asked how they could help.

"I plan to stay here and work with you and Papa until I've built my house," Sébastien explained. "Maybe you could help me clear the undergrowth and cut down some of the trees this autumn, once I decide on the building site."

"I'm glad you'll be with us a while longer," Bastien remarked.

"I can certainly use your help, but we'll also help you all we can. And now that you're taking on adult responsibilities, you'll also have extra expenses, so I'll be paying you full engagé wages as long as you continue to live here and help me with the crops."

That seemed fair enough to everyone.

Antoine promised that he and his own engagé would be available to help Sébastien while they worked on the adjoining lot. He looked forward to living next door to his brother-in-law, and this greatly pleased his wife Marie.

His older brother Louis offered to help them clear the land.

Aubin proposed a toast: "To Sébastien, our new neighbor at Bécancour!"

A week later, Étienne Pépin de Lafond's widow filed a complaint in court against Aubin, charging him with failure to meet the requirements of his lease. Marie Boucher claimed that he had failed to deliver to her twelve *minots* of peas and twenty-five livres in coin for half the value of a cow that had died under his care. Based on his admission of this debt, the court ordered that he must satisfy his contractual obligations and return to the widow the livestock she had provided under their agreement.

Several days later, news reached the cape that the Mohawks had struck their first blow against Pierre Boucher's seignory at Boucherville, just a few miles downriver from Montréal. Bastien fervently hoped and prayed that his former employer and his family had survived.

British King William III had appointed Sir William Phips as governor of Massachusetts and had ordered him to build a stone fort at Pemaquid at colonial expense. On May 14, 1692, Phips arrived in Boston, with a royal charter ending the English law of 1684 that had banned self-government in the English colonies and had united them under a single royal governor.

Although frustrated in his support of the Catholic counterrevolution in Ireland in 1690, Louis XIV was heartened by the French naval victory over the English and Dutch at Beachy Head that same year. He now gathered another invasion force on the coast of Normandie and summoned his Commander of the Fleet Admiral de Tourville to Saint-Vaast-la-Hougue, where his squadron of forty-four ships was to transport the troops across the Channel.

On June 3, 1692, the Anglo-Dutch fleet sank twelve of the French ships during a heated battle in the vicinity of the Island of Tatihou, seriously diminishing French naval superiority in its war against the Grand Alliance.

Early the following month, Canadian officers led militia volunteers, Penobscot and Kennebec Abenakis to rendezvous with the Malicites and Micmacs at Pentagouet. They proceeded south with a force four-hundred strong to attack the village of Wells, killing the livestock, burning the church and a few empty houses. Fifteen armed militiamen aboard three small supply vessels arrived in time to reinforce the settlement's garrison of thirty settlers.

That summer, an English squadron recovered Fort Nelson of Hudson Bay from French control.

Soon after the autumn grain harvest, Sébastien began to clear his concession with the help of his father and brothers. They hacked away at the brush and saplings, collecting those for burning later that autumn. Then they chopped and sawed away at the lower tree branches, finally revealing to the young men just how large the older trees had grown, and how much work would be required to turn this virgin forest into tillable land. They began to appreciate what Bastien must have faced upon his arrival in Canada.

François told him: "I can't believe that you managed to cut down such giant trees by yourself."

"I didn't," Bastien reminded him. "Jacques Vaudry was also working next door to me, and we helped each other."

"Still, you had no oxen; how did you manage to move the timber?"

"At first we cut down those trees that we could easily hew to form the basic structure of the house; then we chose straight-grained timber that we could split into boards and shingles. We sawed the smaller timbers to length, peeled the bark, and hewed lumber on-site, then pulled them by two-man hand sledge to the construction area. We worked around the giants and cut those down later for firewood."

"Seems like an awful waste. There's enough wood in one of those old trees to build an entire house."

François' imagination wrestled with that possibility. "Can you picture how long it would take two men, with axe and saw, to chop one down, trim off all its branches, cut its trunk to length, and split it into boards, or shingles?"

"Guillaume Barette and I learned to chop away and cut them down that first winter while we worked for Pierre Boucher at fief Sainte-Marie," Bastien told them.

Antoine said: "I've seen how it's done in the winter forest. The foreman decides beforehand in which direction the tree must fall, then he marks the location of two opposing cuts, one above the other. You really need at least two men, facing each other across the cut mark. Starting at the lower notch, on the side the tree must fall, each man whips his axe to cut deep at an angle, causing the wood to split into an even larger chunk than the depth of the axe-cut; his second strike chops off the base of the chip. Both men work toward the middle of the trunk, then repeat other, deeper rows of cuts until they have chopped the notch past the center of the trunk.

"When the first notch is complete, they move to the opposite side of the timber, and whip their axes into the other, slightly higher, notch until it nearly reaches the center of the tree, and the timber is ready for its final swings of the axe. Everyone is warned to evacuate the forward and back areas. Only then do the foreman and his helper deliver the final cuts as they face each other from both sides of the trunk. It sometimes takes several days to bring the larger ones down."

Bastien added: "It's quite an experience to see and hear it fall— It begins with a crack and a moan, and seems to move so slowly at first, but it picks up speed, then kicks up a wind. You hear sharp snapping noises as it breaks through even the largest branches of its giant neighbors. The earth shudders under your feet when it crashes into the ground—It takes a long while for the air to clear."

"And the work of stripping it of its own branches and bark begins," Antoine continued.

"Will we get to cut these down?" asked François.

"Not for a while yet," Sébastien replied: "That can wait until later. Right now, I just need to clear enough land to plant my first crop, and collect enough straight-grained timber to hew into building lumber."

Bastien studied his face and realized that his namesake was now well-focused on his own future. He also recalled that he was Sébastien's age when he had first arrived at Québec.

Bastien and Marguerite's youngest daughter, fourteen-year old Catherine, served as godmother for Marguerite Cottenoire who was born in early October.

Three weeks later, on the south shore of the Saint Lawrence at about twenty miles downriver from Montréal, Madeleine de Verchères and her father's engagé stood on the wharf outside her father's fort, watching hopefully for the arrival of her mother from Montréal and her father from Québec.

The local settlers peacefully gathered their harvests in the fields behind them, when sounds of musket fire and cries of *"Cassee kouee!"* suddenly rose from that direction. The engagé grabbed the girl by the arm and ordered her to run to safety in the fort. They reached it together and pulled in two hysterical widows who had just seen their husbands killed in the field. They barely barred the gates before the Mohawks surrounded the palisades.

Madeleine and the engagé took stock of their defensive force: her two brothers ages twelve and ten, an eighty-year old man, several women and infant children. Two soldiers had stationed themselves in the central blockhouse, and stood ready to blow up the fort rather than allow capture by the Iroquois.

Despite her gender, she was determined to save these people and her father's property. She picked up a musket, borrowed a soldier's cap, rallied the others, and organized the defense of the fort. The women reloaded the muskets while she, the engagé, her two brothers, and the two soldiers ran from one loophole to another, firing at any warrior who dared to test the range of their guns. Madeleine ran back and forth behind the ramparts, shouting orders in a gruff voice and firing all day, and she watched throughout the night, periodically calling "All's well!" By maintaining these tactics for one full week, she apparently convincing the Iroquois that the fort was fully manned, because they did not attack.

On the seventh day, a French army Lieutenant arrived at the quay with a company of forty men and called out to the fort to identify himself. The gate opened and one of its soldiers stood guard, while fourteen-year old Madeleine de Verchères came out to meet the officer and surrender her command.

The construction of an English fort at Pemaquid greatly troubled Frontenac. As a military man, he knew that such a strategic English presence would block the movement of Abenaki war-parties along the coast and provide the New Englanders with an advanced base of operations against Acadia. He therefore placed Pierre Le Moyne d'Iberville in command of two war ships that were anchored at Québec, and ordered him to sail to Acadia with four hundred men, pick up three hundred Abenakis at Pentagouet, destroy the new fort at Pemaquid, then attack Wells, Portsmouth, and the Isles of Shoals. Following these raids, he was to clear the Acadian seas of *bostonnais* fishermen.

But the governor's orders were betrayed to the English of Massachusetts, so that when Iberville arrived at Pemaquid, he found an armed New England vessel guarding the uncompleted palisades. Having lost the element of surprise, he redirected his ships to Pentagouet, then sailed for France.

Meanwhile, Governor Phips strengthened his colonial militia, built other forts along the frontier, and successfully courted the Abenaki chiefs, thirteen of whom renounced their alliance with the French by signing a peace treaty with the English. This new threat to their frontier buffer zone further alarmed the French Acadians.

Once the leaves had fallen and the weather grew colder, Bastien, Louis, Pierre Guillet, and Antoine helped Sébastien locate his building site and mark each tree that he had to clear for construction by using their hatchets to cut crossed notches into the bark at eye-level.

Bastien taught him: "If you cut and peel off the bark in a band as wide as your hand all around the trunks of these trees, the trees won't sprout leaves next season, and it will be easier for you to cut them down right through the coming spring and summer.

Antoine offered him the use of his oxen team and sledge to

move the logs to the building site, knowing that Louis and François would continue to assist him and Antoine through the coming winter. Bastien was now fifty-eight years old.

On January 19, 1693, Bastien's and Catherine's children welcomed their common sibling, Marie-Catherine.

That April, Louis bought another property at côte Saint-Marc for 250 livres, this time from Pierre Le Boulanger who represented Jacques Massé's widow, Catherine Guillet. René Blanchet had granted Jacques a lifetime lease to this lot in 1672. The land was located between the other two lots that Louis had purchased from Pierre Guillet, and its two arpents of frontage now extended Louis' property to ten contiguous arpents along the Saint Lawrence River.

Sébastien and Antoine dug their cellars and wells at Bécancour, while Louis Massé and François collected fieldstone for the foundation walls.

Throughout that summer and fall, Pierre and Bastien guided Sébastien and his brothers in the preparation of lumber for the construction of the house. Pierre measured and marked the sills, posts, and beams for framing, while Bastien taught his sons to hew and mortise the structural timbers, to rive and split straight-grained wooden planks for walls, flooring, and shingled roof.

On the last Sunday of December, based upon the recommendation of that year's three churchwardens, Pastor Paul Vachon named Bastien to replace the outgoing *marguillier* on the parish council of Sainte-Madeleine. This was a highly respected position for an habitant, and one for which candidates were screened on the basis of their combined civil, moral, and religious performance. Bastien was overwhelmed by the community's recognition and trust.

The council consisted of the pastor, and three churchwardens who served for three years. Bastien's term would extend through 1696, during which time he would help oversee the upkeep of church, rectory, and cemetery properties. He would also escort the bishop and his party during pastoral visits, help carry the ceremonial canopy during church processions, and be seated in a place of honor during the various religious services.

On the night of January 11, 1694, Bastien, Catherine, and their older children witnessed a partial lunar eclipse in the northwestern sky; at its peak, a barely visible crescent of the moon remained visible over the cape.

The following April, Minister of Marine Pontchartrain wrote to Intendant Bégon that the king had appointed Iberville to the command of two frigates: one armed with thirty cannons, the other with twenty. He had also provided a fighting force of one hundred men, and had granted Iberville a monopoly over the Hudson Bay fur trade until 1697, to cover the expenses of his expeditions there and in Acadia. Iberville sailed from France in mid-May.

The western fur trade had greatly expanded under Governor Frontenac, as the French had built new trading posts in the Great Lakes area: at the headwaters of the Mississippi River, in Sioux and in Illinois country. The king had subsidized these as a means to provide arms and ammunition to the western allies, and while this encouraged their war of attrition against the Iroquois, three times as much beaver fur reached Montréal than was common before 1675.

Frontenac appointed Antoine de La Mothe-Cadillac to the command of the fort at Michillimackinac. The Jesuit mission of Saint-Ignace had been established at that location by Father Marquette as a haven for the Huron and Algonquin tribes in 1670. Since then, it had gradually become the center of western fur trade and a gathering place for the coureurs.

Father Carheil repeatedly protested against the free flow of liquor and the debauchery that the Jesuits attributed to the coureurs and the French soldiers who were garrisoned at the fort. He and Cadillac constantly quarreled over this issue.

In order to remove his military garrison from Father Carheil's Jesuit mission and to secure the West for France, Cadillac proposed the construction of a strongly garrisoned fort at the strait (*détroit*) between lakes Huron and Erie. He identified that location as the most vital trading link to the three upper lakes and the most direct Canadian route to the Mississippi valley. Governor Frontenac supported his reasoning.

Cadillac also proposed to establish Detroit as the new center and western limit of the western fur trade, thereby controlling the current oversupply of beaver skins. The Montréal fur merchants strongly argued against this attempt to draw native commerce away from Michillimackinac. However, the king and his Minister of Marine agreed with Cadillac and Frontenac, and authorized them to seize that key strait for France in order to block the northern movements of Iroquois warriors and traders, protect the western allies, and guard the French overland route to Louisiana.

Through the terror of those dark days of the Lachine massacre and the repeated assaults by the Iroquois against their frontier settlements near Montréal, the Canadians had finally learned that their only real defense was to counter-attack. Led by the Canadians who had once been captives of the Iroquois, the coureurs who had lived among them, and what they learned from their own native allies, the badly outnumbered French had mastered the tactics of *la petite guerre*.

They initiated their own ruthless attacks against their enemies. In the East, they led the Abenakis against the New Englanders whom they perceived to be threatening their Acadian fishing vessels and villages, and whom the Abenakis saw encroaching upon their traditional hunting grounds.

In the West, the Hurons, Illinois, Miamis, and Ottawas continued their joint retaliation after decades of Iroquois ravages, cutting their common enemy from the fur country and trade routes to Albany. They harassed the Iroquois on their own hunting grounds, raided their camps, burned their crops, and looted their trading parties. The Five Nations bore the brunt of the colonial fighting, as did the eastern Abenakis.

The French and their native allies under the command of Acadian Lieutenant Claude-Sébastien de Villieu the elder, mercilessly raided settlements at Oyster River near Portsmouth, thus breaking off the possibility of peace between the Abenakis and the English.

Twenty-seven

On the fourth Sunday of August 1694, the entire family gathered together for dinner at Bastien's house. While the women prepared the meal and the girls looked after the children and grandchildren, the men gathered outdoors and offered Sébastien lighthearted advice about his pending marriage commitment. The boys had joined them and listened to their conversation.

The bride-to-be, Anne Massé, was getting her share of counseling from the women in the family while they worked together in the kitchen area.

Now and then, Sébastien and Anne would good-naturedly shake their heads and glance at each other through the small open window.

"You're sure you want to sign that contract?" Louis asked.

"Why not? I'm just following your example, big brother."

"You couldn't do any better than marrying into that family—Ask Papa!"

Bastien looked at them, then at Catherine. "I certainly agree," he admitted.

François added, "My biggest regret is that the Massé family is running out of daughters of marriageable age!"

"We'll have to see about that!" Catherine added to everyone's surprise. "I have a niece that you might like to meet."

Twenty-year old François blushed, and everyone had a good laugh.

The tables were cleared, and the dishes washed by the time royal notary Séverin Ameau arrived with the document. Michel Rochereau, his wife Marie Bigot, and the bride's godfather, Guillaume Barette soon followed. Finally, Louis and Simonne arrived in a horse and buggy, bringing with them her grandfather, Pierre Guillet.

The family paid particular attention to Pierre's needs, for his health and strength had noticeably declined during the previous year. Catherine and Simonne had grown concerned about him, yet he had insisted on witnessing and signing this third marriage contract between the two families. Despite his physical frailties, his mind was clear, and he obviously enjoyed the family banter.

The young couple set their marks on the agreement in the presence of their family and guests. Beyond the standard commitments, Sébastien pledged Anne a widow's benefit of 300 livres, should she survive him.

The young couple did not plan to marry immediately but would continue to live and work with their parents on the north shore. In the meantime, François would help his brother develop his concession at Bécancour.

Eighteen-year old Louis Massé now worked Catherine's farm with the help of Bastien and his son Louis. Although the Mohawks continued their attacks, these three trained militiamen felt secure enough to till the fields near Louis' and Pierre Guillet's farms.

Following the October grain harvest, Bastien and Catherine warmly greeted Jeanne Renault and her son François Vaudry when they arrived for a day's visit.

"It's such a pleasure to see you both again, Jeanne. Are things going well for you and the children?" Bastien asked.

"Yes," she replied, "life is much easier now that we've moved to Ville-Marie. My older children are married, you know, and they're living nearby at Pointe-aux-Trembles. They've been very good to us; it's wonderful to have the family together again. But I must admit that it feels good to be back in this neighborhood—I see you've managed to build a larger house."

"Catherine's father helped a great deal with that."

"Is there anything we can do for you?" Catherine asked, as she served some of her herbal tea.

"First of all," Jeanne replied after accepting the cup, "I must congratulate both of you on your marriage; I feel certain that both Marguerite and your Jacques, Catherine, would have approved of merging your two families."

"We all went through a difficult time when we lost Marguerite and both your husbands to that epidemic," Bastien admitted. "Yet, in spite of the Mohawk raids, we've managed to survive the crises. It couldn't have been any easier for you, Jeanne, living so close to Montréal."

"I must thank you again, Bastien. Your full lease payments for our concession helped me pay off our remaining debts after Jacques' death."

"He would have done the same for us," he reminded her.

"Yes, I think he would have. And now François and I agree that it's time for me to reduce the terms of that lease, if you wish to continue with our arrangement."

Bastien and Catherine turned to each other and agreed that they would. They offered to walk the concession with their guests, who readily accepted the invitation. Jeanne and François obviously cherished happy memories of their life on that farm.

Jean Cusson drew up Jeanne's revision of the original lifetime contract. It now required Bastien to continue, in her name, yearly contributions of 14 livres, 8 sols to the parish of Sainte-Madeleine, but it also allowed him to keep 7 livres, 4 sols worth of the wheat due her as yearly rent. Laurent Barette and Louis Gatineau signed as witnesses to their agreement.

Two weeks later, members of the cape militia retrieved the bodies of ten local habitants from their temporary graves near the coulé-de-Jean-Grou, and moved them to the Sainte-Madeleine cemetery. Most members of the parish community attended their memorial service.

On December 28, 1694, British Queen Mary II died of smallpox at Kensington. Her husband, William III of Orange, assumed full responsibilities as King of Britain and Scotland.

1695

Early that May, Pierre Guillet died quietly in his sleep at age seventy-two. Simonne and Catherine rushed to Madeleine Delaunay's side to comfort the widow and do what they could to ease the sorrow they all shared over their loss. Bastien, Catherine, and their children were deeply saddened because Pierre had been such a vital and beloved part of their family. Catherine's brother Louis, Bastien, Antoine Cottenoire, and Adrien Barette served as pallbearers and witnesses to the burial in the parish cemetery. The church was filled with family and friends who attended the requiem Mass.

Two days after the funeral, Michel Arsonneau and his wife Madeleine Leblanc had twin boys. One was named François after Bastien's son, who served as godparent with Marguerite Rochereau. Bastien and Marguerite's youngest daughter, Catherine, and Louis Massé served as godparents for the other twin, Louis. The Leblanc, Arsonneau, and Rochereau families still remained Bastien's close friends and neighbors.

At the end of the month, news reached the cape settlements that, once again, Iberville had seized Fort Nelson from the Hudson Bay Company and renamed it Fort Bourbon.

At his father's house on the morning of June 12, 1695, Louis bought an original concession from Pierre Guillet and Jeanne de St-Per's heirs. Located at côte Saint-Marc, this lot of land was four arpents by forty deep, bordering Louis' own property and that of René Blanchet's heirs. It had no buildings but ten of its square arpents were already cleared, therefore Louis agreed to pay the estate 350 livres in four consecutive yearly payments of solid coin or wheat, due on Candlemas Day. His property at Champlain now extended fourteen arpents along the Saint Lawrence River.

Late that summer, news reached the cape that the English had recaptured Fort Bourbon, restored its English name, and seized 400,000-livres worth of French fur.

Nicolas Perrot had spent several years out west striving to counter the Iroquois and English attempts to draw the western nations away from their military and fur-trading alliances with the French. News now reached the Trois-Rivières area that Perrot had returned to Montréal with an embassy of several wavering western chiefs who wished to meet with the *Onontio*, and that Governor Frontenac had managed to strengthen their loyalty to the French in their mutual conflict with the Iroquois.

Minister Pontchartrain ordered less traffic west; Frontenac turned a deaf ear. By 1695, fur shipments to France reached four times the level of demand. Meanwhile, western allies were effectively cutting off the Iroquois from hunting and trapping furs to trade with the English of New York.

The king's military budget for the protection of Nouvelle France had almost tripled in the previous two years, yet excess expenditures over the allotted funds had amounted to 550,000 livres. The French Minister of Marine was frustrated by the results. Beaver pelts now glutted French warehouses; Canadian shipments had risen astronomically during the previous ten years. The French beaver fur monopoly had generated 500,000 livres annually to the royal treasury, and its lease would expire in 1697; however, the persistent oversupply of furs threatened future renewal of that monopoly.

The king suspected that Frontenac's expansion of western fortifications had stimulated the increase in fur trading, although it had strengthened allied support against the Iroquois. The Minister of Marine suspected that colonial officials and merchants must be profiting at the king's expense, in total disregard of his royal attempts and edicts to limit western trade activities.

On November 4th, the Québec governor wrote to the French Minister of Marine that he had ordered three officers to return to France for bad conduct. Included among them was Jacques François de Bourgchemin who had been cited in an incident of unprovoked brutality against Aubin Maudoux five years earlier. Bourgchemin was now accused of having attempted to poison his wife while conducting an illicit affair with another woman. Both this officer of the Marine and his mistress had disappeared before he could be expelled from Canada.

That following month, fifteen-year old Marie-Catherine Massé signed a marriage contract with Pierre Petit dit l'Homme of Bécancour.

Nouvelle France now claimed 12,786 habitants, less than one-tenth of the English colonial population.

Late in February 1696, François Maudoux was born to Madeleine and Aubin; François Rochereau and Madeleine's sister Marie served as godparents to the child.

By early spring, French commanders of the forts at Michillimackinac, the Miamis, Saint-Louis-des-Illinois, and Nicolas Perrot who constantly visited the tribes of the Mississippi, all complained that French-native alliances continued to be threatened by Iroquois efforts to establish themselves as middlemen between the western tribes and the English of Albany. Some of these native allies were located as much as 2,000 miles from Montréal. Frontenac wrote to the Minister of Marine that if the Hurons and Algonquins succumbed to this Iroquois campaign, the colony would be entirely ruined because the French could never offer trade goods as cheaply as could the English.

The Sunday following Easter, civil announcements declared that Governor-General Frontenac would rebuild the fort at Cataracoui which Denonville had ordered to be destroyed seven years earlier. The reading further announced that the governor would call up militia groups, recruit native allies, and muster whatever regular troops he could spare from the defense of Montréal, to march against the central Iroquois capital of Onondaga.

Bastien and Catherine recoiled upon hearing the announcements. Neither one of them looked forward to seeing a son or son-in-law go off on another government expedition into the center of the Iroquois homeland.

"Do they have any choice?" she asked him.

He shrugged his shoulders. At age sixty-two, he had come to realize that his sons had grown into manhood; he knew that they could best determine for themselves how they should respond to this call.

Many young Canadians were eager for such an adventure; François and Louis Massé looked forward to it. Sébastien, Louis, and Antoine knew how difficult the expedition would be but felt a sense of duty to comply and a responsibility to watch over the untested younger recruits. At age fifty-two, Aubin would stay behind and help Bastien tend the fields and livestock.

The women resolutely began to prepare special provisions for the long voyage.

On July 4, 1696, Frontenac left Montréal with an army of twenty-two hundred men. During the following two weeks, they headed up the Saint Lawrence River, portaged past its challenging series of rapids and waterfalls, reached the quiet part of the upper river, and filed past the Thousand Islands to finally arrive at Cataracoui where Frontenac inspected his partially reconstructed fort.

The French forces started across Lake Ontario, where a fleet of native canoes led the way, followed by another fleet of bateaux filled with two battalions of regulars under Governor Callières' command, and then other bateaux manned by the military, carrying cannon, mortars, and rockets. Frontenac himself was surrounded by canoes carrying his personal staff. Eight hundred Canadians, including the cape militia, followed them under the command of a Canadian officer. The final contingent consisted of more regulars and more natives under Vaudreuil's leadership. They reached the south shore three weeks later.

In another two-days time, they arrived at the Oswego river mouth, and Frontenac sent advance scouts ahead through the forest while the army made its way upriver. The soldiers and the Canadians entered the water along the riverbank, mostly pushing and pulling the bateaux and canoes against a swift current.

Two more days of travel beyond this stage, they reached the falls, where the Canadians and their native allies once again emptied the canoes of supplies and equipment, and portaged their provisions and canoes, while gangs of soldiers pulled the loaded bateaux on rollers up the narrow footpath. They worked at this eighteen hours a day, while the natives chanted and carried Frontenac seated in a canoe held upon their shoulders.

They followed a narrow stream and made their way through a dense forest to Lake Onondaga, where Frontenac ordered that all four hundred canoes and bateaux set sail for the crossing. Bastien's sons were greatly impressed by this sight. On August 3rd, the French forces landed a little over a mile away from Salina.

The next day, they built palisades to protect their river craft, extra provisions, and line of retreat. That evening, the sky ahead of them lit up with a reddish glow, and Frontenac raged in frustration. His officers and native allies muttered among themselves, while the troops and militiamen breathed a sigh of relief. The Iroquois had obviously burned their capital village and had once more fled from a superior force to fight another day, as they had during Marquis de Tracy's and Governor Denonville's campaigns.

Governor Frontenac assigned an officer and men to guard the fort, then at sunrise of the following day, Adjutant General Subercase led the French forces forward in a two-line battle formation. Callières commanded the first line with his regulars flanking the Canadians. Following close behind them, the natives now carried seventy-four-year old Frontenac in an armchair; his staff and guards again remained close by his side. Callières, who suffered from gout, sat mounted on the only horse brought along for this expedition, and directed the forward movement of the artillery which teams of Canadians struggled to move forward through nine miles of difficult terrain.

They reached Onondaga just before sunset and found that the entire village had been torched. Its ashes remained encircled by extensive, ripening corn fields which radiated in all directions. Its clearing lay deserted except for the bodies of two badly mutilated French captives.

Just as Frontenac had expected, Onondaga's English-built defenses would have been useless against French cannon and mortars. In spite of reinforcements from all five of the Iroquois nations, the Onondaga defense force would have been greatly outnumbered by the invading French, and so they had retreated into the forest.

Frontenac ordered that scouts be sent out, guards assigned, and that the troops set up camp in the cornfields.

The French spent two days cutting down the unripe corn, digging up and burning all of the food storage. These were tasks that neither the allies nor the habitant militiamen particularly enjoyed.

An Oneida emissary arrived and begged for peace, but since he refused Frontenac's terms, Vaudreuil led seven hundred men to his people's villages, burned their cabins and food caches, and took several Oneida chiefs hostage.

The English of New York could not protect their allies against such an attack—England was as reluctant as France to send troops to defend its North American colonies. However, the colonists sent corn to the Onondagas and Oneidas which carried them through the winter.

After the cape militiamen returned home in late August 1696, François served as godfather to newborn François Cottenoire.

Sébastien married Anne Massé that autumn, thus officially forming a third marital bond between the two families. With the family's help, they moved into their new home at Bécancour.

Upon his arrival at Québec, Governor Frontenac received a letter from Louis XIV ordering him to cancel all licenses for the western fur trade, to abandon and destroy all western trading posts and forts, and to order all Frenchmen back to the settlements along the Saint Lawrence River. Furthermore, the king warned that any disobedience would lead to a sentence of service on his Mediterranean galleys. The Jesuits were to be exempt from this order so that they could continue their missionary work, but they were forbidden to conduct any trading with the natives. The king further directed the governor to make peace with the Iroquois, even if it meant abandoning the western allies, a French consideration that had imperiled the colony under Denonville.

Frontenac delayed implementation of the royal decree, knowing only too well that if he closed those western forts and trading posts, Nouvelle France would surrender its chief means of influence, and its carefully constructed Algonquin alliance would fall apart.

The governor would have accepted the peace overtures made by the Five Nations in 1696, but unfortunately, after years of warfare that had destroyed half of the Iroquois fighting force, the western allies were not ready to make peace. They insisted on the return of their fellow tribal warriors and relatives who had been captured and adopted by the Iroquois to replace their own loss of manpower.

Governor Callières of Montréal did not trust the peace embassies. He suspected that the Five Nations intended to lull the French into inaction, which would allow them time to strengthen their forces and resume their efforts to negotiate their role as middleman with the western tribes.

When Sunday civil announcements finally reported that all trading licenses had been revoked by the king, an impoverished Nicolas Perrot returned to his family at Bécancour, to work as an interpreter and serve in the local militia, following forty years of negotiating alliances with the western nations. During the last half of the seventeenth century, his efforts had protected the colony and had permitted the expansion of French exploration deeper into the mid-continent, but the value of Perrot's service had never been recognized nor rewarded by the many government officials who had benefited from it.

News reached Québec that Iberville and Simon-Pierre Denys de Bonaventure had encountered and overpowered the British frigate *Newport* in the vicinity of Rivière Saint-Jean in Acadia. Then they had sailed for Pentagouet to join with Acadian Governor Villebon, Saint-Castin, their soldiers and Abenakis who led them by sea to the English fort at Pemaquid.

In mid-August, following a barrage of French cannon and mortar, they had seized and destroyed the fort, captured and protected the Massachusetts commander, his men and their families with the promise that they would be exchanged in Boston for French and allied prisoners.

Iberville had returned the Acadians and Abenakis to Pentagouet, delivered the English captives to Québec, replenished his supplies, then sailed with his own men to Plaisance, Newfoundland.

Early that November, Catherine Massé and Pierre Petit had a son, Pierre, whose godparents were Pierre Robineau, baron de Bécancour and his wife Marie-Charlotte Le Gardeur de Villiers.

PEACE TREATIES

Twenty-eight

1697

That winter, Captain Pierre Le Moyne d'Iberville left Plaisance, Newfoundland with one hundred twenty-five soldiers, Canadians, Norman privateers, and a few Abenakis to march across difficult terrain toward the chief English post of Saint John. They captured and burned Saint John, then pillaged and destroyed English fishing posts for 300 miles along the eastern Avalon peninsula. Iberville then returned to Plaisance harbor to prepare a naval attack against the remaining English settlements at Bonavista and the Island of Carbonnière.

In early March, Madeleine was empowered by procuration to sell a second concession at Bécancour that she and Aubin had held title to since late December 1680. This lot of three arpents frontage was located between Antoine Cottenoire's and non-occupied lands. Although Antoine had paid 150 livres for his neighboring lot of two arpents frontage in January 1680, Gabriel Lefebvre of Batiscan would pay 55 livres for Maudoux' land. Three fur merchants witnessed the agreement.

On May 19, 1697, Joseph Le Moyne de Serigny, younger brother of Pierre Le Moyne d'Iberville, arrived at Plaisance with five ships of war: *Pelican, Palmier, Wesp, Profond,* and *Violent.* He carried orders from the French Minister of Marine that he and Iberville were to proceed to Hudson Bay and retake Fort Nelson from the English. This fort protected York Factory, Hudson Bay Company's most lucrative trading post which was located at the outlet of Rivière Sainte-Thérèse (Hayes River). Iberville and Serigny estimated that the palisaded English fort could not withstand cannon fire.

Late that spring, Bastien and Guillaume Barette spent some time together after Sunday Mass.

"Do you remember, Bastien, how disappointed I was that I couldn't visit my brother Jean when we first arrived at Québec?"

"Wasn't he living at Beaupré at that time?"

His friend nodded. "Near Québec, but we were already preparing to leave for Sainte-Marie. Merchant Péré wrote a letter to him in my name, telling him that I had safely reached Nouvelle France and was sorry that I couldn't visit with him."

"Did you two ever get together?"

"We never could until now. My sons Jean and Adrien have offered to take me on pilgrimage to Sainte-Anne-de-Beaupré so that I can reunite with him. I expect he'll enjoy meeting his namesake, and both boys look forward to meeting their uncle."

"He's older than you, isn't he?"

"By a few years—It's time for us to see each other again, don't you think?"

Bastien chuckled. "That's quite a trip by canoe for an old man like you."

"We'll be traveling by *chaloupe*."

"I'm very happy for you, Guillaume. I sent my last letter to my sister and brothers before Madeleine was born; she's now the mother of four children, and I never received a reply. I can only hope my letter reached them. I often wonder if they're still in Pithiviers."

"Why don't you have Louis write to their pastor and find out what's happened since then? I imagine life has been harder for them than it's been for us, don't you?"

"Judging from how much war they've suffered through, I believe so. Yet they've never faced an enemy like the Mohawk."

Louis welcomed the opportunity to write to his relatives in France. "How would it reach them? And would they be able to read it?" he asked.

"There were no problems with that when I first arrived, but I don't know if it still works the same way. Merchants wrote for me and delivered the letters to France by way of their ships; the Jesuits delivered mail packets to and from France through their own couriers who sailed out on the last ship to leave Québec in the autumn, and returned on the first to arrive in the spring. They all appreciated my need to keep in touch with your mother while she waited to come and join me in Canada. Our messages to each other were all sent through the pastor at Pithiviers."

"I can ask Le Boulanger if he can deliver a letter to France for us, but how can we be sure that it will reach them?"

"I don't know, Louis. Things have changed so much here and in France since then—so much war."

Louis was disappointed. He had never known his father to be indecisive, yet he obviously found it difficult to make up his mind about this.

Bastien considered how much he dared to share with his brothers, and how much they could openly share with him about their own living conditions. Such letters would necessarily pass through many hands and would ultimately be read by a non-family member. Under such circumstances, the exchange of family news would be guarded and incomplete.

Finally, he decided: "It's best for all of us to remember each other as we were when I left home."

That spring, Marquis de Nesmond sailed for Newfoundland with a powerful squadron of fifteen ships of the French royal navy and orders from the king to neutralize an English squadron that threatened French fishermen and shipping. Once it had accomplished this task, his fleet was directed to sail to Pentagouet where it would pick up Abenaki warriors, twelve hundred French troops and three hundred Canadians arriving overland from Québec. These combined forces were to capture Boston and march on to Salem and Portsmouth, looting and destroying all settlements along the way, while the fleet followed along the coast to offer support.

When seventy-five-year old Governor Frontenac learned about this pending campaign, he immediately and enthusiastically planned the logistics, collected the men, canoes and supplies for the overland trek to Pentagouet. In spite of his age, he stood ready to lead French land forces against Boston.

In early June, Louis helped his father negotiate for permission to replace his own church pew. Bastien agreed to pay yearly rent on this allotted space during his and Catherine's lifetimes, with the understanding that his right of rental would be inherited by his children. The contract stated that the pew could be removed to permit winter burials in the church subterranean morgue and facilitate spring transfer to the parish cemetery; the family of the deceased would be held responsible for moving and restoration expenses. Bastien had originally acquired the lease to this space in 1689, and his original rental fee extended into the new contract.

The two Le Moyne brothers sailed from Plaisance early in July, Iberville in command of the *Pelican* and Serigny in charge of the *Palmier*; the three other ships of their squadron followed close behind. Plagued by unfavorable sailing conditions, they finally entered the waters of Hudson Bay on September 4th and became surrounded by fog and masses of floating ice. The ship carrying their provisions was crushed and sank. Iberville lost sight of the other three vessels while he maneuvered to free the *Pelican* and make for open sea. Once freed, he steered toward Fort Nelson where he hoped to meet up with his squadron; his destination was now several hundred miles away, on the western shore of that inland sea.

When he arrived within sight of the fort, three larger English vessels forced him to engage in battle, pitting their one hundred twenty cannons against his forty-four. Their mutual exchange of fire lasted over three hours. Iberville held to the wind, managed to sink the English command ship *Hampshire* and capture the *Hudson Bay,* while the *Daring* sailed away. His own ship had suffered damage to its hull, masts, and rigging; gale winds from the east threatened to drive him against the rocky shore. His anchor cable parted, and he was stranded five miles from the fort. A short while later, the *Pelican* and the *Hudson Bay* both sank near the mouth of Rivière Sainte-Thérèse.

Although most of his crew reached land with arms and ammunition, early northern winter conditions caused several members to die from exposure before they could build huts and fires to warm and dry themselves. They had no food, and their situation was critical until their other three ships arrived with vital provisions, men, cannon, and mortars to provide for the assault against the English fort. Following five days of fighting, English Commander Henry Baley surrendered on honorable terms.

Fort Nelson was once again renamed Fort Bourbon, and by now, Iberville, whom the English called the "Canadian El Cid", had seized all of the Hudson Bay Company stations except Fort Albany; it was too late in the year to make that attempt. He left his brother Serigny in command of Hudson Bay and sailed away in late September.

Frontenac never received word from the Marquis de Nesmond until September, when he was informed that the fleet had suffered a long delay because of strong headwinds, that food provisions had run out, and it was then too late in the year to carry out their planned campaign against Massachusetts.

Meanwhile, Saint-Castin's Abenakis had been idle all summer at the mouth of the Penobscot while they waited to rendezvous with sea and land forces from Québec. Other Abenakis prowled the entire frontier, from the Kennebec to the Connecticut rivers, but the English settlers fended off their attacks at Kittery, Wells and York.

Later that September, Sébastien and Anne invited Bastien and Catherine to serve as godparents for their first child, whom they named Joseph.

On September 30, 1697, Louis XIV signed the Treaty of Ryswick, thereby ending King William's War and initiating peace between France and the Grand Alliance of England, Spain, and the Netherlands. France gave up most of the continental conquests King Louis had gained since 1679; he was also forced to grant trading concessions to the Dutch in the French West Indies and acknowledge William of Orange as king of Great Britain, and his Protestant sister-in-law, Anne, as his successor.

Meanwhile, the colonial war continued, since Québec had not received official news of the treaty from France before winter set in. Nouvelle France remained unaware that the Treaty of Ryswick restored all colonial possessions to their prewar status.

At the end of December, François, and Marie-Joseph Le Boulanger served as godparents for Joseph, who was born to Louis and Simonne.

1698

That February, a Dutch and Iroquois embassy arrived at Montréal to announce that England and France had signed a European peace treaty. Frontenac could not act upon the news until he received official notice.

In mid-April, a third daughter was born to Bastien and Catherine. Marie-Madeleine shared her oldest sister and godmother's name, and Louis Massé represented her mother's side of the family.

At the end of May, a second embassy of English officers and government officials from Albany reached Québec with a French copy of the Ryswick treaty. They also brought all the French prisoners they had held in New York and offered to exchange them for all the English held in captivity by the French. Most of the English prisoners chose to remain in Nouvelle France.

The ambassadors also carried a letter from Richard Coote Count of Bellomont, newly installed governor of New York, New Jersey, New Hampshire and Massachusetts, by which he informed Frontenac that he would personally handle the transfer of prisoners between the French and the Iroquois.

Frontenac replied that the Iroquois were rebellious subjects of the French king, that they had already changed their attitudes and had begged him for peace. He informed the English governor that he would continue to personally and directly negotiate the exchange of their prisoners with the Iroquois as a condition of peace. In spite of the recent European treaty, the next official letters between the two governors threatened the use of force to settle the issue.

The French copy of the document revealed to Frontenac that the agreement canceled all gains made by both the French and English colonies in North America: the English regained Newfoundland; France recovered Acadia. He realized that the Acadians and Newfoundlanders must already know of this, since the English had no doubt arrived to cede Acadia and take possession of Newfoundland before their winter set in. The territorial dispute over Hudson Bay had been submitted to a board of commissioners while the British company retained control over Fort Albany at James Bay, and the French continued to hold the rest of the forts.

The Ryswick agreement also arbitrarily placed the Iroquois League under the protection of Britain, and this explained why Bellomont insisted on acting as intermediary between the French governor and the chiefs of the Five Nations during any negotiations between the two parties. This news would have reached New England and New York by November because of their year round ports. Frontenac knew that the fiercely independent Iroquois would resent this part of the treaty; he doubted that they would have been consulted.

The Five Nations considered their options at great length and resumed peace negotiations with Nouvelle France during which they continued to insist that any agreement must exclude the western allied nations.

The governor already knew that the English had officially estimated the strength of the Iroquois confederacy to be at 2550 warriors when the Lachine massacre occurred in 1689; that estimate had since declined to 1239. The Five Nations had greatly suffered during the colonial war. Frontenac was ready to make peace with them but refused to abandon the western allies who had so successfully kept the enemy in check.

In June, Jeanne de Saint-Per's heirs acknowledged receipt of final payment for the land concession that Louis had purchased from their estate.

The following month, Frontenac received official notification of the Treaty of Ryswick from Versailles, and a message from Louis XIV to the people of Canada, dated March 12, 1698. The governor and the bishop of Québec jointly relayed the king's call for all parishes to hold a Te Deum service in thanksgiving for peace in Europe and in North America.

The peace of Ryswick was discussed and fêted throughout Nouvelle France.

At Bastien's home, Louis declared: "This calls for something very special!"

His announcement took Bastien by surprise.

"How long has it been since you enjoyed a bit of calvados?" Louis asked.

His father's eyes brightened. "That would be very special..."

"How long has it been?"

"I served the last to René le Cordier—shortly before he died."

Louis pulled a bottle from behind his back and said: "Papa, there's enough here for everyone!"

His older sons and daughters applauded, remembering how Bastien and Marguerite had rationed the Norman apple brandy that Pierre Boucher had given them as a wedding present.

"I must share this with all of you on this day," Bastien declared.

"You must keep this for yourself, Papa," Madeleine protested.

"You can all share this one," Louis told her with a wink. "I have another that he can keep for 'medicinal purposes'."

They had set up temporary tables outdoors on this bright midsummer day. Bastien and Catherine's older daughters prepared and spread out the food, allowing the grandparents to relax and enjoy their combined brood of fifteen children and thirteen grandchildren. The oldest child was Bastien and Marguerite's Madeleine who expected another baby in the very near future; the youngest was Bastien and Catherine's Marie-Madeleine, three months old. The oldest grandchild was Madeleine and Aubin's Marie, at nineteen; the youngest was Louis and Simonne's Joseph who was on the verge of taking his first step, which he did to everyone's surprise and delight on that beautiful July afternoon.

Louis had brought Pierre's widow, Madeleine Delaunay, and she, in turn, had invited another granddaughter, Marguerite Moreau, to accompany her. It soon became obvious to everyone that this was the niece that Catherine had in mind for François.

Catherine Maudoux was born the following mid-September and was named after her godmother, Bastien and Marguerite's youngest daughter Catherine, who was now twenty years old.

As ice began to form on the river, civil announcements reported that Governor Frontenac was seriously ill. He died in his sleep on Friday, November 28, 1698 and was quietly buried in the Franciscan church at Québec.

Louis-Hector chevalier de Callières, lieutenant-governor at Montréal, automatically became acting governor-general at Québec and would serve in that capacity until the king officially appointed a replacement for Frontenac. Philippe de Rigaud de Vaudreuil then succeeded Callières as lieutenant-governor at Montréal. The two military leaders actively lobbied for the governor-generalship by sending their own representatives to Versailles.

François bought a lot of land from Guillaume Cartier at Bécancour in mid-December. Since Cartier could not attend this signing because of his duties as miller at Montréal, he had granted a procuration for his wife Marie to sign in his stead. The lot of land was of three arpents frontage, extending to one arpent away from Lac Saint-Paul. François agreed to pay 150 livres, 71 of which he drew from his savings and paid at the signing. He borrowed a second payment of 49 livres from his brother Louis and delivered it two days later. Jean Cusson notarized the contract; Jean Joliet signed as witness to the agreement.

1699

That January, François served as godfather for Marguerite, daughter of Sébastien and Anne Massé. She was named after her godmother Marguerite, her father's older sister, who remained close to her brothers now that they both owned land on the south shore.

Madeleine Delaunay died early that February, and Catherine now became part of the oldest generation as had Bastien so many years ago.

Louis XIV had learned that Spain and England were maneuvering to lay claim to the Gulf of Mexico and the Mississippi River. Early the following month, Iberville and his brother Bienville cast anchor in the Gulf of Mexico in an imperial race to carry out La Salle's dream of planting a French colony in Louisiana. Two weeks later, they explored and sounded their way westward along the present coasts of Alabama and Mississippi in search of the Mississippi River delta.

On March 2nd, their boats were caught up in a strong current of fresh muddy river water. Over the next eleven days, they ascended this river to a village of the Bayagoula tribe and met a chief who wore a blue cloak of French design. He proudly claimed that Henri de Tonti had given it to him.

Further on, Bienville traded a hatchet for a letter from Tonti to Cavalier de La Salle dated April 20, 1686, proving that this river was indeed the Mississippi. Tonti had been searching for La Salle in order to fulfill their proposed rendezvous by land and sea. La Salle had failed to find the river's outlet into the Gulf of Mexico, had lost his way, and had been killed by mutineers within his own party.

The Le Moyne brothers returned to their ships through Bayou Ascantia and two lakes, which Iberville named Maurepas and Pontchartrain.

On May 1st, Iberville completed the construction of Fort Maurepas, a temporary stockade fort on the northeast side of the Bay of Biloxi, thereby founding the first European settlement in Louisiana near what is now Ocean Springs. He left his brother Bienville, another officer, and a garrison of eighty men in charge of the infant colony, with the intention of maintaining a French presence in the area. Three days later, he sailed for France with the *Badine* and the *Marin*.

Meanwhile, on March 3rd, François had made his final payment of 30 livres to Guillaume Cartier, who personally ratified and signed the purchase agreement for the lot at Bécancour. He was still unmarried and although he had continued to help his brother Sébastien on his farm at Bécancour since 1692, he still lived and worked with his father. Both brothers now owned their own land directly across the river from Bastien's original concession.

The following month, Louis XIV officially appointed Chevalier de Callières as governor-general of Canada, Acadia, Newfoundland, and other lands of North America. He also officially appointed Vaudreuil lieutenant-general at Montréal.

Civil announcements reported one hundred deaths in Nouvelle France due to a smallpox epidemic.

On October 27th, Bastien and Catherine were declared debt-free after eight years of marriage.

Twenty-nine

1700

Louis and Simonne celebrated the birth of their second daughter, Marie-Angélique, on February19th.

The region of Trois Rivières suffered a prolonged lack of snow and rain from late winter through spring, so that when Bastien attempted to till the soil late that May, he found the fields and forest to be even drier than during the summer of 1663, and he realized that the family must resort to special measures to nurture their crops.

Food reserves had been low even before the drought had struck the region. At least half of the habitants throughout Nouvelle France had spent at least one year in the fur trade, leaving their land fallow while they were away. Many of the habitants had already abandoned their farms at the cape in search of less sandy, more virgin soil on the south shore.

In addition to all Sundays when labor was forbidden by the Church, there were thirty-seven holy days of obligation when church attendance was compulsory and work was not permitted; thirteen of these occurred during the agricultural season.

Bastien called the family together to offer warning. "Catherine and I remember the summer following the great earthquake, when many farmers lost their entire corn and wheat crop. It was impossible to hunt for meat in the forest because so many of its trees had fallen and barred the way. Fires burned over several

leagues around us, and the animals disappeared from the forest
because there was no food or shelter for them. The earthquake
clouded the waters of the Saint Lawence, so that the fish did not
return until late August. The soil is even drier now."

His son Louis asked: "How did you manage?"

"Jacques Vaudry and I got together and hauled containers of
river water up the sandy bluff with cable rope, pulley, and rope
cradle."

"How did you anchor the pulley?" Antoine asked.

"To the old tree that still stands on the edge of the bluff, near
Leblanc's property. I believe it's still strong enough to carry the
weight. Our oxen helped to pull up the load, but even so, we found
that the barrels were too heavy and awkward to handle; I would
prefer to fill kegs with river water."

Catherine was fascinated by the project. "And how did you
water the fields?" she asked.

"We scraped and dug shallow canals into which we poured the
water. Marguerite dug them with mattock and hoe in the
vegetable garden."

Catherine could picture her friend doing that. Marguerite had
always been so industrious. She herself was seven years old and
living at Québec at the time; now she vividly recalled the
earthquake and its repeating tremors, the cloudy Saint Lawrence
River, the forest fires, and the drought. It had been a fearful
time for her parents.

"I'm sure that the girls and Jean-Baptiste can help you dig the
canals," she offered.

Her son Louis volunteered: "And of course, I'll handle the kegs
for you if you'll direct the oxen."

"I can help both of you," François added.

"And what about you people on the south shore?" the older
Louis asked.

Antoine, Aubin, Sébastien, François, and Pierre Petit agreed
that the soil was in better shape at Bécancour, but that they
would have to watch it carefully.

"This may also affect our livestock," Bastien warned.

His son Louis agreed and considered the winter feed required
by his horse and sheep. The horse alone would require three
hundred bales of hay and twenty-five *minots* of oats.

Bastien continued: "My soil is no longer as fertile as it was when I planted my first crops. Perhaps it's time for me to follow my own papa's example and allow two years of rest for each arpent, rotating different fields each year, so that the soil will have time to recover."

"That's twice as long as we do now!" François reminded him.

"*Oui, mon gars,* and that's what I plan to do with one third of my fields, starting this summer."

Antoine, who had also spent his youth on a farm in France, added: "It might also be wise to sow a *méteil* of wheat and rye, to guarantee enough grain for our own bread."

"What's a *méteil*?" Louis Massé asked.

Aubin explained: "You sow a mixture of two different types of grain seed and hope that either or both will survive the poor soil conditions."

Bastien added: "Wheat and rye—good idea, Antoine!"

Civil announcements reported that on July 18, 1700, an embassy of two Onondaga and four Seneca representatives had arrived at Montréal seeking peace negotiations on behalf of their nations and those of the Cayugas and Oneidas. Mohawk representation was noticeably absent. On the condition that they all return no later than that following September, trusted Jesuit missionary Bruyas, Paul Le Moyne de Maricourt, and French officer Joncaire traveled back with the Iroquois envoys who offered to release their French captives. If this first step in prisoner exchange proved successful, Governor Callières promised to free the Iroquois prisoners held by the French.

In August, another announcement revealed that the first official round of peace negotiations had begun at Montréal. The following month, the French held a second round of talks with nineteen Iroquois chiefs, and representatives from many non-Iroquois tribes. Thirteen French prisoners had been released; others were still captive, as were many from among the French native allies. Callières insisted that they must all be returned by early August of the following year, in exchange for the French release of the rest of their Iroquois prisoners. He informed the ambassadors that in case of disagreement between any two native tribes, the French and English governors would mediate because they were both bound by their kings to maintain peace.

Huron chief Kondiaronk spoke eloquently that his and all upper nations were at peace with each other and with the French, that the Iroquois should do the same, that all native nations suffered because of war. The three parties reached a temporary accord and scheduled another round of talks for August 1701.

The habitants grew more hopeful about the possibility of achieving a lasting peace with the Five Nations.

Crop failures occurred during both summer and autumn harvests, causing extreme poverty in some areas, signaling the possibility of an upcoming winter famine in the area of Trois-Rivières. Family members with younger fields and minimal surpluses shared them with Bastien and Catherine to help feed their siblings who still lived at home.

The farmers concentrated on catching and processing eels and sturgeon, and hunting geese, ducks, and passenger pigeons during their seasonal migrations. Bastien was forced to slaughter some of his livestock for lack of feed grain, hay, and straw. That winter was very hard; forest animals also suffered from lack of food.

The Ursulines at Trois-Rivières reported that some farmers resorted to eating wild roots which led to malnutrition and starvation. Urban people of all income levels suffered most of all because so little food surplus could be traded to the stores.

Officials estimated the population of Nouvelle France at 15,000, with approximately 2,000 residing at Québec.

The General Court of Massachusetts passed an act stating that any Catholic priest caught within their territory would be thrown into prison for life. It was generally believed by the Puritans of that province that French Jesuit missionaries who lived among the Abenaki tribes had incited their converts against the English settlers during the first French and Indian war.

Another smallpox epidemic surged through Nouvelle France that winter of 1700–01, causing additional suffering and death. Cape settlers stayed close to home.

Although the Treaty of Ryswick had brought peace to Nouvelle France, it caused new problems in regards to its fur trade. The king's proclamation to curtail trading in the Great Lakes area had finally been put into effect, closing western forts and trading posts for lack of French trading goods. Although this eased the glut of beaver fur in French warehouses, and ended Jesuit protests against the destructive influence of these posts on native societies, it also weakened French claims over the Great Lakes area and western territories.

At the end of May, shortly after the first ship's arrival at Québec, civil announcements reported that childless and ailing Charles II of Spain had named Louis XIV's grandson Philip, duke of Anjou, as heir to his throne that previous October. The Spanish king had died the following month, and the duke of Anjou had been crowned King Philip V of Spain. His succession was immediately challenged by the Holy Roman Emperor and by the Prince of Bavaria. England and Holland viewed his coronation as tilting the European balance of power in favor of Catholic France.

It was also announced that Governor-General Callières had granted permission to Antoine Cadillac to build a French colony at the *détroit* (strait) linking lakes Erie and Huron, which would strategically guard the passage between the lower and upper Great Lakes. Cadillac had convinced the king's chief minister, Count Pontchartrain, that a permanent community at present-day Detroit would strengthen French control over the upper Great Lakes and block English advances. Minister Pontchartrain had allowed the governor to make the final decision. Callières had hesitated to do so for some time.

Intendant Champigny had argued that even if Cadillac could group all the western tribes in one place, ancient rivalries would soon work against their living together in peace for any extended period of time. The governor feared that the proposed colony, built so close to the Iroquois hunting grounds, would either renew their war against the French, or lure the western tribes toward trade with the Iroquois and English. The merchants of Montréal recognized the strategic value of the Detroit location and realized that whoever controlled it would become master of all the western fur trade.

Because of this intense opposition, Cadillac had returned to France to plead his case again before Pontchartrain who had accepted his arguments. Callières therefore acquiesced.

On July 24, 1701, Antoine de la Mothe Cadillac, a forty-three-year old French army officer, selected a site and began to establish a French settlement on the western edge of the narrow waterway between Lac Sainte-Claire and Lake Erie. The hundred soldiers and workers who accompanied Cadillac built a two hundred-square-foot palisade and garrison which he named Fort Pontchartrain. They also constructed a church, attracted colonists, parceled out land, and gathered the Huron and Algonquin nations from the west and from along the Mississippi River and its tributaries. Cadillac had proposed to civilize these natives by promoting their intermarriage with the French. His wife Marie-Thérèse moved to Detroit and became one of the first white women to settle in the Michigan wilderness.

Meanwhile, the French merchants of Montréal strengthened Fort Michillimackinac in an attempt to preserve their share of the fur trade.

Toward the middle of July, as Bastien and the boys were hauling water kegs up the sandy bluff, they noticed a marked increase in the number of native canoes heading up the Saint Lawrence River toward Montréal. Louis arrived by horse and buggy, and told them the news that a great assembly of tribal chiefs was gathering there to work out a final peace agreement between the Iroquois, Nouvelle France and its native allies. Soon after his arrival, Antoine and Aubin joined them from Bécancour with news that the governor had summoned Nicolas Perrot to serve as lead interpreter during the negotiations.

Louis told them: "If Monsieur Perrot is to participate, they must be very close to an agreement!"

"These canoes must be carrying the Abenaki, Montagnais, and converts from the north and east," Antoine observed. "Just think of how many more will arrive from the Iroquois and western nations!"

Bastien added: "This has to be even more important than Marquis de Tracy's treaty with the Iroquois, following his summer campaign!"

All of them wanted to witness these events. They agreed to travel together in Antoine's canoe, then went home to announce their plan to their wives and prepare for a week's camping trip. Antoine and Aubin promised to return two days later to pick up Bastien and Louis.

As soon as they reached Montréal, Bastien and his son walked into town in search of Jean Cusson's office. The settlement had grown tremendously during Frontenac's and Callières' governorships; most of the furs that had flooded into France had passed through these warehouses. Merchants, traders, coureurs, and their families had built homes and shops in the port area, and new home sites had spread out beyond the confines of the existing fort.

Cusson was happy to see them. "I thought I might see you here, Louis; I'm glad you brought your papa along!"

"Don't flatter him, Jean; I can still hold my own," Bastien quipped back.

"I must tell you that I can't wait to get back to the slower pace at Cap-de-la-Madeleine!"

"But it's so much more exciting here! This is quite a gathering!" Louis remarked. "How many do you expect will attend?"

"I've heard several numbers, but the most common estimate is about thirteen hundred tribal delegates, and close to forty major chiefs."

Bastien and Louis looked out onto the streets and saw natives dressed and groomed in contrasting aboriginal styles. Louis could identify some from his trips out west for Nicolas Perrot, but certainly not all of them. He recognized some of the Algonquin dialects and was surprised that he could still match them with the appearance of the individual native groups. He saw no one that he knew.

They talked with their friend for awhile. Cusson offered them shelter in his temporary home.

"That's very kind of you, Jean," Bastien replied, "but we're not alone. We came with my sons-in-law Antoine and Aubin, and we must return to them before we lose our way in this crowd. It's good to see you again, and I hope to see you back at the cape before too long."

They made their way through the crowded streets and back to the riverbank where they had set up their campsite a short distance away from town. Nearby was a large, oval prairie that seemed to attract a great number of Canadian and Algonquin travelers. Quite by chance, Louis spotted and recognized Red Dawn's son and grandsons.

They were all happy to see each other again. Bastien deferred to Louis who carried on and translated their conversation. They both learned that Red Dawn had died the previous winter during the smallpox epidemic, but that the rest of the family had managed to avoid the sickness. The chief had chosen to segregate himself from them during his illness, and they had respected his wishes.

On the morning of August 2, 1701, the great Huron chief Kondiaronk delivered his final oration. Although he had once misled the Iroquois into believing that Denonville had betrayed their chiefs by ordering their ambush at La Famine, Kondiaronk had since atoned for his misdeed, embraced Christianity, and gained the respect of the French by his positive influence over the other allied tribes. Everyone could see that he was suffering from a high fever that morning. Nevertheless, he harangued them for two hours while he sat in an armchair before the crowd of delegates. Nicolas Perrot translated his words for the French and Algonquin participants.

The great chief was angry because his people had brought all their Iroquois prisoners, having paid high ransoms to some of the families who had adopted the captives and grieved at having to give them up. Now Kondiaronk had learned that the Iroquois had not brought any of their native prisoners. Although the Iroquois promised to do so later, they refused to make the traditional offer of hostages until they safely released their own captives.

The French and their allies already knew of English estimates that the Iroquois warrior force had declined to 47 percent of its level at the time of the Lachine massacre. The Five Nations desperately needed to strengthen their ranks; they obviously had no intention of releasing their male captives, but rather chose to absorb them into their warrior force.

Kondiaronk collapsed from exhaustion at the end of his speech. His kinsmen carried him in his armchair to the hospital, where he died in the middle of the night. His death cast a shadow of grief over the proceedings.

The French carried the chief's body to his wigwam of evergreen boughs, and laid him on a beaver skin robe, wrapped in a scarlet blanket. He lay in state according to Huron custom, with the traditional kettle, gun and French sword at his side. Sixty Iroquois converts came to pay him tribute, while one of their principal leaders expressed the grief of his people for the loss of this great Huron chief.

Callières recognized that this great assembly of native tribes might not have been achieved without Kondiaronk's efforts. Religious, military, and ethnic ceremony marked his funeral the following morning, and it was well-attended by his kinsmen, French officials, officers, and clergy. The governor ordered that three military volleys be fired over his grave.

The grand council reconvened on Thursday, August 4, 1701, on that large plain near Bastien's campsite, and was attended by thirteen hundred natives from the west, north and south of the Great Lakes, and from the Mississippi delta to the Gulf of Saint Lawrence. The chief of the Potawatomis from west of Lake Huron asked for Nicolas Perrot's presence among his people to cement the new peace, but Governor Callières refused to grant his request. The stalwart negotiator and intrepid voyageur was no longer needed, nor respected by government officials. He was not of the nobility and had fallen deeply into debt during his years of service.

Thirty-eight chiefs signed that treaty, which marked the end of the sixteen-year war and of the Anglo-Iroquois coalition. Peace between Nouvelle France and its indigenous allies on one side, and the Five Iroquois Nations on the other, was finally achieved. The native nations on both sides of the conflict jointly declared that from then on, they would remain neutral in any war fought between the French and English colonies.

Pierre Boucher's friend Kondiaronk, had fulfilled their common dream of peace.

QUEEN ANNE'S WAR

Thirty

Early in September 1701, British King William III viewed the Spanish coronation of Louis XIV's grandson as an ambitious step toward French domination of Europe, America, and the world. He reacted by negotiating a renewal of the Grand Alliance; France and Great Britain again moved toward war.

In their rush to insure Iroquois neutrality at the start of another war with Britain, the French accepted the Iroquois claim to the Ohio Valley by their right of conquest during the Beaver Wars. Since the Treaty of Ryswick in 1697 had placed the Five Nations under British protection, this opened up the possibility of British territorial claims to that fur-rich territory.

In the Great Lakes area, Antoine de la Mothe Cadillac asked the northern Hurons and Algonquins of the Michillimackinac area to settle at his new Detroit colony. When he invited almost every other western nation into the region and they all accepted, the French lacked enough trade goods to meet their demands. Consequently, overcrowding and competition for the area's limited resources weakened, rather than strengthened, French-native alliances.

The Jesuit Relations reported to their superiors in France that the soil at Cap-de-la-Madeleine had become more sandy, firewood was scarce, and its farms had been mostly abandoned by its early settlers. Nicolas Gatineau returned to Trois-Rivières after a short stay at Montréal and settled at the cape, but he was frustrated by the quality of his crops.

François and Marguerite Moreau had become close friends through the encouragement of her aunt, Catherine Guillet. In mid-November, they signed their marriage contract at Batiscan, further strengthening the bonds between the two families. François pledged a widow's benefit of 450 livres from savings he had earned from his own initial crops, and by working for Bastien and for his brother at Bécancour.

The couple were married the following day by Recollect pastor Constantin de Challey at the parish of Batiscan, and the bride's family hosted the wedding reception at their nearby home. All of Pierre Guillet's children and grandchildren attended, as did Bastien's and Catherine's.

François and Marguerite moved into Bastien's old house and planned to live there as long as his father needed his help.

On December 31, 1701, King William III eloquently rallied the English parliament to support a Protestant crusade against tLouis XIV's ambitions. He emphasized that Britain now required English political and financial support for his efforts to renew the second Grand Alliance of European nations against France and Spain; that this was a final opportunity to preserve the liberty of Europe, English trade, peace, and safety at home. He specifically called upon Parliament to formally ratify his military alliance agreements and to invest in strengthening English naval and land forces to counter French political and military initiatives.

Winter 1701-02

In the depth of that winter, the Mohawks burned Fort Saint-Louis (Chambly) to the ground. Its location directly east of Montréal, on the western shore of the Richelieu River, required that it be replaced immediately the following spring. Originally built as a wooden stockade by Tracy's troops in 1665, it had served as a base for expeditions to the south against the Iroquois by the Carignan-Salières Regiment, then as a garrison for the colonial *Troupes de la Marine* who guarded Montréal. It had most recently been rebuilt in 1690 to protect the habitants of Chambly following the Lachine massacre.

On March 8, 1702, William III died as a result of injuries suffered from having fallen off his horse, and his sister-in-law Anne succeeded him to the throne of England. Queen Anne's childhood friend Sarah Churchill became her constant companion, and Sarah's husband, John Churchill became the Duke of Marlborough, and captain-general of the English army. A new generation of English political and military leaders now rose to challenge Louis XIV's European and North American ambitions.

England declared war on France on May 4th, but Québec did not hear of it until the following summer. The European War of the Spanish Succession would be fought by the allied forces of Britain, Holland, Denmark, Portugal, Austria and other German territories on one side; France, Spain, and Bavaria on the other. Such news spread quickly throughout Canada that summer.

Bastien retreated within himself. War and peace in Nouvelle France had become hopelessly enmeshed with European continental and imperial rivalry. He thought back over the years, as to why he had left his family and ancestral home. His own life certainly had been more productive since his arrival in Canada, but he had also hoped to provide a better environment for his children and grandchildren. Now it seemed that constant warfare had followed him across the sea. No sooner had Nouvelle France made peace with the Five Nations and protected itself against English colonial incursions, than the European monarchs sought to extend their own battles across that sea.

Catherine grew concerned about his unusually somber mood, yet she could not draw him out of it. She spoke to Louis, who came by the following day and took his father out for a ride by horse and calèche.

They had traveled a good distance and had talked about many things, when Louis finally asked: "What's bothering you, Papa?"

Bastien hesitated a long while as they rode on. Then he spoke barely above a whisper. "My sons and I have been very fortunate; we've all been off to war, and come back home unharmed. Have you ever seen a wounded man, Louis?"

His son was puzzled by his question. "Only from a distance—during the siege of Québec. Why do you ask?"

"Did you ever see such men suffer from their wounds?"

"No, I was too far away to see clearly."

"I envy you, *mon gars*. I first experienced this when I was no older than Baptiste."

Louis knew his youngest step-brother to be too young to serve in the militia.

"I saw it many times before I returned home at age twenty-two. It's an experience that has haunted me all my life."

"But why does it bother you so much now, after all these years?"

"Perhaps because I've come to realize that there will always be war. At first, I hoped to find peace by crossing the western sea, yet from the time of my arrival, the Iroquois warred against us."

"But you had a long period of peace."

"Yes, and Nouvelle France thrived because of it; its farms and settlements multiplied, exploration and trade expanded; we had few epidemics and food shortages. Then the Iroquois returned to making war against us."

"And now, they've signed the Treaty of Montréal."

"Yes, they have, but what about the English colonies?"

Louis had always seen his father as the strong pillar of the family, and now, in the fullness of his own manhood, he realized that he had taken his father's strength for granted. He suddenly noticed that the years had taken their toll on Bastien. His hair, once brown, had turned white, his confident stride had slowed, his proud bearing had slackened. He now realized that his father's shoulders could no longer carry the full burden of the family, that the time had come when he, as eldest son must share some of it.

"You look tired, Papa."

"Perhaps I am."

"Louis and Catherine will soon marry and move on to the Massé farm. François and Marguerite are still living in the old house and running the farm for you. Baptiste is strong enough now to be of help in the fields and forest."

"François has his own farm to worry about," Bastien reminded him.

"He promised to stay here as long as you needed him."

"He should be spending more time developing his own land now that he's married."

"I'll speak to him. If he feels he wants to do that, then we can make that possible for him. You and Catherine have five strong sons; surely we can till, sow, plant, and harvest your crops for you and provide your firewood. We can do this together.

"Angélique and Louise are old enough now to help Catherine with the gardens. Jeanne and Marie-Catherine can help with the minor chores. Marie-Madeleine still needs attention, but she'll be helping too within the next few years."

Bastien straightened his shoulders. His eyes reflected a glimmer of hope.

"Perhaps it's time for me to stop worrying so much about all of you and about what the future will bring."

Louis added: "Didn't you and *Maman* always tell us that we should do the best we can, and God will take care of the rest?"

Bastien smiled. "Yes, Marguerite often reminded me of that."

"And that we should always help each other as a family."

Bastien smiled again in recognition of his own words.

"Then it's settled," Louis said firmly. "I'll meet with the boys and we'll organize the autumn chores. If François and Marguerite need to spend more time at Bécancour, then we'll make it posssible for them. You needn't worry about that."

The long war had exhausted the Iroquois nations, so that all except the Mohawks kept their promise to the French and remained neutral in the renewed conflict.

The fighting spread to North America as Queen Anne's War, but did not seriously extend into the Great Lakes area. At the outbreak of hostilities, the English colonial population was sixteen times greater than that of the Canadian French, however, the several separate English colonies had not yet united against their northern neighbor.

On the second day of August, Bastien and Marguerite's youngest daughter Catherine, and Louis Massé signed their marriage contract at Bastien's home; both were in their mid-twenties. Louis pledged a survival benefit of 400 livres for his future bride, drawing from savings he had earned while farming the Massé concession near Champlain, and while continuing to work for Bastien. His cousin-in-law Barthélémi David served as witness, along with Marie-Charlotte Le Gardeur, her two daughters, and René Leblanc, all of Bécancour. They planned to hold their church wedding the following autumn.

One month later, the Carolina assembly further expanded the North American theater of war by sending an expedition to seize Saint-Augustine from the Spaniards before it could be reinforced by the French. Although they failed to capture the fort, their mixed force of five hundred English colonists and native allies seized, burned, and pillaged the town the following December.

Winter 1702-03

A smallpox epidemic raged throughout Nouvelle France that winter, killing nearly a quarter of its population.

On February 10th, eighteen-year old Marie-Louise Massé signed a marriage contract with thirty-year old François Perrot, eldest son of Nicolas who now served as militia captain at Bécancour. François pledged his bride a survival benefit of 400 livres.

The following month, Bastien's son François, and Marguerite Moreau had their first child, Marie-Charlotte.

Governor-General Callières died in Québec on May 26th. The Sovereign Council now recommended Lieutenant-Governor of Montréal Louis-Philippe de Rigaud marquis de Vaudreuil to succeed as governor of Nouvelle France. King Louis XIV hesitated granting this commission because Madame Vaudreuil was Canadian-born, however, he finally overcame his reservations and signed the appointment.

During the month of July, an epidemic of cholera flared through the region of Trois-Rivières. The cape settlers once more stayed at home to avoid the disease.

The following month, Governor Vaudreuil dispatched a war party across the Kennebec River, which the French had always claimed as their Acadian border. In retaliation for the destruction of the Acadian settlements, including that of Beaubassin, by Benjamin Church in 1696, Monsieur de Beaubassin and Abenaki allies attacked English settlements from Casco to Wells. By laying waste to 15 leagues of country, killing or capturing more than three hundred people, they fulfilled Vaudreuil's goal to stir up Abenaki-English enmity and thus strengthen the eastern frontier.

New England retaliated against the Abenaki villages.

Winter 1703-04

Throughout the winter season, a smallpox epidemic spread through the Illinois and the Miami tribes surrounding the Detroit colony.

That February, Marie-Angélique Massé served as godmother at Marie-Joseph Cottenoire's baptism.

Vaudreuil assigned Jean-Baptiste Hertel de Rouville to lead fifty Canadian volunteers, two hundred Abenakis, and Iroquois converts from Sault Saint-Louis, to destroy Deerfield, a northwestern Massachusetts border village. On the night of March 10th, having crossed the Green Mountains by trekking through the Winooski River valley to the Connecticut River, the French and their native allies conducted a savage raid against the settlers of Deerfield, killing forty-three settlers and capturing fifty-four others who were forced to make the grueling overland trip to Canada with their captors.

New England retaliated against Acadia the following June when Colonel Benjamin Church attacked Pentagouet, Pigiguit, Passamaquoddy, Grand Pré, Cobequid and Beaubassin. He sailed for Port-Royal with seven hundred men, but on July 4th decided not to try to seize that settlement. Instead, he returned to pillage Beaubassin before returning home. French settlers surrendered to superior forces; their houses, crops, and churches were destroyed; one hundred twenty captives were taken to Boston.

The Carolina assembly authorized former Governor James Moore to lead another expedition against fourteen Spanish missions in the Apalachee country, to open the way to Louisiana. But the Carolinians were unable to get past the Choctaw warriors to reach the several French settlements located near the Gulf of Mexico.

In June, despite King Louis XIV's warning that wartime activities made ocean crossing too dangerous at that time, Bishop Saint-Vallier sailed from La Rochelle aboard the same ship that had brought him to France three years earlier. It was crowded with voyageurs, merchants, people of all classes, and much of its deck was overloaded with their luggage.

Later that same month, as their merchant ship *La Seine* guided a fleet of other French vessels toward Nouvelle France, they encountered a convoy of one hundred fifty English ships heading east. The smaller French vessels escaped, but following a ten-hour siege, Saint-Vallier's overladen ship was forced to surrender.

When all French passengers had transferred to the British ships, the bishop stubbornly refused to comply, having witnessed the desecration of his holy symbols and relics. The leader of the fleet took him under his protection, and upon reaching England, the bishop was ransomed by government authorities for 1,300,000 English pounds. He was called to an audience before Queen Anne, then comfortably housed with other priests who waited to be released to France.

In late August 1704, a mixed force of French and native allies from Plaisance, Newfoundland, destroyed the English settlement at Bonavista.

Newly appointed governor at Plaisance, Daniel d'Auger de Subercase, petitioned Governor-General Vaudreuil to send a detachment of Canadians and Abenakis to rid his island of the English. Early that following November, forty Canadians and as many Abenakis left Québec by ship for Newfoundland to reinforce the Acadian forces. They arrived three days later and made their own *raquettes* and travois to march overland to the English capital of Saint John.

On November 26th, Boston Governor Dudley wrote to London, urging the capture of Québec: "In the last two years, the Assembly of Massachusetts has spent 50,000 English pounds in defense of our province, when three or four of the Queen's ships and fifteen hundred men could rid us of the French and end the need for these expenses."

Thirty-one

1705

On January 8th, a French force of four hundred fifty soldiers, Canadians, privateers, and a band of native allies left Plaisance, Newfoundland with the promise of support from a brigantine armed with mortar and bombs for their overland expedition. They seized the English settlement at Béboulle where they stayed two days, posted a garrison, and left to continue their journey through deep snow toward Saint John.

When they reached their destination at sunrise of the last day in January, the Abenakis attacked and surprised the nearby settlers, capturing three hundred seventeen; the French then segregated the women for their own safety. The nearby fort could have been easily accessed because of snowdrifts rising against its palisades, but the English cleared their cannons in time to kill two Frenchmen and repel the rest. While the English fired their cannons against them, French forces took over the farmhouses surrounding the fort and awaited the arrival of the brigantine during the next thirty days. The French ship never arrived.

Finally, on March 5th, the French burned all the English houses and buildings of Saint John and prepared to leave. They released most of their captives but kept eighty of the strongest when they marched back toward Plaisance, continuing to burn all English structures along the way. They later claimed to have jammed or thrown forty cannons into the sea, burned one vessel, destroyed two thousand shallops and chariots, and seized only 2600 livres, but inflicted 4,000,000-livres worth of damage on the enemy.

Late that spring, an official census showed a count of four hundred fifty settlers scattered throughout the various French coastal fishing villages of Terre Neuve (Newfoundland).

That March, Governor Vaudreuil finally responded to Massachusetts Governor Dudley's requests for an exchange of prisoners, and while their representatives carried out these negotiations, they mutually took advantage of such opportunities to estimate their enemy's strength. Among the English envoys was Samuel Vetch, a Scottish merchant with military experience who took note of Québec's defenses and developed profitable French trading connections, while he participated in the negotiations.

The Massachusetts governor's son and Samuel Vetch delivered a letter to Vaudreuil, proposing a neutrality agreement between their two colonies. The French governor was willing to accept this proposal, but only if the other English colonies also signed on to the agreement, and if they would end their fishing in the Gulf of Saint Lawrence and in Acadian waters. Neither condition was acceptable to the English. Meanwhile, they managed to arrange several temporary truce arrangements.

This became an even more cruel war by late April, with scalp bounties being offered by both sides. Boston Governor Joseph Dudley complained to Vaudreuil that the French campaign was uncivilized and unchristian against farmers, women and children, many of whom were turned over to the native allies.

The Massachusetts frontier of Maine, the Abenaki villages, and the Acadian settlements were devastated once more as a result of Queen Anne's War. The Abenaki became impoverished by depressed French trade values and often traded with the English of Boston. Vaudreuil and the Intendant reported to the king that this diversion of trade might be drawing the natives closer to the English who offered them better terms for cheaper goods.

Tragedy struck at Bécancour toward the end of June, when Marie-Louise Massé and her husband François Perrot both died together by drowning barely two years after their marriage.

A legal dispute developed over the inheritance of the childless couple's estate. François had bequeathed to his mother, Madeleine Raclos, the Bécancour lot that he had won by court order three years before his marriage. His mother-in-law Catherine Guillet contested this bequest, while Nicolas Perrot defended his wife's rights before the tribunal at Trois-Rivières, then again before the Sovereign Council of Québec.

The final judgement awarded the Perrots half of their son's property, while Catherine received all of her daughter's property, and half of that year's harvest. The notary was subsequently censured for embezzlement through negligence in his preparation of the original bequest, which had been dated the day of the couple's marriage contract. Consequently, he was suspended from his notary duties for one month.

That summer, father and son, Jacques and Antoine-Denis Raudot, were named intendant and assistant intendant of Nouvelle France. Their first commission was to initiate mail service between Québec, Trois-Rivières, and Montréal, thus marking the beginning of the first postal system in Canada.

Early in August, Marguerite-Louise was born to François and Marguerite Moreau.

The following mid-November, civil engineer Levasseur de Néré reported to Québec authorities that the fort at Trois-Rivières held thirty-two houses and an additional seventeen homes were located outside the village palisades. The cape settlement was slightly smaller.

1706

Early that June, Governor Vaudreuil and Governor Dudley of Boston exchanged forty-three English captives for fifty-seven French prisoners.

By mid-September, the Abenakis complained that the French were not paying them for English scalps. Vaudreuil reminded them that the English were enemies of both their peoples, that he had warned them three years earlier that he did not care to buy scalps, but had offered them rewards for English captives. They had not taken advantage of his offer.

The Canadian fur monopoly finally collapsed, and a new system was instituted for the depressed trade. Beaver fur exports remained under monopoly control, but the sale of other furs were declared to be free and competitive. Much of the western trade now flowed toward Albany.

Late that December, Bastien's son Louis was named to serve three years as *marguillier* for the parish of Sainte-Madeleine, as was his father in 1694.

1707

On May 1, 1707, Scotland joined England and Wales by formally adopting the Act of Union, thus creating the United Kingdom of Great Britain during Queen Anne's reign.

Two weeks later, Colonel John March sailed from Boston with twenty ships and a New England force of over one thousand militia volunteers and four hundred fifty sailors to capture Port-Royal in Acadia. Subercase and Saint-Castin succeeded in repelling the invasion. The New Englanders sailed back to Casco Bay, where they picked up a few more ships, Colonel Wainwright, and an additional six hundred men before returning to Acadia for another attempt. This time, Subercase and Saint-Castin led their men on the offensive to repel the second invasion. Colonel March and his forces returned to Boston in mid-August.

That summer, French civil authorities called on Jean Cusson, now seventy-three years of age and retired, to fill in as acting king's attorney at Montréal.

François and Marguerite Moreau welcomed their first son, Jean-Baptiste, who was born in mid-July.

The following autumn proved to be difficult for the settlers of Port-Royal. The two English sieges had caused few casualties but had ruined their properties and crops, and France did not send the badly needed provisions. Subercase had appealed for help from the home country, but France was already suffering severe losses in its European war; whatever assistance it sent was negligible: untested recruits, defective muskets, no pay for its officers and men. The Acadian governor finally resorted to recruiting the help of French privateers from Saint-Domingue, who brought provisions, cloth and ammunition to Port-Royal. This tactic alleviated the poverty and misery of the Acadian settlers, but coupled with Hertel's continuing raids against New England settlements, it inspired Samuel Vetch and Francis Nicholson to seek help from England, where they were well received.

Expecting fresh attacks by the English, Subercase again pleaded for assistance from the Minister of Marine. He was told that France could not afford to send any more help, and that if Acadia continued to be such a burden, the king would abandon it. Conditions continued to deteriorate at Port-Royal; the Acadians already felt abandoned by their king.

1708

Monseigneur Laval died at Québec May 6, 1708, at the age of eighty-five. Although he had retired for health reasons in 1685, and had been replaced at that time by Bishop Saint-Vallier, Laval had functioned as acting-bishop of Canada during Saint-Vallier's long absences from Canada. Since his arrival at Québec in 1659, Monseigneur Laval had devoted nearly half a century of his life to the first Roman Catholic diocese of North America.

Based on his evaluation of French defenses during negotiations for prisoner exchange at Québec, Dutch merchant Samuel Vetch produced a long memo to the British queen. It stated that the Canadian French were troublesome neighbors with a small population who claimed to possess territory extending over more than 4,000 miles of North America, thereby pressing back the British continental empire toward the sea. He argued that the French managed to reduce English commerce everywhere in America, hoping to ruin it completely. If the French population was allowed to grow, it would have an army of twenty thousand men who would fight rather than farm, and who could easily force the English colonists out of North America. He estimated that half of what it cost England in lost trade in one year would cover the cost of expelling the French from Canada, Acadia, and Newfoundland. Once that was accomplished, the English forces could move to the Gulf of Mexico and seize the Spanish colonies, thus ensuring Her Majesty's peaceful and exclusive possession of the North American continent which had a land mass four times greater than that of Great Britain.

Vetch won the queen's approval for the "Glorious Enterprise"—
the takeover of the French colonies. His arguments earned him
a commission of colonel and the promised governorship of Québec
should he succeed in his campaign.

Early that summer, Governor Vaudreuil received a letter from
French Minister Pontchartrain expressing the king's great
disappointment over Québec's lack of military support for his
Acadian colonists.

The French governor had already organized an expedition
against Portsmouth (New Hampshire). Led by Jean-Baptiste
Hertel de Rouville and Jean-Baptiste de Saint-Ours Deschaillons,
two hundred Canadians and hundreds of native converts:
Iroquois, Abenakis, Hurons, and Algonquins, traveled up the
Chaudière, Saint-François, and Richelieu rivers to rendezvous
before striking the seaport. But when sickness spread among
the troops, and their native allies withdrew, Hertel then chose to
attack the small village of Haverhill on the Merrimack River.
English accounts later reported forty-eight men, women, and
children were killed. Hertel went on to lead his Canadian
volunteers against other Massachusetts and New Hampshire
settlements, including: Groton, Lancaster, Exeter, Dover, Kittery,
Casco, Kingston, York, Berwick, Wells, Winter Harbor,
Brookfield, Amesbury, and Marlborough.

On December 21st, a mixed force of French and native allies
left Plaisance, Newfoundland, to capture the major English
fishery port at Saint John and bring the other eastern shore
fisheries under French control.

1709

Early that June, Marie-Angélique Massé married Michel Crevier
dit Bellerive. And a daughter, Marie-Joseph, was born to François
and Marguerite Moreau.

By the end of that month, France had lost ground in Europe,
while Nouvelle France had gained in North America. Scottish
Colonel John Higginson wrote to Queen Anne: "It is imperative
that Canada submit to the British Crown."

The English knew that France was in no condition to defend

its North American colonies, since Louis XIV had repeatedly sued for a peace that Queen Anne had consistently refused to consider. In answer to Higginson's plea and those of her other North American colonial officials, the British queen ordered that the English settlers invade and defeat French Canada.

That summer, rumors spread throughout Nouvelle France that an English attack was imminent; that a British fleet would sail for Boston with silver, munitions, and men; that four thousand English colonists and their native allies from all along the Atlantic seaboard were preparing to attack overland by way of Lake Champlain. The French governor at Plaisance confirmed these rumors on July 23rd.

Panic spread throughout Canada as New England mounted the greatest challenge it had ever waged against the French colony. Bastien sensed that his greatest fear for his family was about to be realized and fervently prayed that this was not so. He knew that such a threat to the Saint Lawrence River valley settlements would require a full call up of the militia, and rightfully so, but who would work the farms? At age seventy-five, he no longer had the strength to do so. Pierre Guillet must have felt this way when Jacques Massé died, he thought ruefully. He himself was so much stronger then. The years had passed all too quickly.

He quietly watched Catherine as she prepared the evening meal and considered how fortunate for all their children that she had agreed to join her family with his after Jacques and Marguerite had died. How could they have managed otherwise? Although twenty years younger than he, her hair had also grown gray, but she was just as energetic as ever. What a woman she was! No wonder she and Marguerite had been such close friends; they were very much alike in their common patience and firmness with the children, their sense of organization and creativity. Their families had never lacked for warm clothing. Even in times of food shortages, Catherine had managed to stretch what she had to feed everyone. It had not been a quiet house, but it had been a happy, well-managed home. Even now, they still looked forward to Sunday reunions after Mass, when everyone contributed to the joint family meal, and shared their news of the week.

Twenty-two-year old Baptiste Massé still lived at home and

worked as engagé for Bastien, while teenagers Jeanne, Marie-Catherine, and Marie-Madeleine helped their mother with her gardening and household chores.

Bastien's thoughts roamed back to the pending English invasions of Montréal and Québec. No doubt his sons and sons-in-law would be called upon to join a major defensive campaign. I must talk this over with Louis, he decided.

Governor Vaudreuil traveled to Montréal to confer with Lieutenant-Governor Claude de Ramezay, civil and religious officials. On their way back to Québec, he and military engineer Jacques Levasseur de Néré assessed all of the Saint Lawrence River valley defenses. Following their inspection, the entire cape community joined together to reinforce its neighborhood redoubts and palisades. Bastien helped the only way he could, by forming trunnels and joint ends with his hand tools.

Vaudreuil called up all militiamen between the ages of sixteen and sixty.

Bastien's three sons and Catherine's two became part of that French force, as did their other sons-in-law Antoine Cottenoire, Pierre Petit, and Michel Crevier. Aubin was excused from military service and remained nearby to help Bastien and other family members as best he could. Louis had also found a young, experienced engagé, Charles Lemerle, for his father.

The women once more prepared batches of trail food for their husbands and Baptiste.

Governor-General Vaudreuil ordered Montréal Lieutenant-Governor Claude de Ramezay to lead fifteen hundred French regulars, Canadian militiamen, and native allies to Pointe-à-la-Chevelure on Lac Champlain (across from Crown Point, NY), to determine the strength of the English army that was moving against Montréal. His orders were to avoid engaging in battle with the English and their Iroquois allies, but to destroy their boats and canoes and dump their munitions into the water.

By late July, English commander Francis Nicholson had deployed his Connecticut, New York, and New Jersey colonial militiamen and Iroquois allies among a chain of stockaded forts extending along the Hudson River from just north of Albany to the southern end of Lake Champlain. His troops now built a fleet of bateaux and canoes at Wood Creek to transport men and provisions for their final move toward Montréal.

From Pointe-à-la-Chevelure, Ramezay assigned his nephew to lead an experienced scouting party to learn the size, location, and activities of the colonial land forces. Louis and Antoine kept their kin close together as the cape contingent followed through difficult terrain and dense virgin forest.

Louis grew uneasy as the pace accelerated. He glanced over at Antoine and saw that he was scowling. Louis reached out and applied enough pressure on his arm to signal that they should slow down. Their entire group matched Louis' pace until they had positioned themselves in the center of the force. They dared not speak, but remained exceptionally alert. Louis detected increased wariness among the native allies. The rapid movement of so large an advance group stirred the birds and forest animals into flight. The density of the undergrowth made progress difficult, but also made it impossible to see what lay ahead. Louis and Antoine both knew that it was unwise to reconnoiter at such speed through this kind of environment, but young Pierre-Thomas Tarieu de la Pérade maintained his quick pace, intent on catching the English by surprise.

Shots suddenly rang out. Ramezay's nephew had clumsily betrayed their presence in the area. The French force scattered among the trees, virtually unable to identify friend or foe. Louis and Antoine were determined to keep their party together; Antoine signaled them to stay low and not to shoot unless they saw the enemy. Men were firing at shadows; some fell to friendly fire.

Hours later, the shooting ended as the English scouts retreated toward Wood Creek; the French, Canadians, and their allies straggled back to rejoin their own main force. Louis and Antoine found one lost English colonial and led him back with them to Pointe-à-la-Chevelure.

The English captive informed Ramezay that Nicholson's colonial forces numbered three thousand men. Two Dutch captives estimated the force to be at one thousand militiamen and two hundred Iroquois.

Ramezay reassembled his forces and withdrew to Fort Chambly.

On their way home from Fort Chambly, Louis and Baptiste noticed a change in François' demeanor, he seemed more quiet than usual. Louis became concerned about his youngest brother and asked Baptiste if he knew what was bothering him.

Baptiste shrugged his shoulders. Although he and François were close, he knew of no special problem.

Louis managed to find some private time with François, and asked him directly. "You seem to have a lot on your mind since we left Pointe-à-la-Chevelure, *p'tit frère*. Would you like to talk about it?"

François' ears reddened, and he was hesitant. "That was one scary experience back in the woods, when everyone started shooting at shadows. Am I the only one who was upset by it?"

"No, of course not. It's something you never get used to, unless you're a professional soldier—even then, I expect that there are some pretty rough moments. We're all farmers, here, François; we're not used to shooting at people, nor at being shot at. Your reaction is quite normal."

"I'm not ashamed, just surprised by it."

"Well, you're a family man now, and you have a wife and four children to worry about. I'm sure you're concerned about what might happen to them if anything happened to you. We all worry about that."

"Do you?" François asked him.

"Yes, I always work to provide security for my family."

"And so do I, but now I feel that I need to do more."

"Is that what you've been worrying about?"

François finally shared his thoughts. "Now that Baptiste is twenty-two, and is strong enough to work the farm by himself, I feel that it's time for me to move my family to Bécancour. Do you think that Papa and Baptiste would understand?"

SENESCENCE

Thirty-two

In mid-August of 1709, Vaudreuil received word that eight vessels had been sighted 45 leagues downriver from Québec. The governor immediately ordered that all livestock be turned loose into the forest, and that all women and children return to their farms while the men worked in the city to strengthen its defenses. That initial warning later proved to be a false alarm.

A month later, Governor Vaudreuil wrote to French Mimister Pontchartrain: "All habitants must seek safety in the town forts for their families, their belongings, grains and animals, in order to withhold provisions of food for any sizable invasion force, especially along the more exposed south shore."

The British fleet had been scheduled to reach Boston by mid-May. Nicholson continued to wait at Wood Creek through the hot late summer, drilling his troops, and daily expecting Samuel Vetch's signal that the fleet had left Boston for the Saint Lawrence River. Nicholson's forces became restless through boredom, fatigue, and supply shortages. Once dysentery and smallpox began to spread, the native allies left. The colonial forces burned their bateaux and headed back to Albany.

When the cape militia returned home in time for the September grain harvest. Louis, François, and Baptiste found that engagé Charles Lermerle had managed to keep up with Bastien's farmwork. Baptiste and Charles worked well together, and seemed to enjoy each other's company. François became more confident that this was a good time for him to move his family to the south shore.

Louis initiated the discussion with Bastien one day when he stopped by the house on his way home from town.

"Was it difficult for you while we were away?"

Bastien shrugged his shoulders. "Not at all. Charles is a good worker, and had everything under control. I did what I could." Bastien replied.

"Do you think that he and Baptiste could run the farm for you?"

"Why do you ask?"

"I think it's time now for François to move on to his own farm, don't you?"

Bastien thought this over, considered carefully what such a change would mean for him and Catherine. He deeply appreciated what his youngest son had done for him by helping with the heavy work while Baptiste was still too young to manage alone. He knew that this was no longer necessary. François had traveled a lot across the river to work his fields as well as his father's. He had a wife and four children to take care of...

"You're right, Louis. It's time he concentrated on his own family's needs. Does he know about this?"

Louis smiled at him. "He's been struggling with that decision. He doesn't want to disappoint you."

"I see. Well let me take care of it."

The following Sunday, the family gathered together after Mass for their joint family meal, which now included Charles Lemerle, and Bastien offered a special prayer when everyone was seated.

"We thank you God for all the gifts you have given us, especially for the safe return of all our young men from their military campaign. We thank you for sending us Charles who has proven to be such a good worker. Bless this family and its three healthy generations. And bless François and his own family as they move into their own home on the south shore. He and Marguerite will go with our blessing. *Ainsi soit-il*."

His eyes locked with those of his youngest son. They were very much alike, he and François, and for that reason, they intuitively understood each other.

The young couple approached Bastien and hugged him.

Antoine told them: "You're welcome to use my bateau to move your belongings. For larger articles, like furniture, I'm sure I can borrow Jean Lemoine's shallop."

Those who already lived at Bécancour told them that their neighbors would be excited to hear this news. "You already know most of our neighbors; we all grew up together on this side of the river," Sébastien explained.

Bastien and Catherine glanced at each other and smiled at this familiar display of sibling help and cooperation. They would miss having the grandchildren living so close to them, but both realized that this change would be good for the entire family.

On October 11th, Boston Governor Dudley received word from England that London authorities had decided in early August not to send a fleet or land reinforcements to Boston. Great Britain needed all of her resources for the European war and had diverted its ships to Portugal.

Nicholson and Vetch sailed back to England to rescue the military venture. Meanwhile Vaudreuil and Ramezay had begun to upgrade the wooden fort at Chambly. It had served well against Iroquois assaults but would surely be vulnerable to British cannons and mortars. They began construction of a stone fortress strong enough to withstand any such overland threat to the safety of Montréal, and subsequently to the entire colony of Nouvelle France.

1710

Near the end of March, Queen Anne appointed Francis Nicholson as commander-in-chief, and Samuel Vetch as subordinate officer of a renewed New England campaign to recover Nova Scotia for the English crown. Both men had wished to attack Québec, but since major English reinforcements and support would not be available, Nicholson directed his expedition toward Acadia, which was more easily accessible and vulnerable.

Nicholson left England in May 1710, with five hundred English marines and a naval flotilla consisting of frigates, transports, and an artillery supply ketch.

Marie-Charlotte Crevier was born to Michel and Angélique Massé on July 17th.

Commander Nicholson picked up the provincial troops and supplies in Boston, then sailed for Port-Royal in mid-September. On October 6th, thirty-four hundred Englishmen, supported by a squadron of British ships, laid siege upon the fort's garrison. The troops landed under cover of naval artillery and began an assault that lasted a full week before Governor of Acadia Auger de Subercase surrendered the fort, his two hundred fifty-eight officers and men, and the French-Acadian population residing within *la banlieue*, a three-mile radius surrounding the walls of Port-Royal. Nicholson triumphantly renamed this sheltered port Annapolis Royal in honor of his queen and claimed English control over all of Acadia.

According to the surrender agreement, the victors provided English ships to deliver the French troops to La Rochelle and to provide for the evacuation of the French privateers based on the surrounding islands who wished to return to France; the French would guarantee safe return of the ships and their captains. The habitants were guaranteed freedom to remain on their farms with all their belongings for a maximum period of two years, after which time they must swear loyalty to the British Queen. Canadians wishing to return to Nouvelle France had the right to do so during the following year.

Subercase managed to settle all French debts with the local population before boarding ship for France.

On October 21st, Colonel Nicholson addressed a letter to Vaudreuil from Annapolis Royal, warning the French governor that any mistreatment of the English colonial population, through further raids against the New England frontier, would result in like treatment of the Acadians. He demanded that a truce parley to be held the following May, at which time he expected to collect all English captives held by the French and their native allies. Otherwise, a like number of Acadians would be delivered to native tribes allied to the English.

Then Nicholson left Samuel Vetch in command of Annapolis Royal and sailed back to England with his troops.

A few weeks later, Vetch wrote to London that England must

send a naval force to deport the entire French-Acadian population, otherwise there could never be peace in Nova Scotia.

An influenza epidemic began to spread through the Saint Lawrence River settlements in November 1710. A few weeks later, Baptiste developed a headache and began to cough. Bastien moved him into the old house, and treated him with herbal medicines but by the following day, Catherine's youngest son was bedridden with chills and fever. Catherine prepared bouillon and herbal teas and delivered them to Bastien, who remained in isolation with his patient.

When their three daughters developed the same early symptoms, Catherine refused to move them to the old house and insisted on personally administering the same treatment to them in their own beds.

Bastien and Catherine tended day and night to their children's needs. Christmas came and went before their four patients recovered enough to leave their beds. Then both parents became sick with chills, fever and cough.

Charles Lemerle alerted Nicolas Leblanc, who relayed the news to Michel Rochereau. Michel sent one of his sons to the village by horse and sled to bring physician Duguay to Bastien's home. At age seventy-six, Bastien was more seriously affected than the others; Catherine also became quite sick. Their children now became the caregivers.

In spite of the physician's treatment, both patients continued to weaken, their coughs deepened into pneumonia, and it finally became apparent that there would be no hope for recovery. As they lay in bed together and shared their thoughts during their more lucid moments, they reminisced about their early years in Nouvelle France, the dangers and challenges they had faced, and the joys and sorrows they had experienced. Baptiste and his three sisters listened intently to their stories.

"Is there anything else that we can do for you?" Baptiste asked.

Bastien looked thoughtfully into his eyes and told him: "If you look under my workbench, you'll find two wooden plaques that I carved some time ago—they're wrapped together in a piece of cloth—When the time comes, give those to Louis and Sébastien— They'll know what to do with them."

Baptiste nodded, and asked again: "Is there anything else I can do to make you more comfortable?"

Both parents coughed weakly and turned toward each other. Bastien caught something in Catherine's eyes and turned to answer: "I think it's time to call your brothers and sisters together."

While their daughters prepared to receive the rest of the family, Bastien and Catherine spoke quietly to each other.

"Do you have any regrets about things left undone?" she asked him.

"None whatsoever. Do you?"

"None. Our children all know how to take care of themselves—and each other."

"They face a difficult future but so did we."

"We struggled and survived, and so will they—don't you think?"

"I firmly believe that," he tried to reassure her by tightening his hold on her hand. It felt more frail than ever, but so was his grip.

Their thirteen sons and daughters by previous marriage and their own three daughters quickly and sorrowfully arrived from Batiscan, Champlain, and Bécancour for their parents' final counsel and blessings.

In a voice barely heard above the sound of the crackling fire in the hearth, Bastien told them that he had two major concerns that they needed to consider.

"First of all," he began, "Jeanne, Marie-Catherine, and Marie-Madeleine are still too young to marry—they'll continue to require shelter, guidance, and protection for awhile yet—we're confident that Louis and Simonne will offer those to them—We hope that you will always continue to help each other—and instill that in your own children...

"This house is the only home your youngest sisters have ever known—Once we're gone, it must be shared in equal shares among all of you—If you divide the land among so many shares, each portion will be too small to support a family—None of you has asked to assume title to the entire property...

"I took on a large debt to build this house—that had to be paid off before we could marry and merge our two families—Louis lent me 400 livres—from what he had earned during his voyage for Perrot—I was never able to repay him— that money is still due him from the estate—We all greatly benefited from his generosity—That debt can be repaid—if you all cede your shares to him—Then Louis can maintain the property—at least until your sisters have married…"

Louis could see how much of an effort this was for his father, so he spoke up: "I assure you that I have no personal interest in owning this property other than to carry out Papa's wishes, but I would accept that arrangement, with the understanding that if a buyer for the property comes forward within the next two weeks, I could sell it, and any profit realized beyond the 400 livres would be shared with all of you."

His siblings accepted this as a reasonable solution.

"But they could not manage—to live here on their own," Catherine added.

Baptiste Massé, who had known no other father but Bastien, quickly set their minds at ease. "I promise to stay here and support them until they're all married."

Holding his wife's hand, Louis promised: "Simonne and I will always remain available to help and support our brothers and sisters."

Simonne gently wiped the tears from her mother's eyes, while Bastien breathed a sigh of relief.

His younger sisters wept quietly as all these arrangements were made on their behalf. They were reassured about their future, but marriage seemed well beyond their imagining at ages of eighteen through twelve. They smiled in gratitude to their brothers and took turns to gently hug their mother and father. Bastien blessed them all.

Bastien and Catherine both died several days after Christmas 1710, and were deeply mourned by their sixteen children, thirty-seven grandchildren, and Bastien's two great-grandchildren. That night, Baptiste led his brothers to Bastien's workshop and told them of the promise he had made to their father. They were all curious about the package Bastien had described. François found it carefully tucked in a wooden box on the barn floor under the bench. He handed it to Louis who smiled when he uncovered the two wooden plaques, stored back-to-back, with the familiar hand-carved reproductions of the family symbol.

Sébastien sighed and explained: "Louis and I watched while Papa carved one of these for *Maman's* casket; it was his family's custom to do so. He explained to us that this flower represents the origin of our family name. It was very special to him; that's why he had carved it onto their bedstead and onto the wooden chest that he had made for her."

Louis told them: "He expects us to mount these onto both caskets."

"What flower is it?" Baptiste asked.

Louis replied: "*La pervenche.* He once told me that it's a blue-flowered groundcover that grew in the woods near his family home in France.

1711

On January 6th, the family met with royal notary Jean-Baptiste Trottier. Louis served as guardian for the three minor daughters of Bastien and Catherine. Aubin, who could not attend this meeting, had also empowered Louis to serve as legal representative of his oldest sister Madeleine. Antoine represented Marie-Marguerite's interests, Louis Massé represented Catherine's, Sébastien and François their own.

Jacques Massé's heirs had met the previous day and had all agreed that Bastien and Catherine's unmarried daughters should be granted double shares of the joint estate's personal property, house, farming equipment, and provisions.

Bastien's and Catherine's children followed his advice, thus passing on ownership of the family homestead to Louis, and allowing Baptiste Massé to continue to support his three young half-sisters until they married. The document was signed by Louis, Antoine Cottenoire, and Louis Massé.

The final inventory of Bastien's worldly goods was notarized by Jean-Baptiste Pottier on February 4, 1711. This showed that Bastien had built up his livestock, especially among the working oxen and dairy herd; three of his cows were with family members who lived at Bécancour. It also reported that his children were working together to flail and winnow Bastien's grain in order to settle his outstanding debts, most of which were as a result of medical, funeral, burial, inventory and notary expenses. Perishable surplus grain, butter and lard were not included in the inventory and would be shared equally by the co-heirs by common consent.

The following week, the family learned that the influenza epidemic had spread to Île-Dupas near Sorel, where it claimed the life of Bastien's twenty-seven-year old granddaughter Marie-Renée Cottenoire. It spared her husband Antoine Brûlé dit Francoeur, who was nearly thirty years older than Renée, and their three sons and a daughter, ages two through seven. Four days before her death, an infant son had died at the age of nine months, and Renée had suffered a miscarriage that same day.

Since he was already spending much of his time in nearby Montréal through his continuing involvement in the fur trade, Antoine and Marie-Marguerite moved their family to Île-Dupas so that she could take care of their only grandchildren.

Thirty-three

Spring 1711

Late in March, Sébastien bought a lot of land from Thomas La Forest at Seigneurie Godefroy de Tonnancour with a cash payment of 100 livres. The land measured three arpents frontage by twenty deep and was located directly across from Trois-Rivières.

French naval power had greatly declined by that spring. English parliamentary power and influence had switched from the Whigs to the Tories. On April 11, 1711, Queen Anne of Great Britain selected Sir Hovenden Walker, rear-admiral of the white fleet, as commander-in-chief of a major expedition against Québec. She withdrew five highly-disciplined regiments from the Duke of Marlborough's forces in Flanders and assigned them to the North American campaign, under the leadership of Colonel John Hill, brigadier-general in charge of land forces. Plans for this major land and sea expedition to take over Canada developed under tight secrecy. Only three-months worth of provisions were requisitioned for the troops, with the idea of making up the deficit from the New England food stores. A force of fifty-three hundred soldiers, six thousand sailors and marines assembled for the assignment; more men would be added from among the colonials.

François and Marguerite Moreau's fifth child, Madeleine, was born at Bécancour on April 16th.

Six days later, François purchased a lot of land from Pierre Bourbeau at Seigneurie de Dutort for the sum of 100 livres. He paid 25 livres as downpayment, and committed to satisfy the balance by clearing five arpents of Bourbeau's other forest within five years; he had already stripped one arpent of its trees and brush, and cut its logs to ten-foot length. François' new acquisition was of three arpents frontage on the Bécancour River and ran inland for twenty, bordering land owned by René David.

On June 25th, Admiral Walker's fleet arrived at Boston where it rendezvoused with the militias from New York, New Jersey, and Connecticut, reaching a total force of sixty-five hundred infantry, eighty-eight ships and transports. Walker was outraged to learn that the New England merchants were profiteering from the fleet's supply purchases. This situation created friction between officers of the colonial and regular contingents.

New to planning on so large a scale, Walker underestimated the possible complications, particularly regarding the availability of experienced pilots and charts to guide his navigation up the Saint Lawrence River. The captured master of the French sloop *Neptune*, and Phips' 1690 journal of his siege of Québec, were the best resources the admiral could find. Alarmed by what he learned about the hazards Phips had faced in the gulf and river of the Saint Lawrence, Walker transferred his flag to a smaller ship, the seventy-gun *Edgar*, and planned to leave two battleships and four cruisers to protect his line of retreat into the gulf.

When the English armada set sail from Boston on July 30th, it consisted of nine warships, two bomb vessels, sixty transports and tenders; it carried some seventy-five hundred troops and marines onboard. The entire force consisted of close to twelve thousand men. Samuel Vetch guided the fleet past Cape Sable, then around Cape Breton, but he refused to lead it beyond the Gaspé peninsula and into the Saint Lawrence River.

By August 13th, light winds and favorable weather eased their entry into the Gulf of Saint Lawrence. Five days later, as they were about to enter the river, the northwest wind began to blow, and Walker had to shelter his fleet for two days.

When the wind finally reversed and blew from the southeast, the admiral advanced slowly beyond the western end of Anticosti.

Then the wind died down and heavy fog rolled in.

Another two days later, the southeast wind picked up again and the fog partially lifted. On the evening of August 22nd, when they were 50 miles beyond Anticosti and about 20 miles off the north shore, Walker ordered a heading toward the south, but he was not at midstream as his pilots had led him to believe. Strong currents carried his fleet towards the northwest, and an easterly wind pushed them relentlessly toward Île-aux-Oeufs which ran lengthwise north to south.

That night, fully believing that he was heading south, Walker was roused from his sleep by the ship's captain who announced that land had been sighted. In response to this report, the admiral ordered the ship to tack toward the north.

Roused abruptly a short while later, he rushed on deck and found his vessel surrounded by breakers; several vessels ahead of them were already trapped on the shoals. Walker recovered quickly and called for all available sail so that the remaining vessels could maintain position at mid-channel.

The wind finally abated by two o'clock the following morning, allowing the remaining ships to drop their anchors and assess the fleet's losses. Seven transports and one store ship were lost. Approximately nine hundred of seventeen hundred men, and some women onboard, had died from drowning and exposure. This number also included immigrants from Scotland who would have become colonists in an anglicized Canada.

Walker cruised near Île-aux-Oeufs for two days in an attempt to rescue as many survivors and salvage as much as he could. Then he called a council of naval officers which unanimously decided that he must abandon his mission against Québec.

On September 4th, the rest of his fleet arrived at Cape Breton, and took stock of the fleet's remaining provisions. These were low enough so that a second council of war unanimously decided that they must also forgo their planned attack against Plaisance, Newfoundland. Consequently, the colonial vessels headed back to Boston and Walker's fleet sailed for England. The British frigate of thirty-six guns *Feversham* and three transports sank in the Laurentian gulf before reaching the Atlantic Ocean.

Walker arrived at Portsmouth, England on October 10th, and left his ship, the *Edgar,* in order to travel overland to London, where he was to report on the success or failure of the largest joint expedition England had ever attempted against Nouvelle France. Shortly after his departure, the *Edgar* blew up during routine maintenance, killing all four hundred seventy crewmen on board. All of Walker's public papers, books, journals, and charts, including William Phips' original journal dating back to his expedition to Québec in 1690, were lost.

Colonel Nicholson had once more led a colonial militia force of fourteen hundred, and six hundred Iroquois from Albany toward Lake Champlain to attack and seize Montréal, but this time, he had chosen to travel by way of Lake George.

The colonel learned of Walker's naval disaster before he reached Lake Champlain. He immediately abandoned his part of the joint expedition, burning Fort Anne at Wood Creek before returning to Albany.

Meanwhile, the people of Nouvelle France had prepared all summer in fear of seeing another, even stronger English attack against Québec and Montréal.

Fort Chambly on the Richelieu River was now a great stone fortress, strongly garrisoned and provisioned against a possible European-type siege. It was well-equipped to survive against British cannon and mortar.

On the western front, the British incited the Outagamis and Mascoutins to destroy the French colony at Detroit, but six hundred friendly warriors fought in defense of the Canadians and repulsed the invaders. However, the unfriendly tribes continued to harass the French and block their travel routes between trading posts in Canada and in the Mississippi area.

Charles Le Gardeur de Croisille and Marguerite Renée de Bécancour served as godparents for Charles-Antoine Massé who was born to Louis and Catherine on August 22nd.

Two months later, when initial reports of the British naval disaster reached Québec, joyful religious, civic, and social celebrations were held throughout Nouvelle France.

Upon hearing the news, two Québec officials: Georges Regnard Duplessis, receiver of the Admiralty, and Charles de Monseignat, tax agent for the colony, chartered and outfitted a ship large enough to accommodate forty men with provisions to winter at Île-aux-Oeufs. Their instructions were to salvage whatever they could from the wreckage of Walker's Fleet.

1712

The French salvage party returned to Québec that following June, aboard five ships heavily laden with great anchors, cannons and cannon-balls, iron chains, clothing, blankets, silver swords, guns, muskets, dishes, furs of all kinds, bells, a great variety of provisions, all of which had been easily accessible; much more had been left under water. Their crews reported seeing close to two thousand corpses strewn along the shore, some partially buried in the sand. Judging from the documents found by the French salvage crew, many among those who had already been assigned to government positions had brought their wives and children with them. The island had offered no adequate shelter for those who had managed to reach shore; most of them had died from exposure.

The Canadian crewmen had found copies of Queen Anne's proclamation which declared English sovereignty over Canada based on Cabot's discoveries.

The French had restored, strengthened, and heavily garrisoned their fort at Michillimackinac. Farther west, The Fox nation began to war against the French, closing the trading routes of the Fox and Wisconsin Rivers, and disrupting trade throughout the upper Mississippi region.

That November 12th, the governor and the intendant wrote to the French minister: "We can arm the completed fortress of Chambly with forty cannons and thirty-six stone-firing guns; five hundred men could be garrisoned there, but one thousand would be more effective; we could provision it with enough food to withstand a one-year siege, and munitions for as long as we found necessary. Finally, this fort can be regarded as the upriver rampart guarding Canada."

1713

The War of the Spanish Succession had seriously weakened French naval and land power. France had lost control over the

European territory it had gained through Louis XIV's extensive European campaigns; its people were heavily burdened with debt and oppressive taxes.

Separate treaties were finally negotiated between France and Britain, the Dutch Republic, Prussia, Portugal, and Savoy. Spain worked out its own separate agreements with each of the same countries. Through every one of these negotiations, France and Spain lost more than they gained.

Both the War of Spanish Succession and Queen Anne's War between England and France were officially ended on April 11, 1713 with the signing of the treaty with Great Britain, the major settlement of the Peace of Utrecht. France ceded control over Acadia, Newfoundland, and the Hudson Bay territory to the British, but retained Cape Breton Island and the Îles-de-la-Madeleine in the Laurentian gulf which allowing it to retain some of its fishing rights. Great Britain also gained the Caribbean Island of Saint-Kitts and a protectorate over the Iroquois.

England thus seized the outposts of Nouvelle France and reduced the French colony to the length of the Saint Lawrence River valley. The century-old French territory of Acadia became Nova Scotia, and New Brunswick. The boundary lines between Canada and the British colonies remained unsettled, as were the boundaries between the British colonies and the western territories claimed by France.

Through the Spanish treaties, Philip V gained recognition as King of Spain, but gave up to England both Gibraltar and Minorca, two key bases that guarded the entrance to the Mediterranean Sea. On March 26th, Great Britain was also granted an assiento, a contract agreement awarding the recently formed English South Sea Company the right to send one trading ship a year to the Spanish colonies and to provide them with forty-eight hundred African slaves a year for thirty years.

EPILOGUE

1714

Late that February, the parishioners of Sainte-Madeleine were asked to pray for the soul of Jeanne Renault Vaudry who had recently died at *l'hôtel-Dieu* of Montréal.

On May 13th, the pastor of Sainte-Madeleine parish read a decree by *Monseigneur* de Saint-Vallier authorizing that a stone church be built at Cap-de-la-Madeleine to replace Pierre Boucher's original chapel of 1661 which had fallen into disrepair. The bishop further declared that the habitants of Bécancour and Nicolet must contribute to this effort before receiving diocesan permission to build their own church on the south shore.

An unknown epidemic began to spread through the Mississippi Valley in 1714 and marked the beginning of a rapid decline in the Miami and Illinois native populations. Recurrent epidemics weakened the influence of the older chiefs who had traditionally sided with the French; the younger leaders of the Miamis preferred to develop trade with the English.

Queen Anne of Great Britain died on July 31st at age forty-nine. In fulfillment of the Act of Settlement enacted by the English Parliament in 1701, she was succeeded by her German cousin, the elector of Hanover, who became King George I of England and Ireland. The Whigs returned to political power. Walker who had been favored by the Tories, was now held accountable for his naval disaster and suffered for it. John Churchill, Duke of Marlborough, returned to England after Queen Anne's death and was restored to some of his former influence under King George.

News of the Treaties of Rastatt (March 6, 1714), and of Baden (September 7, 1714) reached Québec before winter set in. King Louis XIV declared the War of Spanish Succession between France and the Holy Roman Emperor Charles VI of Austria to be officially ended and ordered celebrations in Canada. Governor Vaudreuil, Intendant Bégon, and the Sovereign Council celebrated the Te Deum at the Cathedral of Québec. Cannon salutes sounded from the capital's fortress and from all ships lying at anchor in the harbor below.

The French celebrated in like manner throughout Nouvelle France and all of its claimed territories, but not in Acadia, which already had been taken over by the English authorities.

1715

Louis XIV died on the first day of September. He had reigned longer than any other European king: seventy-two years from his ascension to the throne at less than five years of age. His five-year-old great-grandson, Louis XV, youngest son of the duke of Burgundy, succeeded the "Sun King" who had outlived both his son and his son's son.

A few days before his death, the ailing king had summoned his heir to his bedside, and had given him this advice which was recorded for history: "I have been too fond of war. Do not imitate me in that, nor in the too great expenditures I have made. Lighten the burdens of your people as soon as you can, and do that which I have had the misfortune not to accomplish myself."

On September 3rd of that year, Aubin Maudoux died at Saint-François-du-Lac at the age of sixty-three. He was survived by his fifty-two-year old widow Madeleine, and five surviving children, ages thirteen through thirty-six.

On November 17th, Bastien and Catherine's oldest daughter, twenty-four-year old Jeanne, signed a marriage contract with Médard Carpentier *Sieur* Bailly de Champlain. Serving as witnesses were her guardian Louis, his wife Simonne, and their children: Louis the younger, Joseph, Angélique, and Madeleine who had married Pierre Picard on November 6, 1713. Louis the younger, Joseph, Angélique, Pierre Picard, and François Rochereau all signed their names to the document.

Their church wedding took place the following day in Pierre Boucher's old chapel, the church of Sainte-Madeleine. Pierre Guillet's, Jacques Massé's, and Bastien's descendants were all in attendance.

The wedding reception was held at Louis and Simonne's home.

GLOSSARY

Ainsi soit-il: 'So be it.' 'Amen.'

Algonquin: early native ally, first befriended by Champlain; applies to many native tribes, each speaking a variation of the Algonquian language; historical enemy of the Iroquois nations

Amerindian: American native; more appropriate ethnic term than 'Indian'; applicable to all early native groups

Anjou: region and former province of western France. Angers, its historic capital, and Saumur were its chief towns

arpent: old French unit of land measure equivalent to about 0.85 acre. Used both as a linear and as a square unit of measure

auberge: French inn, or pub

banique: a traditional flat bread of Algonquin origin, consisting of cornmeal or whole wheat flour, oil, sugar, salt, dried berries, and water; baked over the campfire; kept well during travel; high-caloric trail food

banlieue: outskirts of a fort, or town

bateau(x): a small, flat-bottomed, wooden boat with raised bow and stern, and flared sides; rowboat

bostonnais: used both as an adjective and as a noun; particularly in reference to the Puritans and privateers of New England; often used in reference to all English colonists

calèche: two-wheeled horse-drawn vehicle with a driver's seat

calvados: French apple brandy which originated in the Calvados region of Normandie

canadien: was used during the 17th century to distinguish members of the first generation to be born in New France, as opposed to their French immigrant parents

cens et rentes: annual land-rent (quit-rent) owed by a settler to his seignior; like a franchise payment; although an habitant had control over his concession, and could pass title on to his heirs. If he sold the land, he was required to share 1/12 of the sale price with the seignior. This effectively prevented land speculation on the part of the concessionaire, yet was set low enough in the colony to encourage the conversion of virgin forest into agricultural land

chaloupe: shallop; small open river boat with oars and sails

chapelle: standing sheaf of freshly harvested flax, set to dry naturally in the field

charpentier: carpenter, shipwright

cordier: ropemaker

corvée: unpaid labor which could be required from a peasant by someone with authority over him

coureur, coureur-de-bois: unlicensed French fur trapper or trader who traveled through the wilderness to deal directly with the natives

denier: a small silver coin, equivalent to 1/12 sol

eau-de-vie: clear brandy distilled from fermented fruit juice

engagé indentured servant, or employee

fille du roi: 'King's Daughter'; unmarried women of marriageable age who lacked a dowry, many were orphans. They were recruited by the king's agent to travel to New France and receive a dowry at the king's expense when they married a settler and raised a family in Canada.

Five Nations: Iroquois League consisting of the Mohawk, Oneida, Onondaga, Cayuga, and Seneca nations. Their chiefs regularly met at Onondaga, the central nation's major village.

Foxes: Outagamis of Green Bay area; of Algonquian stock; once western allies of the French; laid siege to Detroit in 1711

gavotte: French peasant dance which requires raising rather than sliding the feet in moderately quick quadruple meter

gigue: lively dance movement in compound triple rhythm

habitant: settler of French origin who had successfully developed and lived on his own Canadian land for one year or more.

hôtel-Dieu: chief hospital of the town

Île-aux-Oeufs: one of the Seven Islands (Sept Iles)

Jacobites: supporters of Catholic King James II of England

joie de vivre: joy of life

Lac Saint-Sacrement: present-day Lake George, south of Lake Champlain

l'Enfant Jésus: 'Baby Jesus'

lieue: one league; 4 kilometers; 2.5 English miles

livre: French pound; ancient unit of coin money equivalent to twenty sols/sous

Loups: most likely Mohicans; members of the Delaware group

ma fille: 'my daughter'; 'my girl'

Maman: 'Mother'

Manatte: French reference to the original name for the island of Manhattan, bought by Dutch traders from the Indians in 1626 for 60 guilders of trade goods. Dutch reference is *Manhattes*. Site of New York governor's colonial residence

marguillier: churchwarden, member of the church council

Métis: the family's mixed-breed dog; Guillaume originally gave him to Bastien when Bastien moved alone to his new house

minot: an old French measure of grain, equivalent to 8.75 gallons, or 39 liters; compared to an English bushel which is equivalent to 35.239 liters

mon ami: 'my friend'

mon (p'tit) gars: my son; young man

mon vieux: 'old friend'

notre jolie canadienne: 'our lovely Canadian friend'

Nouvelle France: French for New France

Onontio: Iroquois title for the French governor of New France, or for the French king

patois: provincial variation of French speech

pemmican: concentrated trail food used by North American natives and French voyageurs; consisted of lean dried meat pounded fine with dried berries, ground nuts, and mixed with melted animal fat; light-weight, high-caloric, non-perishable

Pentagouet: present day village of Castine, Maine

Pepère: 'grandpa'

Perche: a 17th-century province of France dating back to 1114 A.D. Since 1790, a region consisting of the departments of Eure et Loir, Orne, Loir et Cher, and Sarthe. Native of that region: *percheron*

pervenche: Vinca minor; blue-flowered, woody trailing evergreen herb and groundcover

Père: 'Father'; deferential title in reference to a priest

Plaisance: early French naval base of operations on Placentia Bay, Newfoundland. The English called it Placentia

Port-Royal: now Annapolis, Nova Scotia

quadrille: square-dance with four couples

Québec: Canada's first European settlement; the capital of New France; now also the French-speaking province of Canada

raquettes: Amerindian webbed snowshoes

redoubt: small, temporary, enclosed defensive shelter

réveillon: traditional French family feasting and celebration following Midnight Mass on Christmas Eve or New Year's Eve

rivière: river

rivière puante: 'stinking river'; so-called by the natives who fought a great battle there and lost many warriors; later renamed Saint-Michel, then Bécancour River

ropewalk: ropemaker's equipment used to twist several strands of twisted hemp yarn into rope or cable

sabot: carved wooden shoe worn by habitant families in early Canada

Sault Saint-Louis: Jesuit mission for the Iroquois located near Montréal

seigneurie: seigniory; landed estate under the control of a feudal lord (a seigneur)

Sieur: deferential title of address for landowner, or nobleman

sol: copper coin; unit of money equivalent to one sou; 1/20 of a livre

Te Deum: joyous liturgical hymn of praise and thanksgiving to God

Tories: major conservative British political group of early 18th–early 19th-centuries who favored royal authority and Anglican Church; sought to preserve the traditional political structure by defeating parliamentary reform

tourtière: French-Canadian meat-pie; mostly enjoyed during the winter holidays

travois: simple native carrying device consisting of two trailing poles to which a platform or net is attached to carry a load

Trois-Rivières: Three Rivers; smallest of the three major settlement areas in the Saint Lawrence River valley during the 17th century; located halfway between Québec and Montréal

Troupes de la Marine: French colonial troops, as opposed to French regular troops

trunnel: tree-nail; wooden dowel used to fix joints in lieu of iron nails

Ville-Marie: original European settlement on the Island of Montréal; already completely encircled by the growing community's houses and trading commercial buildings during this historical period

voyageur: In early Canada, simply referred to any traveler, explorer, or fur-trader; eventually referred to an employee of a licensed merchant who legally transported trade goods and fur pelts to and from remote fur trading posts.

Whigs: major English political group, late 17th–early 19th centuries, which sought to limit royal authority and increase parliamentary power.

CAST OF CHARACTERS

BASTIEN and MARGUERITE:
  m. January 22, 1663

  BASTIEN: b. 1634, Pithiviers, France
  MARGUERITE: b. 1637, Artenay, France
    d. January, 1688
  Their children:
    Marie-MADELEINE: b. 1664; m. Aubin Maudoux, 1676
    MARIE-Marguerite: b. 1666; m. Antoine Cottenoire, 1682
    Louis: b. 1668; m. Simonne Massé, 1691
    Sébastien: b. 1670; m. Marie-Anne Massé, 1694
    Jean-FRANÇOIS: b. 1674; m. Marguerite Moreau, 1701
    Marie-Catherine: b. 1678; m. Louis Massé, 1702

JACQUES MASSÉ and CATHERINE GUILLET:
  m. November 28, 1669

  JACQUES: b. 1631, Saint-Pierre-Chaussé, Anjou, France;
    d. November, 1687
  CATHERINE: b. 1656, Québec
  Their children:
    Simonne: b. 1670; m. Louis, 1691
    Marie-Anne: b. 1673; m. Sébastien, 1694
    Louis: b. 1676; m. Bastien's Marie-Catherine, 1702
    Jacques: b. 1678; d. August 13, 1687
    Marie-Catherine: b. 1680; m. Pierre Petit, 1694
    Marie-Angélique: b. 1682; m. Michel Crevier, 1709
    Marie-Louise: b. 1685; m. François Perrot, 1703
    Jean-BAPTISTE: b. 8/13/1687; m. Geneviève Leblanc, 1716

BASTIEN and CATHERINE GUILLET m. May 14, 1691
  Both died late December 1710

  Their children:
    Jeanne: b. 1692; m. Médard Carpentier, 1715
    MARIE-Catherine: b. 1693; m. Pierre Bourbeau, 1717
    Marie-Madeleine: b. 1698; m. François Didier, 1734

ABOUT THE AUTHOR

Doris Provencher Faucher holds a master's degree in Education and is now retired from teaching. She and her husband live in southern Maine. The oldest of their four children was born during their year-long stay in France.

Based on ten years of research, her series of historical novels depicts the French ethnic experience in North America, beginning with Bastien's and Marguerite's arrival and settlement in New France in the mid-17th century.

Her first novel, *Le Québécois:* THE VIRGIN FOREST, related the challenges they faced in establishing their family in the Canadian wilderness.